Praise for

SILENT ENEMY

"Aviation thriller aficionados will cheer, and readers of any genre will gnaw their fingernails to the quick."
—*Publishers Weekly* (starred review)

"Young's follow-up to *The Mullah's Storm* is better than its predecessor . . . Full of the kind of military jargon that aficionados love, the novel also boasts intense action and surprisingly deep characterizations for a military thriller. Fans of Clancy, Coonts, and Dale Brown need to add Young to their must-read lists."
—*Booklist*

"The story is as lean and mean as they come . . . Parson is as unforgettable a character as you are likely to encounter in thriller fiction."
—Bookreporter.com

"If you liked *The High and the Mighty*, you'll love *Silent Enemy*. Young's airlift pilot makes John Wayne look like a weakling."
—*St. Louis Post-Dispatch*

"A thrilling ride that maintains mach speed from liftoff to landing . . . or however the plane comes down."
—*Shelf Awareness*

"Young wields the language with a deft hand."
—*The Washington Independent Review of Books*

"Don't bother to set your alarm clock . . . you'll be reading this book when it goes off in the morning!"
—*Military Writers Society of America*

continued . . .

THE MULLAH'S STORM

"Digs in its hooks from the first chapter and never lets go. There are writers, and there are fighters—readers are lucky that [Young] is both."

—Alex Berenson,
#1 *New York Times* bestselling author of *The Shadow Patrol*

"A gusty, gritty thriller . . . You will long remember this terrifying, timely tale—and its terrific new writer."

—W.E.B. Griffin and William E. Butterworth IV,
#1 *New York Times* bestselling authors of *The Spy Masters*

"A page-turner that might've been torn from today's headlines. An engrossing, enlightening, and extremely entertaining debut."

—Doug Stanton, *New York Times*
bestselling author of *In Harm's Way* and *Horse Soldiers*

"Gripping and impressively authentic."

—Frederick Forsyth,
#1 *New York Times* bestselling author of *The Cobra*

"Courage and honor in the face of the enemy have not been so brilliantly portrayed since the great novels of the Second World War . . . [A] magnificent novel."

—Jack Higgins, *New York Times* bestselling author of
The Eagle Has Landed and *A Devil Is Waiting*

"Impressive . . . Young is an excellent storyteller, creating memorable characters with Hemingway-like understatement and precision. His descriptions of the terrain, the sound different weapons make, the feeling of fingers and toes succumbing to frostbite, the way things look through night-vision goggles, are superb. A smart, unsettling, timely novel that puts a human face on the Afghanistan conflict while conveying the immense challenges the United States faces there."

—*Kirkus Reviews*

"The plot and the action move with the speed and power of a B-1 bomber."

—Bing West,
New York Times bestselling author of *The Wrong War*

"Young draws on his own war experiences for verisimilitude, which, along with believable characters and an exciting plot, makes this one of the better thrillers to come out of the Afghan theater."
—*Publishers Weekly*

"An irresistible adventure story."
—*USA Today*

THE
⬥RENEGADES⬥

Tom Young

Berkley Books
New York

THE BERKLEY PUBLISHING GROUP
Published by the Penguin Group
Penguin Group (USA) Inc.
375 Hudson Street, New York, New York 10014, USA

USA | Canada | UK | Ireland | Australia | New Zealand | India | South Africa | China

Penguin Books Ltd., Registered Offices: 80 Strand, London WC2R 0RL, England
For more information about the Penguin Group, visit penguin.com.

THE RENEGADES

A Berkley Book / published by arrangement with the author

BERKLEY® is a registered trademark of Penguin Group (USA) Inc.
The "B" design is a trademark of Penguin Group (USA) Inc.

For information, address: The Berkley Publishing Group,
a division of Penguin Group (USA) Inc.,
375 Hudson Street, New York, New York 10014.

ISBN: 978-0-425-26096-8

PUBLISHING HISTORY
G. P. Putnam's Sons hardcover edition / July 2012
Berkley premium edition / May 2013

PRINTED IN THE UNITED STATES OF AMERICA

10 9 8 7 6 5 4 3 2 1

Cover photo copyright © Walter Van Bel.
Cover design by Richard Hasselberger.

For Professor Richard Elam,
a great teacher and friend, and veteran of the U.S. Navy

PROLOGUE

Even from a thousand feet in the air, Lieutenant Colonel Michael Parson could see the earthquake had shaken Afghanistan to a new level of misery. The slums of Mazar-i-Sharif stretched below the Mi-17 helicopter like a vast, disturbed hive. People milled in the streets. Black columns of smoke seethed into the sky above a city of collapsed ceilings and crumpled walls. An untold number lay dead or dying beneath the rubble.

The quake had happened only about an hour ago, and the U.S. Geological Survey rated it a preliminary 7.2. A smaller magnitude than the quake that had devastated northern Japan in 2011, but worse in its own way. Afghanistan's construction standards were prehistoric.

Parson stood in the back of an Afghan chopper with an Afghan interpreter and an Afghan army colonel. Up front, Captain Rashid commanded the aircraft, accompanied by his copilot and a flight engineer. Wind from the helicopter's open door rippled the sleeves of Parson's tan desert flight suit. Reeking whiffs stung his nostrils. Not aircraft exhaust, but something closer to the smell of coal and charred wood. Black flecks whipped through the air: soot from the fires on the ground.

Rashid, the colonel, and the interpreter conversed in Pashto. Subdued tones on the interphone like whispers at a funeral. Parson didn't understand a word, but he could guess what they were saying: *What a fucking mess.* And Parson imagined the colonel was taking the thought a few steps further: *These people will need everything—food, shelter, medicine. How will we ever airlift enough to make a difference? Oh yeah, and still fight the war.*

Parson wished his old Army friend Sergeant Major Sophia Gold had already arrived. She spoke Pashto so well, she seemed to read minds. Parson had requested that she come work with him as an individual augmentee, and she'd agreed immediately; she just had to finish up some training back in the States. There was no better translator/interpreter in the business. And as a paratrooper, she'd been around aircraft enough to speak a little of that language, too.

Parson had been back in-country only a month, in a new role as an adviser to the Afghan Air Force. His third tour, but his first in a nonflying position. In his other tours, he'd flown as a C-130 Hercules navigator and then as a pilot on the C-5 Galaxy. He'd never piloted helicopters, but as a rated officer he could help teach the Afghans the basics of running a squadron: maintain currency records, give regular testing, retrain the guys who bust their check rides, and always, always, always treat maintenance with respect.

The Afghans were making progress toward a professional air force. However, Parson doubted they were ready for anything like the job ahead of them now. For that matter, he didn't think he was, either. To fly his own plane, manage his own crew—that was one thing. To build an air force from scratch was another.

The chopper began to descend for a flyover of the Mazar Airport. The field lay to the east of town, surrounded by a dusty brown expanse highlighted with a meandering strip of green—the weeds and trees that grew along a river. Rashid banked the helicopter toward the airfield and attempted the radio call himself. "Mazar Tower," he transmitted, "Golay Two-One."

An answer came back weak but readable: "Golay Two-One, Mazar Tower. Go ahead." Louisiana drawl. The weak transmission probably meant the controller was using a handheld radio. So power was out, and backup generators were not yet running. The quake must have hit the airport hard.

"Mazar Tower," Rashid called, "Golay Two-One requests . . ." The pilot paused. The interpreter said nothing.

"Low approach," Parson said on interphone.

"Low approach," Rashid repeated on the radio.

Great, Parson thought. The pilot doesn't speak good English, the interpreter doesn't speak pilot, and the controller talks with an accent they've probably never heard before. A triple language barrier. Even the call signs were strange. Like most fliers, Afghan aviators liked macho words for call signs—in their own language. Rashid had told him *golay* meant *bullet*.

"That's approved," the tower said. "Golay Two-One is cleared for low approach. Be advised the field is closed to fixed-wing traffic."

Parson gave Rashid a thumbs-up. To most people in South Asia, that would have been an obscene gesture. But Afghan pilots quickly accepted its American meaning. To give them that signal meant not only *I agree*, *it's working*, or *okay*. The sign meant you considered them part of the international fraternity of aviators.

Out the window, Mazar's runway two-four began to materialize through the haze. Parson knew the field well. In previous deployments he'd landed there in pitch-black on night vision goggles, in winter with snow blowing sideways, and on instruments—right down to minimums—in driving rain. But today something really didn't look right.

Dark smudges appeared in two locations along the runway. As the Mi-17 flew nearer, Parson realized the smudges were fissures, wide gaps in the pavement. Other sections of asphalt also looked cracked up.

No wonder the field was closed. The runway had stretched more than ten thousand feet, but now no more than four thousand feet seemed undamaged. The biggest transports couldn't get in here anymore. At best, the civil engineers could mark off a short assault strip. C-130s and C-27s bringing relief supplies could slam-dunk into the touchdown zone and deliver a few pallets at a time. But the C-5s and C-17s would need to off-load their large pay-loads at Bagram and Kandahar and let the smaller aircraft shuttle the cargo from there. Like digging a quarry with a spoon. And digging it under fire. Relief missions in a disaster area challenged pilots enough. What would crews face when natural disaster combined with war?

Broken pavement passed underneath the helicopter as Rashid overflew the runway. The colonel muttered some-thing Parson could not understand. Epithets, Parson sup-posed. He noticed a hangar leaning as if a giant hand had tried to push it over. The control tower had suffered dam-age, too: A crack in the shape of a lightning bolt extended the length of the front wall. It probably wasn't safe for anyone to remain in the building.

More Pashto on the interphone, and the helicopter climbed away from the airfield. "What are we doing?" Par-son asked the interpreter.

"The colonel wishes to go into the city."

Parson hoped he meant *over* the city. The chopper lev-eled at what he guessed to be a thousand feet, though he could not scan the altimeter from his seat. Not seeing the instruments rankled him. He looked across Mazar. Near its center he saw the Blue Mosque, also known as the Shrine of . . . somebody. Gold would know. He couldn't see any obvious damage to the mosque.

The helicopter slowed, turned, accelerated, slowed again. Rashid seemed to be hunting for a place to land. Why were they landing? This is stupid, Parson thought. If Gold were here, he could explain why it was stupid. Parson started to order Rashid not to touch down, but then he remembered he wasn't in charge. Under his breath he muttered curses, but profanity did little to ease his frustration.

People on the ground watched the aircraft, and some ran in whatever direction the helo headed. Parson could see at least a hundred Afghans milling around, and he hoped they'd have sense enough to stay out of the helicopter's downwash and away from the tail rotor. That tail rotor could take off somebody's head.

Rashid selected a street with no traffic. The street looked barely wide enough for the Mi-17 to clear the power lines sagging along either side. Parson knew helo pilots always worried about the radius of that rotor disc spinning overhead. But sometimes they gave themselves very little room for error.

The *whop-whop* of the main rotor thudded harder as the blade angle changed. The helicopter began descending, and the Afghans below started sprinting toward the landing zone. Two men carried children who must have been hurt in the quake.

The power lines came so close now, they swayed from the wind blast. Below them, some of the locals used scarves or bare hands to shield their faces from flying grit.

"What are we doing?" Parson asked the interpreter.

"The colonel wants to pick up some patients."

Was the colonel nuts? With no support, no plan, just drop into a city full of desperate people?

Up and down the street, buildings lay in ruins. More locals gathered as dust billowed underneath the helicopter. Some limped alone; others leaned on assistants. Still others seemed uninjured, but they waved their arms and shouted. Parson supposed they wanted help for relatives trapped in rubble. And every one of them, he thought, wants to get on this helicopter. His heart pounded faster.

Dust enveloped the aircraft. Parson could see nothing in the brownout as Rashid touched down. How those rotorhead chopper drivers kept from getting vertigo, Parson would never understand. Dust poured in through the open door, and the interpreter coughed and squinted. He turned his face as if looking for clear air, but there was no escape from the blowing grit.

Parson felt a bump, and the dust cleared as Rashid throttled back to idle. The crew chief kicked the door ladder into place. Locals began running toward the aircraft. Under his breath Parson muttered, "Oh, shit. Stay away from the tail. Stay away from the tail." Landing was a bad idea.

A man holding a little girl with a crushed leg reached the helicopter first. He came so close to the tail rotor that wind from its spinning blades tousled the girl's hair. The man seemed not to notice. We're committed now, Parson thought. Might as well help who we can. He and the crew chief pulled the man and daughter aboard. The child's blood dripped from a yellow blanket and spattered onto the floor. She held on tightly to her father's shirt, tiny handfuls of fabric clutched in her fists.

The crowd surged around the aircraft, and people began to try to climb inside. The crew chief and interpreter shouted to them and to each other. An apparently unhurt man pulled himself through the doorway, and the crew chief shoved him back out. A woman with burns across her face stumbled against the side and started up the crew steps. The interpreter grabbed her by the arms and yanked her aboard.

The colonel forced his way down the three steps. Then he lifted two more kids into the chopper. He let two men come with them, presumably the fathers. Then he pulled aboard several more patients until the cabin was full.

"No more," the interpreter yelled. "Captain Rashid says we have room for no more."

The colonel tried to climb back inside. Some of the locals also tried to get aboard, and they got in his way. The colonel pushed back at them, then began waving his Walther P1. Parson thought he looked like a martinet, brandishing that German pistol. You shouldn't pull a weapon if you weren't prepared to fire it.

When the colonel made it back inside, Parson pressed his talk switch and said, "Go." He knew Rashid understood that much.

The noise of the engines and rotors rose, and the Mi-17 began lifting off. A man started climbing through the doorway, and the crew chief punched him. The man dropped outside and fell three feet to the ground.

A boy hung on to the lip of the doorway. His feet dangled in midair, and the crew chief tried to push him off by the shoulders, but the kid wouldn't let go.

The helicopter was about nine feet off the ground and climbing. Parson feared the child would fall to his death if he didn't let go before the aircraft got higher.

"No more," the interpreter shouted. "Rashid says we

are too full." The aircraft yawed to the right, settled, then yawed left.

Seeing no other options, Parson kneeled and pried loose the kid's fingers. Despised himself for doing it. The boy yowled in protest, kicked his sneaker-clad feet, dropped into the dust cloud. When he hit the ground, he got back up and gestured with his thumbs. Parson met his eyes for a moment before losing sight of him in the dust. The boy seemed unhurt, but with a look on his face that said the Americans had just made a new enemy.

Parson hated to think why that kid wanted to get on board so badly. Was he trying to get help for a trapped mother? An injured sister? Parson had used force before; he had killed when necessary. He'd never lost a night of sleep over it, either. Those terrorists deserved what they got.

But this boy hadn't done anything wrong. Parson was glad Sophia wasn't here to see what he'd done. But then he wished he could talk to her about it.

Half a world away from Afghanistan, Sergeant Major Sophia Gold stood on the open ramp of a C-130 Hercules as it flew at twenty-five thousand feet. The slipstream whipped at the sleeves of her uniform. Beneath her stretched an expanse of evergreen forests and tobacco fields, and the brown S-turns of a river called the Cape Fear. She took a breath from her oxygen bottle, then launched herself into the void. The growl of turboprops surrendered to the pure white rush of wind. Gold arched her back, spread her arms and legs, and flew.

That's what free fall felt like: not a sickening plunge, but flight. In fact, at Fort Bragg's Military Free-fall Simulator—essentially a vertical wind tunnel—her instructors had spoken of "flying your body." In her arched position, she controlled her center of gravity so she wouldn't tumble and cause her chute to tangle when she opened it.

But she didn't have to open it yet. She glanced at the altimeter on her left wrist the way a civilian might check a watch. The needle unwound through twenty thousand feet as she dropped toward the world at about one hundred and twenty-five miles per hour. Gold wished she could freeze this moment, live in it for longer. The wind and the speed swept away all worries about the future and despair over the past.

Slightly above and to her right she saw one of her five partners on this high altitude/low opening jump. All five were men: four Special Forces troops and an Air Force pararescueman. Gold was one of very few HALO-qualified women.

The sun glinted in her visor and reflected against the cumulus beneath her. Cool mist enveloped her as she fell through a cloud. For an instant she felt stationary as the grayness took away all visual references, and then *FLASH*: The trees and ponds and roads of eastern North Carolina reappeared, larger now. Green loblolly pines stood among the orange and yellow of sweet gums and maples. Brilliant scarlet encircled a few of the trunks: the odd beauty of poison ivy at the height of autumn color. Lush hues and flatland varied in all respects from the stark mountains of Southwest Asia.

Her altimeter rolled through ten thousand feet. The terrain beneath her expanded by the second, and she knew this nirvana must end soon. The altimeter needle crept toward the red. She hated to do it, but knew she must. As she passed through four thousand feet, she brought in both arms, put her gloved fingers on the D ring, and yanked the rip cord.

There came that luffing sound. Then a giant hand yanked her from her reverie. The harness dug at her armpits and legs. The earth stopped rushing at her. Her feet swung in her paratrooper boots. The opening shock made her think of an animal running free until it reached the end of a long leash. She noticed a slight pain in her mouth: She'd bitten the inside of her lip. This sudden and violent deceleration always hurt just a little, but this time something else felt wrong.

Gold looked up and checked the rectangular canopy and its risers and suspension lines—so that was the problem. The lines were twisted. She had a good chute, but she couldn't steer it.

She could see green smoke on the ground marking her aim point on Fort Bragg's Sicily Drop Zone. The smoke billowed across the drop zone and into the woods. She guessed maybe six or eight knots of wind at the surface, but it was stronger at her altitude. And it was taking her, just like the smoke, over the trees.

She reached above her head, grabbed the risers, and pulled them apart. As they began to untwist, her body rotated under the canopy, and she found herself looking away from the drop zone. Into the forest.

The lines wouldn't unwind completely. And her steering toggles were still fouled. Green beneath her now. If she couldn't fix this twist, she would come down through the pines. She wasn't equipped for a rough-terrain landing. Without the right gear, a tree landing could kill you.

She considered cutting away the main canopy and landing on her reserve, but she was getting a little low for that option. With this malfunction, a cutaway became a judgment call. There was an old saying about your reserve parachute: *How long do you have to deploy it? The rest of your life.* But using the reserve required some altitude, and she was running out of that.

She unclipped her oxygen mask, checked her altimeter. Less than two thousand feet. Not much time left.

Gold pulled harder on the risers. Her body rotated a quarter turn. Why had the chute wound itself up like that? Had she not held a good arch as she fell?

The lines still had one twist in them. Toggles still fouled. By now the reserve was out of the question. Gold pulled at the risers again with the last strength in her biceps and triceps. The tangle released, and her body rotated all the way around.

Now she had some control. She pulled a steering toggle to turn toward the drop zone. But she had too much distance ahead of her and not enough beneath her. She gave up on the DZ and prepared for a rough landing in the trees.

She placed one foot on top of the other to keep branches

from striking between her legs. Bent her knees slightly. Folded her arms and cupped her gloved hands inside her armpits to shield the arteries there. Shut her eyes tight.

In the next moment, terrorists beat her with truncheons. A blow to the feet. A punch to the thigh. To the chest. To the back of her head. A slap to the face. All amid the weirdly pleasant scent of evergreen.

For a moment, the assault sent her back in time. She'd been hit like that only once before, and then the terrorists had been real, when she'd been taken hostage in Afghanistan. Her ordeal had begun with a beating, and the beating was nothing compared with what came later. The blows from tree limbs laid open emotional wounds. Fear and panic, the certainty that an awful death awaited her. She saw the faces of her tormentors. Her skin flushed instantly with sweat. She fought the urge to cry out.

Then the beating stopped. Gold opened her eyes. Dappled shade, pine needle floor. She hung from her risers about a foot off the ground. The chute remained tangled in the tree, ripped in several places. She felt her arms and legs. No broken bones, but lots of scrapes and scratches from bark.

She fumbled for the cutaway pillow, a soft red handle that would release the main canopy. When she pulled it, she dropped to the ground and collapsed to her hands and knees. Struggled to control her breathing. Willed her heart to stop racing.

How did I let that happen? she asked herself. The sound of running boots interrupted her dark thoughts. She saw the DZ control officer and two of the Special Forces guys, who had, no doubt, landed right on target.

"Sergeant Major, are you okay?" one of them asked.

"I'm fine," she said. "I'm fine."

She walked out of the woods with them, and a Humvee picked her up at the DZ. She supposed some private would have to go back and recover her chute, or what was left of it. On the ride back to the base, no one criticized, but she imagined what they were all thinking: *HALO is not women's work.*

And it usually wasn't.

"I've never seen a woman on a HALO drop before," the DZCO asked. "What's your career field?"

"I'm a Pashto interpreter/translator," Gold said.

"So how does a translator get a slot at HALO school?"

Gold had come to expect that question on every jump. The Army didn't consider the interpreter/translator specialty a combat job; that's why it was open to women. But if the Army needed noncombat jobs done in combat zones, then women went into combat. Simple as that.

The military even wanted a few women who could accompany special ops forces—purely as interpreters in a noncombat role. As a Pashto expert with the 82nd Airborne, Gold qualified as an obvious choice for HALO training. Now if the boys needed a woman who spoke the language, she could go with them no matter how they got there.

"So far it's just been training," Gold added. "I've never done this in combat."

"Let's hope you don't have to."

There were a couple different ways to take that comment, but Gold assumed he meant well. She wasn't sure why her risers had twisted; a twist could happen even with a well-packed parachute used with perfect technique. The malfunction reminded her she could never let her guard down, never get distracted, never take anything for granted. Especially with another deployment to Afghanistan coming up. Counselors had told her to expect symptoms of post-traumatic stress disorder from time to time: difficulty concentrating, depression—and in worse episodes, nausea and sweats.

The night sweats had started after Parson had rescued her from her Taliban captors and still happened at least once a week. Five years. The sweats always came with dreams of the sneering men and their knives in that bombed-out village in the mountains. The blades inserted under her fingernails, the pain and blood, the nails ripped off. One by one.

With each fingernail, the insurgents reminded her: "You suffer alone. You are a harlot. You will die, and you will go to hell."

But she hadn't suffered alone. Somewhere in the ridges above, Parson had waited, watched through the finely ground glass of a precision rifle scope. A downed aviator out of his element, he could have given up on her. At that moment, her chain of command certainly had. But Parson refused to let her die.

He'd brought her back alive. Alive but damaged, trace elements of toxin in her psyche. And now she prepared to return to the source of it all, where the bleak terrain matched the bleakness of spirit Afghanistan had brought her.

She told herself she could hack it. She was a professional. Her career had included interpreting for interrogations, serving with Provincial Reconstruction Teams, and running a literacy program for Afghan police officers. She and Parson had received Silver Stars for keeping an important Taliban prisoner alive and in custody after they'd been shot down.

The thought of working with Parson during her new deployment brought mixed feelings. Gold wanted very much to see him again, yet she could not look at him without recalling the worst moments of her life. He had arranged for the Joint Relief Task Force to assign her as his interpreter, however, and she could hardly tell him no. And Afghanistan needed her again.

She still ached all over from the tree landing. She knew she'd be sore in the morning. One of her fingers hurt, and she pulled off her glove to inspect it. Despite the glove, the nail on her left middle finger had somehow torn off. The blood and exposed flesh sickened her.

Gold closed her eyes, breathed deeply. The injury reminded her of things best not remembered.

❧ 1 ❧

It took Gold three days to reach Mazar-i-Sharif. In that time, a refugee camp sprang up. The collection of blue-and-white tents on the airport grounds sprawled across the tarmac. The tents' entrance flaps bore stenciling that read UNHCR. Big, Russian-built helicopters pounded in and out of the airfield. Each helo displayed the roundel of the Afghan Air Force—a circle enclosing a triangle of green, red, and black. Gold saw a few American Black Hawks, too.

A familiar odor filled her nostrils: trash fires and sewage, along with the smell of dust. Even if she'd been blind, she would have recognized the location. The scents filled her with both dread and familiarity, almost a homecoming. She'd left part of herself here, and that part now belonged to Afghanistan.

Gold had talked to Parson by Skype when her plane made a fuel stop in Kuwait; as an individual augmentee, she'd made some of her own arrangements to get to her duty station. He'd told her he'd meet her at the MASF—

the Mobile Aeromedical Staging Facility. No sign of him yet, though. Just doctors and nurses moving among patients lying on green cots set up in brown tents.

An Afghan helicopter landed. Though its rotors quit turning, some sort of power unit inside continued to operate. The chopper emitted a jetlike howl, and exhaust gases shimmered from a port.

Crew members opened clamshell doors in the back and began unloading patients. The injured lay on stretchers, and crewmen lifted them out of the aircraft and lined them up on the tarmac. All the fliers looked like Afghans, except one who was taller than the rest. From his short hair and clean-shaven face, Gold knew he was probably an American. He carried a faded green helmet bag covered with patches. When she noticed the slight limp and the way he pulled at his flight suit sleeve to check his watch, she knew it was Parson.

Gold found a set of foam earplugs in a pocket of her ACUs, and she twisted them between her fingers and inserted them into her ears before approaching the helicopter. As Gold strode toward the aircraft, Parson looked up and smiled at her. She waved, and when she reached him he extended his right hand, and she took it in both of hers. She wanted to embrace him, but not in front of the other troops, and certainly not in front of the Afghans.

He looked tired. The skin below his eyes sagged, and grime gathered in the creases of his neck. He wore his usual desert tan flight suit, only this one had blue oak leaves on the shoulders. The command patch over his right chest pocket read US CENTAF. He had a few flecks of gray in his hair now, but he looked pretty good for someone who'd once been blown up. Since their flight through hell last year, they had kept in touch, and she'd last seen him about two months ago. That was before his deployment, and he'd still worn a major's brown leaves then.

"Damn, it's good to see you," Parson shouted over the noise.

"Likewise," Gold said, "but I'm sorry about the circumstances." It seemed in Afghanistan, there was always reason to be sorry about the circumstances.

Parson nodded, then leaned inside the helicopter's crew door. "Hey, Rashid," he yelled, "kill the APU."

Indistinct words came from the cockpit, and Parson repeated: "APU. Turn it off." Then he slashed his finger across his throat. The screaming whine subsided. Parson turned back toward Gold and said, "It's not always that easy to communicate. That's why I need you."

"Where did you just fly from?" Gold asked.

"Balkh. It's pretty rough up there."

Gold looked at the patients. Dust covered some of them, as if they'd just been pulled from rubble. A girl with a bloody bandage around the stump of her arm stared up at Gold. Her hair shone with an auburn tint, and her eyes were blue. The sight nearly brought Gold to tears. She wished she could take the child in her arms and carry her to a better time and place for a little girl. Gold figured she was probably a Tajik, but those eyes and hair could suggest Russian, British, or even Macedonian. A lot of armies had entered Afghanistan and then retreated, but they'd left their chromosomes. Two medics picked up the child's stretcher and carried her into the MASF.

Another patient, a young man, moaned and kept rocking from side to side. He wore a bloody T-shirt and black trousers. He had a tennis shoe on his right foot, but his left foot was bare, and a broken bone protruded from the skin. The man clutched at his abdomen as he cried out.

"What's wrong with him?" Gold asked.

"Internal injuries, maybe. I think a ceiling fell on him."

"I'll help you get him inside."

Gold took one end of the stretcher by its wooden handles, and they brought the man into the medical tent. As they put him down, Gold asked in Pashto, "Does your stomach hurt?"

In addition to the broken foot, she could see bruises and scrapes all over the man's face and arms. The blood on his shirt appeared to come from those injuries. His midsection seemed to pain him more than anything else, but the cause was not apparent. The man did not respond to Gold's question.

"Where does it hurt, my friend?" Gold asked. *"Pohaigay?"* Do you understand?

"I cannot say to you," the man said.

"Whatever is wrong," Gold said, "let us help you. *Meh daarigah.*" Do not be frightened.

Inside the MASF, flight nurses and medics tended rows of patients lying on cots. Murmurs of conversations babbled through the tent in several languages. Amid the usual English, Pashto, and Dari, Gold heard snatches of French,

German, and Russian. Some of the medical workers wore uniforms, and others wore civilian clothes. Several countries had contributed help from their military services, and Gold assumed the civilians came from the UN and from NGOs such as Doctors Without Borders. Gold retained a special fondness for people who worked to ease pain; she had spent so much time fighting those who inflicted it. But right now she just wanted to get this guy to talk.

"We have doctors for you," she said in Pashto. The man still did not respond.

A medic kneeled by the man's stretcher. The medic wore MultiCam fatigues with flight crew wings and airborne jump wings, along with badges for combat diver and free-fall parachutist. A sleeve patch from the 83rd Expeditionary Rescue Squadron. The five stripes of a technical sergeant. Close-cropped black hair. Rolled-up sleeves bulged around muscles that looked hard as Kevlar. His name tag read REYES.

"Are you pararescue?" Parson asked.

"Yes, sir," Reyes said. He did not look up at Parson and Gold. Instead, he pulled medical shears from his pocket and began cutting away the patient's shirt.

"He's been holding his stomach, but he won't tell us what's wrong," Gold said.

Reyes touched the man's abdomen. "It's not hard or discolored like you'd have with a bad internal injury," he said. Reyes's accent suggested someone whose first language was Spanish. Puerto Rican, perhaps.

The patient continued moaning, and sweat beaded on his forehead. Reyes took a multitool from a sheath on his belt and opened the blade. "These guys don't like to be stripped," he said, "but I gotta examine him." The para-rescueman cut the man's rope belt and checked his groin area. Gold saw blood there, and she turned away. She knew the patient wouldn't want an American woman to see him like this.

"Poor guy," Parson said. "That's a bad place to get hit by debris."

"He'll need surgery," Reyes said, "but I don't think he'll lose anything."

"So what's with his stomach?" Parson asked.

"I don't know."

"Cover him and let me talk to him," Gold said.

Reyes left and came back with a towel that he draped over the patient. The man still looked sick and uncomfort-able. Gold kneeled beside him and said in Pashto, "These people can treat you, but you must talk to us. Your injury is not a punishment from God; it is merely an accident. You have no reason to feel shame."

The man looked at her with moist eyes and said, "I—I cannot urinate."

Gold translated what the man said. "I sure hope his bladder hasn't ruptured," Reyes said. He touched the man's abdomen again. "Yeah, the bladder area's distended."

"What can you do?" Gold asked.

"I'll be right back."

Reyes returned with a plastic container, a small needle and syringe, a larger needle, and an IV cannula with a length of tubing.

"What's that for?" Gold asked.

"He's going to get a suprapubic needle cystotomy. Talk to him. See if you can get him not to look at what I'm doing." Reyes pulled back the towel, then ripped open a Betadine pad and rubbed it on the man's skin. With the small needle, he injected something just under the skin.

"What are you giving him?" Gold asked.

"Local anesthetic," Reyes said. "Lidocaine."

Gold tapped the man on the shoulder and said in Pashto, "Where are you from?"

"Balkh," the man said.

Reyes raised the large needle and uncoiled the tubing. He left one end of the tubing in the plastic container.

"I have never seen Balkh," Gold said. The man glanced down at his waist, and Gold asked, "Is it a pretty place?"

"No."

Reyes inserted the needle straight into the patient's bladder. The man cried out and clutched at the towel. Even if he didn't feel the pain, Gold imagined, he knew something cold and metal had just pushed inside him. Yellow fluid began to flow into the container. Reyes taped the IV cannula into place. The man closed his eyes and sighed.

"Tashakor," he said.

"He says thank you," Gold said.

"Glad I got that right the first time," Reyes said. "I'd hate to stick him like that twice."

"Tashakor," the man repeated.

"Will he be okay?" Parson asked.

"Yeah, but I think it would have ruptured before the end of the day if you guys hadn't brought him in."

Gold looked down the rows of patients. Some had suffered amputations. Some cried out in agony. Some looked near death. Only the man Reyes had just treated showed any sign of relief. A drop of mercy in an ocean of pain.

Just then, the lightbulb fixtures suspended overhead began to sway. Gold felt a strange rolling sensation through the soles of her boots, as if for a moment the earth had turned to jelly. Patients cried to Allah.

"Aftershock," Parson said.

Parson reached into his helmet bag and took out his satphone. He dialed a duty officer with Joint Relief Task Force at Bagram Air Base. When the officer picked up, Parson said, "Felt like we just got hit again up here. What kind of damage reports do you have?"

"A few more buildings down in Mazar. Other than that, we don't know much. A lot of the outlying villages didn't have phone service to begin with, and those that did have lost their cell towers."

"I'm in Mazar with an Afghan flight crew," Parson said. "What do you need us to do?"

"The ops commander wants all available helicopter crews to survey the villages. Find out how much worse it is now."

"There are some PJs up here with us," Parson said. "Can I get some of those guys on board the Mi-17s?"

American pararescuemen didn't normally fly with Afghan crews, but in the aftermath of the quake, a lot of regs had been waived. Parson hoped he could bend one more rule.

"Stand by," the duty officer said. When he came back on the line, he said, "Commander says okay. We'll cut the flight orders and fax them up there."

With more people probably hurt, headquarters wanted him to wait for paperwork? Parson started to swear into the phone, but then he caught himself. He looked at Gold, decided to stay on his best behavior.

"Fine, fax the flight orders when you can," Parson said. "But can we go ahead and launch on the commander's verbal approval?"

"Stand by, sir."

Parson waited, fuming. It seemed the most common phrase in the Air Force was *stand by*. When the duty officer came back, he spoke a less common phrase—one Parson liked better: "That's approved."

"Roger that," Parson said. So somebody showed some sense down there at Bagram. He cradled the phone against his shoulder while he pulled a Tactical Pilotage Chart from his helmet bag. He unfolded the TPC across an empty cot. "All right, then," he said. "Which villages?" Parson jotted in the margins as he listened, circled a dot on the chart.

After the phone call, Parson found Rashid and his crew. "They want us to check Ghandaki," he said. "We have some American PJs we can take with us, and I got an interpreter you're gonna like."

"PJs?" Rashid asked.

"Pararescue jumpers," Parson explained. "Badass medics."

Parson reminded himself to stop throwing acronyms at Rashid. The guy was smart, but he had a hard enough time with standard English, let alone Air Force jargon. Rashid probably didn't know what *badass* meant, either.

Reyes and another PJ, Sergeant Burlingame, brought a wheeled cage filled with equipment out to the Mi-17. Parson helped them lift it into the chopper. When he raised his end of the cage, it felt like it weighed at least a couple hundred pounds. Inside it, he saw a crash ax, a sledgehammer, a power saw, and some other items he did not recognize.

"What the hell is this?" Parson asked.

"A REDS kit," Reyes said. "Rapid extrication tools. We use it for pulling you flyboys out of wreckage. But it'll help get people out of collapsed buildings, too."

Rashid looked on with a puzzled expression. Gold spoke in rapid-fire Pashto, and Rashid said in English, "That is very . . ." Then he and Gold had another exchange in Pashto.

"Impressive," Gold said finally.

"Yes," Rashid said. "That is very impressive."

"If you ever need a PJ," Parson said, "it means you're in a world of hurt."

Rashid nodded, but he didn't look like he really understood until Gold translated. Then he said, "I fear many Afghans are in hurt."

"Yeah," Parson said. "We might as well go find out." He pulled on his flak vest, clicked its snaps into place. Then he put his arms through the sleeves of his Nomex jacket and zipped it over the vest. Now he wore protection from both fire and shrapnel.

Rashid and his copilot and flight engineer strapped into

the cockpit and donned their white helmets. Parson, Gold, and the two PJs buckled into troop seats in the back.

The Afghans spoke just a few words on interphone, and the two Klimov engines spun up. Parson did not understand the terse conversation, but it didn't sound like enough talk for a proper engine start checklist. He'd have to work on their checklist discipline: Someday these guys might go on to fly more advanced aircraft, and you didn't just jump into an Apache and fire it up from memory like starting a Chevy. But for now, the fine points would have to wait.

As the rotors increased speed, Parson felt the vibration in his molars. He'd never get used to that. He'd spent his career in machines that rode the air. This one beat it into submission.

The Mi-17 lifted off, lowered its nose, gathered speed, climbed. Through the door on the left side, Parson could see the refugee camp and then the city of Mazar as Rashid made a turn to the southeast. The helo's shadow flew across the ground ahead of the aircraft like its own disembodied spirit.

Wind whipped a few strands of blond hair across Gold's face. She raised her right hand and brushed them away with her index finger. When she caught Parson looking at her, she did not change her expression, though he felt her lean into his side. Perhaps she was just cold, but he took it as a gesture of affection—one she could get away with here.

The gesture gave him a warm turn in the pit of his stomach. Parson didn't know where this relationship was going. But he liked it that a woman he respected so much would treat him with that kind of familiarity.

She still looked good. Parson knew she was pushing forty, though he didn't know her exact age. But the Airborne kept her fit. The lines around her eyes looked just a little deeper now, but that was all right. Someone so well-conditioned could remain attractive all her life.

The helicopter leveled, and Parson stretched to look over the flight engineer's shoulder into the cockpit. All three crew members seemed to peer outside. So they were navigating from memory, too. A bad habit. A good way to get lost. And at night, a good way to fly into a mountain.

Parson pressed his talk switch and said, "Charts, Rashid."

"Sorry."

Rashid spoke to his copilot in Pashto, and the copilot said something back. Gold smiled. The copilot opened a VFR chart and clipped it to his kneeboard.

"What?" Parson said, off interphone.

"He says you are like a hawk that sees everything," Gold said.

"They're good guys. I keep on them because I want them to live."

The terrain changed as it flowed underneath the chopper. The brown plateau of Mazar gave way to green patches of agriculture. In one field tucked into the cove of a hill, Parson saw scattered purple and white flowers—the telltale blooms of opium poppies. Most of the harvest had already ended. Maybe the guy wanted a late second crop. Sometimes Parson wished he could find an American or European drug user, beat the shit out of him, then show him photos of Taliban atrocities and tell him his money paid for the bullets and blades.

The opium field receded into the distance. It gave way to more hills, then a village.

"That's Ghandaki," Rashid said over interphone. The aircraft slowed and banked. Parson saw part of the village flash by under the crew chief's door gun. He unbuckled his seat belt and rose to look out a window.

It could be hard to assess damage from the air, even from a low and slow helicopter. An exploded home or a cratered courtyard might have been bombed yesterday or in 1984. Parson found it tough to distinguish war destruction from earthquake damage in these mud-brick towns. He had spent his career as an airlifter; he knew little of aerial surveillance. But even Parson could see Ghandaki had just lost its mosque.

He saw the collapsed dome, the toppled minarets. Judging by the brick walls that remained, Parson figured it a crude structure—nothing like the Blue Mosque in Mazar—but surely the best Ghandaki could afford.

Rashid and his crew chattered in their language. Gold furrowed her brow and checked her watch. She got up and looked outside.

"It might have been full of men praying," she said.

The Mi-17 made a low pass. Below, villagers climbed over the rubble. Some waved their arms. Men wearing *pakol* berets and white prayer caps pulled at lumber and crumbled masonry. They worked with only their bare hands.

"Put us down there, sir," Reyes said.

"All right," Parson said. "Rashid, did you copy that?"

When Rashid didn't answer, Parson looked to Gold for help. But then Rashid said, "I search for place to land."

Parson leaned forward to peer out the cockpit windscreen. Rashid had his work laid out for him. The mosque—or what was left of it—lay within the cut of a mountain stream. Mud huts surrounded it. A steep hillside dotted with scrub rose above the town. No spot within a half mile looked clear and level enough to serve as a landing zone.

Rashid twisted the grip throttle on the collective and pulled back on the cyclic. The helicopter cleared the hill, then turned back toward the mosque. Parson didn't consider the Mi-17 the best-designed aircraft he'd ever seen, but the damn thing had power. And unlike some U.S. aircraft, it wasn't junked up with electronic components from every congressional district. The Russians clearly intended a simple machine, maintained easily at a forward base by Ivan the mechanic with his vodka hangover. Perfect for Afghanistan.

The PJs looked out, and Reyes sized up the problem. "Sir," he said, "if they can give us a good hover, we'll put the REDS kit down on its lowering harness."

Parson raised his eyebrows at Gold, and she translated. Rashid gave a thumbs-up. The crew did not have much experience with helicopter suspension techniques, but Rashid was qualified, and he seemed game. They all needed to learn to think on the fly, literally, so they might as well start now.

The last time Parson and Gold had flown together, he'd certainly needed to think beyond any normal procedures. He'd mustered all the know-how he and his crew could find to crash-land a jet crippled by a terrorist bomb, and he still carried the scars. Like elderly people whose arthritis got worse when it rained, Parson's leg ached whenever the altimeter setting was low. He wondered if Gold carried scars, too. She had none he could see, but the invisible ones could be just as bad.

Reyes clipped a carabiner to a tie-down ring on the floor of the helicopter. He attached another to the top of the cage that contained the REDS kit. Then he looped a bight of rope around a figure-eight belay device and attached the figure-eight to the carabiner on the REDS cage. Parson, a lifelong outdoorsman and hunter, remembered mountain climbers used a similar belay system to protect themselves from falls.

The PJs placed suspension harnesses around their waists, and they moved the REDS cage near the door. Rashid pulled into a hover near the collapsed mosque, and dust began to swirl below. The chopper seemed to sway for a few seconds, but then Rashid stabilized his hover. When Reyes was satisfied he had a steady platform, he called, "Ropes." He and his partner positioned the REDS kit out the door and lowered it to the ground.

Then the two pararescuemen looped lines through their own belay gear. They stood in the door, facing inside the Mi-17, with their boots on the bottom edge of the door frame. Both men braked their rappelling lines by holding the ropes behind their backs. In unison, they brought their hands forward, bent their knees, swung themselves outward, and descended down the lines.

After the men reached the ground, Parson unclipped the lines, dropped them, and said on interphone, "Ropes are clear." Just as he saw the PJs remove their gloves and unstrap their harnesses, Rashid climbed away.

"There is a field outside of the town," Rashid said. "I land there."

"Copy that," Parson said. "You guys stay with the aircraft, and Sergeant Major Gold and I will walk to the mosque."

Rashid acknowledged with a double click of his interphone button. Another bad habit, but Parson tolerated this one. It meant *I heard you and understand*.

❧ 2 ❧

As the helicopter descended into the field, dry carostan grass undulated in the rotor wash. The wind blast seemed to turn the blades of grass to liquid, flowing in waves the color of mocha. The sight made Gold a little dizzy. She brought her eyes back inside the aircraft to give her brain and inner ear something that made more sense.

The crew chief watched the ground and talked Rashid down. "Ten meters, sir," he said. Heavy Pashtun accent. Gold wondered if numbers were the only English words he knew. She just hoped he could count down accurately. "Five meters. Two. One."

The chopper settled tentatively, as if it did not trust the stability of the earth. But when the rotors slowed, the machine finally surrendered to gravity. All pitching and rolling motion ended, and Gold realized Rashid had made as smooth a helicopter touchdown as she'd ever felt.

The fliers shut down the engines. The only noises that remained were the metallic clinks of harness buckles unlocked and dropped to the floor. The crew chief and flight engineer rose from their seats, climbed down the boarding steps, and stood guard outside the helo with their AK-47s. Ghandaki wasn't considered particularly dangerous, but Gold appreciated that they took no chances.

Rashid removed his helmet and took off his gloves. The helmet left his black hair matted, and he ran his fingers through his hair. He placed the heel of his hand on the edge of the main panel, pushed himself out of his seat, and sat in the back with Gold and Parson.

"Have you known Lieutenant Colonel Parson for a long time?" Rashid asked in Pashto.

"We have been through much together," Gold said.

"If you are his friend, then you are my sister."

"Thank you, sir."

Rashid unzipped a leg pocket on his American-style flight suit. He withdrew a half-empty pack of Camels, shook out a cigarette, and held it between his fingers.

"Rashid," Parson said, "you guys just hang out—I mean, stay here. Gold and I will go to the mosque."

"We stay," Rashid said.

Parson took his Beretta out of his thigh rig. He checked the weapon, holstered it, then picked up his helmet bag and satphone. The helmet bag didn't look particularly heavy, and Gold realized it didn't actually contain a helmet since Parson preferred to use a headset. She noticed all the patches sewn onto the bag's nylon exterior: OPERATION JOINT FORGE, OPERATION ENDURING FREEDOM, OPERATION IRAQI FREEDOM, OPERATION UNIFIED PROTECTOR. Missions in Bosnia, Afghanistan, Iraq, Libya. An unofficial patch, too:

TERRORIST HUNTING PERMIT. He tromped down the boarding steps and into the grass. His limp was a little more apparent, maybe because he'd just stood up. Gold lifted her rifle, exited behind Parson, and slung the M4 across her shoulder. Rashid came out last, placed the cigarette between his teeth, and fired it up with a Bic lighter.

"Tell him those things will kill him," Parson said.

Gold translated, and Rashid said, "Something else will get me first." He exhaled twin plumes of smoke from his nostrils and looked into the distance.

His fatalism saddened Gold, but didn't surprise her. So many Afghans adopted that same outlook. Yet they got up every day and did whatever they did.

"Let's go see what we got down there," Parson said.

Parson led the way through the field of knee-high carostan. The mere sight of him walking ahead of her brought back a particular hell: Following Parson through the snow, pursued by the Taliban, dragging along a prisoner. Fear and pain twisting through her like a chronic sickness.

She stopped. Looked around at the mountains. Parson looked back at her. "You coming?" he said.

"I'm all right."

She glanced at the finger she'd injured in the HALO jump. The nail was starting to grow back. Parson said nothing else, just waited for her to catch up.

At the edge of the field, Gold saw a group of women by the stream. The women were wrapping a body in a white shroud. Afghans did not embalm their dead, and they preferred to conduct the burial by sundown on the day of death. Gold supposed the women had just washed the corpse. The deceased must have been female; otherwise, men would have done the job.

Two of the women looked over at Gold. When she met their eyes it felt like regarding a person's reflection in a pool of water, staring at someone not really there. She wondered about their stories; everyone in Afghanistan had lost someone to war and disaster. And to whatever extent Afghan life was hellish, it was doubly so for females. Gold knew mullahs who preached that a woman found her place in the home or in the grave.

The grind of an electric saw rose from the mosque. From a distance of a couple hundred yards, Gold saw only the outer courtyard walls. Apparently the pararescuemen had opened their gear and gone to work. When Gold and Parson entered the courtyard, they found Reyes cutting into a wooden beam amid the jumble of bricks and stones. Nearby, Burlingame shone a light into the eyes of a man lying on the ground.

Nothing remained of the mosque's structure. The building had collapsed so completely that Gold could not distinguish one room from another. Only the courtyard walls survived, and not without damage: Chunks of stone and mortar had fallen away, and one section appeared warped, as if the earth had somehow exerted torque from underneath.

Villagers dressed in *shalwar kameez* climbed through the rubble. Several small boys wandered among the adults, along with one girl who looked about eleven. Wails came from underneath the rocks, audible even over the cordless saw. The cries of the unseen trapped carried special poignancy. Discarnate voices of pain.

The locals showed no open hostility. Infidels were forbidden to enter a mosque, but nothing remained to enter. And the Americans had obviously come to help. Still, Gold felt a few hard glares when the Afghan men noticed her hair tied in a bun.

"Salaam," Gold said to the girl. The child's almond eyes widened as she stared. It wasn't likely she'd met a foreigner before, Gold thought, let alone a foreign woman who spoke her language. Gold asked, "May we speak to the imam?"

"God willing, you may," the child said. "But he is trapped. Are you an American?"

"I am," Gold said. "My name is Sophia. What is your name?"

"Fatima."

Fatima's shoulder-length hair shined a deep black. Evidently someone cared enough about her to wash and cut it. The girl seemed to be uninjured, and she moved with the grace of an ibex. Another of Afghanistan's special tragedies: The girls could look so beautiful, but then age hit them early like a sudden illness. Gold marveled that Fatima was so well-spoken. A candle flame of intelligence that some here would like to extinguish.

"Where are your parents?"

"My mama is at home. My papa died a long time ago. My brother is over there." She pointed to the boys lifting stones out of the ruins.

Gold expected the girl to run off and join the other

children. Most Afghan kids were painfully shy. But Fatima followed Gold around at a respectful distance, perhaps trying to understand the strange sight of a blond woman dressed like a man, carrying a rifle, and walking around as if she had every right to appear outside her home.

More cries came from within the rubble. "How many people are in there?" Parson asked. He had to shout over the noise of the saw.

Reyes eased off the trigger, and the saw hushed. "I've heard five or six," he said. "The locals have pulled one out already."

"You guys are going to need some help," Parson said.

"Yes, sir."

Parson took out his satphone and began punching numbers. Reyes went back to work with the saw, and its cacophony filled the courtyard again. Beyond him, three dead lay under blankets. Gold felt sick to her stomach; the scene appeared like a vision of hell from some woodcut image out of the Dark Ages: crushed bodies, slicing blades, religious symbols broken.

Some of Gold's own nightmares looked a bit like that, and recently the bad scenes even came during waking hours. Intrusive memories, the counselors called them. Remembrances of things past with a motive force of their own, returning unbidden and unwanted. Things like Parson's beheaded crewmate, found in an insurgent hideout. Her favorite student, Mahsoud, getting a field amputation in the ruins of the police training center.

She forced it all back into that deep place where she kept such memories, and she tried to get to work.

"What can I do?" she yelled to Reyes. He released the saw's trigger again. His cut went only about halfway through the wooden beam, more than a foot thick. A dark slot in the lumber and a dusting of sawdust beneath it marked the blade's progress.

"Come up here where I am," he said. "Watch your step, and don't put your weight on that slab there." He tipped his chin toward a wall-size section of concrete; with his hands on the DeWALT saw, he could not point. "Somebody's under it."

Gold climbed what amounted to a slag pile. Bricks and debris shifted under her boots and caused her ankle to twist. She regained her balance and tested with her heel for better footing. When she reached Reyes, she saw a hole that revealed the head and torso of an elderly man. The half-cut wooden beam loomed above him. Dust covered his gray hair and beard. His cheeks looked like wrinkled, dirty leather. He gazed up at Gold and Reyes with pleading eyes.

"Kum zai de dard kawee?" Gold asked. Where are you hurt?

"Laingai," he said.

"He says his leg is hurt," Gold said.

"I gotta cut this lumber out of the way before I can even get to him," Reyes said. "I think part of the ceiling fell across his legs. Tell him to turn his face down. I don't want to get sawdust in his eyes."

Gold explained in Pashto, and the man said, "Do not let that piece of wood fall on me."

"We will catch it when we cut it," Gold said.

"Allah's blessings upon you."

The saw roared. Gold noticed Parson talking with the satphone in his right ear. He put his finger over his left ear and turned away from the noise.

The blade cut deeper into the wood, and sawdust settled into the rubble like snow. Gold adjusted her rifle sling over her shoulder. Then she took gloves from her pocket, put them on, and grabbed the end of the beam. She saw Fatima watching it all from just a few feet away.

"It'll be heavy when it comes loose," Reyes said. "Their masonry is shit, but that's good lumber."

"I got it," Gold said.

Parson turned off the satphone and put it back in its case. Gold hadn't heard the conversation, but from the look on Parson's face, it hadn't gone well. He climbed the rubble and took hold of the crossbeam with Gold.

"Get ready," Reyes said as the saw bit down to the last inch. The severed section splintered away, and Gold and Parson held it suspended over the trapped man. Despite Reyes's warning, it was heavier than Gold expected. Newly sawn edges dug into her palms. She and Parson shuffled down the debris pile and dropped the beam. As it tumbled among the bricks, Gold slipped and fell.

Her wrists stung as she caught herself with the heels of her hands. Shifting stones pinched her fingers. The stock of her M4 dug into her side.

"You all right?" Parson asked. He extended a hand and helped her get to her feet.

"I think so."

Gold felt a flush of anxiety she could not explain.

The villagers seemed harmless, or at least not openly threatening. They kept glancing up at her as they pulled at masonry and hauled debris, but the stares could have come from curiosity alone. I'm just tired, she thought. My body clock hasn't adjusted to crossing all those time zones.

She forced her mind back to the job. "So what did you learn in your phone call?" she asked.

"There aren't any more pararescue guys available. They're all tied up in other places. The aftershock hit Mirdshi real bad, and a lot of Kariz is on fire."

Reyes sighed. "We'll just deal with it, then," he said. Then he called out, "Hey, Burlingame. Let's try the spreader to get this slab of ceiling off this guy's legs."

"I'll set it up," Burlingame said. He left the patient he'd been helping and lifted a gasoline-powered pump from the REDS case. Then he hooked up lines leading to a tool that appeared vaguely like a tremendous set of shears with the blades closed.

Burlingame yanked a cord to crank the pump engine as if he were starting an old lawn mower. The pump coughed, belched blue smoke, and then settled into a steady hum. The noise bothered Gold, and she hoped they wouldn't need to run the equipment for long.

"Okay," Burlingame said over the engine's racket, "we got pressure."

Reyes took the spreader and groped his way into the crevice where the old man lay trapped. The man's eyes widened, and he demanded to know what the pararescueman planned to do.

"He's worried you're going to cut him with that thing," Gold said.

"I'm going to pry the concrete off him," Reyes said.

Gold explained in Pashto. The man stopped talking, but he still looked scared. Reyes jammed the spreader underneath the slab and twisted the tool clockwise.

"Ma'am," he said, "tell him to let us know if this hurts."

Gold spoke to the man, and he replied, "It already hurts, my daughter."

"Tell us if it gets worse," Gold said.

She was starting to like the old man. Some Afghan clerics considered her very existence a blasphemy. Gold remembered one in particular, the mullah she and Parson had dragged through a winter storm. But this imam didn't seem to despise Americans, and he had called her *daughter*. Not words you'd expect from a hate-monger, even one in need.

"All right," Reyes said, "here goes." He adjusted something on the spreader tool, and its jaws began to move apart. The slab over the man's legs shifted. He cried out.

"My foot," he said in Pashto.

"Watch out for his foot," Gold explained in English.

"I can't see his feet," Reyes said. "Can he move at all now?"

Gold asked the imam if he could try to pull out his legs. He twisted his mouth as if in intense concentration. Veins emerged under the skin of his neck, and he groaned through gritted teeth.

"No, my daughter."

"He still can't move," Gold said.

"Let me see if I can help brace him," Parson said. Parson slid down into the crevice where the old man lay. He held the imam by the shoulders.

"Thank you, my son," the old man said in Pashto.

"We'll probably have to do him a little more damage just to get him out," Burlingame said.

"That's what I'm afraid of," Reyes said.

"Can I get down there and help you?" Burlingame asked.

"There's no more room," Parson said. "Go see who we need to work on next."

"Yes, sir." Burlingame began searching the debris, looking where the locals pointed.

Down in the hole, the imam stared at the spreader with an apparent mixture of fear and fascination. Looked up at Gold, then at Parson and Reyes.

"Tell him to hold on," Reyes said to Gold. "I'll have him out in a minute."

The spreader jaws separated farther, and the slab moved. The old man screamed. Blood ran from underneath his legs and dripped from stone to stone. When the blood flowed through dirt, it separated into rolling, burgundy beads.

The sight of blood never used to disturb Gold, but it did now. She began to sweat. Saliva flooded the back of her mouth like she was about to throw up.

She looked away, tried to regain her composure. Her eyes focused on small details within the scene of destruction: A comb missing half its teeth. A toy car without wheels. No telling how those things came to be in a mosque.

Reyes put down the spreader, and Parson heaved the man up by his arms. Reyes helped pull the imam from the hole in the debris, and they laid him down in the flattest spot they could find. Blood had soaked his clothing from the thighs down. One foot was mangled, and the other had twisted around nearly backward. Gold figured he'd probably lose both of them.

"I'll see if I can stop this bleeding," Reyes said. He turned off the pump and went for his medical ruck.

With the rattle of the small engine hushed, Gold could hear the imam praying. She kneeled beside him, and when he finished, she said, "You are in good hands. We will get you to a hospital."

"Some of my people are still inside," he said.

"We will do all we can."

Gold looked around for Fatima; she worried about the girl seeing blood. But the child had disappeared.

In the meantime, Burlingame apparently found someone else alive and trapped. He repositioned the pump and spreader tool, and he started the engine again. That's when Gold noticed three men on the hill beyond the mosque. They wore black turbans, and they seemed to be the only people not doing anything. All three stood watching, and the sight of them made Gold's skin grow clammy. They did not speak. Their eyes conveyed nothing but maledictions. Their inactivity seemed even more hostile than their cold expressions.

―――――――

Parson had known people who couldn't stop talking when they were drunk. Apparently, morphine had the same effect on the imam. He kept yammering away with Gold. Parson almost wished they'd shut up. But he knew nothing could help the cause more than a chatty cleric who had bonded with Sophia. He'd seen her have that effect on people. Most of the Afghans she met wanted to tell her their life stories—unless they were trying to kill her. He figured the talking would do Gold good, too. She seemed a little rattled.

Reyes and Burlingame loaded the old man into the helicopter. He lay on the floor of the Mi-17, still speaking with Gold. His face bore scars that looked like he'd been burned by grease splashed from a frying pan. Parson had wondered why so many Afghans suffered kitchen accidents. But then he learned the disfigurement came from leishmaniasis, a parasitic disease spread by the bite of a sand fly.

The PJs put nine other patients on the aircraft, even though the helicopter's cargo compartment was not configured for a medical flight. It carried no stanchions for mounting stretchers, but at least it had plenty of room: The passenger version of the Mi-17 seated twenty-eight people. Reyes and Burlingame spread their patients on the floor and tried to make them as comfortable as possible. In all, they'd pulled six from the ruined mosque and treated a dozen other villagers for contusions and broken bones.

Ten needed a doctor, so Parson decided to fly them back to Mazar.

He suspected a lot of other chopper crews were making the same decision, and he hoped the MASF wouldn't be overwhelmed. Nothing he could do about that, though.

The setting sun glowed a burnt orange just above a distant ridge. Dying light deepened the reddish tint of mineral deposits along the slopes. The air grew chillier by the minute; coolness at dusk marked the hinge of seasons. And though the village seemed relatively safe, Parson did not want to remain here after dark.

Rashid stood outside the front of his aircraft, smoking. The crew chief and flight engineer waded through the carostan grass, looking up and inspecting the rotor blades. The copilot studied a chart.

"Let's get the hell out of Dodge, Rashid," Parson said. He'd used that Americanism often enough that the Afghan officer understood it.

Rashid flicked the cigarette butt with his thumb and middle finger. It arced away like a tracer round. Rashid put on his helmet, and with a vertical index finger, he made a rotary motion to signal his men. A good sign, Parson noted. When guys could communicate without talking, they were becoming a tight crew.

Gold strapped in beside Parson as the igniters started clicking inside the APU. It lit off with a turbine howl, and its exhaust wafted into the chopper.

"So what did you two find so much to talk about?" Parson shouted over the noise.

"He says he hates the Taliban," Gold said.

"I bet they all say that when we save their asses."

"Well, he says he hates the Taliban because they made him stop raising pigeons."

"A man's gotta have his pigeons," Parson said. Then he put a gloved hand over hers for just a second, and he said, "Hey, are you all right?"

Gold pursed her lips and nodded her head. Parson didn't buy it, but he chose not to press her further. Yelling in a helicopter probably wasn't the way to have a conversation about post-traumatic stress. He wouldn't have wanted careless questions about his own issues: *Hey, flyboy, still seeing your loadmaster with his head cut off?*

The main rotor began turning. Parson noted the rotor's shadow moving across the ground just outside: one blade, two, three.

Suddenly:

"RPG!" Reyes shouted.

Parson felt a cracking boom. The blast seemed to crush his eardrums. Something knocked away his headset.

The world went white.

Stings nettled the back of Parson's neck. The helicopter bounced, rocked. For a moment he heard nothing. But he knew there had been an explosion.

In blurred images, he saw the crew chief depress the trigger on his door gun. A cascade of brass rattled from the automatic weapon. The Afghan patients screamed and called to Allah.

Gold snapped open the clasp of her seat belt buckle. In a single motion, she brought up her M4 and clicked the fire mode selector. She jumped out the door without touching the three steps of the boarding ladder. Reyes and Burlingame leaped from the aircraft with their own rifles.

Parson's bearings came back like gyroscopes reinitializing after a power loss. He unbuckled, drew his Beretta. Pops of gunfire sounded far, then near. Attackers shooting, the PJs returning fire.

He scrambled for the door. Something soft under his boots; he'd stepped on a patient. He ducked through the doorway and stumbled outside into the grass. He kneeled among the blades of carostan, tried to make himself invisible.

Rashid remained inside the cockpit, shouting orders in Pashto. Through the glass, Parson saw the crew struggling out of their harnesses. A bullet punched through the center windscreen. Minute cracks instantly spread outward from the hole, and the crazed glass went cloudy. Blood streaked across the inside of the windscreen. The flight engineer slumped forward.

Gold, Reyes, and Burlingame lay prone, firing. The carostan concealed them well. Parson saw little of Gold except her boot heels, her rifle muzzle bouncing with each round, and her ejected cartridges spinning end over end.

"Cover the other side of the helo," Reyes told Burlingame. As Reyes spoke, he fired two rounds at a turbaned figure running toward the helicopter with an AK. The man went down.

Burlingame rose and dashed around the aircraft. Parson followed. The PJ dropped into the grass and did not fire. Blood spurted from an exit wound at the back of his thigh.

Not this again, Parson thought. Dear God, not again. He pressed himself as low against the ground as he could, scanned for the enemy. A man with a grenade launcher kneeled in the grass down the hill. Maybe forty yards away. Long shot for a handgun.

Parson fired three rounds from his pistol. Pulled the trigger a fourth time. Nothing happened. Jammed.

The jihadist with the grenade launcher was down in the grass. Hit, maybe. Parson struggled to clear his weapon. Slapped the bottom of the magazine. Racked the slide. Fired again.

Rounds whacked into the side of the Mi-17. From where, Parson couldn't tell.

Grenade guy raised up on unsteady knees. Still not disabled, then. Parson dropped his Beretta, reached for Burlingame's M4. The jihadist leveled the grenade launcher.

Parson opened up with the rifle. The terrorist in his sights crumpled, fired the grenade launcher. Smoke wisped from the launcher's breech as the man fell. The grenade flew wild, arced over the helicopter, and exploded behind it.

Rashid appeared under the tail boom. He shot at two insurgents approaching from the rear of the Mi-17. One dropped. The other turned back.

The shooting died down. Parson held his breath, kept his weapon raised, waited for another attack. None came. But under the whine of the APU, Parson heard screams from within the town. One shot echoed from among the houses. A moment later, two more.

Parson wondered what was going on. Why hadn't they

been overrun? A lightly armed aircrew on an exposed hill-side made for an easy target. But the firefight seemed to have ended, though something was still happening down the hill.

He glanced over his shoulder at the aircraft. The RPG had torn open the right engine cowling, ripped away the accessory gearbox, and damaged the main rotor. The Mi-17 wasn't going anywhere soon.

"Colonel Parson?" Gold called from the other side of the chopper.

"I'm good, Sophia," he shouted. "You?"

"Yes, sir. But the flight engineer is dead. The copilot's wounded."

Parson checked Burlingame. The injured PJ was trying to pull something out of his medical kit.

"I got gauze pads in here," he said. "Put some pressure on both sides of the wound."

Parson found the pads and opened them. He placed them over the entrance and exit wounds, and he pressed down. Blood soaked through the pads and into the fabric of Parson's flight gloves. The PJ grimaced but did not cry out.

"Reyes," Parson called. "Your buddy's hit."

"How bad?" Reyes shouted from inside the helicopter.

"Shot in the leg."

"Stop the bleeding as best you can," Reyes yelled. "The preacher's hit bad in here."

Parson found a triangular bandage in Burlingame's medical ruck. He tied it around the PJ's leg, over both gauze pads. By now the dressings were saturated with blood.

"Just put fresh bandages over the old ones," Burlingame said. He spoke like a man overtired. Parson supposed the blood loss was starting to affect him. Red smears darkened the grass beaten down around the PJ. The reddened blades of carostan reminded Parson of the blood spoor he'd once followed when tracking a wounded elk.

He tied on more gauze pads. The bleeding slowed. "Are you going to be all right if I make a radio call?" Parson asked.

"Yeah, just leave me my rifle."

Burlingame sat up, still in obvious pain. Parson handed him the weapon. Rashid walked up to Parson, removed his helmet.

"Please get help for my men," he said. The Afghan pilot's eyes glistened. The lines in his face seemed deeper.

"I will, buddy." Parson knew all too well how Rashid felt. Years ago, Parson's C-130 had been shot down in the midst of the worst blizzard Afghanistan had ever recorded. He managed to survive with Gold and their prisoner, but all his crewmates had died. The hurt remained with Parson as if the crash had just happened.

When Parson stepped inside the helicopter, he saw Reyes examining the imam. The old man had been shot in the side, and Gold held a bandage on the wound.

"Don't die on me, grandpa," Reyes said. "I worked my ass off to dig you out."

Gold looked at Parson as he stepped around the flight engineer's body, but she did not speak. Rashid's copilot held pressure on a wound to his own arm.

Parson's boot slipped in the blood on the floor. He

nearly fell, but he caught himself against the cockpit bulk-head. He gathered up his headset, lowered himself into the pilot's seat, and plugged the headset into a comm cord.

On that unfamiliar helicopter panel, it took Parson a second to find the control head for the UHF radio. Blood stuck to the frequency selector. The radio and all the avionics remained powered up as if the Mi-17 still waited to fly. Parson pressed the talk switch on the cyclic.

"Mayday, mayday," he called. "Any aircraft. Golay Six-Four is down. Enemy fire."

To his relief, an answer came quickly: "Golay Six-Four, Cyclops One-Eight. Go ahead."

"Cyclops," Parson said, "we are an Mi-17 with about ten wounded U.S. and Afghan personnel." Parson followed up with his location, and he described the injuries. "Who am I talking to?" he added.

"Cyclops is an RC-135 on station."

A Rivet Joint bird. A Boeing filled with electronic eavesdropping gear. Not the first aircraft Parson expected to reach in the midst of an earthquake recovery, but he'd take any help he could get.

A few moments later, the Rivet Joint called back. "Golay," the pilot said, "be advised an MV-22 is inbound your position."

"Golay copies," Parson said. So the Marines were on the way in an Osprey. Maybe once the wounded got out, he could learn what the hell had happened in the village.

Parson turned off the APU and kept the radio alive with battery power. No sense tormenting the injured with that turbine screaming. And this way, the crew could hear better if those insurgent bastards tried to sneak up on them again.

The silence felt strange. Nothing but the whimpers of the patients and the grainy hum of UHF. In the quiet, Parson thought he heard distant thunder. Then he realized nothing could have come out of that clear sky but an air strike. Around the natural disaster, the war went on both near and far. Pain did not stop for pain.

3

Gold kept direct pressure on the imam's wound like Reyes had told her. She held little hope for the man's survival. Judging by the angle of entrance, the bullet might have ripped through his lungs. Pink foam flecked his lips. Reyes performed a chin lift to help the imam breathe. Then he moved on to the other wounded. Triage, Gold realized. He doesn't think the imam will make it.

The old man's eyes grew glassy. He stopped bleeding. In a few minutes, Reyes came back, put two fingers to the imam's throat, shone a light into his pupils. "He's gone," Reyes said.

Gold ripped the soaked compress off the wound, slapped it onto the floor. Blood dripped from her fingertips. Some of it had seeped under her nails and formed burgundy stains as if she'd dug barehanded into red soil. She wiped her fingers on her ACU trousers.

"I'm sorry," she said.

"I thought the old guy was home free when we got him out," Reyes said.

There's no such thing as home free, Gold thought. But why had the insurgents attacked now? Couldn't they see this was a relief operation?

In her training, she'd studied not just language but religions and cultures. Her own faith and interests led her deeper into philosophy and theology. And as she looked down at the imam, she thought of an old Talmudic teaching: *To take one life is to kill the whole world.*

Beside him lay two other patients who had died in the RPG explosion. One had no fresh wounds that Gold could see; he was just dead. The other had a metal fragment the size of an ax blade embedded in the flesh under his chin, and the blood had gushed out of him in such quantity that he appeared to have been dipped in red. She looked away, but it was no use. Some things, once seen, could never be unseen.

But she still had a mission to accomplish. The dead needed to be taken back to the village as soon as it was safe. Their families would want to bury them today, if possible. That burial might prove difficult; Gold could already feel night's approach as shadows climbed the mountains. And until help arrived, Parson and the crew couldn't leave the wounded.

Gold wondered what they might find in the village. The bad guys should have pressed the attack when they'd disabled the helicopter. They could have murdered all the crew and passengers. But they'd chosen not to, and there had to be a reason.

Up front, Parson stopped fiddling with the radio. He took off his headset, unplugged it, and placed it on the center console. Muttering curses, he climbed out of the pilot's seat and stood over the flight engineer's body. To get out during the firefight, Rashid had pushed the engineer off the jump seat. The engineer lay sprawled on his back with a single gunshot wound to the upper chest. The engineer's helmet remained in place, its boom mike still positioned above lifeless lips. Parson unzipped his jacket and placed it over the dead flier's face.

The wounded copilot looked on from a troop seat. He said in Pashto, "The lieutenant colonel is still like a hawk. He sees what must be done." Gold nodded in agreement but said nothing.

"Let's go keep Rashid company," Parson said to Gold.

At that moment, she didn't feel like facing someone else's pain. But it was part of her job. She picked up her rifle and followed Parson outside. The copilot came with them and sat in the grass beside Burlingame. The wounded PJ was sitting up, wrapping a new bandage around his leg. His bleeding seemed to be under control, so Gold figured the bullet must have missed his femoral artery. Rashid stood and stared into the hills, his helmet in his left hand and his pistol in his right.

"I am very sorry about your crewman," Gold said to Rashid in Pashto.

"When he first enlisted he could barely read," Rashid said. "He came to know this machine the way a mullah knows the Quran."

"Perhaps he has found paradise," Gold said.

"God willing. But we need him here."

Gold wanted to say something by way of consolation. Before she found the words, a rhythmic pulsing rose in the distance, like the beat of a helicopter, but with a slightly higher frequency. The thrumming grew louder.

"What is that?" Rashid asked in English.

"Our Osprey," Parson said. "The jarheads are here."

"Must be a TRAP team," Burlingame said.

"They are trapped?" Rashid said.

"No," Parson answered. "Tactical recovery of aircraft and personnel."

"Almost as good as pararescue," Burlingame said. He shifted his weight onto one hip, shut his eyes for a moment.

When the Osprey appeared just above a ridgeline, its twin rotors made Gold think of the wings of a dragonfly skimming a millpond back home in Vermont. The aircraft began descending toward the field. Two helicopter gunships accompanied it: wasps guarding the dragonfly. Gold eventually recognized them as Cobra attack choppers.

The gunships remained aloft as the Osprey landed. They circled the village and the field in a show of force, but they did not fire. Dust and blades of dry grass swirled through the air as the Osprey settled to the ground. On its open ramp, a crew chief manned a machine gun mounted on a pintle. A belt of ammunition fed into the weapon from one side, and a black hose for catching empty brass extended from the other.

Gold squinted and turned her head from the blast of wind. When the gale subsided, she looked up to see Marines pouring off the Osprey's ramp. She knew they'd make no assumptions about who was friendly, so she pointed her rifle away from them and kept her hand off the trigger.

The TRAP team set up a perimeter: Riflemen dropped to the ground in a semicircle around the Mi-17, weapons aimed out at anything that might approach it. A few of the Marines trotted over to the helicopter.

"What do you have, sir?" a gunnery sergeant asked Parson. The gunny was the biggest human being Gold had ever seen. A black man well over six feet, maybe just shy of three hundred pounds, and none of it fat. Fingers the size of .50-cal cartridges. Arms like the cypress roots in the lakes near Fort Bragg. Accent of the Deep South. His name was Blount.

"Four dead Afghan nationals inside the Mi-17," Parson said. "That American PJ over there has a gunshot wound to the leg. The Afghan flier sitting next to him is also hurt. More wounded in the aircraft."

"Aye, sir," Blount said.

"There's something else," Gold said. She explained about the gunfire and screams heard from down in the village.

"We'll evac the wounded, and we'll leave some Marines to do a recon down there," Blount said.

"This is my interpreter, Sergeant Major Gold," Parson said. "We'll go into the town with you. I tried to get some help in here even before we got lit up, but nobody was available."

"There's problems all over the place with the aftershocks," Blount said. "We were headed somewhere north of Mazar, but we got diverted when y'all called in under fire."

One of the TRAP members examined Burlingame's leg wound. The medic wore the chevrons of a Navy petty officer—a hospital corpsman. His sleeves were rolled up in the Marine Corps style, and as he treated Burlingame, Gold saw a blue tattoo on the inside of his forearm: a column of names, all of them sergeants and lance corporals. Fallen comrades, Gold supposed. Nine of them.

The corpsman rolled Burlingame onto a litter, and Gold helped carry him into the Osprey. As she maneuvered her end of the litter up the steel ramp, she noticed the inside of the aircraft still smelled like a new car. Strange, modern war.

Gold and the corpsman, along with Parson and Reyes, loaded the wounded Afghans aboard the Marine aircraft one by one. Rashid's copilot walked on board, assisted by the crew chief.

"We will fly together again," Rashid told the two Afghan fliers.

"Inshallah," the copilot said.

With all the patients transferred to the Osprey, Parson went forward into the cockpit and conferred with the pilots. Gold couldn't follow the conversation, but the pilots also seemed to be talking on the radio. Then they'd speak to Parson again. He shrugged, then nodded. Finally he gave a thumbs-up.

When he returned through the back of the Osprey, he said, "If you have anything left in the helicopter, go ahead and get it now."

"Why?" Gold asked.

"The Cobras are going to blow it."

Gold understood. She'd heard from air cav and medevac soldiers about helicopters disabled by enemy fire. If you couldn't fix it quickly and fly it out, you destroyed it. That way the enemy wouldn't get any use out of the parts or intel out of the electronics.

Parson retrieved his headset and helmet bag from the chopper, and Gold picked up her rucksack. Reyes gathered the medical gear he'd scattered while working on the wounded. Rashid never spoke as they moved the dead well away from his aircraft, and he never entered the helicopter. Parson picked up Rashid's checklist binder and flight bag. When they were finished, nothing lay on the floor of the Mi-17 but smears of blood.

"The snake drivers want us way down the hill," Parson said. "That'll keep us away from any debris that goes flying."

Blount and four other Marines led the way out of the field, toward the village. Gold, Parson, Rashid, and Reyes followed. Gold looked back over her shoulder to see the Osprey's crew chief jog over to the Mi-17. Still wearing his flight helmet, cord dangling from his shoulder, the Marine flier climbed aboard and satisfied himself that no one remained inside. Then he ran back to his own aircraft.

A few moments later, the Osprey's rotors picked up speed. Gold felt the staccato beat vibrate through her rib cage as the MV-22 levitated into the air like a helicopter. The Osprey rocked slightly, rotated into the wind, and accelerated. As the aircraft climbed and gathered speed, its nacelles tilted forward until the rotors positioned themselves like giant propellers. Now the tilt-rotor flew as a fixed-wing airplane. It grew smaller and smaller until absorbed by the cumulus that cloaked the horizon to the north.

The thick grass made for difficult walking even downhill. Blount bulldozed through it more easily than the rest; the rustling blades came up above Gold's knees but only to Blount's calves. The Marine wore a combat utility uniform in MARPAT digital camo. He carried a Squad Advanced Marksman Rifle, a scoped M16 larger than Gold's M4 carbine.

Parson followed close behind the Marines. From the set of his jaw, Gold could see he was angry—at the loss of Rashid's flight engineer, at the destruction of an aircraft. She knew how deeply he felt the loss of his own crew years ago, and she could imagine what must be going through his mind.

Reyes seemed to take it all in stride. He scanned to the left and right, held his index finger across the trigger guard of his rifle, took long steps through the grass. Gold didn't know him, and she'd had little contact with Air Force pararescuemen; she'd met them only on a few HALO training jumps. But she knew PJs were taught to expect anything and assume nothing when they parachuted or rappelled to reach a downed pilot or wounded soldier. A patch Velcroed under the flag on his left sleeve displayed his blood type: AB POS.

Rashid held his pistol and kept looking down at the village. Gold thought that was a good thing. She knew he was upset about his crewmates, but at least he seemed to have his mind on what was happening now.

"This is probably far enough," Parson said eventually. The carcass of the Mi-17 was at least a half mile away, silhouetted by the rising terrain behind it. He stopped, turned to look at the stricken helicopter.

Gold supposed Parson wanted to see the fireworks; she felt too heartsick to care. The run of events, the big picture, haunted her now. Things would get worse before they got worse.

A spray of sparrows settled into a birch by a low stone wall at the edge of town. One of the Cobras orbited overhead while the other rolled onto its firing run. It descended at a steep angle, then lined up on its target. Everything about the gunship—its hard edges, stingerlike shape, smudged trail of exhaust—seemed to threaten. Gold thought that even someone from centuries past could look on that thing and know it was a weapon.

Smoke boiled from underneath the Cobra. A dot of light—Gold could make out no more than that—shot from within the smoke. It corkscrewed for an instant and then straightened itself on a direct path to the Mi-17.

When the projectile struck, the helicopter swelled with fire. The entire mass lifted off the ground. Then, in apparent slow motion, its components disassociated from one another. The main rotor spun free like a flaming pinwheel. The tail boom danced end over end through flickering billows. Sparks arced away like embers kicked from a banked campfire, bounced as they fell back to the ground. A half beat later came the noise. Not a blast, more like a hard crump from the very inside of Gold's head. The sparrows exploded from the birch.

"What in God's name?" Rashid asked in English.

"A TOW missile," Parson said.

Not in God's name, Gold thought. All these things around us man has brought on himself, claims for God notwithstanding.

The helicopter and the grass around it burned. The flames and towering smoke made Gold think of old-time New England farmers firing their fields. But the smell wasn't the same. Too much odor of oil, fuel, and high explosives.

What kind of stance to take going into the village—that was Parson's next decision. Ground tactics weren't his field, but he was the highest-ranking officer present. And this wasn't the first time circumstances had forced him to take command without the preparation he'd have liked.

He could go in soft: Knock on doors and let Gold make introductions. Or go in hard: Let the Marines kick down doors and, if they found nothing threatening, let Gold smooth it over.

Parson chose the latter. They'd taken fire. If some bad guys remained behind to set a trap, no sense making it easy for them to spring it. Later, somebody might say he should have been nicer. But Parson knew an old joke about that kind of thing: *How many stateside second-guessers in air-conditioned offices does it take to screw in a lightbulb? Two: One to screw in the bulb and one to kiss my ass.*

He explained his plan to his de facto team. "I don't know what we're going to find," he said. "I've seen those sons of bitches massacre a whole village. But I don't think I heard enough shooting for that to have happened here."

"We got it, sir," Blount said.

A smoke haze from the burning Mi-17 hung over the settlement. Tires had cut deep ruts in the muck of its one dirt street, but Parson saw no vehicles. Just a pair of chickens pecking at grains of spilled rice and a goat near enough to starving that its ribs protruded.

Wails and cries emanated from some of the houses. Blount chose the nearest one, pointed to the door, whispered to his men, gestured with his hand. One Marine moved toward the back of the mud-brick hut. He kneeled and held his weapon ready. The other four, led by Blount, stacked themselves by the front door.

Parson sent Reyes and Rashid to the right side of the structure. He crouched with Gold in what little cover they could take by a courtyard's rock fence on the left. Nobody could slip out of the house unseen.

Blount did not use a ram or any other tool to breach the door. He just slammed his boot against the rough planking. It splintered and slapped open.

A woman screamed. Then she began what sounded like a singsong lament in Pashto. No one fired. Parson heard boot steps thudding through the hovel.

"Clear," Blount shouted.

Parson and Gold rose from the fence and ran inside. Gold began speaking to the woman. Parson didn't really know any of the language, but he'd heard Gold utter those syllables before: *We will not harm you.* The woman wore a drab brown dress and a purple *hijab.* Apparently she saw no reason to hide her face, and she seemed past caring, anyway.

"What's she saying?" Parson asked.

"There is nothing more you can take from me," Gold translated. "Kill me, burn my house. Nothing is left."

"What does she—"

Gold held up her hand to silence Parson so she could listen. Right now, her expertise trumped his rank, and he knew it.

"They took her boy," Gold said.

"Who did?" Parson asked.

"The Talibs."

Parson was puzzled for a moment. Afghanistan had an awful problem with pederasty. In a society where unmarried men and women could not be seen together, far worse things happened than boys and girls stealing kisses. But the Taliban, for all their crimes against humanity, generally did not tolerate child molestation.

Gold spoke to the woman again. The mother answered back in short sentences, a calmer voice. She seemed at least to understand that the strangers who now invaded her home posed no further danger.

"Her son was—is—ten," Gold said.

"Why did they take him?" Parson asked.

"She doesn't know."

Rashid watched the woman, his brow furrowed. He looked at the scene around him as if trying to make sense of it.

"What do you think, Rashid?" Parson asked.

"I hope not what I think."

Whatever was happening, it did not accord with what Parson knew of the Taliban. When they hit a village they didn't like, they usually left behind nothing but bones and ashes. Killing civilians was one of the few things at which they excelled. It certainly figured that in a time of natural disaster, they'd find a way to add to the misery. But whatever they'd done here had more method than madness.

"Did she recognize any of the bad guys?" Parson asked.

"No," Gold said. "But she probably wouldn't tell if she did."

True enough, Parson thought. It's hard to convince people you'll protect them if they don't know how long you'll stay.

"Let's see what else we find," Parson said.

In the next house, they found nothing. Half the walls had collapsed in the quake or one of the aftershocks. The dirt-floor dwelling smelled of mold and stale bread, along with the cold soot of a burned-out cooking fire.

At the house after that, Parson walked through the door and stopped short. The sight before him ripped through all the barbed-wire fences he had strung around his emotions.

The little girl who'd been following Gold around lay clinging to the body of her mother. The child cried silently, could not form words or even sounds.

Blood had flowed along the edge of an overturned table and pooled in a corner of the room. Blood had spattered a shelf of crockery, apparently ejected from an exit wound.

Tracks of blood wound through the hut: large boots, small shoes.

Gold kneeled by the girl. She put her hand on the child's back. The girl spasmed as if in a seizure but made no other response.

When Gold spoke, the child turned, buried her face in Gold's lap. Scarlet smears covered her hands and arms.

"Let me check her out," Reyes said.

"Her name is Fatima," Gold said.

Gold whispered in Pashto, stroked Fatima's back. The child shook her head. Parson could imagine the conversation: -Let the strange men examine you. -No, strange men have done enough today.

Finally, after much talk, Fatima stood and let Reyes look at her. The PJ opened his medical ruck, checked her for wounds, took her pulse.

"She's not hurt," Reyes said. "Physically, I mean. That must be her mother's blood all over her."

"She says they came and took her brother," Gold said. "Their mother tried to stop them."

Reyes unsnapped the tube to his CamelBak and offered it to Fatima. "Tell her to drink from this," he said. "She's dehydrated."

Gold spoke. Fatima took the tube in her hand, which looked to Parson like the fist of a doll. She paused before placing her mouth on the tube, sipped once and then stopped. Too distraught to want water or food, Parson supposed. She was only doing as she was told because she felt some small connection to Gold, and because she simply didn't know what else to do.

"This is so fucked up," Blount said.

"You got that right, Gunny," Reyes said.

"My daddy used to slap me and my mama around," Blount said. "Ain't nothing lower than hurting a little one."

"I bet he didn't slap you around for long."

"I fixed it so he didn't do that no more."

For just an instant, Parson thought he saw a thousand-yard stare in Blount's eyes. But then the big man focused again, watched for threats, monitored his men.

"Ask her if she knows why they wanted her brother," Parson said to Gold.

Gold cut her eyes at him without turning her head. Parson knew that look: *You're pushing it, sir.* She never hesitated to tell him when she thought something was a bad idea, and for that he was grateful. But this time she allowed one more question. Gold spoke again in Pashto.

"She says the men told him he'd become a soldier of God," Gold said. "They shot the mother and took him away."

So they were kidnapping boys for child soldiers? Using the chaos of the earthquake, perhaps, to pull off something they might not get away with otherwise.

Turning disaster to their advantage certainly sounded like the Taliban. Even when they'd ruled, they'd taken no responsibility for their people's welfare. No real department of social services. No functioning ministry of agriculture. A government uninterested in governance. Only their militias and religious police took their duties seriously. Beyond that, Allah would provide.

By the time Parson's team finished searching the rest of

the settlement, night had fallen. A broken cloud layer scudded away to reveal a full moon bright enough to throw shadows. The search found two other murdered parents, as well as the existence of one other missing boy.

Parson couldn't quite get his mind around what he was seeing. Disaster relief was hard enough without these assholes coming up with something like this. What God could they imagine they were serving? The problems he faced had changed now. Not just earthquake recovery anymore. He and Gold had a dragon to kill.

His head still ached from the RPG blast that began the attack on the helicopter. In much of his experience with RPGs, they'd appeared as harmless green pinpoints on night vision, ineffectual arcs in the blackness, fired upward at his aircraft and not even reaching his altitude. But this one had caged his gyros.

At least the weather was cooperating. Parson knew the Osprey crew would fly back on night vision goggles, but with the clear sky and lunar illumination, they'd hardly need them.

He worried whether darkness would bring back the bad guys, and he ordered everyone to stay alert. But all seemed quiet. Apparently, the insurgents already had what they wanted.

4

In the quiet of night, Gold watched and listened for signs of life. At first she heard only the distant tapping of automatic rifle fire, the music of destruction in sixteenth notes. Some skirmish in the next valley. Closer, she made out the yowl of a cat.

Parson had sent the rest of the team to bring back the bodies of the imam and the two other villagers killed in the attack on the helicopter. Now he walked ahead of her, safety off on his Beretta. With one hand, Gold took Fatima's hand; with the other, she held her M4.

They stopped at a hut where lamplight shone through an oil-paper window. Parson knocked at the door. Gold let go of Fatima and gripped her rifle with both hands.

"We come as friends," Gold said in Pashto. "We are Americans. We will not hurt you."

From within the home came the sounds of wooden clatter, metallic clinks. Perhaps a grab for a weapon. Gold snapped her fire mode selector to the AUTO position.

"Leave us," a voice called from inside.

"We have with us a little girl from your town," Gold said. "Her name is Fatima. Her mother is dead. We want only to leave her in someone's care."

"I know no one by that name."

"Sir, can you take in this child?"

"Leave us!"

Gold moved away from the door, put her rifle back on SAFE.

"My cousin lives here," Fatima whispered.

That did not surprise Gold. Cousin or no, Fatima would be another mouth to feed, and a worthless girl at that. A goat probably carried more value here. She explained the situation to Parson, and he summed it up in his own way: "Bullshit."

It seemed not a shred of mercy remained for anyone in Afghanistan, but especially not for females. During previous deployments, Gold had heard of parents selling girls to buy food. Even in antiquity, Afghanistan had been a bad place for women. Gold thought of a nearby historic site, the Tomb of Rabia Balkhi. Rabia Balkhi was a medieval poetess who'd died in an honor killing. Her brother had killed her for having sex with a slave lover, and she'd written her final poem in her own blood.

Parson and Gold knocked at two other homes. At one, they got no answer, though a cooking fire burned inside. At the other, the answer came: "I will not open my door to infidels."

"We'll just have to take her back with us," Parson said.

"Don't we need to get clearance from Task Force first?" Gold asked.

"We'll just ask forgiveness instead of permission."

That worked for Gold. She worried about how Fatima might react to an aircraft ride and getting dropped off with strangers at the MASF, but it seemed better than leaving her to fend for herself.

Gold kneeled to speak with the girl at eye level. "Fatima," she said, "you will have to come with us. We'll take you for an airplane ride and get you some food and a place to sleep."

"I want to go home."

Gold fought tears. "I know you do, my dear," she said. "But your mother is gone. I know this is hard, and I am so sorry. But there is no one to take care of you here."

Fatima began to cry. "My brother might come back," she said. "I have to be at home if he comes back."

Now Gold's eyes watered too quickly to control. She blinked, felt the tears escape. Droplets fell onto her arm, her rifle barrel. She let the M4 lean into the crook of her elbow, and she embraced Fatima. Against her arms she felt the softness of the little Afghan girl and the hard angles of the weapon.

Gold sniffled, tried to regain her composure. "I do not think he is coming back, Fatima," she said.

The girl's shoulders quivered. For a moment she wept so hard, she could not speak. When she found words again, she asked, "Is he dead like Mama?"

"No, Fatima. We do not believe he is dead. But some very bad men took him."

"Can you bring him back?"

Gold did not know what to say. She wanted to offer the girl some hope, but to offer false hope would be unforgivable.

"We will try," she said finally. "But we do not even know where they took him."

"Please bring him back. He wants to come home. He was crying when they took him away."

Gold released Fatima from the embrace, then held her by the arms. "We will do all we can," Gold said. "That is all I can promise."

Even if some miracle brought the boy back, Gold could see little but misery in both children's futures. Mortal life presented few crueler fates than that of an orphan in Afghanistan. At best, grinding poverty. At worst—Gold hated to think of the abuse that happened to kids of either sex.

"What is your brother's name, Fatima?"

"Mohammed. He is Mohammed."

Parson had remained near enough to listen. Gold knew he'd have understood not a word, but the situation required little interpreting. She half expected him to tell her not to get involved with one Afghan child; that wasn't their mission. But he only watched and listened. A pool of darkness hid his face, so Gold could not judge his expression.

When she'd first met him years ago, he seemed insensitive, even profane. Then she saw how he bonded with friends and crewmates. Like most military men, he didn't spend a lot of time talking about his feelings. But if he saw a threat to one of his own, he made his feelings clear through action—even violence. In the beginning, he blamed all of Afghanistan, all of Islam, for the loss of his C-130 crew. But now he loved some of the Afghans like brothers, though he'd never express it that way.

Above, the moon glowed bright like a coin of mottled fire. The planets of early evening joined it as cold points of silver. At the edge of the village, a few local men gathered where Reyes, Rashid, and the Marines had brought the dead.

"Do any of you know this child?" Gold asked.

No one answered. Rashid repeated the question, and the men pretended not to hear him. Gold wanted to slam the butt of her rifle into their cheekbones. Then she thought to herself: You're thinking like Parson. At least they were taking responsibility for burying their imam.

"I guess we're done here," Parson said. He sounded tired, disappointed.

"Then I'll get us a ride," Blount said.

The Marine took out his PRC-148 and made a call. In his huge hands, the radio looked like a miniature model of itself. He used an antijamming system that hopped frequencies, and the voice that answered seemed to come from within a shaking echo chamber. Gold could make out only one word: "Inbound."

"I guess the girl's coming with us?" Reyes asked.

"Yeah," Parson said.

"Let me tote her up to the field," Blount said. "She's been through enough today without having to walk up that hill."

Fatima cowered, held on to Gold when the Marine bent toward her. "It is all right," Gold said in Pashto. "He is my friend, and he is your friend." Then she said in English, "Thanks, Sergeant. Just don't put your hand on the top of her head."

Blount searched his pockets until he came up with a Hershey's bar. He unwrapped it and handed it to Fatima. Then he slung his rifle over his right arm and picked her up so that she sat on his left shoulder.

"I got one about this age back home in Beaufort," he said.

Fatima ate as Blount carried her up the hill, away from the village. Gold doubted the girl had ever tasted chocolate before, but she showed little reaction to it.

In the grass field, a couple hundred yards from the burned-out hulk of the Mi-17, Blount set Fatima on the ground.

"Just sit tight, honey," he said. "I gotta get ready for our ride to come in." Then he added, "I don't reckon you understand me, do you?"

By now, the girl seemed to have lost her fear of the gunnery sergeant, who must have looked to her like a giant from a fairy tale. Fatima listened to him speak as if she did understand, but when Blount busied himself with something in his rucksack, she moved over to Gold and looked up quizzically.

"Where are we going?" she asked.

"Mazar-i-Sharif," Gold said. "Have you ever been there?"

"No."

Fatima had probably never traveled half a klick out of her village. The rest of the child's life would turn on this night, and Gold wondered what events were being set into motion.

Blount found what he was looking for in his ruck. He pulled out four chemical light sticks, sliced open their wrapping with his KA-BAR knife. Using his thumb and forefinger, he bent the first one until the glass vial inside the plastic tubing popped. The two chemicals flowed into each other to form a radiance of neon blue, and Gold thought it looked like a tiny molecular re-creation of the pulsars and quasars above. Starlight writ small. Blount repeated the process with the other three chem lights. He walked the field and dropped the light sticks to form an inverted *Y* landing signal.

After a few minutes, Gold became aware of a distant buzz, like the thrum of a cicada but in a lower key. The sound slipped in underneath the night, and she realized she'd heard it for several seconds before it registered in her mind.

A warbling came from Blount's radio. He pressed a talk switch and said, "The LZ is cold, sir."

Gold wasn't wearing night vision goggles, but in the moon's glow she could still pick out the shape of the Osprey. It flew with all strobes and nav lights off, a black shadow against the sky.

As the aircraft approached to land, Gold shielded Fatima's eyes from the blowing grit. The Osprey touched down, and Blount spoke again into his radio, turned up the volume. He gave a thumbs-up to Parson. This time Parson picked up Fatima.

Blount led the way around to the Osprey's open ramp. Gold walked behind the dim outlines of Parson and Fatima, Reyes and Rashid. She sat on the nylon webbing of a troop seat and turned her rifle muzzle down so any accidental discharge wouldn't strike a rotor.

The Osprey rose into the air. Closed off in the privacy of darkness and engine noise, Gold fought back tears, managed to compose herself. If she suffered from post-traumatic stress disorder, she'd make *post* the operative word. Deal with it later. Now she had a job to do. And it involved a new kind of enemy.

The makeshift command post at Mazar reminded Parson of the early days of the Afghanistan war: plywood walls, folding chairs. Permanent headquarters had grown up in Kabul and at the big air bases. Kandahar airfield, with all its new hangars, would have been unrecognizable to troops who hadn't seen it since the start of the war.

But with a new crisis centered in the north of the country, the evolution of a military presence started over at the beginning, with tents, cheap wood, and HESCO barriers. The CP door even had a makeshift counterweight to keep it pulled closed: a plastic water bottle filled with sand, strung up by parachute cord.

Parson had made an initial report to intel last night when they'd landed. Now, this morning, he wanted to debrief more thoroughly. He joined Rashid and an American intel officer in a secure teleconference with Task Force at Bagram and with CENTCOM headquarters at MacDill Air Force Base, Florida. It was seven in the morning at Mazar, and at MacDill, nine and a half hours behind, it was nine thirty at night. Parson had put on the same flight suit he'd worn yesterday, and it smelled like smoke and sweat. The officers on the TV screen in front of him wore clean ABU fatigues.

"They lit us up pretty good," Parson said. "But I don't think we were who they wanted." He explained about the missing boys.

"The Taliban has used child soldiers before," a CENT-COM colonel said. "But they were recruited out of madrassas in Pakistan. Taking them by force is something new."

As Parson listened, he found foam cups and poured coffee from a pot placed atop a stack of MRE cartons. He handed one to Rashid and drank from the other. The coffee had gone bitter from too much time on the hot plate.

"This stuff sucks," Parson said.

"Indeed it does," a major at Bagram said. Parson had meant the coffee, but he agreed with the major's statement.

"Some Taliban rank and file have taken us up on the amnesty program," the colonel said. "And even a few of their commanders have put down arms. But this seems like two steps back. It's hard to see how this fits in."

Parson didn't care how it fit in. Divining the intentions of terrorists seemed a waste of time. Analysts fretted over how to interpret a statement, how to view an action. To

Parson, the only way to view the Taliban was through crosshairs—which he'd done more than once.

Rashid sipped his coffee and frowned. Parson knew how the Afghan pilot felt this morning. He'd lost a crew member and an aircraft. That was a special pain Parson well understood. But the man still had a job to do, and Parson figured the best thing was to get him back in the air as soon as possible. At the moment, Rashid twirled his lighter between his fingers like his mind was somewhere else and he wanted a cigarette.

The major in Bagram excused himself from the teleconference, then returned. "Intel shop says Al Jazeera has a new video from the bad guys," he said. "We'll try to put it up if you like."

"Please do," the colonel from MacDill said.

"Yes, sir."

Parson looked at Rashid and the intel officer, shrugged. The screen went to snow, and when the picture returned, it showed a bearded man in white robes and a black turban. No salt in his beard; he looked to be in his thirties. On the wall behind him hung a green flag. Two AK-47s leaned against the wall, beside another weapon Parson had not seen in terrorist videos before: a curved Arabian sword, called a *saif*, resting in its scabbard. Silk tassels dangled from the hilt. The scabbard's chape and locket gleamed of old silver. The man in front of the weapons spoke in accented but fluent English.

"With great regret we note that some of our former Taliban brothers have capitulated to the crusaders," he said. "They have entered talks with the puppet government in Kabul, which is religiously forbidden. Some have announced they will cease offensive operations due to the natural disaster.

"We view these measures as apostasy and declare these former brothers *kafirs*. The earthquake was an act of God, a holy punishment for cooperation with infidels. Therefore, we forbid any acceptance of relief from infidel nations. Likewise, we forbid the pigs and monkeys of Jewish and Christian aid organizations from entering the Islamic Emirate of Afghanistan. God alone shall provide according to His will."

The man reached for the sword, drew it from the scabbard. Engraving ran the length of the blade—words in Arabic that Parson could not read. He'd seen such weapons on display in Kuwait and Saudi Arabia. Some of them were hundreds of years old and fetched high prices from collectors.

"In addition," the man said, running his thumb along the flat of the blade, "we shall strengthen our numbers with the youth of Afghanistan. We shall redouble our jihad under the symbol of the Black Crescent and the sword of Islam. This holy weapon has been blessed by God and shall never know defeat."

The video then cut to a graphic: a black sliver of moon against a green background, two swords crossed in front. Well, Parson thought, at least now we know our enemy. One crazy enough to bring a sword to a gunfight.

"Bastard," Rashid mumbled. A word Parson had taught him.

"Who is that dipshit?" Parson asked.

"We don't know," the major said. "And we've never heard of a group called Black Crescent. A splinter organization, apparently."

"I guess the Taliban was too moderate for them," the colonel said.

"Well, I saw last night what he means about strengthening numbers," Parson said.

"No doubt," the colonel said. "Problem is, we can't guard every village. We were stretched thin even before the earthquake."

"How about ISR assets?" Parson asked. He'd take all the intelligence, surveillance, and reconnaissance he could get. Keep an eye on things, at least.

"The Predators have a pretty high ops tempo already," the colonel said. "I'll check, but I can't promise anything."

"What about taskings for the Afghan Air Force?" Parson asked.

"I wouldn't expect that to change," the colonel said. "Get the supplies where they need to go."

Parson had mixed feelings about that. He wanted somehow to chase after these Black Crescent lowlifes. But the pallets of relief supplies stacking up at Mazar and the other airfields couldn't do anybody any good sitting on the tarmac. Maybe the best thing for Rashid would be to take a new Mi-17, fill it up with rice, potatoes, and cooking oil, and go fly a mercy mission. Rashid came from a culture and a religion Parson would never understand. But Rashid was a guy. A crew dog. Parson could relate to that part of him. Nothing better for a crew dog than a good day's work with his buds. Especially if at the end of that day he could think about how people would eat that night because he had flown them some food.

That video, however, sucked away any satisfaction Parson might have felt about a relief flight. What kind of sword-wielding asshole would tell those people they couldn't have the food?

Parson knew such people existed. Very early in his career, he'd flown loads of Unimix into Somalia. The stuff didn't look appetizing. Unimix consisted mainly of corn flour and soybeans, with the smell and appearance of cattle feed. But dangerously malnourished people could eat a porridge made of it and not throw it up. Then, as they got stronger, their stomachs could tolerate real food again.

Those missions purified him, Parson had believed. Nullified a few of his sins and justified the space he took up on the planet. The Somalis would help push the pallets of Unimix off the airplane and then dance a little jig, perhaps a dance of gratitude, of happiness. But later, Parson learned most of that food had just lined the pockets of warlords. The end result was a failed military intervention in a failed state. A Black Hawk down, then another, and eighteen dead Americans.

That's when Parson quit trying to save the world. He could save only the person right in front of him, the buddy next to him. At best. A harsh lesson in a harsh world.

In a way, it had liberated him, taught him to leave infinite problems to an infinite power. But it had also broken his heart.

❧ 5 ❧

Gold wanted to get Fatima to eat something. The UNHCR staff at the airfield passed out boxes of Humanitarian Daily Rations—like military MREs except in yellow packaging. Gold took one marked VEGETABLE BARLEY STEW and carried it to Fatima's cot. The child lay curled under a woolen Army blanket, eyes open.

"*Sahaar mo peh khair,*" Gold said. Good morning. She lowered herself onto the edge of the cot.

Fatima did not respond.

"Are you hungry?" Gold asked. She opened the pouch of stew. Lettering on the side read FOOD GIFT FROM THE PEOPLE OF THE UNITED STATES OF AMERICA.

Fatima shook her head. Gold held her hand, tried to smile at her. No telling how the horrors of yesterday affected the girl. Not even an adult should have to witness the things she'd seen. Gold wasn't sure what else to say, so she just sat with Fatima to keep her company. After several minutes, Fatima finally spoke.

"Is my brother here?"

The sadness in that question struck Gold with tactile force. Her palms grew clammy. She felt that clutch of anxiety in her chest, the same burning under the breastbone that came when bad memories intruded on the present.

"He is not, Fatima. We do not know where Mohammed is."

Gold struggled for more words. Then Parson came into the tent. He was dressed to fly. Body armor over his flight suit, survival vest over the armor. The weight of the gear seemed to make his limp more pronounced. Gold felt unaccountably glad to see him at this moment, as if the weapons and gadgets in his pockets offered some kind of deliverance.

"How's she doing?" Parson asked.

"About like you'd expect. She's asking for Mohammed."

Gold rubbed the back of Fatima's hand, thought her skin was the color of the pistachios that grew in the orchards around Mazar. Fatima looked up at Parson, then at Gold.

"Is that man your husband?" she asked.

Gold half smiled. "No, Fatima."

"Is he your brother?"

"No. Well, no," Gold said. "He is a military officer. We work together. He brought you here to keep you safe."

Parson seemed to realize they were talking about him. He kneeled beside the cot to be at Fatima's eye level. Gold could see scratches in the back of his neck from the RPG attack yesterday. Shards flung by the blast had left claw marks still red and raw. The wounds weren't serious, but they had apparently bled a little since Parson's shower in the latrine trailer that morning. He smelled of soap, though he wore a dirty uniform. Gold knew he'd been busy, and she supposed all his other flight suits were balled up unwashed in a laundry bag.

"Hello, Fatima," he said.

"Salaam," Fatima said.

Parson stood and said, "They've already assigned Rashid to another aircraft and crew. We're taking some bags of rice to a refugee camp over in Samangan Province."

"I'll get my things," Gold said.

"Don't rush. We still have some flight planning to do. Just meet us in command post."

Gold found one of the UN staff, a French nurse, and told her about Fatima. The nurse agreed to keep an eye on her, but Gold could see the medical workers were busy. The Mazar refugee camp already held about two hundred occupants, and it wasn't hard to imagine two hundred personal tragedies like Fatima's. Some refugees wore casts and bandages; some stared at the tent walls as if catatonic; a few wailed aloud.

In her own tent, Gold donned her MOLLE gear, the field vest that carried her hydration pack, ammo, and other equipment. She checked the magazine in her rifle and the three spare magazines that were snapped and Velcroed into pouches of heavy-duty nylon. Gold opened another pocket to make sure she had sunglasses, a rainproof writing pad, and her two black ballpoint pens labeled SKILCRAFT—

U.S. GOVERNMENT. She tied her hair in a tight bun, put on her Kevlar helmet, and headed across the tarmac to command post.

In the flight planning room, she found Parson and Rashid poring over a chart spread across a card table. Parson clenched a blue highlighter marker between his teeth. Gold wasn't trained to use aeronautical charts, but she noticed he'd drawn a course line that zigged and zagged.

"The scenic route to Samangan?" she asked. Samangan was the next province over to the southeast.

Parson removed the highlighter from his mouth and said, "The minimum risk route. A couple of Mi-17s have come back with bullet holes since yesterday."

"Anyone hurt?"

"Not this time."

"Anything new on the abductions last night?" she asked.

"Yeah, there's a video from what looks like a Taliban splinter group."

When Parson finished telling her about Black Crescent, she felt sick to her stomach. She remembered talking with Afghanistan's national directorate of intelligence about reports that the Taliban forced teenagers to carry out suicide bombings. Unfathomably heinous—but isolated incidents. A renegade campaign to gather up child soldiers, to create child terrorists in quantity, was another thing entirely. Few people would suspect a ten-year-old was the one wearing a suicide vest in a crowded market.

Worse, terrorist trainers could work with the children well into adulthood, indoctrinating them, teaching them skills. By the time those kids taken last night reached their twenties, they might speak good English with an American accent. They might take jobs in government agencies in Afghanistan or anywhere else. They might learn to make bombs, mix poisons, fly airplanes.

Most terrorists were radicalized in early adulthood, Gold considered. But kids brought up to kill would not *come* to radicalization; they'd have little memory of anything else. Robbed of their childhoods and the affection of family and friends, the children could be trained to have the remorselessness of psychopaths.

That people could even think of such a scheme ran against all Gold wanted to believe about humanity. Ultimately, this plot could create a new strain of terrorist free of all conscience and empathy, just when coalition forces were drawing down in Afghanistan. Gold didn't know what it would take to stop it. But she knew somebody had to try.

Two Afghan crew members came into the flight planning room, a sergeant and a lieutenant. Rashid's new engineer and copilot, Parson assumed. He didn't know either one of them, but Parson had not yet found time to meet everyone involved in NATO Air Training Command–Afghanistan. Both wore American-style desert flight suits with the black, red, and green flag of their country on the right sleeve. The engineer was a clean-shaven man in his twenties, with friendly, almond-colored eyes. The copilot looked older, closer to Parson's age. His beard was trimmed close, so wiry it reminded Parson of steel wool, and his thin build bordered on gaunt. The man carried himself with an intensity, not merely looking at his surroundings, but staring. Rashid spoke to them in Pashto, and Gold joined in.

"This is Sergeant Sharif and Lieutenant Aamir," Gold said. "I'm afraid they don't speak any English."

That didn't surprise Parson, especially with regard to the sergeant. The Afghan military had a problem getting NCOs who could read and write in their own language, let alone speak English. There wasn't much of an educated class left in Afghanistan after decades of war, and real fluency in English was rare even among the officers.

"No problem," Parson said. "Are they ready to aviate?"

"They sound like it."

"Good. Tell them we have some help today, too. A couple of Mi-35 Hinds are going to ride shotgun." The Mi-35s, Russian-built gunships, would provide armed escort. Parson looked forward to seeing them work.

When Gold spoke to the Afghans, they nodded but said nothing. Parson figured they were old enough to have seen Hinds flying for the wrong side. He put the cap back on his highlighter, folded the chart, picked up his helmet bag, and said, "All right, let's do this."

Out on the flight line, the Mi-35s seemed to threaten even when sitting still. Like the Marine Corps Cobras that had escorted the Osprey, something about a helicopter gunship just looked mean. The Hinds had stubby fixed wings in addition to their main rotors. Parson supposed the wings generated some lift at high speed, but they also provided pylons for mounting bombs and rockets. With a nose gun for a beak, the Mi-35s looked vaguely like ptero-dactyls. Ugliest damned flying machines he'd ever seen, but effective as hell.

Parson followed Rashid and his crew into the Mi-17, and he strapped into a troop seat along the side of the cargo compartment. Gold sat next to him on his left. Reyes was already on board with his medical pack and weapon. PJs normally worked in groups of two or three, but the earthquake response had spread medics so thin, Parson felt grateful to get even one for whatever injuries they found at the refugee camp. A three-ring binder with the aircraft's maintenance forms lay on the seat to Parson's right. He opened it and leafed through the pages.

The forms showed a fairly new helicopter: only a little more than two thousand hours on the airframe. Inspec-tions up to date, oil serviced in both engines. Recent sheet metal repairs for a hairline crack in the door frame and a bullet hole in the tail boom. Signatures from an American maintenance supervisor and Rashid's Afghan crew chief.

Good. They were learning to document everything.

He took his headset out of his helmet bag, put it on, and plugged its jack into the interphone system. Clipped commands in Pashto: the crew running checklists and the engines about to start. Parson thumbed a switch on the battery pack connected to his headset cord, and a green indicator light began flashing. Green meant a good battery for the noise-cancellation circuit, so maybe those Russian turbines wouldn't give him a headache today.

Gold wore her own headset. She pressed the talk button, uttered just a couple words in Pashto. Then she said to Parson, "They have their flight clearance."

"Good."

The muscles in Gold's jaw tightened like she was nervous about something. Parson knew she had no fear of flying, and she'd almost certainly spent more time in helicopters than he had. She was still upset about what she'd seen yesterday, he supposed, especially since it involved kids.

Gold was made of stronger alloys than most people, Parson still believed. But every substance had limits. He thought of the airplanes he'd flown. Each had a performance envelope, and you could fly it to the edge of that envelope with no problem: a certain speed, a certain angle of bank, a certain power setting. But when you demanded more, you could expect consequences.

As Parson looked forward through the cockpit door, he saw gloved fingers punch the start buttons one at a time. The engines above his head ignited, and then he heard the whine of gearboxes as the main rotor began to turn.

The lead gunship called for takeoff clearance in passable English. "Golay flight, cleared for takeoff," the tower answered. "Wind calm."

Rashid waited for the Mi-35s to depart ahead of him. Peering out the window, Parson saw the Hinds hover-taxi into position. As they accelerated into the air, a cloud passed over the runway, and the pavement dimmed and brightened as if the gods turned a rheostat.

Rashid throttled up. Parson felt a rocking motion as the Mi-17 lifted itself off the ground. As Rashid climbed and banked onto a heading to follow the gunships, Parson could not help trying to watch the instruments. He was not able to see much of the panel over the flight engineer's shoulder, but when the engineer leaned forward, Parson noted the HSI's compass card spinning with the turn. The helicopter lacked the modern computer displays found in newer American aircraft. It had old-fashioned round dials—steam gauges, as pilots called them—set into a panel painted that shade of barf green the Russians liked so much for aircraft interiors. Every switch was labeled in Cyrillic.

Rashid leveled off just underneath scattered clouds that were dissipating rapidly. The forecast called for clear conditions the rest of the day. The remaining clouds obscured a few of the mountaintops, but that didn't matter. Parson and Rashid planned a route that cut through passes instead of overflying ridgelines. The course would avoid the known threat areas, or at least minimize exposure to them.

The tactics binder showed where the enemy might have shoulder-fired missiles, antiaircraft artillery, or rocket-propelled grenades. For each weapon, the classified text gave odds with a cold algebraic symbology: $P(h)$. $P(k)$. Probability of hit. Probability of kill.

Parson knew better than most what those weapons could do to an aircraft. But he did not dwell on that now. He wanted to keep Rashid's confidence level up. So Parson focused on what went well, which included decent weather and a smooth ride. With no wind roiling across the slopes, the chopper flew as if sliding along sheets of silk. Such lack of turbulence was rare in Afghanistan. Parson pressed his talk button and said, "A good day to fly, huh, buddy?"

"A good," Rashid said.

As the helicopter flew over a dry, uninhabited plain, the crew chief peered out and swiveled his door gun. Reyes leaned back in his seat with his eyes closed, dozing as if he had not a care in the world. He propped his feet, one boot crossed over the other, on a stack of rice bags labeled UN WORLD FOOD PROGRAMME. Gold looked through the circular window above her seat and watched the terrain roll past. She wore a pair of dark sunglasses with a Smith & Wesson logo on the frame. On her right shoulder, her infrared-feedback U.S. flag patch gave off a slick sheen. The Army-style flag patch had its star field to the upper right, which looked backward to Parson. But its main purpose was to show up on night vision devices, not to look spiffy.

After a few minutes, the barrens below gave way to tended land. A wheat field flowed underneath, followed by a walled compound, then a well, then a cemetery with three open graves. A mound of freshly turned soil stood by each pit. Shadows filled the graves themselves; the holes in the earth appeared to contain nothing but blackness of infinite depth.

Rashid banked over a valley. Parson remembered that crease in the terrain as one of the turn points they'd marked on the VFR chart. Movement caught his eye: Down at treetop level, a pair of F/A-18s flew low through the valley like two pintails swooping along a river channel. Parson wondered what target they sought.

Gold turned away from the window and looked to Parson. "What can you tell me about this refugee camp where we're going?" she asked.

"Civilian agencies set it up just a few days ago," Parson said. "I haven't even been in this province before."

After what he'd seen in Ghandaki, he hoped the camps would provide some security for quake victims. Perhaps there would be safety in numbers by gathering refugees together instead of letting them fend for themselves in remote villages. If the camps needed to stay in operation for more than a week or two, maybe the Afghan National Army could guard them. Like the Afghan Air Force, the ANA still had a lot to learn, but Parson figured they ought to be able to handle sentry duty.

The flight continued through a mountain pass, along another valley, down a stream cut. Parson caught glimpses of the Hinds as they flew close escort. The gunships made S-turns along the route ahead of the Mi-17. The aircraft riding shotgun in front of him reminded Parson of C-130 missions he'd flown here, as well as in Iraq and Bosnia. Warthog attack jets would fly alongside and ahead of the Hercules, crisscrossing and banking in a show of force. The tactic usually intimidated bad guys into keeping their heads down, but occasionally some knucklehead would be dumb enough to shoot at the jets. The Warthogs would roll into a hard turn, come back around with nose guns spinning and smoking. No more bad guys.

Rashid's voice on the interphone brought Parson back to the present. "Ten minutes," the Afghan pilot said in English.

"Copy that," Parson said.

"Leader cannot talk camp," Rashid added.

"How's that?"

Gold spoke in Pashto, and Rashid answered. Then Gold said, "The lead Mi-35 pilot can't raise the refugee camp radio."

He's probably on the wrong frequency, Parson thought, or maybe they just can't understand him. Parson unzipped a lower leg pocket of his flight suit and pulled out a comm sheet. He looked up the call sign and freq for the new camp. From the call sign, he guessed USAID or some other American agency manned the radio.

"Put me on UHF, will you?" Parson asked.

Rashid gave a command in Pashto, and the flight engineer reached forward to one of the panels. Parson pressed his talk button. The whine of his headset's sidetone told Parson he was transmitting on air and no longer just on interphone.

"Clara Barton," he called, "Golay flight is two Hinds and an Mi-17 inbound your station. How copy?"

No answer. Only the whine of radios, the rush of wind, the pounding of rotors.

"Clara Barton, Clara Barton," Parson transmitted, "Golay flight is ten minutes out."

Nothing but static. Parson met Gold's eyes, shrugged. The corners of her mouth shifted in a gesture Parson took for puzzlement or worry. He tried the call again.

Still no answer.

Finally the squelch broke, and Parson heard voices off mike. Babbles of Pashto. Shouts. Then a click, and dead silence.

❧ 6 ❧

Sweat beaded on Gold's upper lip as she considered what she'd just heard. Please let it be an aftershock, she thought. But the panic in those transmitted voices suggested something worse. The only words she'd made out were *no*, *Allah*, and *mercy*.

"Do we land?" Rashid asked in English.

"Let's take a look first," Parson said. Then he added, "Sophia, tell the gunship pilots something's wrong at the camp. I don't know if they heard what we just heard."

Parson put her on UHF, and she pressed her talk button. "Golay lead," she said in Pashto, "this is Colonel Parson's interpreter. The camp may be under attack. He wants to recon before we land."

"Golay lead copies," the pilot answered. "What are our rules of engagement?"

Gold pulled her boom mike away from her mouth. She shouted to Parson over the wind and engines, "They want to know the ROE."

"Weapons tight," Parson said.

Good call, Gold thought. It meant the gunships wouldn't fire unless they identified a clearly hostile target. There were a lot of friendlies and civilians down there. She put her mike back into place and relayed Parson's order.

"Roger," the gunship pilot said in a thick accent. Then, in his own language, "We copy weapons tight."

These gunship guys spoke even less English than Rashid. Gold knew that in the Mi-35 training program, the Afghans talked with their Czech instructors in Russian. She considered it a small miracle that any of them managed to communicate anything at any time, let alone while flying high-performance aircraft armed with deadly weapons.

The Mi-17 turned and descended. "I see camp," Rashid said.

Gold stood, tried to see what she could through the windows and front windscreen. One of the Mi-35s flashed by. It flew just a few feet lower than the Mi-17, and Gold saw the helmeted pilots, one seated behind the other in the tandem cockpit. The gunship banked and descended, then disappeared from view.

Rashid turned as well. Gold didn't know much about helicopter tactics, but she guessed the changes in heading and altitude would make the choppers harder to hit with a missile or RPG. During the turn, the refugee camp appeared in the windscreen. People ran among the tents. Smoke churned upward from a blackened spot on the ground. As the smoke rose, a breeze caught it and stretched it into a black arc across the sky. Gold looked down at the flames; she couldn't be sure, but she thought she saw a truck or some other kind of vehicle burning.

"Clara Barton, Clara Barton," Parson called, "Golay flight."

Still no response.

Gold braced herself at the side window nearest her. The other Mi-35 streaked low across the ground.

"Golay Two, break left!" the lead gunship called in Pashto.

An instant later, Gold saw why. The smoke trail of a shoulder-launched missile corkscrewed a diagonal path in front of the M-35 below. Brilliant globules of light, so bright they hurt Gold's eyes, rippled from the gunship. Defensive flares, she realized, hot enough to confuse a heat-seeking missile.

The heat-seeker missed by mere yards. The Mi-35 banked hard and punched off more flares. The aircraft spewed fire, looked vaguely like a giant spawning insect. Gold watched the gunship climb and turn. She heard one of its pilots ask, still in Pashto, "Did you see where that came from?"

"*Ho,*" the other Mi-35 called. Yes. "I have them," the pilot added.

Gold did not see the other gunship. She struggled to follow the air-to-ground battle developing around and beneath her, but she couldn't keep all the combatants in view. Ground forces usually fought in two dimensions, but aircraft fought in three.

Reyes stood up. Like Gold, he moved to one window, then another to watch the fight.

Rashid turned his helicopter again and then said on interphone, "There. Some men on the road from the camp."

Gold moved to a window on the opposite side of the helicopter and saw about a dozen insurgents on a dirt path. They had apparently jumped out of the two white pickup trucks stopped nearby. She still couldn't see the other gunship, but the insurgents could. They tried to scatter. Too late.

The second Mi-35 came into Gold's view, flying so low it seemed nearly on the ground, guns smoking.

Geysers of dust erupted among the enemy fighters. Some insurgents emerged from the dust cloud, running. Others, caught by the rounds, disintegrated into flying limbs. The gunship zoomed across the road, and its rotor wash swirled the dust kicked up by its own fire.

"All right!" Parson said. "Get some."

Rashid seemed to watch something intently. He leaned toward his side window, nearly touched the glass with his helmet.

"Cease fire," Rashid said in English. Then he repeated the call in Pashto.

"What?" Parson asked.

"Say again," the lead gunship called.

"Cease fire," Rashid said. "There are childs with them."

"You gotta be shitting me," Parson said.

"Look," Rashid said. He banked left and pointed. Gold moved again, this time to see through the windscreen. Two small figures sprinted away from the road. Larger men ran behind them. Just before the Mi-17 flew over them,

Gold saw one of the men chase down a boy and grab him by the shirt. Instant human shield.

"We are off the target," the gunship lead said. "Weapons safe."

Even through the official terminology and the warble of UHF, Gold could hear the pain in that voice. Had he just blown up some children?

"I come around," Rashid said. He began descending, and he turned until he had reversed course. Ahead, insurgents and at least three boys ran for cover.

"What are you doing?" Parson asked.

"I fly past," Rashid said. "Make them run. Maybe childs escape."

The Mi-17 leveled just a few meters above the ground. The helicopter flew so fast now that the bare earth underneath it flowed like molten iron. The bad guys out in front threw themselves into the road ditch.

Except for one. The man raised an AK and fired as he disappeared under the nose. Gold heard three impacts on the underside of the helicopter like stones striking the wheel wells of a Humvee speeding down a mountain path.

She looked forward at the crew, over to the side at Parson, toward the back at Reyes. All appeared okay. The bullets, she supposed, had penetrated the floor and buried themselves in the rice bags.

Rashid climbed, then began another turn.

"That's enough," Parson said. "We won't get that lucky again."

"What can we do?" Rashid asked in Pashto. Gold translated for Parson, though she suspected Rashid asked a rhetorical question.

"Damn little," Parson said. "They'll disappear before we can get a Quick Reaction Force in here. Just watch which way they go." The Mi-35s broke off their escort, flew among the mountains in an apparent effort to track the insurgents.

Reyes leaned across a stack of rice bags to look through a window. "I bet they hurt some civilians at the camp," he said. "Sir, let's get on the ground. Somebody might be bleeding out right now."

"Okay," Parson said. "Rashid, give me a flyover of the camp. Put it down right outside the perimeter if it looks safe."

Rashid rolled the Mi-17 toward the collection of tents. Two ravens, black as the inside of a rifle muzzle, wheeled over the camp. They soared out of sight to the left. When the birds came back into view, they almost filled the windscreen. Gold nearly ducked; for a second it appeared the ravens would hit the glass. But in the last instant they folded their wings and dropped like shards of obsidian. She remembered Parson's stories of bird strikes: If birds see you in time, they'll dive. If they don't, they'll splatter themselves across your windscreen or even punch through.

Gold's mouth tasted faintly of stale milk; her stomach churned. Her palms grew moist. All the banking, climbing, and diving made her a little airsick. And she worried about what she'd seen on the ground.

She sat on a troop seat and buckled in. She put her rifle

across her lap and held on to the steel tubing of the seat frame, then inhaled a long breath through her nostrils. She didn't want to throw up in the helicopter and subject everyone to the odor, and she hadn't brought an airsick bag. Most chopper flights in the past just took her straight from point A to point B, firebase to firebase. Sometimes the helo flew a low-level run, but none of this tactical maneuvering stuff.

Gold swallowed hard, exhaled. Her gut began to settle, and she thought she could manage not to vomit if Rashid didn't yank the chopper around anymore.

Fortunately, Rashid flew straight and level for a few minutes. Parson leaned toward the windscreen, and she heard him say on interphone, "I don't see any bad guys down there."

The chopper slowed, and Gold figured Rashid was looking for a place to land. She wondered what they'd find on the ground. It seemed pretty clear Black Crescent had just carried out another raid. And this was miles from Ghandaki, the site of the first attack. The terrorists must own some resources, Gold thought, vehicles and drivers. Either that or they operated a number of separate cells around the country.

Now some civilians who'd already lost their homes had just lost so much more. With terrorism overlaid onto natural disaster, misery squared and cubed itself like explosives in a roadside bomb. Four times the compound, sixteen times the hurt. Exponential suffering.

Gold felt a queasiness at the back of her throat. Not airsickness now, but a trace of that old anxiety again. Brought on by the needless cruelty she witnessed. When people got hurt through an act of God, she could reconcile it. Chalk it up to mysterious ways, things beyond her understanding. But here was an act of man.

R ashid landed upwind of the burning truck. Through the flames, Parson saw the flatbed carried bags of something, but he could not identify the cargo. When one of the bags burned open, the contents spilled and ignited. The stuff flowed out in a glittering cascade of fire. Flour, maybe.

Parson saw no driver in the cab, but anyone inside that truck would have been dead by now. Flames boiled through the broken windshield, over the hood, around the fenders warping in the heat. The tires melted off the rims. Parson wondered how those bastards started the fire. Maybe with an RPG.

The smell reminded him of his own burning aircraft, damaged by a terrorist bomb the year before. He'd managed to crash-land more or less in one piece, but a lot of the patients and crew on that aeromedical flight never got out.

That fire still burned inside his soul. Now he was angry. Attacking a refugee camp violated every custom, every law and tradition of every culture. To Parson, a natural order extended to all things, even man-made objects. His own profession provided examples: An airplane always sought the speed for which its controls were trimmed. Let go of the yoke, and the plane would fly that speed. Didn't matter if the plane had to climb or dive to achieve that speed. Some rules allowed no exceptions. So Parson could hardly assign words to the crime unfolding before him. It was something, quite literally, unspeakable.

Reyes grabbed his rifle and medical ruck. He bounded from the helicopter before the crew chief even installed the boarding steps. The PJ hit the ground flat-footed, and he left deep boot prints in the soil. Gold got out behind him, and the two ran along coils of concertina wire at the camp's perimeter until they found an opening.

When Parson caught up with them inside the camp, it seemed the concertina encircled some earthly cantonment of hell. Bodies lay scattered among the tents. Wounded men and women writhed and screamed. Laments pierced Parson's eardrums in languages he could not understand. He had seen brutal acts before, individual crimes, but never a visitation of atrocities like this.

Reyes kneeled beside an Afghan man who'd apparently taken a round in the chest. The pararescueman donned a headset connected to the PRC-152 radio in his tactical vest. With one hand he held a wad of hemostatic dressing on the Afghan's wound, and with the other he pressed a push-to-talk switch already tacky with blood.

"Fever Eight-Niner," he called, "I need some help from you guys or from Pedro."

Parson could hear only half the conversation, but he knew Fever was the call sign of HC-130s flown by rescue units. *Pedro* meant their choppers, HH-60 Pave Hawks. The rescue assets were stretched pretty thin; Reyes would need luck to get any assistance.

The PJ seemed to listen closely. He said nothing, and he looked over at Gold. She stopped beside a man lying on his stomach. Blood pooled underneath him. She rolled him over to reveal slashes across his torso, as if giant talons had clawed into him. Shrapnel wounds from an oblique angle, Parson guessed, probably from a grenade. Without a word, Reyes unzipped a black pouch strapped to his thigh, pulled out a gauze pad, and threw it to Gold. Parson walked over and held out his open hand, and Reyes slapped a dressing into it.

"Sir, don't waste it on someone who won't live," he said.

Parson looked around for a person he could help. A few yards away he saw a woman sitting up, holding her left hand over the mangled remains of her right. She didn't look like an Afghan, and it took a moment for Parson to piece it all together. When he sat beside her, she said in clear English, "Please help me." Then she began to sob. Her hair was black, and she looked east Asian.

Parson gently lifted her left hand from the bleeding hamburger meat that had been her right hand. It wasn't a clean tear; blood vessels and strands of torn muscle hung like roots from her wrist. He wondered what weapon inflicted such a wound. Grenade shrapnel, probably. Parson couldn't quite decide how to apply the dressing, so he just wrapped it around the entire mess.

The woman wore a cream-colored correspondent's

jacket, now dusty and spattered with blood. On the ground beside her lay a broken video camera with a placard that read NHK. A Japanese reporter in the wrong place at the wrong time.

"I know that hurts," Parson said. "We'll get you out of here."

"My sound technician's dead," the woman said. "Cameraman killed, too." Then she sobbed again.

Reyes was still talking on the radio. He reached for his transmit switch again and said, "Fever Eight-Niner, we got a mass casualty event. Advise when you're ready to copy the nine-line."

From a pouch in his vest, Reyes withdrew a GPS receiver. He thumbed its controls with one hand and read off the coordinates of the refugee camp. Then Reyes transmitted the other items required in a 9-line medevac request, though Parson knew the PJ guessed at some of it. The number of patients: still undetermined. Dozens at least. Special equipment: ventilators, oxygen, everything. Security of pickup site: Well, we're not under fire at the moment.

After Reyes relayed all the medevac information, he said, "Roger that, Fever. Tell 'em I got at least two sucking chest wounds, probably a lot more than that. We copy you're inbound with jumpers." The PJ wrapped bandaging on his first patient, then moved to the man Gold was helping. Gold took her hands off the man's wound, and they came up bloody.

She stood up and said a few words in Pashto. Uninjured refugees crowded around her, gestured with their arms, shouted. A woman in a blue burka wailed and pointed until she collapsed at Gold's feet.

Rashid entered the camp at a jog. He was by himself, and Parson felt glad Rashid had told the rest of his crew to guard the helicopter. Rashid had removed his flight helmet, but he still wore his body armor, and he carried two first-aid kits from the aircraft. Both of the green canvas pouches bore a red cross.

"What to do?" he asked.

"Just find—" Parson said, but Gold interrupted him with a stream of Pashto. Rashid joined her. Both of them talked with the refugees as Rashid opened one of the first-aid kits.

Parson took the other kit from Rashid. As he unzipped it and unwrapped a dressing, he asked, "What are they saying?"

"Men came in two pickup trucks," Gold said. "They shot all the Westerners, and they captured some of the boys. At least four, I think."

Parson had wondered why no camp staff appeared. But it hardly surprised him that they'd been among the first killed.

Gold and Rashid conversed in Pashto again. Then Gold said, "They demanded to know the time. When a man told them, they eviscerated him with a sword. They killed everyone wearing a watch."

"What?" Parson asked. Terrorists could always find excuses to murder, but he wondered what malign creed had produced this new twist.

"Not many Afghans need to know the exact time," Gold

said. "Insurgents assume anyone with a watch is working with the Americans or with the government."

"Son of a bitch," Parson said. He thought of his old man's stories from Southeast Asia. The Khmer Rouge had killed anyone wearing glasses because intellectuals presented a threat. This shit just never ended.

⚡ 7 ⚡

Flies buzzed around Gold's face. The flies kept landing on her cheeks, tickling her skin with their legs, trying to drink the water in her eyes. She shook her head to scatter them. She couldn't brush them away because she had both hands busy. With her left, she held a QuikClot pad on a woman's forearm. A bayonet or machete had cut to the bone and slashed downward, peeling away a shank of flesh like a butcher carving a fillet.

The pad wasn't big enough to stanch all the bleeding, so Gold kept her right thumb clamped around a pressure point on the inside of the woman's upper arm. From Gold's combat first-aid training, she knew she held the pressure point correctly, because below that point the pulse stopped. She just hoped she could keep the woman from bleeding to death until Reyes took over. Right now he worked twenty yards away, checking a man's pulse at the wrist.

Parson and Rashid were busy with other patients, both

officers now following instructions from the enlisted para-rescueman. Gold watched Parson tape down a bandage on an old man's foot. Then he moved to a woman lying motionless in the dirt. Two young girls clung to her, crying. Gold could not see what wounds the woman had suffered.

"Don't waste your time on that one, sir," Reyes said.

"But—"

Gold felt the same as Parson. *Please let that one be okay.*

"I already checked her," Reyes said. "Apneic and no heartbeat. She's dead. Three entrance wounds."

Amid the flies, Gold heard another buzzing in a lower register. The sound grew louder, and she recognized the turboprop groan of a C-130. She looked up and squinted, and she saw the Herk thousands of feet above her, inching into the sun. The brightness hurt even through her shaded glasses. She shut her eyes, but not soon enough. The glare left a yellow corona that remained visible even with her eyelids closed.

She looked at the ground and blinked. The hot spot still burned on her retinas, but now the circle was red. When it finally faded and she looked up again, the C-130 appeared on the other side of the sun as if it had flown through it.

The noise of engines and props dropped half an octave, and Gold knew the aircraft was slowing for the drop. She tried to discern the ramp coming open, but the C-130 flew too high for her to see that. After several seconds, the engine noise rose again.

She knew some PJs should have just exited the aircraft.

Yet she saw no one falling through the sky. If you found a last-second problem with your rig, then of course you wouldn't jump. But that was rare.

A few seconds later, she spotted them: three specks dropping toward the earth at terminal velocity. She'd seldom seen a HALO jump from this perspective. Watching from the ground, it became obvious why this was such an effective way to insert troops covertly. You could hardly see them even if you knew they were coming.

For a moment she wished she were with the jumpers. But parachuting was just transportation. She was doing her real job now, blood up to her wrists, comforting the wounded in their own language.

One by one, the jumpers' main chutes fluttered, inflated. The pararescuemen used that new Special Operations Vector rig that was so maneuverable. Two of the PJs began steering toward the refugee camp, but the third appeared in trouble.

His chute took on the shape of a bow tie, and it began to spin.

A line-over. One of his suspension lines had wrapped itself over the canopy. The resulting bulges imparted a rotation to the parachute and left the jumper little control.

He spun down below his two teammates. Gold couldn't gauge his rate of descent except to see it was somewhere beyond lethal. The refugees looked skyward and pointed. Even they knew something was wrong.

"Cut away," Gold said under her breath. "Cut that thing."

Now the PJ drew close enough that Gold could make out his flailing boots, his ruck, and the individual shroud lines. The offending line seemed to tighten its choke on the canopy, and the spin grew faster. The man moved his hand toward his harness, and he grasped the cutaway pillow. He yanked hard.

The misshapen canopy collapsed. It twisted around itself and fell away as the reserve parachute billowed.

The riggers had packed the reserve canopy well. The reserve snapped open like the crack of a whip, and the jumper pulled a steering toggle to make a smooth turn into the wind.

"Allah-hu akbar," whispered the woman whose arm Gold held. Gold hadn't realized she'd been watching.

"Yes, He is," Gold said.

"I did not wish to see more death today," the woman said in Pashto.

"God willing, you will not," Gold said. "Those are men of medicine."

The pararescueman under the reserve canopy landed first, and the other two touched down a few seconds later. Once they were on the ground, Gold could not see them; the camp's sandbag walls blocked her view. But a few minutes later they strode inside, rucksacks over their shoulders.

All three gathered around Reyes. As he briefed them, he pointed to Gold. One of the men came over to her and put down his medical ruck.

"Nice work," he said. "We can probably save that arm."

"You want me to let go now?" Gold asked.

"Hold the pressure point, but let go of the wound itself."

Gold took her hand away from the pad, and the pararescueman wrapped fresh dressings over it. "Okay," he said. "I got it now." Gold released the woman's upper arm and stood back to let the PJ do his job.

She took a handkerchief from her pocket and wiped her fingers. The effort left bright red blotches on the white cloth. She shuddered, then folded the handkerchief into a neat square and put it away.

"Was that you with the line-over?" she asked.

"Yeah, that was a little more excitement than I wanted."

"Good save."

"Thanks," the PJ said. He inserted an IV needle into the woman's good arm, then glanced up at the badges on Gold's ACUs. "I bet you've had one or two malfunctions yourself."

"One or two." Gold switched languages and said to the woman, "I will leave you with this medical man. He thinks you will not lose your arm."

"Peace be upon both of you," the woman said.

With the injured now in the hands of four pararescuemen, Gold decided to see what she could learn. She wanted to talk to more of the people in the camp, but first she needed to get an idea of the damage. In front of a row of tents, she found the man the refugees had spoken of—the one gutted for wearing a watch.

The witnesses had not exaggerated. The man's blue entrails coiled about his waist and legs, covered with flies. He lay on his back, staring with dead eyes into the sky. To Gold, his expression seemed to ask whether any ultimate authority had seen what had happened to him. His blood dampened the ground around him as if someone had poured oil to settle the dust, and the blood turned the soil the color of copper. His left hand had been hacked off at the wrist. The hand rested in the dirt beside him, palm up, callused by whatever had been his work.

She turned away, tasted bile at the back of her throat. A deep breath helped fight her retching reflex. She took hold of a tent rope with both hands and tried to steady herself.

What manner of human being could do this to another? Gold was starting to believe a certain amount of evil always existed in the world. Like matter, it could not be destroyed. Only moved around and changed in form.

And those young boys, Fatima's brother, were in the hands of the men who did this. What would those kids turn into?

Gold kneeled and closed her eyes. Asked a higher command for strength and composure. Skill and judgment. *If there's a right thing to do here, please help me find it.*

For a moment, she concentrated on sounds. That infernal buzzing of flies. In the distance, the chirps of a starling. The crunch of footsteps.

She felt a hand on her shoulder. Before she opened her eyes, she knew it was Parson.

"These sights don't get any easier, do they?" he asked.

"No, they don't. Will you please help me up?"

Her joints still felt stiff from sitting in an awkward position while holding on to that wounded woman's artery.

Parson took her hand and pulled her to her feet. Through his flight glove, she felt the grip of his fingers and remembered that frostbite had shortened some of them. He had a way of showing up at her lowest moments, like during her capture in that winter storm. Parson had called on all his survival training and outdoor experience to keep the two of them from freezing to death. Now it wasn't the elements she faced, but the cold, thin edge of despair.

"Intel will need all we can find out," Parson said.

"I know," Gold said. "We have work to do." She took her writing pad and one of the pens from her MOLLE gear, clicked the ballpoint pen.

"I guess we better find the people who ran this place," Parson said.

"The refugees say they're all dead."

And they were. Gold and Parson found three American men and two women lying in a row, shot execution-style, close range. Each had taken a bullet to the head. On the ground just a few feet away, five cartridge casings gleamed in the dust.

The victims still wore their ID cards on lanyards around their necks. Gold flipped up one man's card so she could read it. He'd been a USAID employee, part of a Disaster Assistance Response Team.

All of them looked to be in their late twenties. Gold thought she knew the type. During a six-month TDY tour at the Pentagon, she'd seen them every day on the Metro. Fresh out of Ivy League graduate schools, idealistic enough to choose government over Wall Street, hoping to change the world. Not a bad sort by any means, just naive. Riding to work carrying leather briefcases and bottles of spring water, texting with iPhones, talking on Bluetooth. Looking at her uniform with the proper dose of respect, but way too much pity. And never expecting to meet an end like this.

P arson had never seen Gold in such an intense conversation. She spoke to a group of women gathered around her, taking notes, gesturing with her pen.

Though Parson did not know Pashto, he usually had some idea of what Gold said just from the context and the expressions. Not this time. When she wasn't making eye contact with the women, she seemed to gaze into distant hills, looking at something not visible to him. At every pause, he wanted to jump in and ask her what was happening. But he told himself that would be stupid; just let her do her job. Moments like this were why the Army had spent so much to teach her what she knew.

Rashid came over, and even he kept a polite distance from the discussion. If there was something those women had a hard time discussing with Gold, Parson figured, they sure as hell wouldn't tell a man. Maybe they recounted sexual assaults, and Gold was trying to get the women to report it. Rashid reached into a leg pocket of his flight suit and took out a nearly empty pack of unfiltered Camels. The cellophane crinkled as he fished out a cigarette.

"Can you hear what they're talking about?" Parson asked.

"Not all of people live . . ." Rashid struggled for the

word. "Near," he said. "Not all live near. Some flown in from other damage place. Some from Taliban village."

"So?"

"Some women say other women know something. Know where bad men hide."

Go on, girl, Parson thought. If she could find that out, it would be the best intel victory since the Navy SEALs dropped in on Osama bin Laden.

"Is she getting anywhere?"

"I cannot hear. She say, 'Do you not want more for childs than to die?'" Rashid placed the Camel between his front teeth. In the breeze, he had to flick his lighter three times to get the cigarette burning.

"Sounds like a good approach to me."

"Those women very afraid," Rashid said. He exhaled blue smoke and removed a fleck of tobacco from his tongue. "They have need to be afraid." He swept his arm across the camp, across the dead and wounded.

Rashid had a point. No wonder Gold needed to make such a hard sell. Parson decided to change the subject. "I think once the PJs get the worst patients ready to go, they'll call some HH-60s in here for medevac," he said.

"There are more than we carry on Mi-17," Rashid agreed.

"How do you like those two new crew members?"

"Sergeant Sharif very good," Rashid said. "Lieutenant Aamir not talk much."

"How's his flying?"

"I do not know yet. I fly all way here. I let him fly back to Mazar."

Good idea, Parson thought. You couldn't make a new guy a good copilot if the aircraft commander was a stick hog.

Parson monitored not just the individual talents of these Afghan fliers, but how they worked together. They came from different regions and tribes, which could be a big issue. To apply for enlistment, they needed two letters from village elders affirming their identity and their fitness for service. That certification meant Afghan crew members carried the honor of their families with them on every flight. They faced all the challenges of any student trying to earn wings—and they did it in a combat zone under constant terrorist threat. Parson wished he could buy every one of them a round of beers every day, but that high compliment shared among American aviators wasn't the thing to do here. Culture and faith banned alcohol for Afghans, and General Order Number One forbade it for Americans.

The knot of women around Gold began to break up. Parson thought he recognized the blessings of parting, syllables he'd heard Sophia say before. After the last two women drifted away, Gold reviewed her notes, folded the writing pad closed. She zipped the pad and pen into her MOLLE rig, took off her helmet, retied her blond hair. As she replaced the helmet she looked at Parson in a way that suggested she wasn't satisfied with what had just gone down.

"Sounded like you touched a nerve," Parson said when she joined him.

"I don't know," Gold said.

"Rashid said it seemed like some of them might know where these bastards hang out."

Gold adjusted her rifle sling across her shoulder as she looked over the camp. "It's not that simple," she said. "You know how it goes—somebody knows somebody who might know."

"Good job," Parson said. "All we can do is tell intel what they said."

"Yeah."

Parson thought it a little odd that she hadn't said *Yes, sir*. Not that he cared. She'd long since earned the right to speak with him casually. But Gold was usually wrapped so tight, so professional and regulation, that she observed military courtesy by instinct. Something was on her mind.

He had mixed feelings about having brought her back to Afghanistan. From a command perspective the assignment was a masterstroke. No male interpreter could have pulled off whatever she'd just accomplished. The last twenty minutes alone justified detaching her from the 82nd Airborne and flying her halfway around the world. But now Parson didn't know if it was best for her.

The throb of distant helicopters interrupted his worrying about Sophia. He scanned a sawtooth ridge to the west and could not find the choppers. Parson adjusted his aviator's glasses, shaded his eyes with his hand.

There they came, three dots moving in unison. Parson caught them as they emerged from behind a pinnacle of shale. Two of them were Air Force HH-60 Pave Hawks. Their refueling probes jutted forward like the proboscises of moths. Behind them flew an Osprey tilt-rotor.

All three aircraft banked toward the camp and began descending. Parson watched for smoke trails or tracers coming up at them, but for now at least the sky remained clean and tranquil. The blue stretched all the way into China; he knew that from the morning's weather brief. Not ideal tactical conditions, but better than having turbulence knock the fillings out of your teeth. He'd once flown a low-level mission on a gusty day during the first months of the Afghanistan war. One particularly evil downdraft slammed the C-130 with so many negative Gs that the oil pumps cavitated in all four engines. The Herk damn near scraped the ground as the oil pressure needles drooped. But then the pressure climbed and so did the airplane, and the crew lived to fly again. For a while.

The Pave Hawks fluttered toward landing. As they skimmed low to the ground, dust billowed behind them and churned in the air rent by their blades. Helmeted gunners manned M134 miniguns that protruded from the sides of the choppers. Parson watched the crewmen as the HH-60s touched down and shrouded themselves in dust.

The Osprey drew nearer and tilted its rotors to vertical. When it turned, the word MARINES became visible, painted in light gray on the aft end of the fuselage. The twin tail fins bore the letters EH. Parson had to think about that squadron code for a moment: It was the Black Knights of the 2nd Marine Aircraft Wing. Parson hoped it was that same TRAP team he'd met in Ghandaki; he liked that big gunnery sergeant.

Grit swirled as the Osprey landed. Dust collected on Parson's sunglasses; its chalky taste irritated his throat with every breath. The aircraft dropped its ramp. From Parson's view, tan combat boots appeared at the ramp crest, camo trouser cuffs bloused over the tops of the boots. Sure enough, the first man off the Osprey stood a head taller than the others.

Blount waved to Parson. He did not salute; in a combat zone a salute could identify an officer as a valuable target for a sniper. The gunnery sergeant barked orders to his men, and the TRAP team helped the pararescuemen load patients onto the helicopters. Parson briefed him beside the body of a woman shot through the head.

"They took some more kids, Gunny," Parson said.

For a moment, Blount did not speak. A vein bulged along the side of his neck, underneath scar tissue that looked like a burn.

"Sir, I thought I seen some shit," he said, "but I never seen nothing to beat this."

"That makes two of us."

"If them sumbitches want seventy-two virgins, I'll be their date counselor."

Blount took a camera from one of his cargo pockets, and he snapped a photo of the woman at his feet. Parson led him through the camp, and Blount shot more images. Outside the fence, they found Rashid's crew bringing the rice out of the Mi-17. Blount carried the last of the hundred-pound bags, one over each shoulder. At the camp's mess tent, he swung them off his back like they were pillows. Then he took one last photo of the man gutted by a sword.

The stain was already fading as the dry dirt soaked it

up. Afghanistan's soil knew how to do that, Parson thought. Afghan soil had absorbed blood from the Soviet 40th Army, from the troops of Queen Victoria, from the hoplites of Alexander the Great. From women, children, and rescue workers. And from too many of Parson's friends.

8

The rescue team landed back at Mazar under a dusk sky the color of wine. Gold helped Reyes and the other PJs take the wounded from Rashid's Mi-17, the Osprey, and the two Pave Hawks. She worked in silence, pondering her talks with the refugees. She hadn't briefed Parson on all of what the women had told her; she was still trying to make sense of it herself.

There was a village in Samangan, the women said, just north of a stream they called Goat's Gut. Maybe the creek's twists and turns resembled the intestines of an animal. Whatever the name's origin, Gold doubted she'd see it on anything produced by the National Geospatial-Intelligence Agency.

In that village—just a collection of a few mud-brick homes—lived an elderly woman who knew things. Was she connected to the insurgents? Yes, one refugee said. No, she hates the Taliban, another said. Still others claimed she was the mother of an important cleric, one who had laid down arms.

Gold didn't feel much encouraged about that business of a former Talib putting away his guns. In Afghanistan, loyalties and peace agreements came with price tags and expiration dates. She remembered attending a reintegration ceremony for some ex-insurgents in Paktika Province. You couldn't kill all the lower-level fighters, the reasoning went. So you needed an amnesty program for those willing to come back into the fold. That amnesty was part of the overall COIN strategy: counterinsurgency, as opposed to counterterrorism. Easier to take away reasons to join the insurgency than to take out every terrorist.

With a group of U.S. officers and Afghan politicians, she had ridden to the reintegration ceremony in a convoy of MRAP vehicles. Gold watched the MRAPs' antennas sway with every bump in the dirt road, and she thought it ironic to have to travel to a peace ceremony in a truck engineered to be mine-resistant and ambush-protected. At the reintegration, the Talibs stacked their AK-47s, magazines removed. They stood in a line, wearing their flat-topped hats, field jackets of old Soviet bloc camo, and white *shalwar kameez*. An imam offered a prayer and said, "May God reward you for joining the peace process."

The government in Kabul gave them jobs, and in some cases new identities. Within months they started turning up captured in night raids on insurgent hideouts, or dead on the battlefield from firefights with American troops. For coalition forces, ISAF soldiers, or NATO training command advisers, staying alive meant learning not to trust.

Gold still thought about that as she went to a briefing with Parson, Rashid, and Reyes. In just the time they'd been gone at the refugee camp, the Air Force had set up a forward command and control center at the Mazar airfield. The facility amounted to a small Air Operations Center in a tent. Parson called it the C2-Forward.

Inside, live video feeds, radios, and satphones hummed. The place looked like every other deployed ops center Gold had seen: laptops glowing, electrical cords snaking across the floor into power strips, plastic water bottles and yellow Post-it notes everywhere.

The intel officer displayed one of Blount's digital photos on a computer screen. The photo showed the remains of the five Americans executed at the camp. Gold sat next to Parson at a folding table, and she looked down at the table's aluminum surface. She didn't feel like seeing these images again, though she knew she had to explain each one to intel.

She described the victims, gave every detail she could remember about all the dead and injured—the flies and the blood, the slash wounds, the hacked wrists. Parson and Rashid told what they'd seen from the air—the abducted boys, the pickup trucks. Then they filled out a SAFIRE report, jotted down the particulars of the surface-to-air missile fired up at the helicopters.

"You got some good stuff in your interviews, didn't you?" Parson asked Gold as he scribbled on the SAFIRE form.

"Maybe," she said. She still could not decide how much of her informal *shura* with the women was worth reporting. Might as well let intel do its job, she figured. So she told the officer everything she'd heard.

"There's a mullah in that region who served in the Taliban government," the intel officer said. "Or at least there used to be. He hasn't turned up on the radar in a long time."

"Who is he?" Gold asked.

"Name escapes me," the intel officer said. "Hang on a second."

The officer began tapping on his laptop. Searching the SIPRNET, Gold supposed. Like doing a Google search of classified information. The intel officer opened a document and began reading.

"It might be a guy named Durrani," he said. "None of this stuff is recent, though."

"Did he reintegrate?" Gold asked.

"Nope," the officer said. "He just quit. Or maybe he got so smart, we just stopped picking up his comms."

Entirely possible, Gold thought. The Taliban were brutish, but unfortunately not stupid. If they moved around with cell phones at all, they'd keep them turned off with the SIM card removed. They knew the infidels had big airplanes with funny-looking antennas that could pick up everything.

"What do we know about this guy?" Gold asked.

"Very little," the officer said. "He ran some of the Taliban's madrassas up until 2001. After Operation Enduring Freedom kicked off, we had some SIGINT reports: his voice on the radio, that kind of thing. I got nothing after 2006."

"But at that time he was in Samangan?"

"That's where this says the radio traffic came from."

"So you're telling me our intel supports what I heard at the camp," Gold said.

"It's so sketchy, I'm not sure it supports anything, but it doesn't dispute what you heard, either."

Gold rubbed her thumb across her fingernails, thought for a moment. Why would the women point her in this direction? Did they think this mullah, or his family, or anyone else up there would help? It probably wasn't a setup— not by people who'd just been shot at by extremists.

But acting on tips carried all kinds of perils. People settled old scores by fingering their enemies as insurgents. Some Afghans gave worthless information in hopes of getting paid. On top of that, anything that happened in Afghanistan had a lot to do with who was smuggling what to whose relatives and which officials took bribes from where. Sometimes Gold felt more like a cop in a bad neighborhood than a soldier.

"I wouldn't puzzle over it too much," Parson said. "If you want to go up to that village and ask around, we'll just fly you up there."

"Thank you, sir," Gold said, "but I don't think it's a good idea to fly. If we go in with choppers slamming around, the whole world will know we're there."

"You wish to go on ground?" Rashid asked.

"I think it might be best."

"Have you lost your mind?" Parson said.

Gold answered by way of a half smile—the nearest she'd come to mirth in a long time. She couldn't remember the last time she'd laughed out loud.

"I'll see if they'll give me a squad and an up-armored vehicle," she said.

"Bullshit," Parson said. "The Army assigned you to me. I'm not letting you go get yourself killed on some wild-ass goose chase. You know how dangerous the roads are."

She let Parson's point hang in the air. Of course she knew the roads were dangerous. If she wanted safety, she could get her doctorate in international studies or comparative literature and go teach somewhere. Maybe someday. But now she had responsibilities bigger than herself.

"Sir, I know I'm supposed to be here as your interpreter," she said. "But you said yourself we might have gathered some important intel at the camp. It'll get wasted if we don't act on it."

"I don't want you to get wasted," Parson said.

This would be a tough sell, Gold realized. Parson meant every word he said. Lord knew he had his flaws, but you didn't need to guess what he was thinking. He didn't want her to go, at least not by road. That was that. And the man was as loyal as a German shepherd. If he liked you, and especially if he felt responsible for you, he'd do anything to protect you. And that was the problem. Protectiveness was about to get in the way of the mission.

―――――

Now Parson worried. The best thing about Sophia—as a soldier, as a leader, and as a senior NCO—was her judgment. But this was the craziest damned idea he'd ever heard. *Let my interpreter, my dearest friend in the—* Well, anyway, let a sergeant major with a bazillion dollars' worth of training and experience get KIA while she's on my watch? Look at my name tag, girl. Does it say *stupid* under those wings?

He felt glad she didn't argue. Gold had earned so much respect—from him and from everybody else—that he didn't want to pull rank on her, and certainly not in front of people. But damn, why not just fly in and fly out? Fuck 'em if they don't like helicopters.

Parson considered the matter settled, so he changed the subject. "Anything else for us," he asked the intel officer, "like some info on this bastard who thinks he's Zorro?" He was curious about this new terrorist leader. Who the hell used a sword nowadays?

"Maybe," the officer said. "Remember that video he released?"

"Sure."

"Well, he referred to his 'former Taliban brothers.' But he might not have ever been Taliban."

"Come again?" Parson asked. He began to wonder if this intel guy really knew the score.

"Not all the insurgents are Taliban. You have other groups like the Haqqani network and HIG. And then among the Taliban there are younger members more hard-line than the founders."

Parson looked at Gold, who nodded. Apparently all this

sounded right to her. But so what? The insurgents had factions that went by names Parson could not pronounce. Hairsplitting, as far as he was concerned. Bad guys were bad guys.

"As soon as the communist government fell in the 1990s," Gold said, "the mujahideen began fighting among themselves. Some have had blood feuds for years."

"Fine," Parson said. "Let 'em kill one another till there's one left, and then I'll shoot that one."

"The point is that all this might mean some rift among the insurgents," the officer said.

Parson could see the idea interested Gold, but he was starting to lose patience. Historians could sort this out later, if anybody cared. But he was tired and hungry and wanted to finish the briefing.

"So who is he?" Parson asked.

"No one we've ever seen before this month," the officer said. "In some of his communiqués, he goes by the nom de guerre of Chaaku."

"Pashto word for *knife*," Gold said.

Figures, Parson thought. What's the Pashto word for *asshole*?

"But we think his real name is Bakht Sahar. Middle thirties, educated at Darul Uloom Haqqania madrassa in Pakistan."

"Jihad University," Gold said.

Pakistan again. Some ally. Gold and Parson—shot down and captured—had appeared in a video with another terrorist from Pakistan named Marwan. Parson could still feel the dread, the sick fear, waiting for the blade.

And now there was another Marwan. Parson had given up hoping for sweetness and light in Afghanistan. That kind of hope was like flying an instrument approach through the fog down to minimums: watching the localizer and glide slope needles, your thumb poised over the go-around button, thinking *I'll see the approach lights at any moment*. And if you kept hoping long enough, you could fly your ass right into the ground.

Parson looked over at Rashid. "What do you think about all this, buddy?" he asked.

"I think words of my grandfather," Rashid said.

"How's that?"

"He say how Allah make Afghanistan. When Allah create world, he have things left over. Mountain. Desert. Rock. All the rubbish left over from world go to make Afghanistan."

Parson didn't know what to make of a story that described Afghanistan and everything in it as an afterthought. It was one thing for him to give up on Afghanistan, but to hear Rashid lose heart was something else. But who could blame Rashid if he did? The man had just lost part of a crew, and there was no telling what other friends and family he'd lost over the years. You couldn't ask about that sort of thing, so Parson didn't know Rashid's family history. He just hoped Rashid could keep his head in the game, since he and all the other Afghan fliers had plenty of work cut out for them.

That became even more clear after the briefing, as Parson walked along the flight line with Rashid. Pallets of food, blankets, and other relief supplies were piling up on the ramp. The C-130s brought it in faster than the heli-copters could distribute it. If the Mi-17 crews didn't catch up, pretty soon the Mazar airfield would get mogged out—maximum on ground—and there'd be no room for anything else.

Rescue and medical teams were also getting backed up. Parson saw people walking around in official-looking uniforms and jumpsuits of green, khaki, and blue. He saw patches from organizations he'd not run into before: Los Angeles County Search and Rescue Team, Fairfax County Urban Search and Rescue Team, Air Force Expeditionary Medical Support Health Response Team. The medical crews could treat patients in the camp here at the airport, but those search-and-rescue guys couldn't do any good until they got out into the field.

"Much to fly," Rashid said.

"You got that right," Parson said. He noted that Rashid was looking across the ramp and seeing the big picture, not just his own flight schedule. Another good sign. Senior officer material. The Afghans needed to grow their own leadership class all over again, since so many of the natural leaders had been killed off or chased away. War brought a kind of reverse Darwinism: It eliminated the strongest and the brightest.

"Let us see where we fly next," Rashid said.

"Might as well."

In the flight planning room—just a section of the tents that made up the Air Operations Center—they found Lieu-tenant Aamir poring over a VFR chart. Rashid spoke to him in words Parson could not understand. He got the tone, though. A command voice, but not an unfriendly one. Aamir answered with something that sounded matter-of-fact. To Parson, Pashto had a pleasant ring. It didn't have the hard edges of German or Russian—or maybe he just liked it because he associated it with Sophia.

"He say the . . ." Rashid pointed to the whiteboard.

"Schedule," Parson said.

"Yes, schedule. Aamir say schedule for us to fly tomorrow to village near Kunduz."

Short flight, Parson knew. Less than a hundred miles. He leaned over the chart Aamir had spread across a table. The Afghan copilot drew a pencil line along the straight edge of a navigational plotter. He had erased a previous line and started over again. Good planning, Parson thought. Rashid and Aamir would probably just take a radio compass bearing off the Kunduz NDB, but it never hurt to have a backup. And Parson—a navigator before he was a pilot—had preached chart usage from the time he'd become an adviser. Maybe they were finally listening.

The chart covered the G-6B sector, which included northeastern Afghanistan, parts of former Soviet republics, a section of northern Pakistan, and even a sliver of China. Some of the roughest terrain in the world, with elevations up to twenty-five thousand feet. Arid, too. The color-coded chart wasn't green; it was brown—except the white parts where snow shrouded the mountains all year long.

Aamir's course line ended at a tiny circle without a name. Other nameless circles surrounded it, the grouping of them marked NUMEROUS VILLAGES. The elevation in that area was a little more reasonable—more like six thousand feet. But higher mountains loomed nearby. Not the worst kind of terrain for a helicopter, but certainly not the best.

"Has he looked at the weather?" Parson asked.

More chatter in Pashto.

"He has not," Rashid said.

"I'll get it for you."

Parson tried not to give the Afghans too much help; they'd need to operate on their own sooner or later. But he could log on to the weather computer and get more detailed information than they could get in a verbal briefing over the phone. From a laptop placed on a table made of rough planks and cinder blocks, he printed out the text forecast, the surface analysis chart, and a constant pressure chart.

The text forecast brought lousy news. Winds out of the northwest tomorrow morning at twenty knots gusting to thirty. Moderate turbulence.

The charts backed up the text. The isobar lines on the constant pressure chart bunched up so tightly that the cheap inkjet printer had blurred some of them together. The lines connected points of equal pressure, just the way contour lines on a terrain map connected points of equal elevation. Close isobars meant rapid changes in pressure, which meant strong wind. If anything, the text forecast was conservative.

Rashid looked over Parson's shoulder. "How is weather?" he asked.

"Buddy," Parson said, "we're going to get our teeth kicked in."

❧ 9 ❧

After the briefing, Gold and Reyes stopped by the mess
tent. The cooks there really didn't cook; they just
heated up Unitized Group Rations—MRE food in big
tray packs. The turkey cutlets and green beans tasted
lousy, but they provided a quick way to feed all the flight
crews, relief workers, and refugees at Mazar. The fare
might improve as the chow tent got better established,
Gold knew, but UGRs would do for now.

She sat at a folding table with the pararescueman,
sipped coffee from a foam cup. The coffee was weak, but
at least it was hot. With so much misery around her, Gold
felt guilty about every comfort. The warm cup in her hand
made her think of the newly homeless in the cold. The
food, however tasteless, reminded her of people going
hungry in remote villages. She unzipped her field jacket
and thought of refugees with only the one set of filthy
clothes on their backs.

"What's wrong?" Reyes asked.

Gold gestured toward the mess tent opening, beyond which lay the refugee tents and the flight line. A C-27 took off, turboprops growling. A stray cat slinked across the ramp, the animal's fur as mottled as a New England snowshoe hare between seasons. Somewhere in the distance, a child cried.

"We can never do enough," Gold said.

"One save at a time," Reyes said.

That didn't make Gold feel any better, but she gathered that it was good enough for Reyes. She noticed the patch on his uniform. It read USAF PARARESCUE—THAT OTHERS MAY LIVE. Not a bad guiding creed, she thought. The patch depicted a winged angel with her arms spread across a globe.

"Let me tell you about something that happened during Katrina," Reyes said.

Reyes described flying over an inundated New Orleans in 2005, fetid water the color of Gold's black coffee. He and his Pave Hawk crew picked up a half dozen survivors stranded on rooftops and delivered them to a collection point at Louis Armstrong International Airport. On their second pass over the city, the pilots circled above a house flooded up to the eaves, with three people waving from their perch on the shingles. The survivors had chopped through from the attic; the ragged hole looked like it might have been punched by a bunker buster that pierced but failed to explode.

As the helicopter hovered, its rotor wash whipped the foul water to froth. Reyes strapped onto the forest penetrator, and he let the flight engineer lower him on the hoist.

While he rode the cable down, he thought he felt a grinding through the steel braids, but he paid it no mind. On the roof he found an elderly black man and two boys. Grandchildren, Reyes assumed, maybe eight and twelve.

"Their mama's down there," the man said, pointing inside the attic. He shouted over the helicopter's thudding blades. "She can't climb out, and we can't lift her."

On his hands and knees, Reyes peered through the hole. Splinters pricked through his flight gloves, and he scratched his wrist on an exposed nail. When his eyes adjusted to the darkness inside, he saw a woman, overweight and very pregnant, lying on the attic floor.

Reyes plugged his headset into his radio, pressed the transmit switch. "I'm gonna need some help, boys," he said. "After I send these guys up on the penetrator, put Wilkins down here with the Stokes litter and a crash ax."

"Copy that," the pilot said. "Send 'em up."

Reyes unfolded one of the rescue seats on the penetrator. "Sit on this thing," he told the older boy. "Put this strap around you, and hold on."

The child, eyes wide with fear and face dripping with sweat, clung to the penetrator as Reyes cinched down the strap. "Please don't let me fall out," the boy said.

"I'm going up with you," Reyes said. "All you gotta do is ride, and don't try to climb into the helicopter. Just let my buddy pull you in."

The boy followed instructions better than some adults Reyes had rescued, and so did his brother. When they were both safely in the HH-60, Reyes rode back down and tried to get the old man to go.

"I ain't leaving without my daughter," he said.

"There's nothing you can do to help, sir," Reyes told him. "Let 'em get you into some air-conditioning at the airport, and we'll get her out."

"I'm staying right here, young man."

"Sir, you're suffering from heat stress. You need some cool water and a fan."

"I been hot before."

The man's life wasn't in immediate danger, so Reyes decided not to argue any further. "He wants to stay," Reyes called up to the Pave Hawk. "Tell Wilkins to come on down."

The grandfather watched as Reyes's partner rode the hoist. Once Wilkins touched down on the roof, the flight engineer, aboard the aircraft, reeled the penetrator back up and swapped it with the Stokes litter. Reyes and Wilkins went to work with the crash ax, taking turns and widening the hole the old man had chopped. When they climbed down to the attic floor, the woman could barely speak above a whisper.

"How are my boys?" she asked.

"They're fine, ma'am," Wilkins said. "The helicopter's taking them to the airport."

The woman nodded and closed her eyes. Reyes felt her neck and found her pulse weak and rapid. She had stopped sweating; her neck was dry. Heatstroke.

"She needs to get out of here," Reyes said.

He and Wilkins rolled her into the litter and strapped her in. Sweat dripped off Reyes's nose and onto the woman's face, but she didn't seem to notice. His flight suit was soaked by now, and the stink of filthy water and rotted food was starting to make him a little sick.

When they lifted her from the wooden floor, Reyes felt light-headed. If the heat was getting to him, he could imagine what it did to her. The two PJs turned the litter upright, and Reyes almost dropped his end.

"You gonna make it?" Wilkins asked.

"I'm good," Reyes said. "On the count of three."

Reyes counted, and they heaved the patient through the hole vertically. She must have weighed three hundred pounds. Reyes's arm muscles burned. Up on the roof, the old man helped lower his daughter to the sloped surface. He was stronger than he looked, and he didn't let her slip.

The pararescuemen pulled themselves up through the hole. Even through the leather palms of his gloves, Reyes felt the heat emanating from those shingles, but after the close air of that attic, the rooftop felt almost cool.

A few minutes later, he heard the rumble of the returning Pave Hawk. The helo hovered over the house, and the crew lowered the cable. Reyes connected the cable to the suspension harness on the Stokes litter, feeling good about this hard-won save.

"She's in heatstroke," he transmitted. "Pour some water on her when you get her aboard."

"Roger that. We'll tell the docs."

"Patient's secure," Reyes said. "Take her up."

The cable didn't move.

"I got her strapped in," Reyes said. "Take her up."

No answer for a moment. Then: "The hoist is jammed."

Reyes swore under his breath. Then he transmitted, "You gotta be kidding me."

The flight engineer answered him: "The motor popped the breakers, and I think it's burned out."

Reyes knew what would come next. They'd want to jettison the cable. He considered just having the helicopter lift the woman externally, swinging from the cable. The pilots were skilled enough to set her down gently. But that was dangerous, especially for a patient in this condition.

"You gonna cut it?" Reyes asked.

"Affirmative," the engineer called. "Tell me when the litter's disconnected."

Reyes removed the cable hook from the litter harness and said, "It's clear."

The Pave Hawk drifted away from the house. The cable dragged across the roof and tangled in a television antenna. "Cable's fouled," Reyes called. "Just cut it where you are."

When the jettison squib fired, a tiny explosive charge severed the cable. The cable dropped away from the helicopter, writhed like something in death throes until it slapped into the water. The helicopter accelerated away.

"Where they going?" the old man asked.

Reyes explained what had happened. As he did so, the flight engineer called back to him on the radio: "Anderson's crew has a good hoist. They're coming to get you."

"Copy that," Reyes said.

While he, Wilkins, and the old man waited, the woman went into cardiac arrest. The two pararescuemen performed CPR until they were both exhausted, but by the time the second helicopter arrived, she was dead. The old man had watched it all from two feet away.

Reyes asked himself questions for months. What if he'd suggested carrying her externally? What if he'd mentioned the grinding he'd felt in the cable? What if he'd gotten her out earlier and sent her up first? Questions without answers.

"You have a hard job," Gold said when Reyes finished his story.

"I've made my peace with it," he said. "You do what you can do, and that's all you can do."

Gold knew he was right, but she had a hard time making herself believe it. Maybe she had spent so much time in Afghanistan that part of her could never leave the place, never let go. At least she could get her mind around half of Reyes's philosophy—the part about doing *all* you could do. And right now, that involved a road trip.

The first mortar hit just as Parson and Rashid left flight planning. A concussive force slammed Parson's eardrums as if from the inside. Both men dived for cover by the sandbagged wall of the command post. Shouts erupted from the flight line, screams from the refugee tents and the MASF. The bang left a steady hum in Parson's ears.

"Sons of bitches!" he shouted. His own voice sounded muffled.

"Where that from?" Rashid asked.

"I don't know." A pool of halogen light illuminated the

area around the command post, but darkness lay beyond, punctuated only by the blue dots of the taxiway edge lights.

Parson realized he didn't even know if he was really behind cover. Whether the sandbags protected them depended on where the next mortar landed. He had to wait about five seconds for the answer.

The next round hit so close that his damaged eardrums registered only a dull thud. But the siss of flying shrapnel, in a different range of sound, he heard well. Something stung the back of his hand. Sand dribbled onto his neck from above him, the result of a fragment that had just missed his head and buried itself in the bags.

An oddly idle corner of his mind recalled when he'd emptied an autoloading shotgun at a flight of geese, reloaded, and fired again. By the last shot, his ears had numbed to the blasts. When he'd pulled the trigger, there was no explosion at all, but he'd felt the recoil and heard clearly the cycling of the bolt.

He grabbed Rashid's arm and pulled him flat to the tarmac. "You all right?" Parson shouted.

"Yes. And you?"

"Nothing serious. Stay down."

A call-to-arms bugle tone sounded from the base's loudspeakers. Alarm Red. A helicopter lifted off. Parson could not see it, but he assumed the aircraft was a gunship hunting their tormentors. Maybe the pilots would spot the bad guys on the forward-looking infrared and light them up. Parson had seen gun camera video from the FLIR on Apaches and Cobras, and it was priceless: Jackasses burying an IED by the roadside at night, with no idea anybody could see them. A crisp, understated voice on the radio, saying, "Clear to engage." A white blob washing out the screen. Fragments of glowing warmth flying—the heat signature of disintegrating bodies.

Another mortar exploded. This one hit farther down the airfield, near the departure end of the runway. Parson listened for any clues of the damage: moans, cries, curses. He heard nothing, but he knew his hearing was unreliable now and would stay that way for hours.

A truck engine started. Moments later, two Humvees sped down a taxiway. Marines and Air Force security police, Parson supposed. Good. Now both ground and air charged after the insurgents. Maybe the attack was over.

The all-clear came, and he worried about Gold. Where was she now? More Humvees and trucks began rolling around the base—the post-attack recon teams looking for unexploded ordnance and wounded personnel.

"Let's go count noses," Parson said. "I hope everyone's all right." Rashid looked confused, but he followed Parson without comment.

Under a lamp pole, Parson stopped to examine his right hand. Shrapnel had slashed a scratch through the skin over his metacarpal bones, just deep enough for blood to run down his knuckles and drip from his thumbnail.

"You are hurt," Rashid said.

"Not bad." Parson judged he did not need stitches. He unzipped a chest pocket and took out his handkerchief, dabbed the fabric over the wound. In the pallid light, he could see Rashid was unhurt, and for that he was grateful.

He pocketed the handkerchief, flexed the fingers of the injured hand. The bleeding had slowed, and it didn't hurt too much now. Parson was right-handed, so of course that was the hand that always got hurt.

But this was nothing like last time. When he'd been shot down with Gold years before, he'd cracked his right wrist. Through the frozen hell of evading in a winter storm, he'd endured the pain of that wound. He'd fashioned a crude splint, and he'd gotten by well enough with that. But when they were captured by Marwan's men, the splint gave away the injury. While Marwan interrogated Parson, another terrorist twisted his wrist. Parson had thought he knew pain—until that day when the blinding agony scarred his mind with permanent marks. He even wondered if a neurosurgeon could open his skull and point to the evidence, the way a botanist might find the record of a wildfire in the growth rings of a redwood.

They found Lieutenant Aamir and the rest of Rashid's crew unharmed. But the mortars had damaged more than Parson's hand. The recon team discovered an Afghan mechanic dead of shrapnel wounds. Inside the MASF, aeromeds were stitching up an American crew chief, a German nurse, and an Italian aid worker. And Parson didn't hear the loud noises he wanted to hear: the cackle of a chain gun, the whoosh of a Hellfire—anything that sounded like payback. Apparently, the Quick Reaction Force had caught nothing. And Parson had not seen Gold anywhere.

He finally found her in the refugee tents with Fatima. The girl had been crying, but she seemed calm now as she clung to Gold's arm. She looked up at Parson and spoke in Pashto.

"What's she saying?" Parson asked.

"She remembers you," Gold said. "She says you are the friend of the giant who brought her here."

Parson almost laughed. "I guess that's true," he said.

"Any intel?"

"QRF went out, but I never heard them shoot." Parson also told her about the dead and wounded.

"Black Crescent again?" Gold asked.

"I don't know," Parson said. "Yeah, probably."

At the front of the tent, the plywood door creaked open. Blount walked in. He looked like he'd just come in from the field. The big gunnery sergeant wore his body armor and carried that tricked-out rifle of his. Fatima cried out a greeting and waved. Blount smiled and waved back.

"Speak of the devil," Parson said.

"Not exactly," Gold said.

"Sir," Blount replied. "Sergeant Major. Just came by to check on my new friend."

"She was pretty scared," Gold said, "but she's okay now. Nobody in this tent got hurt."

"That's good," Blount said.

"You been outside the wire?" Parson asked.

"Yes, sir. We were part of the QRF."

"See anything?"

"We didn't catch nobody, but we saw where they'd been. Slippery bastards. We found three mortar tubes with the ground wet underneath them."

"What does that mean?" Parson asked.

"They pack ice around the mortar rounds, and the ice holds the round in the mouth of the tube. By the time the ice melts and the round seats and arms itself, they're long gone."

"Damn," Parson said. You could spend a million dollars on some way to kill terrorists, and they could find a fifty-cent way to get around it.

"I swear it's like stomping roaches," Blount said. "You just can't get them all."

Yeah, Parson thought, but you can keep stomping. He wondered if terrorist groups like Black Crescent, the Taliban, and al-Qaeda were accidents of history, things not supposed to happen. And if they were accidents, were they like accidents in aviation? The result of a chain of mistakes and missed opportunities that line up just the wrong way and lead to disaster? If one link in the chain had broken, if one thing had happened differently, then the catastrophe would not have taken place. He knew pilots who would give anything to go back in time and add power three seconds earlier, or reset that altitude alerter and not transpose the numbers.

"Sir," Gold said. "You know I can help get these guys."

Parson looked at her hard. Wasn't this settled? Then he raised his eyebrows, just to soften his expression. He didn't want to be angry with Sophia—or at least he didn't want her to know he was angry.

"Sir, what are y'all talking about?" Blount asked.

"She got some good intel up at that refugee camp in Samangan," Parson said.

"I heard about that," Blount said.

"Well, now she wants to go back in there to a village to get some more intel, but she wants to go by road."

"What did you tell her?"

"Not *no*, but *hell, no*."

Blount kept silent for a moment. "What if some Marines go up there with her?"

Now Parson was even more annoyed, but he held back his temper in a way he could do for no one except Sophia. "I know you two are smart people," he said. "So what part of *no* do you not understand? It means *negative*."

"Sir, do you know about the Lioness teams?" Blount asked.

"The what?"

"Lioness teams. Female engagement teams in the Corps. Women Marines who speak the language, know the culture. They do a lot of what the Sergeant Major here does; they just haven't done it as long as she has."

"What about them?" Parson asked.

"If you okay it, we could hook her up with Lioness. I'll see if my CO will let part of my platoon escort them up there. So the Sergeant Major wouldn't go by herself, and she wouldn't be the only one who speaks Pashto."

Parson hated the idea. He was still haunted by the last time Gold had been torn from his sight when they were supposed to be together. He had watched helplessly, tied to an overturned chair, as they dragged her away. That image still woke him up at night.

Emotions. They got in the way of the mission. You're not supposed to let that happen, he told himself. But you're not supposed to let people take unnecessary risks, either. Where was the link in the accident chain? Would this asshole who called himself Chaaku become the next bin Laden? Do you have the means to stop him right here?

"You say you'll go with her?" Parson asked.

"Yes, sir," Blount said.

"All right, listen. You check with your CO and these lion women. She can go only if you and your whole squad go with her. In MRAPs, too. Not some light-ass Humvees."

"Yes, sir."

"Rashid and I have to fly tomorrow," Parson continued. "Gold can stay here and work it out with you jarheads. But if I get back and I find out she's gone with anybody but you, in anything but an MRAP, I will kick your ass all over this airfield no matter how big you are."

"We'll take care of her, sir." Blount smiled. "Sir, did you ever consider being a Marine?"

"Hell, no," Parson said. "Do I look crazy?"

✦ 10 ✦

Gold saw a lot of her younger self in Lance Corporals Lyndsey Meacham and Ann Woolrich. Both women were in their early twenties, so Gold had more than a decade on them. Their military bearing and courtesy never wavered; they answered every question with "Yes, Sergeant Major" or "No, Sergeant Major." However, Blount had misunderstood their language ability. They spoke a few words of Pashto, but unlike Gold, they had not studied at the Defense Language Institute.

What Pashto they knew they had picked up on the job in the Lioness program. The Lionesses could come from any Marine Corps job specialty. They were originally intended to search local women, who, under cultural norms, could not be searched by men under any circumstances. But their role had expanded to include more than searches. Ann and Lyndsey told of accompanying infantry as the men kicked in doors. The Lionesses would talk to the women inside, with or without interpreters. Lioness teams had lost at least three of their number to roadside bombs, and Gold imagined history would record them as the military granddaughters of the WACs, WAVEs, and WASPs of World War II.

The two younger women sat across from Gold in the back of the Cougar MRAP vehicle. They wore Marine Corps camo like Blount and his men, and they carried full-sized M16A2 rifles, larger than Gold's M4. Each wore the standard Kevlar combat helmet and body armor, with spare magazines in pouches at the front of the armor. Both had tied their hair in long ponytails instead of tight buns. Given their role, Gold presumed they wanted to make their gender immediately apparent. A private took the wheel, and Blount rode in the right front seat. A gunner manned the .50-cal in the turret. Gold could see only his boots and legs.

She carried her usual field gear, with one other piece of equipment. One of her pouches contained a Blue Force Tracker, an electronic device that looked like a handheld GPS. It was that, and more. The BFT let the command post know her position at all times, and it could send and receive text.

Gold also brought an item to use as a gift for villagers, a token to ease the conversation along, if things went well enough to have a conversation. She'd talked one of the camp's cooks out of a twenty-four-ounce bag of Domino sugar.

When the driver started the engine, the diesel clatter sounded to Gold like an incantation, a prayer for safe passage. The rear ramp clanged shut, and she heard two other

Caterpillar engines rumble to life, the rest of Blount's team in a pair of identical Cougars.

The MRAPs rolled from their parking spots on the tarmac, through a sandbagged checkpoint with unsmiling Afghan sentries, and out onto a perimeter road left crumbling by the earthquake. Gold watched through steel louvers that shielded windows of bulletproof glass as thick as her thumb. She knew the ride might take at least two hours, though her destination was less than eighty miles away. It all depended on the condition of the roads.

The paved portion of the route did not last long. The three Cougars, Gold's in the middle, jounced onto a dusty road that amounted to only two ruts across a rock-strewn valley floor. They passed a small village—just four houses of stacked shale. A cow grazed behind the stone huts, ribs visible underneath its hide.

The village gave way to a *qalang*—a flat expanse of wheat. The wind picked up, and the wheat stalks bent and flowed like green-amber breakers on an inland sea. Beyond the fields, the terrain began to rise and the road to twist. The rough path hurt the bones in Gold's hips, and her shoulders strained against the aircraft-style harness; the Cougar's suspension offered strength, not comfort.

"So how much did they tell you about this mission?" Gold asked.

"Not much," Ann said.

"Only that we would talk to some women in a village, and you didn't want to go in loud with helicopters," Lyndsey added.

"That's right," Gold said. "And do you know about this new insurgent group?"

"They briefed us that there have been attacks from something called Black . . ." Ann seemed to struggle for the word.

"Black Crescent," Gold said. "The Taliban played too nice for them, so they went into business for themselves."

"Sergeant Major," Ann asked, "aren't you the one who brought back that detainee from the C-130 that got shot down a few years ago?"

"I helped," Gold said.

"I remember hearing about that on the news," Lyndsey said. "It was right after I graduated from boot camp."

Gold couldn't recall what the media had reported at the time. For her safety, the Army refused to release her identity, and she had never given any interviews. The Air Force had done the same for Parson. Given his bluntness, Gold imagined Air Force public affairs would never let him anywhere near a television camera, anyway.

But within the military grapevine, their reputations had spread. Gold didn't like to talk about the incident, and she certainly didn't like attention resulting from it.

"We just did what the mission required," Gold said. "Nothing more, nothing less."

For her, the lesson learned was Charlie Mike. Continue Mission. You were put here for a reason, and if you remained alive, then you still had a job to do. As Parson might say, it wasn't over until all your friends were standing around the funeral home talking about how natural you looked.

Terraced hills rolled by Gold's window as the terrain began rising. Some of the layered fields grew more wheat, and others held rows of small trees. The orchards were too far away for Gold to identify the trees, but she guessed they were mulberries, or perhaps almonds or walnuts.

Blount twisted around in his seat, handed back three bottles of water. Gold took one and passed the others to Ann and Lyndsey. "Have you done a lot of these KLEs?" Blount asked.

"Not recently," Gold said.

She'd done many key leader engagements back when she worked with the Provincial Reconstruction Teams. The groups would meet with tribal elders and try to coax them into helping build schools and roads, or at least not attacking schools and roads. It usually worked for as long as the company or battalion remained in the area. But when the troops left, the insurgents returned, often with the cooperation of villagers. She was beginning to wonder if all the schools, hospitals, and hydroelectric generators did any good. Did they win hearts and minds or just generate disappointment?

And Gold wasn't sure she'd call this mission a KLE. More like a long shot in the dark on iron sights. She twisted open the water bottle and took a drink.

The road wound past a bluff pocked with small caves. Gold noticed Ann and Lyndsey gripping their rifles a little tighter. She knew what they were thinking. Hiding places near the road meant good spots for an ambush—or for a lone jihadist to sit with a cell phone or a radio, waiting for coalition forces to drive past. A press of a button would set off the IED. The gunner must have thought the same thing. His boots shifted around on the turret stand as he swiveled his weapon.

The bluff receded in the dust, and the dust got whipped away by the wind. The team drove past another farm where long-haired sheep roamed unfenced. The animals bleated and ran from the road as the Cougars rumbled past.

Around the next bend, Gold saw two boys walking a goat through a field. Both looked about twelve, and one held a length of hemp looped around the goat's neck. The animal had black fur, two stubby horns, and yellow eyes. The goat twisted and pulled against the rope in what seemed a halfhearted attempt at escape. Gold waved at the boys, though she doubted they could see her through the window shields.

One of the kids—in an Adidas T-shirt—reached down and picked up a stone. He hurled it at the Cougar. Gold watched it spin toward her like a rifled bullet. The rock clanged against the steel plating over her head. The gunner's feet shifted again, but he did not fire. Gold heard him mutter, "Bite my ass, you little shit."

"Takes balls to attack an armored vehicle with a rock," the driver said.

"They know we won't open up on them," Blount said.

Gold sighed, moved her rifle from the crook of one elbow to another. Hearts and minds. She wondered if there was anything she could ever do, any good she could accomplish, by which she might arrive at contentment. Of course she would press on, do her best. But her continued efforts reminded her of Samuel Johnson's line about the triumph of hope over experience.

Her Blue Force Tracker chimed. She unzipped its pouch and saw she had a message. She pressed on READ and saw: HOW GOES IT? MP.

She pulled off her gloves to compose her answer: OK. ABOUT HALFWAY THERE. U?

A moment later the BFT chimed once more: GETTING READY TO FLY.

Gold considered ending the exchange, but somehow texting with Parson pulled her out of the sour mood brought on by the thrown rock. She wrote one more message: SOME KID JUST BOUNCED ROCK OFF MRAP. When the BFT chimed again, it said: DID U THROW ROCKS BACK?

She smiled, cleared the screen, looked outside. The vehicles splashed through a muddy spot. The water came from a narrow stream that cut through a wheat field and ran across the road without benefit of a culvert. It had not rained since Gold's arrival in Afghanistan, so she guessed the stream was fed year-round by snowmelt from higher elevations.

At the edge of the field lay a rusting hulk, the wreckage of a Soviet aircraft. A wing had broken off, but the fuselage remained pretty much intact. Part of a red star was still visible on the tail. From the condition of the wreckage, Gold surmised the plane had not burned, but that its crew had crash-landed. Reminded her a little too much of her first day with Parson.

The aircraft looked like some kind of transport, though

she had no idea of the model. Parson would know. Vines grew around the two bent propellers.

Beyond the field came a barren stretch of ground. The ride grew rougher, and Gold could see why. The soil was so choked with rocks that the ground seemed almost paved in cobblestone.

The Cougars drove past a bombed-out compound. Roofless mud-brick walls crumbled against wooden beams. The gunner's feet shuffled. More hiding places here, too.

The compound disappeared behind them without incident. Next, Gold noticed a pile of stones beside the road, maybe six inches high, as if to mark something. She puzzled over that for just an instant.

An explosion slammed the vehicle from underneath. The Cougar lifted into the air a few inches, thudded back to earth. All of Gold's bones seemed to rattle against one another. Her ears popped. She could hear the shouts of the Marines, but from far away.

Parson didn't like the look of the sky. Lens-shaped clouds hovered over the mountains, paralleling the ridgelines. An untrained observer might have called them pretty, but Parson knew standing lenticular clouds resulted from strong wind flowing across high terrain. The wind carried moisture that condensed as it got lifted higher, forming a telltale convex shape. That meant turbulence. Maybe it was better that Gold had gone by road after all. But he and Rashid's crew had no choice but to fly.

He took one final look up at the cloud formations,

tromped up the boarding steps. The air was cool again today, but he wore no jacket. His body armor and survival vest kept him warm enough.

Inside the Mi-17, Rashid punched a start button for the left engine. When the engine reached the proper RPM, he moved an overhead stopcock lever to feed fuel, and the Klimov lit off. Rashid repeated the process for the right engine, then let both of them stabilize at idle.

Parson listened to Rashid, Aamir, and Sharif clean up the engine start checklist, their Pashto incomprehensible to him. He hadn't bothered to replace Gold with another interpreter for this flight. It was a simple mission—just take a load of food and two passengers up to another devastated village. Reyes rode along in case the crew ran into more injured refugees, and the crew chief manned his door gun. The passengers were civilians from that urban rescue team in Virginia, and one of them brought a cadaver dog with him. The Belgian Malinois whined and pawed in its kennel.

I'd whine, too, if I had that dog's job, Parson thought. Or maybe she just doesn't like riding in helicopters any more than I do.

Parson turned off his Blue Force Tracker so its emissions wouldn't interfere with the helicopter's electronics. Then he pulled his laptop out of his helmet bag and turned it on. When it booted up, he left-clicked to open a moving map display. A tiny airplane icon in the center of the screen rested atop a blue circle that represented the Mazar airfield. As the flight progressed, the airplane would fly across the moving VFR chart.

Rashid and Aamir had to navigate the old-fashioned way, with a paper chart, NDB bearings, and VOR radials. Parson felt tempted just to hand up the computer, but that would have turned into a crutch. He was supposed to let them use what was installed in the aircraft.

When the helo lifted off, it flew smoothly for several seconds, and Parson began to hope the forecast and his instincts were wrong. Then a gust slammed the aircraft as if it had flown into a wall. Parson's seat belt dug into his gut. His headset slipped, and he had to readjust it over his ears. The Mi-17 rose through air filled with stones and potholes.

Aamir was flying, and not doing a bad job for the conditions. He held attitude and rotor pitch for the climb, and he didn't try to chase a certain speed. If you couldn't stay out of turbulence, at least you shouldn't make it worse by yanking around your aircraft.

When the chopper leveled, still rocked by a tormented sky, Parson noticed a whiskey-stained haze softening all shapes on the ground. At lower altitudes, enough dust rode the wind that it colored the air itself.

The Mi-17 flew as a single ship; the Hinds were escorting other missions deemed higher risk. That was too bad. Parson liked having the gunships close by—not so much for their guns as for their cabins. If one chopper got forced down, another could land and pick up its crew. Good insurance when you could get it, but making do in less-than-ideal situations was just part of military life.

Parson waited for the opaque chatter to clear from the interphone and radios. Then he pressed his talk switch and said, "Good job, copilot." He knew Aamir spoke no English, but he wanted to encourage him anyway. Rashid uttered about four words in Pashto. Translating the compliment, Parson assumed. Aamir did not respond.

A lunar landscape passed below. Dry seams and folds of hills flowed underneath the helicopter. Eventually, a ribbon of green relieved the lifelessness on the ground; grass and brush marked the course of a mountain creek that meandered along a valley.

Rashid had his chart out now. Good. And Aamir fiddled with the nav radios. Not so good. He should have let Rashid do that for him. Sometimes these guys didn't make enough distinction between the pilot flying and the pilot monitoring. The PF was supposed to fly the aircraft; nothing else. The PM was supposed to do *everything* else: handle the radios, navigate, work out systems problems with the engineer.

Parson decided not to say anything. Aamir wouldn't understand him anyway, and Rashid should take care of it himself. Parson wanted to do his job as an adviser without undercutting Rashid's authority as aircraft commander. And rattling along in this damned turbulence didn't make it easier to work on the fine points.

The two urban rescue guys looked sick. Reyes twisted in his seat to scan outside, his rifle sling wrapped around his arm, the weapon's muzzle pointed to the floor. Rashid and his crew kept talking in Pashto. Although Parson had no idea what they were chatting about, he hoped Rashid was saying "Keep your paws off the radios." However, that shouldn't have taken this much discussion.

Parson checked his moving map. The airplane cursor crawled in an easterly direction, but not quite the heading he would have expected. He hadn't plugged in all the waypoints; Rashid knew how to navigate, and Parson didn't want to insult his intelligence.

Rashid and Aamir were still talking. Sharif, in the flight engineer's seat, fell silent. In the back, the crew chief kept looking toward the cockpit. He seemed more worried about the pilots than about manning his gun. What the hell was all the yammering about? Parson knew the Afghans had a joke about advisers like him: If you speak three languages, you're trilingual. If you speak two, you're bilingual. If you speak only one, you're American. Now he wished he'd never let Gold out of his sight. A bonehead idea from the start.

"Hey, Rashid," Parson asked on interphone. "What's wrong?"

No answer for a moment. Then Rashid said, "Wrong radial, I think."

He had to be kidding. To Parson, an old navigator down to his marrow, the first step toward not being an idiot was knowing where you were. Now he was ticked off at those two—and at himself for not backing them up. They should have worked out an MRR—minimum risk routing—and done a good study of that route. Rashid knew how to do that; he'd done it a hundred times.

"They gotta be bullshitting me," Parson said, off interphone. "Whiskey tango foxtrot."

Reyes turned around. "What's the matter, sir?" he asked.

Still off interphone, Parson answered him: "I think they're lost."

Reyes frowned. It occurred to Parson that you didn't need to be a pilot to know this wasn't supposed to happen. Ever. But if it did, there was only one thing to do—climb and confess. He unbuckled his seat belt, got up, and looked over the flight engineer's shoulder.

"Rashid," Parson said, this time on interphone, "tell him to leave the radios the fuck alone and get some altitude."

In the next instant, the helicopter banked so aggressively, Parson felt himself grow light in his boots. The crew shouted phrases that told him nothing. His mind struggled to understand what was happening.

Rashid grabbed the cyclic on the pilot's side. *He was fighting his copilot on the controls.*

Aamir gripped the cyclic on the copilot's side with his left hand, drew a Makarov pistol.

"Tah yaw bandee yeh," he yelled.

Sharif grabbed Aamir's pistol arm, pulled it down toward the floor. The helicopter turned hard to the left. Parson lost his footing and stumbled to his knees. Felt his kneecaps whack against steel. Then the Mi-17 veered right.

The Makarov fired. Sharif screamed as blood spewed from his thigh.

Parson groped for a handhold. Struggled against the turbulence and the pain in his knees to get up.

The chopper skimmed just above a rock chimney that

towered over a gorge. More stone spires loomed ahead. Rashid punched at his copilot, wrested the cyclic away from him. Then Rashid banked to avoid the rock formation. Sharif slammed Aamir's arm into the center console, and the Makarov clattered to the floor.

The two pilots were fighting over which direction to fly, Parson realized. Aamir wasn't trying to crash the chopper; he could have done that pretty quickly. He apparently wanted to commandeer it. Without Gold here, Parson couldn't tell what exactly was going on. A jihadist had once tried to bring down Parson's C-5 Galaxy. The man was a patient on that aeromedical flight with Gold, an Afghan thought to be a trustworthy police officer. When allowed into the cockpit, he'd pulled fire handles to shut down the engines.

But this was something else. Parson could figure out the details later, but whatever it was, this madness had to stop right now. He unsnapped his pistol holster, tried to stand. Turbulence punched the chopper again and sent Parson reeling backward.

The nose of the Mi-17 dipped. Aamir grabbed the cyclic and tried to yank it to the left. The aircraft skimmed along a valley floor as the pilots fought. Ahead, an evergreen stood by a bend in a stream.

Parson fell against the cargo of food. He drew his Beretta and pushed himself away from the stacks of rations. Behind him, one of the civilians shouted, "What's happening?" The dog yowled.

The helicopter banked left, turned hard right, yawed.

Something smacked into its chin. Absurdly, Parson caught a whiff of Himalayan cedar. He realized they'd skimmed the top branches of that tree.

He braced himself against the flight deck bulkhead, brought up his pistol with both hands. Parson leveled the weapon at Aamir, thought to punch a round right through that bastard's helmet, through his brain, and out the other side. But just as he placed the joint of his finger to the trigger, the copilot did a strange thing. He took his hands off the controls, raised his arms. Tears streamed down his face. He uttered syllables in Pashto that sounded like pleading.

Parson took his finger off the trigger but still pointed his pistol at Aamir. Maybe the man had just gone crazy.

Whatever the hell had just happened, Parson knew Rashid couldn't explain it now. The Mi-17 teetered on the ragged edge of controlled flight, and Rashid fought to recover it. The chopper pitched down, banked, and then climbed. It veered toward the valley wall, a steep rim of mountains. Rashid pulled up hard to avoid an outcropping.

Too hard. The Mi-17 shuddered and pitched up higher. Rashid dropped the collective lever. The helicopter leveled and slowed, just above a rock ledge. It began descending toward the ledge.

Rashid twisted the grip throttle on the collective, adding power. The engines screamed. The chopper kept descending.

What the hell was the problem? At this moment Parson couldn't help Rashid, could only stay out of his way and try to hold the weapon on Aamir. He wasn't even sure what was wrong, until he remembered an aerodynamic weirdness about helicopters: settling with power. If a helo descended too quickly, the chopper's own downwash kept the rotor blades from generating lift.

Satan himself might have designed this special hell for pilots. All your instincts told you to add power. And more power made it worse. Right now the aircraft had the flight characteristics of a brick. The only way to recover was to fly out of the vortex. And that required altitude Rashid didn't have.

The Mi-17 hit the rock ledge so hard, Parson collapsed to his knees. His kneecaps still hurt from the first time he'd fallen, and the pain made him nauseated. Rotor blades disintegrated as they crashed into a wall of stone just above the ledge. Metal splinters and rock chips gouged the windscreen.

Parson turned to his right, scanned for fire. No flames, no fuel odor. He still held on to his Beretta. His headset cord coiled around his shoulder. He could see Rashid and Sharif reaching across the panels, shutting down the aircraft, jabbering in Pashto.

One of the civilian passengers held his leg, cursed. The other civilian peered outside, perhaps worried about enemy nearby. The crew chief looked stunned. He leaned on his weapon, swiveled the door gun on its mount. The engines' turbines whined down to silence. Parson heard groans and profanities. Reyes unbuckled his seat belt, checked his rifle. The dog whimpered in its kennel, trembling.

Then for a moment, no one spoke. No sound but the moan of wind as it coursed over the ridge and swirled around the wreckage. A gust rocked the bent cabin of the Mi-17. Parson felt it shear through the open door. The wind caressed his cheek and tousled his hair.

An unseen specter seemed to touch him, mock him, whisper threats and condemnations. He had heard Gold talk about Muslim mythology, jinns and spirits. Now one of them swept through the Russian-built helicopter, and its passing left Parson amid his worst memories and greatest fears.

❧ 11 ❧

All five of Gold's senses worked, but not together. The inputs did not compute. She heard muffled shouts, grinding noises. The Cougar filled with dust. The dust carried a burning smell, but Gold saw no fire. She had a metallic, chemical taste in her mouth. Where did that come from? She held on to her seat; she could feel its frame through her gloves. She felt pain from . . . somewhere. Her head. Her head hurt.

She realized her helmet had slammed against a bulkhead inside the vehicle. Her mind began to clear, the facts to connect. They'd run over a roadside bomb. Would an ambush follow?

Now she recognized the voices. The loudest was Blount's: "Gunner, you all right?"

No answer, but the gunner's boots moved around on the turret stand. He was still on his feet.

More voices on the radio: "IED! Two's hit."

"Cover the left!"

"Got it."

The Cougar rested at an angle. It must have rolled into the ditch. Lyndsey got up. Ann appeared unconscious. Gold unbuckled, clicked the fire selector on her rifle.

She looked out the window, saw no enemy. From the radio, she knew the gunners on the undamaged vehicles watched for bad guys. She heard no firing, so she went to the back of the vehicle, pulled a quick-release pin, and kicked open the ramp.

The blast had carved a crater that could have swallowed a small pickup. The pit of stones and fresh soil looked almost like something at a construction site. Sometimes insurgents used a particularly evil type of bomb known as an explosively formed penetrator, which could send molten copper right through armor. Gold doubted this bomb had been an EFP. Still, she was amazed the Cougar hadn't overturned. More importantly, the interior hadn't been breached. Evidently the V-shaped hull had divided and deflected the force of the blast.

Gold stepped down the ramp, still a little unsteady on her feet. She felt numb, tried to gather her thoughts. Glanced up at the gunner. He remained at his weapon, but he looked woozy. The man leaned back in the turret. Blood ran from his temple. He wiped at it and examined his fingers.

Marines from the other two vehicles ran toward Gold. Others stopped, pointed their rifles left and right of the road. Still no shots fired. So it could have been a lot worse, she thought. Occasionally, terrorists would rain fire on a vehicle after the bomb had hit it. Gold supposed this road was so seldom traveled that insurgents didn't bother to man a kill zone. They probably hadn't planted a command-detonated bomb, just a pressure plate left waiting for something to drive over it.

"Are you all right, Sergeant Major?" a Marine asked.

"I think so," Gold said. "Check the gunner. One of the lance corporals inside might need some help, too."

More grinding and crunching came from underneath the vehicle. Sounded like a blown-out transmission. The wheels didn't move at all. Even if they had moved, the Cougar could not have gone far. Some of the tires were burned and torn away.

"Shut it down," Blount said to the driver. "This thing ain't going nowhere." The engine clattered to a stop.

A corpsman walked up the ramp and entered the vehicle. He was the same medic who'd treated the wounded when Rashid's helicopter got hit at Ghandaki.

Gold placed her weapon back on SAFE, then followed the medic back in to check on Ann. She sat up now. No blood, no obvious injury. The corpsman kneeled in front of her. He shone a light into her eyes, then held up two fingers on his left hand.

"How many fingers am I holding up, Lance Corporal?" he asked.

"Two."

"What day is it?"

"Monday."

"Good. Keep your head still. Follow my fingers with your eyes."

He moved his hand up, down, left, right. Ann's eyes, a

little bloodshot but apparently working, tracked the movement.

"TBI?" Gold asked.

"Too early to tell," the corpsman said. "She's all right from what I can see now."

Gold realized he was right about diagnosing too early. She knew of soldiers who'd had their bells rung by roadside bombs but escaped with no immediate impairment. Weeks later, however, traumatic brain injury cropped up. Problems with memory and concentration, headaches, depression.

The gunner climbed down from the turret. The corpsman cleaned the cut on the Marine's head and placed an adhesive bandage over it. Then he checked the gunner's responses the same way he'd checked Ann's.

"I think you've had a concussion," the corpsman said. "You're lucky that's all you got."

"I know it," the gunner said.

"We'll get you guys back to Mazar," Gold said. "You need to take it easy after a knock on the head like that."

"I'm good to go, Sergeant Major," the gunner said.

"Me, too," Ann said. "Let's get this thing done."

Gold looked at the Marines around her. She admired their willingness to press on, but she wondered if it was smart. The corpsman had done his best, but if Ann and the gunner suffered from concussions, a doctor needed to look at them.

"Can you hang with it?" Blount asked. He twisted around in his seat, looked at the gunner, the Lionesses, and Gold. Clearly, he wanted to keep going.

"Yes, Gunnery Sergeant," Ann said.

"Affirmative," the gunner said.

Was it worth the risk? Gold knew she'd have to make the decision herself. She'd received approval for this mission because Parson and officers above him trusted her judgment. The whole point of combat: Stop the enemy—and not let him stop you. If this mission was worth starting, it was worth finishing.

"It'll be tight," Blount said, "but we can get everybody in the two good Cougars."

A jingle truck sputtered toward the three halted MRAPs. The truck was the only vehicle Gold had seen since they'd turned onto this road. To her, the flatbed looked bizarrely festive with its ribbons, decorative chains, plastic flowers, medallions, and reflectors that adorned the sides. For whatever reason, truck drivers in this part of the world dressed their vehicles like automotive clowns. Blue smoke chugged from a corroded exhaust pipe that nearly dragged the ground. Tarps covered its cargo. For all Gold knew, the truck could have carried canned goods, bricks, or artillery rounds for the Taliban.

The driver stared straight ahead as he steered around the MRAPs. He seemed to want no eye contact with any of the Americans. The jingle truck rocked on its rusted, leaf-spring suspension as it receded into the distance.

"You can bet our boy there will tell somebody we're here," Blount said. "I suspect he's picking up a radio right now."

Blount had a point. Whether the team turned back or pressed on, Gold thought, they needed to do one or the other quickly. And after this morning, the bad guys would know they'd come this way. The route back might present more danger than the way forward.

She hoped she wasn't making people take chances for a fool's errand. But the tip from the women at the refugee camp represented her best hope for progress. It might actually lead to something useful. Gold remembered the car bombing of a hospital in Logar Province back in 2011. She'd been stateside at the time, but she'd followed the intel reports. Not only did the Taliban deny responsibility, they condemned the attack. Very unusual. Had that been Black Crescent's debut? If rifts existed among the insurgents, the coalition needed to exploit them. Now.

"Are you two sure you're all right?" Gold asked.

"I'm good," Ann said.

"Semper fi," the gunner said.

"Then let's saddle up," Gold said. "Thank you."

"*That's* what I'm talking about," Blount said. "We don't stop for no firecracker buried in the dirt."

Blount and the Marines from the disabled MRAP boarded the other two Cougars. Gold squeezed into the lead vehicle with Ann and Lyndsey. She wanted to keep an eye on Ann and make sure the injured Lioness got a seat. At the moment, though, Ann looked fine. Gold sat on the floor and balanced her rifle on the heel of its stock to keep the muzzle pointed in a safe direction. The bag of sugar rested beside her; it had come through the IED blast without breaking open. Gold took a little satisfaction that she'd remembered to bring the sugar from the damaged MRAP.

She couldn't help thinking about what might have happened if they'd taken lighter vehicles. More than likely, most would have died. The survivors would have been disfigured and maimed for life. Gold had visited blast victims at Walter Reed and Bethesda, and she'd been awed by their grit as they faced years of painful rehabilitation and surgery. She offered a silent prayer of thanks as the two remaining Cougars started moving.

The grade of the road grew steeper, and the vehicles wallowed through another stream that bisected their path. Gold checked her map. She thought that creek might be the one the women had called Goat's Gut. Beyond the stream, corn grew along both sides of the road so close that the drying leaves and tassels brushed the Cougars' windows. Gold tensed; the cornfield made another good place for an ambush. But when no ambush came, she relaxed enough for the corn to remind her of vegetable gardens in New England and farms outside Fort Sill and Fort Campbell. It was late in the season, and the rustling field stood ready for harvest.

As the team climbed deeper into the hills, they met no other trucks, encountered no more pedestrians. Gold had never traveled this route before, so she didn't know if the absence of traffic was unusual. Maybe the IED had scared everybody off the road. By some means Westerners could not understand—not even Gold—Afghan villagers seemed to communicate all events instantly. Most owned no phones or computers, but they always knew what was happening in their districts. Whether they'd tell an American soldier, however, was another matter.

After several more miles of fields, barren rock, and a thinned-out pine forest, the Cougars slowed to a crawl.

"Up ahead," Blount said.

Gold crouched to look forward through the windshield. Nestled into a cove in the hills she saw a village of about six homes. The wood-latticed structures were made mainly of stone, with rough planking and thatch for roofs. A gray tabby prowled among boulders between two of the huts. A rooster flew from the cat's approach and alighted atop one of the houses. At another home, a white flag fluttered from a rough-hewn tree limb that served as a pole.

The white flag was not a signal of surrender. It was the banner of the Taliban.

On his knees in the cabin of the downed helicopter, Parson held his pistol ready. His legs hurt like hell from when he'd fallen during the crash landing. He sniffed again for spilled fuel, smelled only normal engine odors. Rashid killed the battery switch, and the interphone went dead. With not even static on the circuit now, Parson tore off his headset and pitched it onto the troop seats by his helmet bag. The Afghans shouted in Pashto.

"What the hell just happened, Rashid?" Parson yelled.

Rashid barked a command, apparently an order for silence. Then he said, "Lieutenant Aamir want to give you to ransom."

A chill went through Parson. Not caused by the rising wind, but by stirrings of rage. As a lieutenant colonel, an adviser to the Afghan Air Force no less, he would have made one hell of a prize. The military would not have paid ransom for him, but the insurgents didn't know that. One group might have sold him to another. Or perhaps they'd have simply murdered him on video. No wonder that bastard flew off course. He'd never been lost; he was just heading for a different destination.

Parson had narrowly escaped a beheading on camera a few years ago. The memory still gave him nightmares. *And this son of a bitch had just tried to deliver him to a terrorist's blade.* An animal fury overcame Parson. He scrambled to his feet, pointed the Beretta at Aamir.

"I'll blow your fucking head off!" Parson shouted. He held the weapon with both hands; his hands shook with anger. The muzzle danced and bounced, but it didn't matter. He couldn't miss at this range.

Aamir's mouth dropped open and he froze. Parson began to squeeze the trigger. The hammer was down; Parson was firing double-action. The Beretta's parts linked up and moved as the hammer began to rise.

"No!" Rashid said.

Damn it, Parson thought. Rashid was right. Damn it, damn it, damn it. Parson released the trigger, holstered his weapon. He couldn't just blow Aamir's head off, not if the man wasn't resisting anymore. But he could sure as hell kick his ass.

Sergeant Sharif, in the flight engineer's jump seat, sat in Parson's way. Parson reached over Sharif's shoulders, popped the quick-release on Sharif's harness, and pulled him out of the cockpit by the armpits. The flight engineer's leg left gouts of blood on his seat. Parson put him down in the cargo compartment. Sharif's face twisted in agony. Blood ran along the canted floor to the crew entrance door and dripped onto the ground. The two civilian passengers stared, one groaning in pain and holding his leg.

Parson grabbed Aamir by the front of his survival vest, dragged him over the jump seat, and threw him to the floor.

"You wanted to let them cut my head off?" Parson yelled. Picked him up by the collar, slammed him against the steel plating. Aamir still wore his flight helmet, so the manhandling did little damage.

That angered Parson even more. He aimed a straight punch, rammed his fist into the copilot's cheek. That felt a little better. He drew back to hit him again.

Aamir held up his hands toward Parson, pleading gibberish.

"His son," Rashid said. "He keeps talking about his son."

Whatever. Parson wasn't listening. He kneed Aamir in the groin. The copilot gagged, doubled over. Parson pushed him upright. Grabbed him by the collar with one hand, unsnapped his helmet strap with the other. If he could get the helmet off, he could hurt that bastard worse.

One of the civilians spoke up. "Sir," he said, "what are you doing?"

"I'm gonna bust his head . . ."

Damn it, Parson thought. A witness. If Gold were here, she'd have stopped him, too. And she'd be translating all this babble.

Parson still held Aamir by the collar. Couldn't decide whether to beat him up more. "All right, Rashid," Parson said, "what the fuck is he saying?"

"Insurgent have his son. He want trade for you."

"Who has his son?" Parson asked.

"Bad men. Maybe Black Crescent. Maybe no."

Parson had no children. He'd never even been married. But he knew how it felt to be responsible for someone else. He shook Aamir by the collar.

"Why didn't you tell somebody, shithead?" Parson asked. Shoved the copilot onto a troop seat. "Don't you fucking move."

Rashid climbed from the cockpit, removed his helmet. Gave orders in Pashto, and the crew chief found duct tape and parachute cord in his tool box. Rashid took the cord.

"We tie him," Rashid said.

"Damn straight we tie him," Parson replied. He grabbed Aamir's hands, yanked them together behind the copilot's back, held them tight as Rashid bound them with the parachute cord.

Parson tore off a strip of duct tape, nearly slipped in Sharif's blood on the floor. Slapped the tape over Aamir's mouth.

"Sir," Reyes said, "if he's congested, that'll keep him from breathing."

Parson started to tell Reyes to mind his own damned business. But the man was right. Parson tore the tape from Aamir's face. The copilot cried out.

"Quit whining," Parson said. He wadded up the length

of duct tape, threw it down. Tore off a longer strip and taped Aamir's boots together.

Reyes had been tending to Sharif's injuries; now the PJ opened an Israeli bandage. The device consisted of a length of elasticized cloth with sterile pads on one side and a closure bar on the other. Reyes adjusted the pads to cover Sharif's wounds, then wrapped the cloth leader several times until he locked it down with the closure bar.

The uninjured civilian spoke up again: "We'll need a medevac for that gunshot wound."

Who the hell was this guy to be putting in his two cents? For a moment, Parson wanted to tape the civilian's mouth, too. But at least the man's advice made sense. Seemed to know the lingo, too. Maybe the guy wasn't a complete idiot.

"Yeah," Parson said. "I know it."

All he really wanted to do was beat Aamir to death. But other things needed doing. He tried to think past his anger. Regaining his self-control was like recovering an airplane from a spin. Part of you wanted only to pull the nose up. But if you wanted to live, you had to put the nose farther *down*. You had to use your head, not your gut.

Parson ducked through the crew door to look outside. Nobody had installed the boarding ladder, but he didn't need it—the landing gear had collapsed on impact, and the helicopter's deck rested only about a foot off the ground. Parson's knees hurt from falling during the hard landing, and that made his limp worse. Instead of jumping right out, he stepped down from the aircraft one boot at a time.

Small cumulus raced overhead. But other clouds remained stationary. Roll clouds, like long cigars, formed over the ridges. Far above them, Parson saw a layer of mother-of-pearl. Not good. Signs of severe turbulence, with updrafts and downdrafts approaching five thousand feet per minute.

So the winds were picking up, but at least the visibility stayed decent. He reached inside the Mi-17 and pulled the satphone out of his helmet bag. Somehow his laptop still worked, still set up with the moving map display, so he jotted down the coordinates it showed. Then he turned off the computer and punched the number for command post at Mazar.

"This is Parson," he said when the duty officer answered. "Golay One-Eight is down." He gave coordinates for the rock ledge where the helo had crash-landed.

"Do you have casualties?"

"One gunshot wound to the thigh. Maybe one broken leg." Parson reported Aamir's attempt to commandeer the Mi-17, the struggle for control. Relating the story made him angry all over again. He wished his brain could work like some aircraft systems, that he could put his emotion switch on BYPASS.

"Oh, shit," the duty officer said. "Not again."

Parson knew what the guy was thinking. The year before, an Afghan officer had opened fire on American advisers during a meeting at the Kabul Airport. He'd killed eight USAF troops and an American contractor before taking his own life. The Taliban had claimed him as an agent, but his family denied it and said he'd had money problems. Other reports suggested the officer may have been involved with suspected opium trafficking.

Nearly all members of the Afghan Air Force were like Rashid—competent, committed, hardworking, and trustworthy. Their vetting included a family background investigation, drug screening, and record reviews. Recruits even had their biometric data checked against a criminal database. But this was a different situation, and Parson knew no amount of background checks could have prevented it. In Afghanistan, nothing was simple and nothing was safe.

So where exactly had Aamir hoped to land? The Mi-17 hadn't gone down where he wanted it, but he'd tried to put it somewhere around here. Parson realized the bad guys who'd waited for Aamir to deliver him might be close.

He heard Rashid in the helicopter, interrogating Aamir.

"Did you find out where he was trying to go?" Parson asked.

"A bandit camp four kilometers north," Rashid called.

"So they might have seen where we crashed."

"Yes," Rashid said. He gave a command in Pashto, and the crew chief began to work at the hardware that attached the door gun to the aircraft structure. The weapon represented a blend of Russian and American technology: a PKM automatic weapon installed on a Dillon Aero mount. The crew chief detached the PKM from its pintle, wrapped a belt of ammunition across his shoulder. He and Rashid carried the weapon out of the helicopter. They spoke, pointing to terrain beyond the aircraft, apparently considering how best to set up a field of fire.

The lay of the land both hindered and helped, Parson judged. The Mi-17 had come down fairly high along the mountainside, on a flat shelf. The ledge overlooked a steep draw studded with gullies, scrubby hawthorns, and stones the size of aircraft tires. Bad guys would most likely attack from below. Infantry troops always loved the high ground, to fire on the enemy from an elevated position. Though Parson had never been a grunt, he knew any rifleman would call this a good spot.

But from an airman's perspective, it sucked. A helicopter coming to pick them up would have to fly into the wind cascading over the ridge. Mountain wave turbulence could roll a helicopter inverted. The rescue might have to wait until the wind calmed.

"Hey, Reyes," Parson called.

"Yes, sir," Reyes answered from inside the cabin.

"We're thinking we might have the wrong kind of company pretty soon. I know you got patients to treat, but keep your rifle close."

"Always, sir."

The passenger who'd spoken up earlier climbed out of the helo and stood beside Parson. The man had short-cropped brown hair tinged with gray. Salt-and-pepper stubble on his cheeks. He wore a beige equipment vest like the ones Parson had seen on photographers, except this one read USAID across the back. A shoulder patch said VIR-GINIA TASK FORCE ONE.

"Do you know how to shoot?" Parson asked.

"Gulf War," the man answered. "First Cav."

So maybe this guy was useful. Parson stuck out his hand. "Michael Parson," he said. The man gave a firm handshake.

"Jake Conway."

Parson briefed Conway on the situation with the weather and the chopper pickup. Then he climbed back inside, found Aamir's pistol on the aircraft's center console. After checking the chamber and magazine of the Russian-built weapon, he handed it to Conway.

"This will have to do," Parson said.

"At least we know it works," Conway said. He placed the Makarov in a vest pocket.

While Parson and Conway spoke, Rashid toiled silently. He helped the crew chief pile stones around the PKM to set up a better fighting position. Occasionally he looked inside the helicopter, regarded Aamir.

"May I let the dog out and give her some water?" Conway asked.

"Up to you," Parson said. "If it runs off, we can't go chasing it."

"She won't do that."

Conway disappeared inside the Mi-17. He emerged a few minutes later with the Belgian Malinois on a leash. He also carried a bowl and a bottle of water. The fur on the animal's back remained bristled, but the dog made no sound. The Malinois looked at Parson, wagged its tail once, and lay on the ground, head upright, ears perked.

"Here you go, Ingrid," Conway said as he placed the

bowl in front of the dog. He cracked open the water bottle, poured some into the bowl, took a swallow. The dog lapped as Conway handed the bottle to Parson.

Before Parson could take a sip, the dog stopped drinking. It looked up, muzzle dripping, at something downslope. Parson shaded his eyes with his hand, saw nothing but shale, dust, and gnarled vegetation.

The animal kept staring. Wind tousled the hair raised along its spine. The dog emitted a low growl.

❖ 12 ❖

Gold and the Marines remained inside their two Cougars and watched the village, especially the house flying the Taliban flag. She half expected gunfire to chatter from the stone huts. But she heard only the Cougars' idling engines, the flag's fluttering, and the rush of wind whipping dust across the path.

"Sergeant Blount," she said. "Let's not dismount your men just yet."

"What do you want to do?" Blount asked.

"I guess I better go ring the doorbell," Gold said. "Let's not look any more threatening than we have to."

It was pretty hard for two armored vehicles full of Marines not to look threatening, Gold knew, but she could at least not make things worse. She put down her rifle and removed her helmet. Taking an idea from Ann and Lyndsey, she even untied her hair.

"You're walking out there unarmed?" Lyndsey asked.

"If they open up on me from the inside, my rifle won't

help," Gold said. She realized she was taking a chance. But the whole point of counterinsurgency was not to intimidate the locals. The bullets you didn't fire were the most important.

Blount seemed to get it. "Hey, gunner," he said. "Lower your weapon."

"Sergeant?" the gunner asked.

"I didn't say take your hands off it. Stay ready to shoot. Just don't point it at the houses right now."

"Aye, aye, Sergeant."

"Let us go with you," Ann said.

Gold thought for a moment. "Watch me go to the door," she said. "If it seems safe, then you two follow me." In her work as an interpreter, she had visited many Afghan villages, but she'd never sauntered right up to a hut flying the enemy's flag. She felt she'd entered some gray area between brave, creative, reckless, and stupid.

"I don't like this one bit," the gunner said.

"Nobody asked you," Blount said.

"I don't like it, either, for what that's worth," Gold said. "Let me out."

The ramp at the back of the Cougar whined open. Lyndsey raised her gloved fist, and Gold tapped it with her own. Gold added one more instruction: "If it looks *real* good, bring the bag of sugar."

The sun hurt Gold's eyes as she stepped down the ramp and onto the ground. She'd left her shades in a pouch on her MOLLE gear, one more little thing to look a bit less formidable. Also, she wanted to make eye contact when she spoke with the villagers.

At the back of the Cougar, she took a deep breath and scanned her surroundings. No one in sight. Just more chickens. Another cat, sleeping on a doorstep. She began walking toward the house with the flag.

Gold tried to move as casually as possible. Too fast a pace might have appeared aggressive. Too slow might have seemed like stealth.

This could be a trap, she knew all too well. Back in 2009, she'd served at a base in Khost where CIA spooks planned to meet with a hot contact. A Jordanian doctor claimed to have access to al-Qaeda's number two, Ayman al-Zawahiri. Gold wasn't in on the meeting; the Jordanian spoke Arabic, not Pashto, and so her services had not been required.

She was walking to the chow hall when the doctor detonated himself. Gold knew what had happened the instant the blast wave took her breath away. The suicide bombing killed seven agency people. For her, not being needed on that day meant not needing to die.

Now she wondered if her next step might bring an explosion or the crack of a tracer. The wind felt good against the back of her neck; the day was bright but cool. Her head had cleared from the IED blast earlier, and she felt focused on her mission. Not bad for a last moment, she considered, as long as the end came quickly.

It did not come at all. She reached the door, glanced back at the MRAPs, and knocked. *"Salaam,"* she said.

Shuffling sounds came from inside. Whispers in Pashto. Gold could not make out the words. She listened hard for anything metallic—rifle safeties, fire mode selectors, or grenade pins—but she heard none of that. Finally a female voice said, "*Assalamu alaikum*. But why do you defile our village with these machines?"

"Only to talk, my sister," Gold said. "I believe we have a common enemy."

"You are not my sister. And we all have enemies."

"Then let us discuss them," Gold said.

Inside the house, a long silence. Gold breathed just a little easier. If a burst of automatic weapons fire was going to come through that door, it would have happened by now. She thought she heard whispers within. A vast chasm of culture and religion stretched between her and the women inside; Gold wondered what common reference points she could call on if the conversation continued.

She thought of only one: The taproot of every faith, the core of every philosophy, was human suffering. Maybe the women here had seen so much of it, they'd want to try something different to stop it.

"My sister," Gold said, "I am still here. If you wish to talk, I would like to meet you. If you wish me to go, I will leave you in peace."

After several seconds, the door unbolted, swung open. A woman in a blue burka stood at the entrance. Gold could see only her eyes. They were black, surrounded by creased skin. In the room behind her stood two other women dressed the same way.

"Thank you," Gold said. "Peace be upon you. May two of my colleagues enter? They bring a small gift."

The woman at the door peered outside at the MRAPs.

"No men may enter."

"They are two women," Gold said.

The Afghan woman looked at Gold in apparent surprise. "They may come inside," she said.

Gold motioned with her arm, and in a few seconds Ann and Lyndsey came from the back of the Cougar. Lyndsey carried the sugar. Suddenly Gold had second thoughts about the gift. Would it seem patronizing? Too late now.

When Gold and the Lionesses entered the home, Gold said, "We have sugar for your tea."

"That is generous," the woman at the door said. "Times are hard. We have not had that luxury in a while." From her tone, she didn't seem especially impressed, but neither did she seem insulted.

"May we be seated?" Gold asked.

"You may."

Gold gestured to Ann and Lyndsey, and all three sat cross-legged on jute rugs spread across the stone floor. What little light entered the room came from glass mounted at an angle in an irregular-shaped window. Daylight showed at the top edge of the ill-fitting sash. In the ceiling, Gold saw rafters cut from birch trunks, bark still peeling, thatches of grass and brush stuffed between them. A fire burned in a corner hearth.

The woman who'd been doing the talking sat and removed her head covering. Her gray hair was tied tightly, and her lined face was dark and leathery, a record of a difficult life. The other two women kept their faces hidden.

"Why have you come to us?" the elderly woman said.

"Children have been taken for soldiers," Gold said.

"Refugees from the shaken earth have been killed merely for accepting help. I am told that even among the Talibs, some do not approve."

"I know of these things, but they are the business of men."

"Indeed," Gold said. She paused, considered whether to press further. Well, she had come this far. "Perhaps it is the business of a Mullah Durrani. Do you know him?"

The woman looked down at the rug on which she sat. In the colors of its jute strands, Gold saw the pattern of a mosque, dome and minarets.

"We shall have tea," she said, "with your gift of sugar." The woman gave orders to the other two. They dipped water from a pail and placed a kettle over the fire.

When steam rose from the kettle, the women added green tea leaves. After the tea had brewed, they poured it into clay cups and added sugar.

"Hamdillah," Gold said. Literally, *Praise be to Allah*, but often used as a thank-you.

The two women who gave out the cups never uttered a word. Daughters, perhaps. Only the older woman spoke, and she never offered her name. She sipped her tea silently. Finally she said, "I am one of Mullah Durrani's wives. My husband has retired from jihad and all public matters."

Despite the burning hearth, Gold shivered. She hadn't expected to get this close to Taliban leadership. One of the daughters rose to add dry sticks to the fire. The flames sizzled into the twigs, flared yellow to orange.

Gold watched the fire for a moment, then asked, "Does your husband know of Black Crescent?"

"I am certain he does. He keeps informed in his retirement."

"Do you believe he would speak with us?"

The woman stared straight at Gold. "Never," she said. "He will not hold counsel with infidels."

Two steps forward and one step back, Gold thought. If this never went further, she'd accomplish little.

"I would like to talk with my colleagues in English," Gold said. "They do not understand your language well. We do not mean to be rude."

"You may speak among yourselves," the woman said.

Gold briefed Ann and Lyndsey on the conversation so far. Like Gold, they had expected to meet a distant cousin of Durrani's at best. A lucky break to find a wife. But if she wouldn't help, then so what?

"I have an idea," Ann said. "Appeal to the maternal instinct."

"Maybe so," Gold said. That approach had worked when she talked to the women at the refugee camp attacked by Black Crescent. Perhaps it would work here, too.

"What mother wants her child taken from her?" Ann said.

Gold sipped her tea while she gathered her thoughts. The tea was not too sweet; the Afghan women apparently intended to make that bag last a while. Steam rose from the liquid, and it burned going down.

"My sister," she said in Pashto, "I know your husband has waged jihad. I know your family has produced warriors. But do you not want something more than war for your children? At least until they are old enough to fight as men?"

The wind strengthened outside. A gust shifted some of the thatch overhead and made the birch poles creak. Gold wondered if this was a freak event or some seasonal wind. She'd heard of a dry northwesterly called the *Bad-i-Sad-O-Bist-Roz*, but she couldn't recall if it came this time of year. Parson would know.

"We do not carry sons for nine months only to see them disappear," the older woman said. "Jihad is blessed by God, but for fighters old enough to wear the beards of Muslim men."

"Then will your husband speak with us?" Gold asked. "When the Talibs came to power, they punished pederasts. Your husband can still protect Afghan children, despite our differences."

"How could he help you, if he so wished?"

"Perhaps he or his contacts know something of Black Crescent, where its leader hides."

That was pushing it, Gold knew. But now she'd laid it out, exactly what she wanted. Either she would get it or not. If not, better to find out now.

"Call on me in two days," the woman said. "I will have an answer by then."

"That is all I can ask," Gold said. She placed her right hand over her heart. *"Hamdillah."*

"Assalamu alaikum."

Gold rose to leave. The two Lionesses stood up with her. When she opened the door, the wind nearly tore it from her hands. The gust filled the room behind her. She looked back at Ann and Lyndsey and saw ashes swirl from the hearth. Banked embers glowed and crackled. Gold sensed she had set new forces into motion, on courses yet unclear.

R ashid lit a Marlboro. Parson started to tell him he knew better than to smoke that close to a downed aircraft. But the fuel tanks hadn't ruptured, and Parson figured the poor guy needed a cigarette. Rashid pulled the filter from his lips and exhaled. The wind whipped the smoke away instantly. He hunkered beside his crew chief in the fighting position they'd built up with rocks in front of the helicopter. Both of them stared down into the draw and across the valley, where the dog kept looking. The Malinois lapped at its water dish, then looked up again.

Nothing down there that Parson could see. Maybe the dog had spotted or sniffed some animal it didn't like. A wolf or something.

Parson had experienced his own encounter with Afghan wolves. A starving pack had stalked him and Sophia as they trekked through the snow after the shoot-down of their C-130. When the wolves had finally attacked, the first one hit Parson like a linebacker, all teeth and muscle, hard enough to knock him off his feet. He'd used his rifle, his pistol, even his knife to fight those damned things off. Sophia killed a couple of them, too.

And now he found himself forced down in Afghanistan again. The air itself felt heavy, more like currents of water than gusts of wind. He forced himself to concentrate, to think about the tactical situation. Parson wondered if he lived his life like a timberline spruce in his native Colorado, clinging to existence at the ragged edge, holding on to alpine soil that just barely kept it alive. Such a tree survived one day at a time, through adaptation and perseverance. Parson knew he had to do the same.

"I'll build a little defilade for us," Conway said. The Gulf War vet began piling stones and slabs of shale in a semicircle near the Mi-17's broken tail boom. "Too bad not to have sandbags," he said.

"How do you think we should set up?" Parson asked.

"If we put the M4 back here with me, and the crew chief's weapon up front, we'll have an interlocking field of fire."

"Sounds like you've done this before," Parson said.

"A little bit. Are those the only two rifles we have?"

"Yeah. But maybe we won't need them. Task Force is sending helos out to us. The question is can they get to us in this wind."

"Can't we just hump it down to a flat spot in the valley?" Conway asked. "Maybe the choppers would have an easier time landing down there."

"They would," Parson said. "I've been thinking about that. But I'd rather not leave a defensible spot to go traipsing over ground with no cover."

"Hmm." Conway placed his hands on his hips, looked at the terrain below him and above him. "Me neither," he said.

Reyes stepped from inside the helicopter and surveyed

the preparations going on around the aircraft. Dried blood stuck to his hands; he'd worked without latex gloves. Parson had heard pararescue guys talk about what they called "dirt medicine." In a combat zone, you had bigger problems than germs. If your patient bled to death through a clean wound, you hadn't done him much good.

"Sir, you're setting up like you think we'll be here awhile," Reyes said.

"I hope not," Parson said. "I just don't know if a chopper can get to us right now."

"How's everybody doing in there?" Conway asked.

"Your partner's leg is broken, but it's not a compound fracture," Reyes said. "Could have been worse. And I have Sharif's bleeding under control."

"Rashid will be glad to hear that," Parson said.

"I don't want to use a tourniquet unless I have to," Reyes said, "because then he could lose the leg."

"Good thinking," Parson said. The last thing Afghanistan needed was one more amputee. The carpenters who carved crude prosthetics represented the only growth industry in the country, except maybe the poppy growers. And it took a lot of time and money to get an aircrew member trained. You couldn't keep losing them at this rate.

Work would settle his mind, Parson decided. He removed his survival vest, but kept on his body armor. He pushed his flight suit sleeves up above his elbows and helped Conway pile rocks. The two men created a low wall of stone, with a notch left open for a rifle barrel, much like the rock berm Rashid and the crew chief had built near the front of the aircraft. Reyes, still busy with his patients, gave his M4 to Conway.

Parson picked up his survival vest and took his radio from its pouch. He'd kept the PRC-90 on ever since his initial satphone call, hoping to hear the rescue choppers announce their approach. But so far, he'd heard only hiss.

He placed the radio atop the stone wall, and beside it he put other tools in case he needed them quickly. They included a signaling mirror and a flare launcher roughly the shape of a thick pen. The little pen-gun launcher didn't look like much, but it could throw a gyrojet flare so high that rescue pilots wouldn't miss it.

"Gentlemen," Parson said, "collect your gear so you can grab it quick. If the helos do get to us, we don't want to screw around."

Reyes positioned his medical ruck in the door frame of the Mi-17. He unrolled a Skedco litter—a sheet of hard green plastic with black nylon straps, ready to move the two injured men since neither could walk. Rashid and his crew chief had already stowed their helmets in bags beside the chopper's nose. Parson dropped his own bag near his survival gear and kneeled on the ground behind the rock wall.

Every gust blew harder. One flung grit into Parson's face, stung his cheeks and eyes. He blinked, rubbed his eyes, pulled his sunglasses from a zippered pocket, and put them on. Maybe the shades would provide at least a little protection. He wished he'd brought a jacket; it was a little cooler at this elevation. The wind died to near calm, then threw dust again.

So the gust increment would be a bitch today, Parson realized. High winds were always a pain. But you could deal with up to thirty knots pretty easily as long as it blew steady. However, ten gusting to thirty beat the daylights out of you. He guesstimated current winds at ten knots gusting to, hell, forty. And it wasn't even noon yet. The winds would pick up during the afternoon. Afghanistan seemed to want to show Parson its worst weather in every season.

A distant rhythm rose with the gusts, nearly imperceptible at first. Parson realized he'd listened to it for several seconds before it registered: the sound of helicopters. The howl of wind and slap of rotors intertwined in a counter-beat until the chopper noise dominated.

The same rhythm, with an electronic hum, emitted from Parson's radio: a chopper pilot pressing a transmit switch but not yet talking. Gathering his thoughts, apparently, in a language not his first.

"Golay," the pilot said finally. Afghan accent. "Lightning flight. We are two-ship Mi-35."

That would work. The Mi-35 cabins had enough room to evac Parson and all of Rashid's crew and passengers.

"Lightning, Golay One-Eight," Parson said. "I hear your aircraft. Do you have my position?"

Another vibrating pause on the radio. Then, "Affirmative. Do you visual?"

"Negative, Lightning," Parson said. "I'll advise when I see you. The LZ is cold, but hostiles might be nearby."

"Copy."

The Mi-35s grew louder. They appeared against a ridge

in the distance, farther away than he'd expected, small as hornets. The pair of helicopters throbbed into the valley. Parson keyed his radio.

"Lightning," he called, "Golay has you in sight. We're about three miles off your two o'clock. I'll pop a flare."

Parson twisted the orange flare cartridge into the launcher's chamber. With his thumb, he pulled down the spring-loaded trigger handle, held it above his head, looked away from it. He released the trigger and felt the firing pin snap against the cartridge. The flare spat like a bottle rocket and smoked an arc high over the stone ledge, but the wind flattened its trajectory. Parson put down the launcher and picked up his radio again.

"Lightning," he transmitted, "you get a visual on that flare?"

"Negative, Golay."

"Okay, come right about ten degrees. I'll pop another one."

He carried bigger flares in his survival vest, but he preferred not to use them in this wind. They'd spew sparks that could fly anywhere and start a fire. Parson cursed under his breath and loaded another round.

With the launcher held above his head, he thumbed the trigger and let it snap forward. The flare rocketed straight up, but again its velocity gave in to the wind. The dot of light sailed down the mountainside toward the valley floor. Parson made another radio call.

"Lightning, Golay One-Eight," he said. "You pick up that one?"

"Negative, Golay."

Parson tossed the launcher onto the ground beside his helmet bag, pressed his talk button again: "All right, Lightning," he said, "I'll try a signal mirror."

He held the mirror between his thumb and middle finger. The glass was about the size of a playing card, only thicker. Parson aimed through the sighting port in the middle, angled the mirror until he centered the sun's fireball on the first helicopter.

"I visual you," the lead pilot called.

Sometimes low-tech's the way to go, Parson thought. He put down the mirror and keyed his radio again. "Copy that, Lightning," he said. "We're on the south end of a ledge. There's room for one of you to land just north of our aircraft."

"Understood."

"The surface winds are real squirrelly," Parson added. "Be careful."

Long pause. Then the Mi-35 pilot said, "We careful."

Gotta remember to avoid American slang when Gold's not around, Parson noted. That poor guy just took part of his mind away from flying to wonder what squirrels had to do with wind.

Parson stuffed the pen-gun launcher back into his survival vest. He pulled himself inside the Mi-17 and helped Reyes put Sharif on the Skedco litter. Bloody bandages swathed the engineer's leg. Sharif propped himself up on his elbows, but kept his eyes closed.

When Parson stepped back outside, the Hinds were close, setting up their approach so near that he could feel the pounding in his ribs, see the pilots' helmets through the canopies.

One chopper began descending. The other stayed high for overwatch. Maybe this will actually work, Parson thought.

Now the lower aircraft descended so close that Parson could read its tail number, see the Afghan roundel. Its exhaust shimmered and blurred the terrain behind it. Then the chopper entered the mountain wave wind effect as if it had flown into an unseen waterfall.

The Mi-35 dropped so quickly, Parson thought for a moment both engines had failed. But they hadn't quit; they screamed at full power. The aircraft rolled hard to the left. Parson felt in his chest a twist of horror. He expected the helo to hit the rocks and explode, but the pilot pulled up just above the ground. The chopper rattled away across the valley floor, then climbed. The twist behind Parson's breastbone released. He took in a deep breath.

"We try again," the pilot called over the radio.

Parson keyed his radio once more, thinking to tell the helicopter pilots to approach from a different angle. But he took his thumb off the switch. These guys knew what they were doing; he'd just let them do it. They couldn't express themselves well in English, but that didn't mean they were stupid. The helo circled, descended, approached again, this time parallel to the ridge.

That turned out even worse. The helicopter entered the mountain wave and rolled almost ninety degrees.

In that attitude the helo had the aerodynamics of a

rock. The Mi-35 plunged toward the mountainside. The aircraft swept over Parson's head so near, he felt the heat. Its tail rotor clipped a sapling just yards below the downed Mi-17. Then the winds released the chopper, and the pilot recovered so low that the rotors left a plume of dust.

"Lightning," Parson called, "pull off." Then he added every phrase he could think of, official or not, to make himself understood: "Abort, Lightning. Retrograde. Return to base. Get the hell out of here."

The Mi-35 climbed. Parson expected to see it grow smaller, but it turned and headed back again. Beside Parson at the rock wall, Conway said, "That dude has more balls than sense."

"Yeah, he does," Parson said. He jogged over to Rashid, handed him the radio, and said, "Tell him to stop being a hero before he kills himself."

Rashid spoke into the radio. A long answer in Pashto. Rashid spoke again, looked at Parson.

"Tell him it's a damned direct order," Parson said.

Rashid made another transmission. Finally the Mi-35s climbed together, joined up in formation, and turned on a heading toward Mazar. Another crackle of words on the radio. Rashid smiled.

"What did he say?" Parson asked.

"He say protection of Allah upon us until helicopters come back and land."

The beat of rotors grew fainter until only the sound of wind remained, rushing over peaks, eddying around passes, resonating in long, low notes of an ancient mountain anthem.

❖ 13 ❖

As Gold and the Marines pulled away from the village compound, she watched through the Cougar's side window. No one appeared in front of the homes. But from the back, a kite lifted into the air. The diamond-shaped kite consisted of two crossed sticks and rough brown paper, with a knotted rag for a tail. Clouds raced above it, and the wind swept it ever higher.

"Sergeant Blount," Gold said, "I think you should see this."

Blount stared back at the village. "All right, people!" he shouted. "Look alive. Gunner, keep your head on a swivel."

"I thought the Taliban frowned on kite-flying," Lyndsey said.

"They do," Gold said, "except when they use it as a signal."

"Oh, hell," Ann said.

The kite soared so high, Gold lost sight of it. She supposed a strong gust had snapped its string. The women at the village had obviously sent a message, but what? Gold kept the tip of her thumb on the fire mode selector of her rifle, but she hoped she wouldn't need the weapon. The Cougars were taking a different route on their return to Mazar, so insurgents would find it hard to set up an ambush even if they knew when the team left the village. Best case, the kite signaled that the woman needed to talk to her husband.

Whatever the message, Gold knew the Taliban never had a problem communicating. They used computers, phones, and Icom radios when they had them. But they could also send signals perfectly well by flying kites or releasing pigeons.

The road—another rutted, rock-infested dirt path—led through a gorge so deep, it blocked the wind. Near the bottom of the gorge, with the Cougar headed downhill on a quiet idle, Gold heard a different kind of signal: distant, evenly spaced rifle fire in a kind of iambic pentameter. Five shots and their echoes.

"What the fuck is that?" the gunner asked.

"A message," Gold said. Probably some kind of answer.

"This is really giving me the creeps," Ann said.

Gold didn't like it, either. What had she gotten herself—and these Marines—into? The very air around her felt strange, as if it were made of some element not on the periodic table. The war had taken weird twists and turns for her, but this was uncharted territory: a parley with the wife of an enemy leader, or at least a former enemy leader. Perhaps a *shura* with Durrani himself. Or maybe an ambush around the next bend.

But you didn't make peace by talking only with your friends, Gold reminded herself. And you didn't win a war by never taking chances.

No ambush took place. The two Cougar MRAPs traveled winding paths where they met no other traffic, and they made it back to Mazar safely. At command post, Gold and Blount briefed an Air Force intel officer on what they'd seen and done. The officer made a phone call, and the Marines launched a Cobra to destroy the crippled MRAP left by the roadside on the journey to the village.

"I've never seen us blow up so much of our own stuff," Blount said.

"Welcome to Afghanistan," Gold said. "By the way," she asked the intel officer, "where is Lieutenant Colonel Parson? I thought he'd get back before we did. He'll want to know all this."

"There's been a problem," the officer said. He told her about what Aamir attempted, the downed Mi-17, the failed rescue attempt.

"Oh, my God," Gold said. A spike of panic churned through her. Sweat began to pop on her forehead. The bad news came on like an illness, a first flush of fever. She crossed her arms and leaned her elbows on her knees. Here came another of those moments. At least Gold recognized the feeling when it happened. The phenomenon had carried different names in different eras, but its nature remained the same: soldier's heart, shell shock, combat fatigue, post-traumatic stress disorder.

And she would control her stress. Or at least delay it. Put it in a box somewhere and wrestle with it later.

"It's all right, Sergeant Major," the officer said. "Parson has been talking to rescue forces. They'll get him as soon as the wind dies down."

"When will that be?" Gold asked.

"Sometime tonight. Tomorrow morning at the latest."

"What can I do?"

"Nothing, really. They'll be okay."

Don't patronize me, Gold thought. They're outside the wire in a hostile area. That's not okay.

But she kept all that in. She said only, "Is there anything else?"

"We do have another video from Black Crescent," the officer said. "Are you up for watching it?"

Gold only nodded, so worried about Parson that she didn't bother to say "Yes, sir." She really didn't want to see the video, especially if it depicted some horror, but she had a job to do.

The intel officer slid his laptop so Gold and Blount could see the screen. He clicked to open a file, then clicked on PLAY. A song in Arabic emitted from the computer's tinny speaker, something about the warriors of jihad. A green flag fluttered on the screen, bearing the Black Crescent symbol.

The flag faded to reveal a horror, though not one of blood. The Black Crescent leader, Chaaku, sat brandishing a sword in his left hand, a Quran in his right. Ten boys stood around him, their ages maybe six to fourteen. Each child held an AK-47 or a bayonet, and the boys wore bandannas emblazoned with verses from the Quran. The verses meant the wearer was ready to die.

"Somebody needs to take away his camera," Blount said.

"No," the intel officer said. "The more he runs his mouth, the more we know about him."

The terrorist leader began speaking. From the cadence of his English, Gold judged him a fluent speaker, and not reading from a script.

"As you can see," he said, "the numbers of our young martyrs are growing. We teach them the principal duty of a Muslim is to pray and to fight. Mortal life has no other purpose than to vanquish the infidels and win the earth for the people of Allah."

At the word *Allah*, the boys raised their weapons. Only the youngest of them smiled. Gold supposed he'd been orphaned a while back and thought this an elaborate game of make-believe by his latest caretakers. Most of the other children looked frightened.

The diatribe continued: "Some of these lion cubs will strike in the coming days. Others will grow to manhood and ever more fearsome capabilities. The spirit of Sheikh Osama bin Laden lives on in the youthful hearts that surround me. You will know their acts when you see them."

The screen went blank; the music rose and faded. Gold wondered if Fatima's brother had stood among the kids on the video. She also wondered if the ten boys were all Black Crescent had, or if there were more. Chaaku, or whatever he wanted to call himself, had not given numbers.

Intel analysts, she knew, would scrutinize every pixel of that video for clues. The wall behind Chaaku, made of baked mud—did its color suggest a possible location? The choice of music—had the same song appeared in other videos? The boys—could any be identified? She considered letting Fatima watch the video to point out her brother, if he was there, but Gold dismissed the idea. It would upset the girl and serve little purpose.

Gold cared more about the big picture—if she could just get herself to concentrate. She found it hard to stop worrying about Parson and imagining how those kids must feel. But she realized this new jihadist leader intended a masterstroke, some way to occupy the pedestal that once belonged to bin Laden.

Nearly all these terrorists said they acted purely out of religious piety, but Gold knew ego had a lot to do with it. This guy wanted to be the new *Amir-ul-Momineen*, the Commander of the Faithful. But other Islamists might not like him to claim that mantle, at least not this way. And maybe that was a wedge she could use.

With little to do but wait and watch, Parson surveyed the valley below him. Scattered birch and pine bowed to each gust. The strongest winds lifted dust from the swales and hills as if the ground smoked. If any insurgents stalked nearby, Parson could not see them.

He was getting hungry. This mission was supposed to be a short out-and-back, and he'd not brought any food of his own. But the crashed Mi-17 had carried relief supplies. Maybe there was something he and the others could eat.

"Keep a good lookout," Parson told Conway. "I'll see if there's any food in the helicopter."

"Yes, sir," Conway said.

"You're a civilian now. You don't have to 'sir' me."

"Yes, sir."

Old habits, Parson thought. Once you've worn the uniform, you don't ever completely take it off.

Inside the helicopter, Aamir remained sitting on a troop seat, staring at the floor. He looked as if he took no interest in anything happening around him. His hands remained tied behind his back, his feet taped together.

Conway's partner lay with his back propped against the cockpit bulkhead. Every few seconds he would close his eyes tight and reopen them; Parson took that as a sign of pain. Reyes had given the man a plastic bottle of water. The injured civilian drank the last of it and dropped the empty to the floor.

Sharif was stretched out on Reyes's litter, apparently unconscious. Reyes fussed over him, checked vital signs.

"How is he?" Parson asked.

"I think he'll make it," Reyes said, "as long as this doesn't drag out too long."

Parson wanted to assure him that wouldn't happen, but he'd learned not to make those kinds of promises. He stepped around the two men lying on the floor and made his way back to the stacked relief supplies.

What he found disappointed him. When he looked closely, he saw the cargo had not been daily rations or Meals Ready to Eat, but bags of rice and even Unimix. Conditions in some of the villages must be getting bad if they were shipping that stuff.

Parson turned to go back outside, but then he realized

he was hungry enough to try the Unimix. He picked up the empty water bottle Conway's partner had dropped. Sitting on a troop seat, he raised the left leg of his flight suit and unclipped his boot knife. The Damascus steel blade amounted to a long razor, and it sliced into the bottle so effortlessly that Parson used no sawing motion at all.

He cut off the top of the bottle to create an open cup. Then he went to a bag of Unimix and lopped off the corner.

The dry, cereal-like substance poured from the opening, and Parson caught some of it in his makeshift cup. He found a full bottle of water, opened it, and poured some into the Unimix. Parson stirred it with his finger until it formed a lukewarm slurry.

Lacking utensils, he looked around for something to use as a spoon, but found nothing. With no other options, he tipped the cup toward his mouth and drank, chewed. The Unimix tasted like coarse, unsweetened oatmeal.

"How is that?" Reyes asked.

"It sucks," Parson said, "but it's food." He imagined his primitive manner of eating the Unimix was probably how the stuff usually got eaten. But even in his present circumstances, he was better off than most people who'd ever tasted it. "Do you want some?" he asked.

"I'll pass," Reyes said.

"There's plenty if you get hungry enough."

Parson supposed, after having delivered tons of Unimix in relief missions gone by, there was a strange irony that he wound up eating it. But he didn't have time to ponder that.

He went back outside to resume his watch. The valley below still looked empty. Just a few stunted trees growing along a narrow stream. A canal extended from the stream at a right angle. Difficult to tell at a distance of a mile or so, but it seemed the weed-choked canal irrigated no crop. The Army Corps of Engineers had built dams and canals in Afghanistan during the 1950s, but most fell into disrepair. Maybe this was one of those relics.

Though Parson saw no threat, something still bothered the dog. She kept staring in the same direction, growling and whining. When Conway stroked her ears, it did little to calm her.

"Something's down there," Conway said. He held Reyes's rifle. Parson noted that he always kept the muzzle pointed in a safe direction.

"Your dog's not happy, that's for sure," Parson said. He envied the animal's simple existence—fully aware of dangers within its view but with most forms of evil beyond its knowing. Living moment to moment with no plans and no concept of time.

Parson shaded his eyes with his hand, wished he'd brought binoculars. His hunter's eye caught a ripple in the canal, and at first he thought of ducks feeding among the weeds. Were there ducks here? He couldn't remember seeing any flying around. Their rapid wing beats would have distinguished them from other birds. And that stagnant canal water probably could not support fish big enough to create ripples like that.

"We got company," Parson said. "Down in the canal. Right where the dog's looking."

Rashid gave an order in his native tongue. He and his crew chief swung their machine gun where Parson pointed.

"The dog is unclean, but is useful," Rashid said.

"Reyes," Parson called. "Gimme your radio." Parson had his old-school survival radio in his vest, but the para-rescueman's newer PRC-152 had encryption and wider frequency capability. Reyes clambered out of the Mi-17 and handed Parson the radio and his headset. Parson dug his comm card from a flight suit pocket, ran his finger down the list of call signs and frequencies. He punched in the channel for the AWACS surveillance aircraft.

"What's up?" Reyes asked.

"Hostiles down in the canal."

"How do you know they're hostile, sir?"

"Because they're sneaking through that nasty water. They wouldn't get in that shit without a reason." Parson put on the headset, pressed the transmit button, and called, "Bandsaw, Bandsaw, Golay One-Eight."

Several seconds went by. Just as Parson started to press transmit again, he got an answer: "Golay One-Eight, Bandsaw Three-Six, go ahead."

So the AWACS was listening up, Parson thought, just like it was supposed to. At least that much was going right.

"Bandsaw," he called, "Golay One-Eight is a downed Mi-17. Search-and-rescue is aware of our position, but they're not the only ones who know where we are. Can you vector some close air support our way?"

"Spectre's on station," the AWACS answered. "I'm standing by to copy your position."

That would work, Parson thought. An AC-130 gunship. Helicopters couldn't land right now, but that monster could sure as hell orbit overhead and lay down some fire. However, it depended on *where* the gunship was on station. Parson transmitted his coordinates.

"Bandsaw copies all," the AWACS responded. "Be advised Spectre Six-Four is about eighty miles from your position."

Parson did some mental math. The gunship could head toward him at about four miles a minute, depending on the aircraft's drag index. So it would take maybe twenty minutes to arrive, plus whatever time the crew needed to spot the target and set up on a firing run.

"Thanks for the help," Parson said. "We'll be here." For a while. The wind blustered strong as ever. Through the blowing dust, Parson saw a distant, dripping figure climb from the canal and take cover behind a boulder. Then another, clad in black. And another, and another.

He gestured to Rashid. Parson pointed two fingers at his own eyes, pointed downhill, then held up four fingers. Rashid nodded, scanned left to right. He spoke in Pashto, and the crew chief shifted the PKM slightly, held his finger over the trigger of the big machine gun.

"Are you seeing what I'm seeing?" Conway asked. He was so focused on the enemy that he hadn't noticed Parson's signal to Rashid.

"Yeah," Parson said, "and I'm worried about the ones we *don't* see."

The insurgents who'd come out of the canal held their positions. The terrorists were too far away to hit with the M4 and the crew chief's door gun, let alone Parson's side-arm. And the longer they stayed put, the more he worried about bad guys coming from other directions. Though Parson and the others had a nearly unobstructed view of the valley below, the mountain's folds offered little visibility to the sides. Above, the top of the ridgeline loomed just a hundred yards or so uphill, with everything behind it obscured.

Reyes made one more check of his patients, then stepped out of the helicopter, holding his Beretta. He lowered himself behind the stone barricade Parson and Conway had built. Even with every able-bodied man now in a fighting position, Parson's de facto fire team seemed a thin force for repelling committed jihadists. Nothing for it but to keep a good watch, and when the shooting started, try to keep them pinned down until air support could get here. The radio would be more important than the guns.

"Spectre's inbound," Parson told Reyes. "You can call in a strike better than I can, so you take the radio." PJs weren't forward air controllers, but they knew how to make an emergency call for fire.

"Yes, sir," Reyes said. He took the PRC-152 and the headset from Parson. Reyes also retrieved a smoke flare from his tactical vest and prepped it. He removed the plastic cap from one end and pried up the pull tab. It was the same kind of flare Parson had elected not to use earlier, but he did not object. If it became necessary to mark their position so a gunship could lay waste to everything around them, sparks would be the least of their problems.

A flicker of movement down in the valley caught Parson's eye. He turned his head to see a man dart from behind a boulder, run several yards, dive for the ground. The insurgent carried an AK-47. Another man leapfrogged ahead of him, holding what looked like a grenade launcher.

"All right," Parson said. "Here they come." He thumbed the safety on his pistol, placed an extra magazine on the stones in front of him.

The dog gazed down at the valley floor, sniffed the air. She growled, whirled, and barked, teeth bared at something behind her.

Parson turned and looked up at the top of the ridge. The wind stung his eyes. He saw figures crouching above him. There was a glint, or maybe a flash. And the smoking trail of a rocket-propelled grenade.

❧ 14 ❧

Gold still kept contacts with the Afghan National Police. She had spent a tour helping run a literacy program for new recruits, and she decided to see if anyone knew anything about this Lieutenant Aamir and his kidnapped son. At the moment, she could do little else to help Parson.

After several phone calls, she finally reached Sergeant Baitullah in Kabul. He had lost both feet in last year's bomb attack on the police training center, but the police needed reliable people so badly, they let him stay on in a desk job.

"*Salaam*, my teacher," he said. "It is good to hear your voice."

"And yours, Baitullah. I have missed you and your classmates." She especially missed the ones she could never talk to again.

"How may I serve you, teacher?"

She told him about Parson and Rashid, the Mi-17 forced down, Lieutenant Aamir.

"Kidnapping was a curse upon this land long before Black Crescent," Baitullah said. "True Muslims consider it among the foulest of sins because it is a sin against family." Gold listened closely to his voice, the cadence of his words. He sounded more self-confident than she'd ever heard him, in command of information. His tone thawed just a little of the ice in her heart, made her feel perhaps not all her efforts were wasted. "I must check our records on these crimes," he added. "Sadly, there are many."

Baitullah promised to call back after he did some research. Cell phone service was still intermittent; she could only give him a landline number that would ring on a field telephone in command post. If we were both Taliban, Gold mused, he could just turn loose a pigeon.

She was taking a walk with Fatima when Baitullah called back. The Giant Voice speakers strung around the base crackled and hummed, then announced: "Sergeant Major Gold to command post. Sergeant Major Gold, please come to command post."

Gold brought Fatima with her. The girl seemed excited as she looked around at the computers, telephones, and radios. Perhaps she thought this strange facility could somehow bring back her brother. Gold felt a twinge of regret; she'd been so careful not to encourage false hope.

When she picked up the phone, Baitullah sounded regretful, too.

"I can find nothing on Lieutenant Aamir," he said. "I presume he has not reported the crime."

"He probably has not," Gold said. Parents who suffered a kidnapping could not count on swift and skillful response by Afghan authorities, so they usually cooperated with abductors.

"These events often end badly," Baitullah said. "In 2011, the insurgents hanged the eight-year-old son of a police officer. The officer had refused to give the terrorists a police vehicle."

Gold knew of that case. She didn't want to talk about it.

"What about Lieutenant Aamir himself?" she asked. "Is there anything to suggest terrorist ties?"

"Nothing. His record was clean until now."

A promising career ruined, then, in addition to everything else. A tragedy within a tragedy.

"Thank you for your help, Sergeant Baitullah," Gold said. "I will keep you informed."

"Allah's blessings upon you."

Outside, gusts roughed the tents of the refugee billeting and the medical teams. The sky took on a beige tinge with the dust lifted into the air. To escape the wind, Gold took Fatima to the chow hall. The serving line had closed for lunch and would not open for dinner for another hour, so Gold took two pint cartons of orange juice from a refrigerator. She opened one for Fatima, inserted a straw, and sat with her in the empty dining tent. Overhead, a cloth plenum rumbled with air from the ventilation system.

"Were you talking on the telephone about my brother?" Fatima asked.

Gold thought for a moment. "I was talking with the police about another boy taken from his home. We are also trying to find your brother. But I must tell you we can make no promises."

A tear slid down the girl's cheek, but after a moment she seemed to compose herself. She examined her straw, then placed it back in the carton and took another sip of juice.

"Do you have a brother?" Fatima asked.

"I do not," Gold said. "I am an only child."

"Do you live in a big house in America?"

"I live in what we call an apartment, near a military base. It is only a little bigger than your house." But palatial by comparison, Gold thought, with its electricity and central air. Luxuries this child might never have.

"Why does your husband let you come to Afghanistan?"

Gold smiled. "I have no husband."

"Then you must get one," Fatima said. "I wish we could go to America together, after we find Mohammed. I could marry the giant soldier who carried me to the helicopter, and you could marry your pilot friend."

Gold wanted to laugh and to break down in tears all at once. She did neither. Instead she said, "Fatima, in my world, women have other choices. They don't have to get married. They can learn things, get jobs. If you get the chance, I want you to go to school. That might be hard. Be careful, but be brave."

Fatima looked Gold directly in the eyes, no tears now. "How did you learn to read?" she asked.

"I went to public schools where I grew up. Then I joined the Army, and they sent me to a special school to learn your language."

"Was it hard to learn my language?"

You bet it was, Gold thought. Pashto had seven vowels, some with no equivalent in English. Emphasis on a consonant could change the meaning of a word.

"Learning Pashto was difficult," Gold said. "Your people are very poetic, and they use language in different ways from English speakers."

Fatima smiled. Afghans of any age seemed to like hearing their native tongue was challenging but rich. To compliment someone's language was to compliment something deep within them. Even kids understood it.

The girl slurped the last of her juice through the straw. When Gold took away the empty carton, Fatima kept the straw and placed it in a pocket of her dress.

"If you go away," Fatima asked, "what will happen to me?"

"I must be honest with you, Fatima," Gold said. "Sooner or later, I will have to go away. But I will try to look out for you." Gold knew of a few options. UNICEF might help, or perhaps one of the private charities working in the country. The Afghan Child Education and Care Organization had done good work. Deciding the best choice would take time and the approval of higher-ups.

Gold walked with Fatima back to the refugee tents. At her cot, Fatima said, "Please come back again and talk to me."

"I will, Fatima," Gold said. "I enjoy talking to you very much."

She felt another pang of regret as she left Fatima in the

tent—alone and with nothing to occupy her but a straw. Gold returned to command post to see if there was news of Parson and the Mi-17 crew.

"He's been talking to AWACS," the duty officer said.

So at least he was still alive, as far as anyone knew. Probably giving well-considered orders in not too well-considered phrases, Gold imagined. Patience was not his strong point.

"How does the weather look for getting them out of there?" Gold asked.

The duty officer pointed to a whiteboard with a forecast written in hieroglyphics only aviators could decipher. Gold felt a flash of annoyance. She wouldn't expect this guy to speak Pashto. Why did he think she could read his technical language? Irritation was a rare emotion for her; concern for Parson was getting to her. Maybe she was even channeling a little of his personality.

She took a deep breath, glanced again at the forecast. Someone had circled part of it with a dry-erase marker. That portion read *BECMG 1719 30020G30.* Gold pointed to it.

"What does that mean?" she asked. The duty officer turned in his swivel chair.

"Oh, that means between seventeen hundred and nineteen hundred Zulu time, the winds will come from the northwest, and they'll drop to twenty knots, gusting to thirty."

"Can the rescue crews fly in that?"

"It'll suck, but they're going to try."

"Sir," Gold said, "I work for Lieutenant Colonel Parson. I'm his interpreter. I want to ride on the first chopper that goes out to get him."

The grenade sailed over Parson's head and detonated behind him. The blast so overwhelmed his eardrums that he heard no boom, just a grinding sound like a knife on a whetstone. With both hands, he raised his pistol and began firing at the enemy above him. Instinct and muscle memory took over. He had no conscious thought of aim and trigger pull, yet he felt the Beretta recoiling in his grip.

Beside him, Conway fired the M4 on semiauto. He unleashed not a burst of rounds but a series of pops, each shot aimed. One of Conway's empty cartridges flipped into Parson's flight suit collar. Parson swatted the hot brass away from his neck.

The insurgents scattered and dived. One of them spun to his right as if hit. That must have been from Conway's disciplined fire, Parson figured. He didn't think any of his own rounds had connected.

Rashid and his crew chief shot in the other direction. Plunging fire from their PKM door gun kept the terrorists below them pinned down. Their tracers rained into the valley like neon sleet. Parson saw one burst streak to a boulder that shielded a jihadist. The tracers bounced off the rock and angled upward until they burned out and vanished. Sputters of the enemy's AK-47 fire died down, flared again.

The rock barricades provided Parson's team good protection from rounds fired up at them from the valley. But the stone offered no cover from the enemy firing down on them from the ridge.

A few feet to Parson's left, Reyes opened up with his handgun, firing toward the ridge. He tried to use the Mi-17 as a defilade, but he had to come from behind cover to see his target. When the Beretta's slide locked back, Reyes ejected the empty magazine and reached into his vest for a spare. Just as he began to reload, he stumbled backward and fell.

Parson lunged toward him. He feared he'd see blood spurt from a chest wound or from Reyes's mouth. But the PJ only coughed.

"Are you all right?" Parson shouted over the gunfire.

"Yeah, but that felt like I got kicked by a mule."

Body armor, Parson realized. Thank God. Reyes slammed a new magazine into his weapon, clambered up on his knees. Released his slide and fired uphill.

"If we don't get some help in here, we're fucked," Conway said.

"I know it," Parson said. "Make 'em keep their heads down as long as you can."

So this is what it means to be flanked, Parson realized. He was no infantryman, but he knew things had gone wrong in a hurry. If the bad guys were only in the valley below, he'd have the upper hand, literally—covering his target from an elevated position. But some of the enemy had come around behind him. Taking fire from two directions, he occupied not so much a fighting position as a kill zone.

Conway's dog huddled beside the Mi-17, tail between her legs, shaking. Bullets cracked from both upslope and down, and the animal flinched with each round. Wailing came from inside the helicopter. Aamir cried out in words that were incomprehensible to Parson except *Allah*.

Parson caught a glimpse of an insurgent's head and shoulder behind an outcropping uphill. He fired two shots. The man ducked below the outcropping. Parson had heard of coalition squads getting into fixes like this. The only way out: Keep the enemy at bay with small arms and wait for air support. The battle's outcome depended on who ran out of ammunition first.

He fired once more, emptied his Beretta. Thumbed the magazine release and let the spent mag clatter to his feet. Inserted a full magazine and kept firing. Odors of burned gunpowder wafted in quick snatches, ripped away by the wind.

The sound of Reyes's voice murmured under the staccato snaps of the M4 and the deep rips of the PKM. The PJ had holstered his pistol and was speaking into his headset.

"Spectre Six-Four," he said, "this is Golay One-Eight. I have an emergency fire mission. Target is riflemen to the immediate northwest and southeast of my position."

Maybe help would get here in time. Rashid and the crew chief stopped firing their door gun, scrambled to feed a fresh belt of cartridges. Parson almost told them they were doing it wrong until he remembered they were working with a PKM. Unlike most crew-served weapons he'd seen, the Russian-built PKM fed from the right and ejected to the left. Parson turned to look downhill. One of the black-clad gunmen advanced, zigzagged to take cover in a gully. Parson raised his weapon, pulled the trigger. Dirt flew from the lip of the gully.

"Request strafing attack," Reyes continued. "Friendlies are all within four meters of the Mi-17. Will mark my position with orange smoke."

The man in the gully rose again, sprinted forward. Parson squeezed off three shots. The man stumbled, dropped his AK. He collapsed face forward, but then he rolled to his side and reached for his rifle. Parson steadied his hands on the stone berm he'd helped build. Took aim at the insurgent's center mass. Pressed the trigger. The man jerked, but still held his weapon.

All right, Parson thought, maybe you got body armor, too. He aimed for the insurgent's head, missed. Just a puff of dust by the man's neck. Fired twice more and the man went limp.

Amid the shooting, Parson listened for aircraft engines. He strained to pick up the sound of turboprops, but he heard only the rush of wind, shouts in Pashto, more shots. All the firepower in the world couldn't help them if it didn't get here quickly. He'd brought only two fifteen-round magazines for his Beretta, and he'd already used more than half of the last one. Conway had emptied at least one thirty-round mag, and Parson didn't know how much ammo the crew chief had for the PKM. Rashid racked the bolt on that weapon and sprayed more fire among the insurgents below. Geysers of dirt spewed upward as bullets flayed the ground.

A sense of hyperalertness came over Parson as he watched for jihadists trying to move closer. The air itself seemed granular, as if he tasted each molecule as he inhaled. Time clicked by in distinct half-second increments. A man on the outcropping above raised his grenade launcher. Parson aimed, focused on his pistol's front sight centered in the notch of the rear sight. When he fired, he felt everything that resulted: the leap of the muzzle, the cycle of the slide, the extractor kicking out the empty brass, the weapon closing itself with firing pin poised over a new primer, hammer at full cock.

The first joint of his finger on the trigger, Parson nearly squeezed it again. But his target had disappeared. Save 'em, he told himself. Save 'em. He'd been in firefights before, but not like this one. They usually turned on who shot first, shot straightest, and shot most—the volume of thrown metal. But this seemed more like some strange and deadly field sport, in a play to run out the clock.

The enemy must suspect an air strike could be on the way, Parson figured. Their usual countertactic was to fire from occupied homes. They knew the coalition's own rules about trying to avoid civilian casualties, so they put civilians in front of themselves whenever possible. Not an option today, though. Nobody lived on this mountainside except snakes and scorpions.

Conway ejected another spent magazine from the M4 carbine. "I'm out," he yelled. Drew the Makarov pistol, fired the handgun until it emptied. Reyes looked up from his radio, patted the pockets of his vest. He ripped open a pouch and withdrew an M4 mag.

"Last one," Reyes said.

"Thanks."

Conway dropped his pistol. Reyes tossed the magazine, and Conway caught it one-handed. Smacked it into the M4's magazine well, released the bolt. Fired two rounds.

"Where's that gunship?" Parson shouted.

"Five minutes," Reyes said.

Parson doubted his group could hold out much longer than that. They were armed for survival and evasion, not an extended gunfight to hold a fixed position.

Please let that thing get here, he thought. The Spectre was an armed version of the C-130s he'd flown during his days as a navigator. But the Spectre carried no cargo; armaments were its only payload. It mounted an M102 howitzer and a forty-millimeter Bofors cannon. Parson imagined the crew running attack checklists, ready to press the FIRE button as soon as they arrived overhead. He didn't know all their procedures, but he did know the flight engineer had a consent switch for firing the guns. The pilot had the trigger, but the FE could break its circuit. Even the gunship's engineering reflected the moral responsibilities of its crew.

Movement caught Parson's eye. Something underneath the crumpled tail boom of the Mi-17. He turned with both hands on his pistol, thumbs along the left side of the grip. An insurgent crouched behind the helicopter.

Before Parson could aim, the man opened up with his AK. The burst hit Conway full in the chest. Conway wore no armor. Blood spewed from three exit wounds as he went down. Droplets spattered Parson's sleeve as he leveled his sights and fired four times. The jihadist crumpled. Parson's Beretta locked open. Empty.

We're about to be overrun, Parson realized. He leaned to grab the M4 from Conway. The civilian's left arm quivered; his body spasmed. Parson snatched the weapon away. He fired at another insurgent sliding downhill toward him. The man held his rifle up out of the dirt, fabric sling swaying, dust rising behind him as he shuffled through the rocks. Parson got off only two shots; the third pull brought nothing. Empty. His target fell, but other insurgents fired down from the ridge.

Parson dropped the M4 and drew his boot knife. He'd fight with that until they shot him; he would *not* let himself get captured.

Reyes was talking on the radio again. The only phrase Parson could make out was *danger close*. The PJ picked up his smoke flare and yanked the lanyard. Orange smoke boiled from the end and billowed downwind into the valley.

Parson heard that familiar turboprop thrum. He looked up to see the Spectre over the ridgeline, higher than he'd expected. It came straight on, grew larger. Banked to the left. That's the side the guns were on.

And then the earth itself came apart.

Stones and soil roared into the air. Blinded by dust, Parson saw only shadows and flashes. The ground trembled and bucked underneath him. A pulsing howl raged in his ears. Grit flailed his skin. An alien force sucked breath from his lungs, burned his throat. His tongue contracted, sensed ashes and steel. The very taste of fire.

Balance left him. Sky and terrain joined, swirled into each other, physical reality gone liquid. Then solid again. He felt something hard against his spine. Parson found himself on his back, but he could not remember falling.

Wind swept away the noise and brought form back to the mountain. The sky returned to its place, and amid the blue, Parson saw the gunship turning.

He rolled onto his stomach and looked up. The ridge above him still smoked, and it had changed form. The outcropping was gone; the profile of boulders and scree had rearranged. Nothing moved but the rising cinders.

Voices echoed below. Parson pushed himself onto his side, sat up, and squinted downhill. Six, seven insurgents ran away toward the canal.

The Spectre completed its turn, leveled its wings. The jihadists sprinted about a hundred yards from Parson, fleeing through the valley with no effort to use cover.

The gunship overtook them in seconds, seemed to float past them. For a moment Parson wondered if the crew had chosen mercy. But then the AC-130 banked left again, and fire speared from the fuselage, long streaks of light. Thunder pealed from a clear sky. The land around the insurgents convulsed, boiled with flame.

When wind cleared the dust, Parson saw no one running. He saw no one at all, not even a corpse. A deep breath filled his chest. The growl of aircraft engines faded, and the mountains grew silent once more.

❧ 15 ❧

After nightfall a broken cloud layer drifted over the airfield at Mazar, an onyx sky with fissures of stars. Gold lacked an aviator's sense of weather, but she'd heard Parson talk about meteorology enough to realize a few things. First, if she could see stars so brightly between the clouds, that meant the dust lofted earlier had cleared. Second, the wind still flicked strands of hair around her cheeks, but now she could face into it without her eyes stinging. Both good signs.

Sometimes flyboys like Parson got so wrapped up in their fancy machines that they didn't think enough about the big picture. But she admired the way they spoke the language of wind and rain, sun and cloud. It drew them more closely to the natural world, the elements of creation. No wonder so many of them spent their off-duty hours with a fishing rod, a hunting rifle, or a hiker's backpack.

She checked in at command post to see when the rescue

flight would launch. Flight orders had already been cut; Gold felt relieved to see the duty officer remembered to put her with the crews. The orders listed her as an MEGP: mission-essential ground personnel.

"When do they go out?" she asked.

"As soon as they get here," the duty officer said. "A pair of Pave Hawks coming up from Bagram."

"Have you heard from Michael—I mean, Lieutenant Colonel Parson?" she asked.

"Yeah, he's okay, but he sounded a little stunned. They had to call in an air strike pretty close, and I think it rang their bells."

That chill of anxiety went through her again. Memories and fear. Thoughts of knifepoints and frostbite, bomb blasts and blood. Focus, she told herself.

"I didn't know they'd come under fire," she said.

"Happened pretty quick. You could hear shooting anytime the PJ keyed his mike."

"You mean Sergeant Reyes?"

"Yeah, that's the one. Puerto Rican guy. That dude was ice cold on the radio. Gave coordinates like he was talking about math homework."

"Is he all right?"

"Yeah, but they have a KIA. One of those civilian workers."

The news of the firefight and the death left Gold feeling unstrung. She wanted to get to Parson, to see with her own eyes he was all right. She thought of the family of the dead civilian, about to get that awful knock at the door. A

strong force of dread settled on everything around her—
the command post, the tarmac outside, the mountains
beyond.

With time to wait before the helicopters came in, she
tried to think of something useful to do. But she could
only pace and worry, imagine the worst. What if they came
under fire again? What if the winds picked up once more,
and Parson and the crew had to stay out there all night?

She was still waiting in command post when the Pave
Hawks arrived. The plywood walls shuddered as the helicopters thudded overhead. After the choppers landed, they
shut down only long enough to refuel. Lettering on the
metal skin of one of the aircraft, near the tail rotor, read
DANGER KEEP AWAY.

A helmeted flight engineer beckoned her aboard, then
resumed his place by the right side's minigun. Another
crewman manned the left gun, and two pararescuemen
rounded out the enlisted crew. Gold knew none of them,
and the pilots did not offer her an interphone cord for
her headset. Parson always treated her as a crew member,
but she knew she was just a passenger to these guys.

The instrument panel shone dimly as Gold watched
from the back. All the crew wore night vision goggles, and
green backglow from the NVGs illuminated their faces.
She felt the turbulence as soon as the Pave Hawk left
the ground. With one especially nasty jolt, her shoulder
smacked into the bulkhead behind her, and she understood why the winds had prevented a rescue until now. She
wished she could hear the crew's conversation; that would

have provided some distraction. But she could only tighten her seat belt and hold on.

Gold felt heavy in her cloth seat. The webbing pressed into the back of her thighs, and she assumed the chopper was climbing. Beneath the cloud layer, the helicopters fluttered along in almost total darkness. Gold saw no terrain down below, just pure black. Then a break in the overcast admitted a shaft of moonlight bright enough to reveal mountains passing underneath the aircraft.

Inside, she noted crew members pointing, checking charts and a photomap. Someone cranked his interphone volume way up, and Gold overheard squelched voices—pops and hums and commands. But with her own headset not connected, she could make out no words clearly.

The moonlight yielded to the whims of the clouds. Light faded, brightened, and faded once more. Gold felt blind and deaf, suspended between mountains and moon. Almost like a ghost: able to move in the world, but unable to alter physical reality to her satisfaction.

In the next pool of pale light, she noticed a hillside dotted with *qalats*—mud houses with adjoining stone fences for animals. A lamp shone in one window; otherwise the village was dark. The village had a name, no doubt, though probably not one indicated on U.S. charts. Too insignificant for that.

She considered the inhabitants, wondered about their fates and their pasts. Had they suffered in the earthquake? More than likely. Had they lost loved ones in the wars and coups since 1979? Almost certainly; every family had.

Gold felt responsible for each life down there, though she knew that made no sense. Her conscience outweighed her powers, her ability to bring about change.

You've spent so much time here, she told herself, that part of you will never leave. Her mind had absorbed the language, the customs, the history, so thoroughly that if a neurosurgeon wanted to separate the American from the Afghan in her, he would not know where to make the cut.

She thought of lines from a poem by Kipling. They had stayed with her because she had lived them:

I have eaten your bread and salt.
I have drunk your water and wine.
The deaths ye died I have watched beside,
And the lives ye led were mine.

The helicopters crossed a ridge, and the village disappeared behind them. The land grew dark once more. The choppers banked, leveled, banked again. After several minutes of flying in blackness, Gold saw where the cloud layer overhead split wide. Through the opening, moonlight shone like a diffused and filtered sunrise, dawn on some shrouded planet in another galaxy.

The moon held low on the horizon, red and near full. Its peaks and craters, plains and false seas loomed so near that the lunar terrain appeared as if on a relief map.

The sight eased Gold's mind. The apparent nearness of another world served as a subtle reminder, or perhaps an assurance: *Someone is in charge, Sergeant Major. And it's not you.*

She began scanning outside. Gold could see well enough to make out tributary creeks twisting through the network of valleys below. Soon she noticed a change in the tone of engines and rotors, and she felt the Pave Hawk slow down. It banked a few degrees to the left, then made a full left circle. Chatter rose on the interphone and radios, but like before, she could overhear only an unintelligible crackle of voices.

When the aircraft flew straight and level again, she noticed a strange light up ahead. A green glow emanated in a perfectly round shape. The light pulsed and wavered, and Gold imagined it would appear much brighter to the crew members on NVGs. In a moment, she realized what it was: a buzz-saw signal, commonly used to hail aircraft at night. It looked like no other light source, and it was low-tech and dependable. Troops made it by cracking a chemical light stick, tying it to a few feet of parachute cord, and spinning it over their heads.

If they were signaling that way, Gold thought, they must be confident the landing zone was secure. You wouldn't twirl a light if you thought bad guys lurked nearby. The air strike had probably taken care of all threats.

She wanted to get Parson on board and out of there immediately. Now she knew he was safe, and that was fine. But she'd feel a lot better with him strapped in beside her.

The Pave Hawks clattered over the valley; Parson could see them in the full moon even with all their lights off. Good thing that Spectre had laid waste to the insurgents so thoroughly. With this much illumination, the helicopters would have made tempting targets for a bad guy with a shoulder-launched missile.

Just to Parson's left, Reyes spun the light stick. Rashid and the crew chief still manned the PKM, though nothing had moved anywhere near them since the gunship did its work. Sergeant Sharif and the wounded civilian lay inside the Mi-17. Reyes had spread a poncho over Conway's body. Parson held the radio; he'd been told the Pave Hawks were bringing more pararescuemen, as well as Gold. He took one more call from the lead Pave Hawk.

"Golay," the pilot said, "we have your buzz saw. Can you confirm the LZ's still cold?"

"Affirmative," Parson said. "There's a flat spot on this ledge big enough for one helo. Surface winds are still gusting, but they're better than they were." With nothing to measure wind speed and direction, he could describe the weather only in the most general terms.

"Pedro Two-Four copies all. We'll come in one at a time."

That decision made sense to Parson. One chopper could fly overwatch with gunners at the ready as the other picked up downed crew members. Landing would go quicker than having the Pave Hawks hover while taking up survivors on the hoists. Parson didn't feel like swinging from a damned cable anyway. A wave of fatigue came over him; he was getting too old for this. He thought his years of military service were wearing him away like the brake discs on landing gear, a little less of him left after each mission.

Parson waved his hand under his throat, a signal that Reyes could stop spinning the light stick. The PJ let the stick rattle to the ground. He rolled up the parachute cord over the plastic stick and stuffed it all into a cargo pocket on his leg. As he worked, he looked uncomfortable. He kept pausing, bending forward, adjusting the straps and buckles on his body armor. The armor had saved Reyes's life, but he probably suffered a deep, sore bruise underneath it, maybe even some cracked ribs.

Been there, Parson thought. He, too, had experienced the sledgehammer of a bullet striking Kevlar. Force equaled mass times acceleration, and acceleration was a bitch.

But soreness beat the hell out of a slug through the chest. A flight surgeon once told him how the gunshot wounds of the Afghanistan and Iraq wars resembled those of Civil War survivors—mainly injuries to the limbs. Back then, if you got shot in the torso you just died. In the present day, you had body armor, and you weren't seriously hurt. So those who showed up in hospitals, then and now, had taken bullets to the arms and legs. Except the really unlucky ones who got shot in the head or had a bullet get under the Kevlar by entering at the shoulder.

Conway, of course, had become another kind of exception. What a damnable shame, Parson thought, for him to survive the Gulf War, then come here to help and lose his life in a firefight.

As the first helicopter approached the ledge, Parson wondered if that aircraft carried Gold. The lead Pave Hawk thudded over the ledge and threw billows of grit into the air. Parson turned his face from the stings, waited for the pitch of the rotor blades to change. The other chopper orbited the mountain, its metal skin bronzed by moonlight.

The lead aircraft touched down and throttled back to idle. Two pararescuemen swung themselves out of the HH-60, brought a litter from inside their helicopter. Both wore black knee pads over their fatigues. As they ran toward the Mi-17, Parson saw they had name tags Velcroed to their upper sleeves. The cloth tags carried a straightforward acknowledgment of the dangers at hand: Rank. Last name. Blood type.

The PJs placed the litter on the floor of the downed helicopter, then lifted Sharif onto the litter. As they moved him, the wounded flight engineer clenched his teeth, but said nothing. Parson and Reyes picked up Conway's partner. The men hauled both patients into the first Pave Hawk. Parson looked around the cabin; Gold was not there.

Rashid and the crew chief unloaded the PKM and lifted it from the fighting position they'd built. "You guys head out on the first chopper," Parson said. "I'll put Aamir on the other one." Rashid did not argue; he seemed to want Aamir out of his presence. He and the crew chief heaved the PKM onto the Pave Hawk. Rashid ran back for his flight bag, then climbed aboard.

Reyes followed them inside. He fussed over his patients, conferred with the other pararescuemen.

The Pave Hawk's engines whined louder. Parson sheltered himself inside the Mi-17 from the blowing dust.

Conway's dog cowered in its kennel, and Parson felt sorry for her. The dog had lost her master, and she seemed to know it. The animal barked over the noise of the HH-60's departure. Aamir sat on a troop seat, looking down at the poncho that covered Conway.

Parson kneeled beside Aamir, drew his boot knife. Aamir's eyes widened. He tried to slide away from Parson.

"I'm not going to hurt you, dipshit," Parson said. He grabbed Aamir's boots, cut the duct tape that bound them, but he kept the copilot's hands tied. "Stay in your seat till I tell you to get on the next helicopter." Parson knew Aamir had no idea what he said, and he wished Gold was already by his side.

With the lead Pave Hawk off the ground, the number two helo settled onto the ledge. Parson was eager to see Gold emerge from the aircraft. He'd let her deal with Aamir, get more of his story. Sophia would do a good job of that. She could put people at ease, calm them down. He'd watched her long enough to realize language skills were only half her powers. The other half was her manner, her approach, stuff you couldn't teach. So many situations went smoother—even safer—if you could just get people to chill out. Not really a big part of Parson's skill set, he had to admit.

Gold jumped out of the Pave Hawk right behind the PJs. Met him inside the Mi-17. "Sir," she shouted over the engines and rotors, "are you okay?"

"I'm all right," he said. "Here's our guy." He took Aamir by the arm, pulled him toward the door. "Just get him seated. Tell him if he gives you any trouble, he'll get his ass kicked again." Gold led Aamir to the Pave Hawk without speaking.

The pararescuemen from the second aircraft helped with Conway. Parson tucked the poncho under the dead man's shoulders, took Conway's feet. When they lifted him, a few drops of blood dripped from the creases of the poncho. They carried him to the Pave Hawk, stumbling and side-stepping with the weight.

Then Parson gathered up his helmet bag, survival vest, and Conway's pack. The PJs loaded the dog and kennel, and Parson boarded last. He sat beside Gold and fastened his seat belt. Now she was talking to Aamir. In the pale glow of a utility light mounted on the helicopter's ceiling, Parson saw Aamir's expression change. The tight set of his lips relaxed as if he'd found some thread of relief.

The aircraft lifted off. The pulse of rotors coursed through Parson's body like his own heart pounding. Turbulence jounced the chopper as soon as its wheels left the ground, but it climbed unencumbered by downdrafts. In the clear air of a country without industry, the moon lit the sky a deep garnet. Parson wondered when a fighter plane or gunship would come along to blow up the crippled Mi-17.

"Do you think Black Crescent has his boy?" Gold asked.

"I don't know," Parson said, "but it wouldn't surprise me."

"I talked to the national police. They said he hasn't reported the kidnapping, and he had a clean record up until now. No connections with bad guys."

"That doesn't surprise me, either. You know what's a

shame? He's actually a damn good pilot." So much about this sucked, and to Parson's mind, what sucked most was the waste of talent. Aamir hadn't started out as a criminal. But he'd been dealt a bad hand, and he'd played it the worst way possible. And now he was going to jail. It occurred to Parson that once again, he and Gold were escorting a prisoner. Different circumstances from last time, thank God. But bad enough.

He wondered how Rashid was coping in the other helicopter. The poor guy had lost two aircraft and a number of crew members all within a matter of days. Enough loss to get any aircraft commander to turn in his wings, but Parson doubted Rashid would do that. He'd come too far, worked and studied too hard, to throw it all away.

Gold and Aamir spoke again. The copilot's lips trembled, and a tear fell from his cheek. But then his face dried up, and they talked in what sounded like matter-of-fact tones. Maybe Gold was filling him in on Black Crescent, the videos, the statements from Chaaku. Parson couldn't think of much in that to offer hope, but the guy needed to know. And the more he knew, the more likely he could help. The more dots out on the page, the more likely the dots would connect. Son of a bitch better help, Parson thought, after what he's done.

That judgment was getting way out of Parson's field. He was an aviator, not a cop. The Air Force had an Office of Special Investigations for just this sort of thing. He supposed the OSI boys would want a long sit-down with Aamir. Parson hadn't noticed any OSI types around Mazar, but that didn't mean they weren't there. Some of them wore civilian clothes, and they had a way of turning up anywhere.

Up ahead the terrain flattened, and the lights of Mazar glowed like crystals on black velvet. So power had returned, at least for part of the city.

At the moment, the city looked so peaceful that Parson could hardly imagine Mazar had been the stage for one of the worst massacres in Afghanistan. Gold had told him how the Taliban tried to take Mazar in 1997 and got routed. Hundreds, maybe thousands of Taliban troops were killed in combat or executed as prisoners. When the Taliban rolled back into town the following year, they went on a payback frenzy for days, charging down the streets in pickup trucks, blasting away with automatic weapons. Witnesses told of bodies decomposing in the streets and dogs eating corpses. Thousands of Shiite Hazaras died before it was over.

The Pave Hawk banked and descended to set up an approach for landing. Parson tried to make his mind stop wandering, but his mind always wandered when he was tired. He looked forward to a shower and a good long rest before dealing with all this shit again in the morning.

When the chopper touched down, the bump startled him awake. Parson realized he had dozed off, leaning on Gold's shoulder.

❧ 16 ❧

Aamir watched the TV screen with a look of pure, undistilled hatred. In the secure room at command post, Gold sat with him as he viewed the first of the videos from Chaaku and Black Crescent. She hated to show him statements from the sword-wielding terrorist who might very well have abducted his son. But Aamir never hesitated; in fact, he wanted to get on with it.

To Gold's relief, Aamir had not appeared in a prison jumpsuit and shackles. He wore the same sweat-stained flight suit he'd had on last night. She didn't know what authority had decided that, but she considered it a good call. If they treated him like a military officer and crime victim instead of a perpetrator, maybe he'd act like an officer and help out. He had to face a reckoning for what he'd done, but that could wait.

Parson, Rashid, and an OSI agent stood by. "Has he ever seen this Chaaku guy before?" the OSI agent asked.

Gold felt sure Aamir had not, but she interpreted the question anyway.

"Never," Aamir answered in Pashto. "I never heard of this monster until today."

After Gold repeated the answer in English, the OSI man asked, "When did his boy go missing?"

More translation. "A little more than a month ago," Aamir said.

So the abduction had happened before the earthquake, Gold noted. Had Black Crescent been abducting kids for weeks now? If so, they might have used the natural disaster as a way to step up what they'd planned all along.

"Ask him what happened the day the kid was abducted," the OSI agent said.

Gold apologized in Pashto for having to ask the question, but Aamir cut her off.

"I do not deserve your respect," he said. "You may ask me anything in any way."

"You faced awful choices, Lieutenant," Gold said. "We understand that."

Aamir showed no reaction to Gold's remark, but went right to the question. "My son, Hakim, went to school that morning in Jalalabad as always," he said. "I was on the other side of the country, flying at Shindand Air Base. When I landed, there was a message from my wife saying Hakim had not returned home. By the time I reached her by telephone, she had received a *shabnamah*."

Gold explained in English that a *shabnamah* was a "night letter," a warning from terrorists. The letter told Aamir not to call the police, and instructed him to fly to a certain set of coordinates as soon as he had a mission with an American officer on board.

"So they did not seek Lieutenant Colonel Parson by name?" Gold asked.

"No," Aamir said, "they wanted any American. But they said the higher the American's rank, the more likely I would see my son again."

"What were they going to do with the rest of the crew?" Gold asked.

Aamir did not speak for a moment. "They did not say," he said finally. His lips began to tremble, and the color went out of his face. He looked over at Parson and Rashid. Rashid stared at him without any apparent emotion. Aamir lowered his gaze to the floor. "I am sure the crew would have been executed," he said. "Me, too, most likely. But I saw no other choice. By now, they have probably killed Hakim."

Gold translated everything Aamir had said while the OSI agent took notes. "I guess we need to show him the latest video," the agent said, "the one with the kids in it. Do you think he'll fall apart if he sees his son?"

"I don't know, sir," Gold said. "He thinks his son might be dead."

Rashid spoke up in Pashto. Evidently he'd followed the conversation in English well enough, but he had thoughts he could express best in his own language. Or maybe he just wanted Aamir to hear them straight from him. "I care not if the video makes him fall apart," Rashid said. "He must help."

"Captain, please—" Gold said.

"You are right, sir," Aamir said. "Show me this cursed video."

Gold nodded, and the OSI agent leaned over, clicked the mouse. The image came up on-screen. Before Chaaku even began speaking, Aamir slid from his chair and fell to his knees.

First he cried out in a moan of anguish that formed no words. Then, with his head on the floor, he shouted, "That is him! That is Hakim!"

Now even Rashid seemed moved. He placed his hand on his copilot's shoulder and said, "Tell us which one, Lieutenant. Show us your son."

Aamir sat up, coughed, wiped his eyes and face with the sleeve of his flight suit. He pointed to the computer and said, "To the immediate left of that monster. Dear God, they have placed upon him the head scarf of a martyr."

With another mouse click, the OSI agent paused the video. Gold looked closely at the boy beside Chaaku. He held an AK-47 with the magazine removed. His face bore no expression. The boy's resemblance to his father became clear now that Gold knew who he was. Hakim had that same penetrating gaze, something about the set of the eyes. In the video, he was looking at something offscreen. Probably an adult pointing a loaded rifle, Gold supposed.

"When was this made?" Aamir asked.

"Within the last week," Gold said. She had translated none of his last few words into English, but she didn't need to. It would have been obvious to Parson and the OSI agent that Aamir had identified his son.

"They will put a suicide vest on him and send him to his death," Aamir said. He began to wail again.

Rashid placed his hand on Aamir's back and said, "Allah is merciful, Lieutenant. He hears your cries."

God is merciful, but people are not, Gold thought. She could hardly imagine Aamir's pain, and she could hardly imagine a good end to this. And what of Fatima's brother, Mohammed?

"Is it not enough for my son just to be killed?" Aamir asked. "Must he die a murderer? Must he suffer?"

No words Gold knew could offer a decent answer to that question. So maybe she could get him to focus on other questions, more ways he could contribute. One thing she'd learned in her years of working with men: In bad situations, they felt better if they thought they had some control. If they faced a problem, you needed to give them something to do about it, no matter how insignificant. If they could do little to help, let them *believe* they were helping. Nearly all men shared that trait, whether they were American or Afghan, flyboys or ground-pounders. She couldn't give Aamir unrealistic hope, but she could get him to focus.

"Lieutenant Aamir," she said, "I know this is difficult, and I will not lie about the gravity of your son's circumstances. But you might be able to help him if we look at some things on a map."

"Anything," he said. "Please tell me anything I can do."

"Let us look at where those coordinates were, and where your helicopter went down."

"Yes, yes. Right away. I want a chart. Where are some aeronautical charts?"

In English, Gold explained what she was doing.

"Good job," Parson said. "I was going to ask him to do that anyway. Let me get a TPC."

Parson went into the flight planning room and came back with a Tactical Pilotage Chart. Gold didn't understand all the different kinds of aviators' maps, but she'd gathered that the white ones with a bunch of lines and circles were for flying on instruments. The colorful ones that depicted terrain were for visual flying. This map had color—mountains and valleys and streams.

Parson spread the chart across a table. He took a pencil from the pen pocket on the left sleeve of his flight suit, marked a spot on the chart.

"This is where we went down," Parson said. "Now, where was he trying to go?"

Gold asked the question in Pashto. With the pencil between his thumb and forefinger, Parson held it toward Aamir. The Afghan flier took the pencil and marked another location. As he looked up from the chart, he locked eyes with Parson. To Gold's relief, Parson did not seem angry or even surprised. He just took back the pencil and placed it in his sleeve. Judging from the scale reference on the chart, only a few miles of ground separated the two points. No wonder the insurgents had seen the Mi-17 go down and had attacked so quickly.

Both pencil marks fell within a spur of mountains called *Kuh-e Qara Batur*. Gold examined the spur's contour lines. The contours ran closely together, indicating steep terrain. The ridge base at the valley floor lay at an elevation of two thousand feet, and the mountain's peak topped out at 5,692. Just a hill, by Afghan standards.

"Have you ever been to that location?" Gold asked in Pashto.

"Never," Aamir said. "They did not even tell me if there was a flat spot to land."

What Gold really wanted to know was whether Black Crescent hid there, in a compound or cave complex. Or was it just a random spot they'd chosen for this single purpose? No way to find out quickly. To Aamir, the location was just a set of coordinates.

On a thread of hope, she thought back to her conversation with Mullah Durrani's wife. If Gold ever got to talk to Durrani himself, perhaps she could ask if there was something in *Kuh-e Qara Batur*. As an old mujahid, Durrani would know about all the old caves and forts that insurgents might use. But if she asked, would he just turn around and warn Black Crescent?

Tomorrow she would visit Durrani's wife again. The woman had said she'd have an answer about a meeting with her husband. That whole exercise could turn out to be a waste of time or worse. But Gold knew only one way to find out.

Once again, Parson found himself in Gold's world. Riding in the Cougar MRAP, even his clothes felt strange. For this ground mission, he wore MultiCam fatigues—officially known as the Operation Enduring

Freedom Camouflage Pattern—instead of his usual flight suit. He'd been issued one set of MultiCams for this deployment, though he'd never expected to use them. Just free hunting clothes for later, Parson had thought. He'd not even bothered to get the cloth wings of a command pilot sewn onto the shirt. Body armor hid that oversight. No one could see he was technically out of uniform.

Blount and his driver rode up front. A gunner stood in the turret. A second MRAP, another Cougar, carried more Marines. Parson rode with Gold in Blount's vehicle, and Gold introduced him to the Marine Corps Lionesses, Ann and Lyndsey.

"Did you have any trouble getting permission to come with us?" Gold asked Parson.

"Yeah, a colonel with Joint Relief Task Force gave me a ration of shit. Said this fell outside my role as an Air Force adviser. He didn't even like it that I'd let you go last time. But I told him it might lead to the people who took Aamir's boy."

"So if it's the business of the Afghan Air Force, then it's your business," Gold said.

"Ah, I didn't put it quite that well, but that's kind of what I said."

He'd actually used words he shouldn't have uttered to a superior officer, but he'd made them a little more acceptable by adding a *sir* at the end. Eventually, the task force commander had seen the logic and told him he could go as long as he filed a full report.

The armored vehicles rumbled through the airfield

checkpoint and out onto the road. Overhead, the rotor-and-turbine pulsing of helicopters rose above the Cougar's diesel. Parson looked up to see a flight of three Mi-17s climbing toward the south. More loads of rice and Unimix, he knew. People had to eat. Parson didn't have Gold's understanding of cultures and history, of human nature and spirit. But he'd seen enough to know that some of the most powerful tools of foreign policy were a bowl and a spoon.

With Mazar receding behind him in the dust, Parson felt vulnerable, out of his element. Here on the ground, roadside bombs presented a constant danger; Gold and the Marines had received a loud reminder of that. Certainly there were plenty of ways to die in the air, but Parson had training and experience to handle those risks. Ground threats seemed more sinister. However, if Gold was going to take these kinds of chances, he wanted to go with her.

Beside him, Gold took off her helmet and untied her blond hair. She shook it out with the fingers of both hands. Parson liked how her hair fell around her shoulders. As she tied it back into a ponytail, Parson glanced down at her helmet on the floor. She had written something in black marker, tiny script on the inside liner. Soldiers often did that. Many wrote their blood type, for obvious reasons. Parson had also seen girlfriends' names, *Remember 9/11*, and *Gotcha Osama*. But this was different—two lines of poetry, something vaguely familiar. Parson thought he might have read it in an English class long ago, though he had no idea who wrote it:

Because I could not stop for Death—
He kindly stopped for me—

Gold caught him looking. "Emily Dickinson," she said as she put the helmet back on and snapped the chin strap into place. "It reminds me not to get careless."

She's too smart to get careless, Parson considered. But he liked the way she could find, in all the stuff she'd read, thoughts that cut to the heart of issues they faced. Parson's own reading seldom ventured beyond flight manuals, newspapers, and *Field & Stream*.

He wondered what experience had inspired that poem. In his own life, he'd come to understand the truth of those lines. Death sure as hell didn't care what plans you'd made. Parson just hoped Gold's musing on the subject didn't mean she'd taken some dark turn in her thinking. She'd seemed different on this deployment, with an undercurrent of sadness. You could hardly blame her, given all the things she'd witnessed. He just wished she'd stop owning all the problems in Southwest Asia. Too big a mission for anybody.

For now, though, she appeared okay. Gold and these Marine Corps women seemed to have hit it off pretty well, too.

Blount turned in his seat to face Parson. "Sir," he said, "we're taking mostly a different route than what we used coming and going last time. But it'll be the same for the last couple miles. There's only one road into that village."

"I'm sure you know what you're doing," Parson said.

He appreciated being kept informed, but the update didn't make him feel more secure.

Parson decided to focus on things he could control. If this op produced some actionable intelligence, what would he do with it? Well, if it led to a fix on where this Chaaku jackass hung out, maybe he could arrange for a little visit. Ideally, Parson thought, from the Spectre gunship that had rained down so much fire two days ago. Parson could not order such a strike himself, but with decent intel he could make a strong case for it up the chain of command.

The Spectre's terrible majesty reminded him of a bird of prey. Thinking of it now, he remembered seeing a red-tailed hawk make a strike—and perform what to Parson was amazing flying. He'd been sitting in a deer stand last fall. His rifle in the crook of his arm, the air spiced with the smell of autumn woods, he saw the hawk plunge through the trees. At maybe a fifty-degree dive angle and at God only knew what airspeed, the bird snatched a squirrel from a fallen log and zoomed up in an escape maneuver. But a hickory tree blocked the egress route. The hawk's tiny brain made an instant calculation worthy of the newest avionics: *The bank angle required to miss the tree causes too high a load factor at my current weight. If I jettison my payload, I can make it.* The hawk dropped the squirrel, made a hard right turn, missed the hickory, and disappeared. When Parson climbed down from his stand, he examined the squirrel. Though the hawk's talons had clutched it for no more than a second, the rodent was stone-cold dead.

That image gave Parson an oblique comfort. He looked forward to taking this fight back into the air one way or another. Find out where Black Crescent hid, then get a Special Tactics Team in there and call down some fire and steel.

The Cougar lurched through a gully. Parson braced himself against the vehicle's pitch and roll, thought of roadside bombs. But no boom came; it was just a lousy road. He'd heard somewhere that Chechen and Uzbek jihadists were especially skilled at building IEDs. No doubt some of them were plying their trade in Afghanistan right now. Gold and the Marines showed no reaction to the Cougar's bouncing. Unfortunately, he thought, they knew the difference between hitting a rut and hitting a bomb.

He looked outside through the louvered window. Morning mist clung to a hillside, but above the hill the sky was clear. Two specks appeared on the horizon. As they grew larger, Parson recognized them as a formation of C-17 Globemasters. They flew low, but not on a course for landing at Mazar. An airdrop run, then.

Their heading took them on a path diagonal to the road, drawing nearer. Now Parson could make out their cargo ramps coming open. From inside both aircraft, pilot chutes blossomed, and then an object slid out of each jet. Twin pairs of main chutes unfurled above the objects. Probably some kind of heavy equipment airdrop. Not the way you'd usually drop relief supplies. By airlift standards, food didn't weigh much. This drop was artillery pieces or ammunition, maybe. Crews with a different mission, different problems. Parson turned away from the window before the loads hit the ground. He had his own mission to consider.

The MRAP vehicles rolled past barren rock, terraced fields, stony hills. Gold and the Marines rode quietly, perhaps considering what might await them. From the start, Parson had wondered if they were driving into an ambush. But he trusted Gold's instincts; she knew about these Afghan villagers. And even if you were a villager who hated Americans, Parson thought, you probably wouldn't set up an ambush if the Americans knew where you lived. He clung to that hope as the vehicles stopped about half a mile from the village.

Blount opened his door, scanned the compound with binoculars. The Cougar's ramp clanged open, and Gold climbed down to look toward the village. She shaded her eyes with her hand. Blount gave her the binoculars. Gold looked through them for a minute, handed them back.

"What do you think, Sergeant Major?" Blount asked. "I don't see any muj."

"Looks just like it did a couple days ago," Gold said. Then she looked at Parson. "Sir?"

Parson borrowed Blount's binoculars, looked for himself. The homes resembled every other mud-brick and stone compound in Afghanistan. He saw no movement, no telltale glints of metal, nothing to suggest hidden jihadists. That didn't mean they weren't there, but Gold seemed satisfied. She was just deferring to his rank.

"Let's go visit the neighbors," Parson said.

❧ 17 ❧

The Cougars moved into position so their guns could cover the village. Gold knew those weapons wouldn't do her and the Lionesses much good if this meeting went badly. But her gut told her not to worry about that.

She stepped down the vehicle's ramp. As before, Ann and Lyndsey held back. Gold wanted to see what kind of reception she got before bringing anyone else inside.

The same white Taliban flag hung from the home of Durrani's wife. Last time, the flag had fluttered in the high wind, but now it swayed gently in a lighter breeze. None of the villagers appeared outside. A goat tied to a pistachio tree eyed Gold as she walked toward the door. In the distance, a rooster crowed.

Her confidence grew with every step. If men with RPGs and rifles lurked inside the homes, she'd be dead already. In the mathematics of military doctrine, threat equaled capability plus intent. Durrani and his associates certainly had the capability of setting up an ambush. So it appeared, at least for now, they did not have the intent.

Gold knocked at the door. The smell of cooking wafted from inside; she took that as another good omen.

"Good morning, my sisters," she said in Pashto. "It is Sergeant Major Gold."

Women's voices muttered in Pashto, crockery rattled, and the door swung open. Durrani's wife stood at the threshold in her blue burka. Gold recognized the crow's-feet around her eyes.

"*Salaam*, American," the woman said.

Gold wondered if the woman had ever put those two words in the same sentence. "*Assalamu alaikum,*" she said. She waved to the MRAPs, motioned for Ann and Lyndsey to join her. Parson watched from the open ramp, Beretta in hand. So he was in full protective mode now. The attack dog side of him. I know what I'm doing, Michael, she thought. Trust me—and don't point that gun at the house.

The Lionesses joined Gold at the doorway, sunglasses off, rifles left behind. They nodded greetings to the Durrani matron. Gold liked the way they worked. Certainly the United States had done some dumb things in Afghanistan, but creating these female engagement teams was brilliant. She remembered the original memo on the Lioness project. Under the heading of UNCLASSIFIED/FOR OFFICIAL USE ONLY, the memo outlined the concept and its execution. The best-qualified women volunteers would get briefings on counterinsurgency and Afghan culture. By law, they could not be assigned to combat units. So they weren't *assigned*; they were *attached*. In war, you did what you had to do.

"Come inside," the matron said. "My daughters and I hope you will join us later for our midday meal."

"That is very kind of you," Gold said. "We shall." Though Gold had not expected the worst, this kind of hospitality surprised her. Apparently she still had things to learn about Muslim attitudes toward strangers and travelers. And if this woman thought of her as a traveler instead of an enemy, that represented progress. The war had brought so many setbacks, so many disappointments. If now it presented an opportunity, Gold didn't want to waste it.

She entered the home with Ann and Lyndsey, sat with the woman on her jute rugs. The two daughters tended cooking at the hearth. One of them bent to a low table and began cutting potatoes. She dropped the potato slices by the handful into an iron pot suspended over the fire.

Whatever the women used to season the food— peppers, maybe—gave the room a pleasant smell, but the fire made the house uncomfortably warm. Gold removed her helmet and gloves. From a cargo pocket on her trousers she took a brown desert scarf. She folded the Army-issued cloth into a *hijab* and tied it over her hair. Sweat still beaded on her face, but the scarf felt a little cooler than the Kevlar helmet.

"You came for an answer," the wife said. "My husband will see you."

Gold smiled, took a deep whiff of the potatoes and peppers. She had begun to wonder if this whole thing was *diwana*. Crazy.

"I am more grateful than I can express," Gold said. Then she added, in English to Ann and Lyndsey, "Yes." The younger women said thank you in Pashto. They didn't know enough of the language to say much else.

"He requires that you visit him alone," the matron said. "You must bring no soldiers, no weapons."

Gold's smile faded. Of course there was a catch. This was Afghanistan, where nothing came easily. The Army, the Air Force, Parson, the whole chain of command would never let her go alone to a meeting with a Taliban cleric. Suicide, they'd say. So getting her hopes up really had been *diwana*.

She tried to mask her disappointment. At least she could share a meal with this woman, make a village contact.

"Your help is most gracious," Gold said, "but I must be honest. My superiors will not likely allow me to attend this meeting alone."

"I thought as much," the woman said. "But this condition is not negotiable."

And why would it be? If I were a former Taliban leader, Gold thought, I wouldn't invite a platoon of Americans to see me, either. From his point of view, that would amount to a one-way ticket to Guantánamo. It was astounding that Durrani would agree to a meeting under any conditions.

"I understand your husband's concerns," Gold said. "I wish things were different, but this is the world in which we live."

"This is what we have made of the world," the matron

said. She met Gold's eyes. Then she turned to her daughters and asked for tea.

Gold considered the woman's last statement, savored the wisdom of it. No talk of *inshallah*, how it's the will of God and we can't help it. No blame, either, though the woman probably had strong opinions about that. What other silenced wisdom existed among the women of Afghanistan? Maybe in this case it wasn't so silent. Durrani apparently let his wives—or this one, anyway—talk to him about important matters.

Though Gold had no sympathy for the Taliban, she had learned not all Talibs thought alike. Maybe a few could be reasoned with. Gold hoped so. The only other way to win the war was to kill them all.

"How long have you been married to Mullah Durrani?" Gold asked.

The woman looked at her for several seconds, and Gold feared she'd asked too personal a question.

"Thirty years," the matron said finally. "He had just completed his studies when we wed."

Well, there was a good bit of information. At least Durrani had studied somewhere. Many Taliban imams had little in the way of credentials, could barely read. His schooling alone set him apart.

"Are you married?" the woman asked. She took a cup of tea from one of her daughters, motioned for the three Americans to be served.

"I am not," Gold said as she took her tea. The matron nodded as if she'd expected that answer. Gold asked where she was from. Kandahar. They spoke of their homes; Gold told her of Vermont's Green Mountains. Eventually the wife said, "Our meal is ready."

The daughters ladled stew from the kettle and poured it into bowls. When they set Gold's dish before her, she noted with surprise that the stew contained meat as well as potatoes and peppers. *Murgh*, as the locals called it. Chicken.

Steam rose from the first spoonful. She blew on it for cooling, but it burned her tongue a little anyway. Hot from the peppers, as well, but not too much. She could have used ice water, but she made do with the green tea.

"This is excellent," Gold said. "We thank you for this meal."

The women ate in silence. Gold contemplated what she had arrived at here. A brief moment of intersecting interests, perhaps. A patch of common ground never anticipated, not charted on any map. She'd visited scores of villages, talked with hundreds of tribesmen and -women. But she'd never gone this deep, sharing a meal with the wife and daughters of the enemy. Or maybe the former enemy. To get this far and not use it . . .

Gold placed her spoon in the bowl and looked over at the matron. "Madam," she asked, "in the unlikely event I am allowed to meet with your husband, how may I find him?"

"There is a telephone number you must dial. The mujahid who picks up this telephone will answer such questions."

The woman reached into a pocket inside her clothing, produced a folded scrap of paper. She handed it to one of her daughters, who passed it to Gold.

"We have lived so long in *Darul Harb*, the house of war," the matron said. "I for one wish to enter *Darul Amn*, the house of peace."

When the meal ended, clouds hung low outside like a sheet of steel. A slanting rain swept the shoulder of the mountain that overlooked the village. Gold said her good-byes and led Ann and Lyndsey back to the vehicles. As the rain began to fall on the village itself, the first drops struck earth so dry, their impacts left puffs of dust.

S ophia was coming unglued. Now Parson felt sure of it. She'd done a hell of a job following up on the tip that led her to a mullah's wife. Good on her for that—it was why the taxpayers had spent so much teaching her the language. But to take seriously the thought of meeting alone with a former Taliban official? Of all people, Gold should know what happened to Americans in Taliban hands. She should know it right down to her fingertips. So on the ride back to Mazar in an MRAP lumbering through hard rain, Parson gave his answer: "Fuck no."

Gold did not argue. She said only, "I understand, sir."

"If Emily Dickinson reminds you not to get careless, what would she say about this?" Parson asked. Gold shrugged. For her, a rare gesture.

"Sounds like they want a high-value hostage," Blount said from up front.

"I really didn't get that feeling," Gold said, "but I can see the security concerns."

The dumbest private in the Army could see the security concerns, Parson thought. Then he said, "They tried to get *me* as a high-value hostage."

"Due respect, sir," Ann said. "That was Black Crescent. Mullah Durrani has nothing to do with them as far as we know. In fact, it sounds as if he doesn't like them."

Sophia Gold Junior, Parson thought. These Marine women would probably grow up to give good advice to some jarhead commander. But Parson had made up his mind. He'd rescued Sophia from terrorists once. He wasn't going to have to do it again. Fuck this whole stupid idea.

During the rest of the drive, Parson turned his thoughts to other responsibilities. Maybe he could get another Mi-17 and crew sent up from Shindand so Rashid could keep flying. All available aircraft were needed to help move the relief supplies still piled up at the Mazar Airport. He'd seen pallets of lumber, too, for rebuilding villages. A good thing, if the aircraft could get the lumber distributed. Move people back into their homes before the cold weather. Parson wasn't a public health expert, but he'd been around this kind of work enough to know you didn't keep people in refugee camps any longer than necessary. The close quarters of those camps invited disease.

As the Cougars rolled up to the airport, Parson had his head down, going over notes in his pocket calendar: *Call Shindand. Weight of lumber? NOTAM for runway repair? Flying time waivers.*

He looked up when he heard Blount say, "Oh, shit." The Cougar lurched to a stop.

Black smoke boiled up from within the airfield perimeter. Sirens screamed. The flashing lights of fire trucks and ambulances strobed across the base.

American security policemen blocked the main gate. A sign at the guardhouse read FPCON DELTA. Force protection level Delta. Attack imminent or in progress. The SPs held their weapons ready, not quite pointed at the vehicle's windshield, but close enough to open up immediately. The sentries would assume nothing about anyone trying to get into the base. Terrorists loved to detonate secondary bombs and wipe out rescue workers.

"I need to see everyone's ID," one of the SPs said. He looked about nineteen and scared. Parson pulled out his wallet, withdrew his card, passed it forward. Gold and the Marines did the same.

The security policeman checked both sides of all the ID cards. Another SP checked underneath the vehicle. Finally, the first SP said, "Proceed."

Parson took back his ID and asked, "What happened?"

"Suicide bombing. We don't know how or when he got in."

Shouting and wailing came from the refugee tents on the airfield. Gold leaned forward to look. "How many are hurt?" she asked.

"We don't know, ma'am," the SP said. "Too many."

"Let's get moving," Parson said. He slapped the back of the driver's seat. "Go."

Both the armored vehicles rolled through the entry

point. The SPs chained the gate shut, and the Cougars turned left onto the parking apron. From this angle, Parson could see the bomb had detonated within the refugee tents.

"Oh, my God," Gold said. "Stop. Let me out here."

The driver stepped on the brakes, opened the ramp. A burning odor filled Parson's nostrils. Gold grabbed her rifle and descended the ramp in two steps, ran for the tents. Parson unsnapped a first-aid kit from its mount inside the vehicle and followed Gold at a jog. Blount and the Marine Corps women caught up with him.

Outside the tents, the medical people had already set up a casualty collection point. A French doctor in blue overalls kneeled among a row of wounded lying on the ground, perhaps two dozen. Farther down the row, Reyes worked with another pararescueman. He held down a screaming man while the other PJ applied a tourniquet above the patient's elbow. Below the elbow, mangled flesh hung from a few inches of bone that ended in a sharp point.

"Fatima!" Gold shouted. Then some words Parson could not understand, and again, "Fatima!" She stopped, looked around, called once more for Fatima. Checked inside a tent, left it, disappeared inside another one.

"What can I do?" Parson asked Reyes.

"Do you know how to make a splint?"

"Yeah."

Reyes pointed to an Afghan boy sitting up, crying, and holding his hand. "Splint that kid's wrist, sir."

Parson made his way over to the child. His face and arms bled from cuts and scrapes. Flying debris, Parson supposed. The boy's left wrist displayed an unnatural bulge, and a dark bruise had formed around the bulge. Parson kneeled beside the child and opened the first-aid kit. He put his hand on the boy's shoulder. The boy turned away, shielded his arm.

"Let me help you, son," Parson said. "I know how much that hurts." He knew the kid didn't understand him, but he hoped it would help to talk anyway. And he knew well the boy's pain. After getting shot down during a winter storm years ago, Parson had trekked through the mountains with Gold for days, all the while nursing a cracked wrist.

Inside the first-aid kit, he found a roll of KERLIX gauze. Now he needed something with a straight edge to immobilize the wrist. Parson got up and searched among the tents—some collapsed, some torn and burned. One of the fallen tents had a wooden floor. With the toe of his boot, Parson kicked at the splintered planking. He found two lengths of cracked wood he could use for a splint.

As he stooped to pick up the lumber, he noticed a lump of some wet substance on the ground. It took a moment for him to realize it was charred human flesh, blown away from the bone.

Around him, medics and nurses moved among the injured, stopping to treat some, abandoning others. Parson had made hard calls in his life, but he did not envy medical workers the rapid-fire decisions of triage: *This one has a chance; give him a tracheotomy. That one won't make it; just leave him alone.*

In the midst of the wounded, Parson heard not just

their screams but a steadier undertone of groans through gritted teeth, cries with no syllables, no form but the breath required to utter them. The moans of the dying.

Shake it off, he told himself. He stepped around tent stakes, lumber, and corpses. So much blood smeared the pavement, it looked as if an aircraft had blown a fitting and dumped red hydraulic fluid across the tarmac.

When Parson returned to the casualty collection point, the Afghan boy still cradled his broken wrist. Parson sat beside the child and tore off strips of gauze.

"Let's see it, now," Parson said. He wished Gold were with him to talk to the kid, but she was still looking for Fatima. Though he didn't see Gold, he heard her calling the girl's name.

Parson placed his hand on the boy's arm. "Let go," he said. "You're a tough kid. You can do this."

The boy took his hand off the injured wrist, held his arm out to Parson. He sniffed, tried to stifle his crying. Parson felt compelled to keep talking. Maybe it was helping.

"That's it," Parson said. "We're going to make what we call a splint." Using some of the gauze as padding, he placed one piece of wood under the child's arm. That must have hurt; the kid cried out but did not jerk away.

Trying to be more careful, Parson put the other board over the arm and secured it with gauze strips. He didn't want to cause more pain by squeezing the injury between the boards, so he tied down the splint just enough to immobilize the wrist. "You're doing good," Parson said. "Tell you what. You study hard in school and then come fly with us. We can use tough guys like you." The boy looked at Parson with what seemed like interest, as if he actually understood the words.

Just a few yards from Parson, Reyes's patient had stopped screaming. Reyes gave him an injection, checked his pulse.

"Have you seen Rashid?" Parson asked.

"Flying, sir," Reyes said. "We've already sent some of the most critical to hospitals. He rounded up enough crew to get a chopper in the air."

"Damn. Good for him."

Gold still called to Fatima, more distant now. Finally, he heard the girl's high-pitched shriek: "Sopheeeeeeeeah!" Thank God for that, at least. He would have hated for the girl to get killed, hated what that might have done to Sophia.

Parson stood, tried to think of words he'd heard from Sophia that he could say to the boy with the injured wrist.

"*Salaam*," Parson said. Wondered if he'd said it right.

"*Salaam*," the boy answered.

Parson left the child to wait for more expert help. Along the rows of tents he saw some of the Marines. Blount, Ann, Lyndsey, and a corpsman searched for more of the wounded. The corpsman pointed, shouted instructions, dropped his medical bag, and kneeled by an injured man.

Farther into the encampment, Parson found Gold with Fatima. Gold led the girl by the hand, steered her away from the dead and wounded.

"You got your hands full," Parson said. "Want me to take your M4?"

"Please." Gold passed the rifle to him, hugged Fatima, said something in the child's language.

"Is she okay?" Parson asked.

"She's pretty scared, but she's all right. When I got her calmed down, the first thing she wanted to know was if the giant black man and my pilot friend were hurt."

Fatima looked up at Parson. "I'm good, honey," Parson said. "So's your buddy Blount."

"What about the others?" Gold asked.

"Reyes is over there. And Rashid's in the air. Scrounged up a crew and already flew out some wounded."

"Thank goodness. Butcher's bill is high enough today as it is."

"How bad, do you think?" Parson asked.

"I counted eleven dead, and I wasn't even looking for them. I was just looking for Fatima."

Parson noticed Air Force security policemen and Army MPs searching among the refugee tents. The men scanned the ground, seemed to look for evidence. At the edge of the camp, four of them gathered around something they'd found on the pavement.

"You two stay here," Parson said. "I want to see what those guys are looking at."

As he neared the four policemen, he began to hear their conversation.

"That's the most fucked-up thing I ever seen," one said.

"It happens," another said. "I've seen it in Iraq."

"Me, too," said the third. Of the four, he was the most senior. A tech sergeant. "Hajji detonates himself. The head goes flying, but it stays pretty much intact."

Down at their boots, Parson saw the severed head of the suicide bomber. It rested on its side, cheek to the pavement. Both eyes remained open wide, as if caught in a moment of surprise. No beard stubble. A boy of about twelve.

❖ 18 ❖

Even before all the wounded were treated, the OSI began investigating the bombing. Inside the air ops center, Gold interpreted for three terrified Afghan gate guards. None looked older than twenty. One trembled as he sat at the table with the other two.

"Will I be imprisoned?" he asked in Pashto. The man looked at Gold with the eyes of a frightened animal.

Gold wasn't sure of the answer, so she said only what she knew: "They have not handcuffed you, Private. Because you are not bound, they are treating you as a witness and not a suspect." She meant for that statement to give the young man relief, but his shaking did not stop.

This OSI agent was not the one who'd questioned Aamir, and he did not give his name. He began by saying in English, "Gentlemen, I ask that you tell me the truth. Whatever you've done or not done, telling me the truth might not improve your situation. But I promise it will not make it worse."

The agent never shouted or threatened. Gold appreciated his manner, but if anything that just seemed to scare
the guards more.

"Please tell him we are not terrorists," the trembling
man said.

The OSI agent placed a photo on the table. The picture
showed the face of the suicide bomber—eyes still open,
head ripped away at the neck by the force of the blast. Skin
remarkably unburned, with the smoothness of childhood.
A sight, Gold thought, that violated every notion of de-
cency in any kind of society.

"I do not remember that face," another guard said.

"Neither do I," the third said. "Truly, I would tell you
if I did."

Gold believed them. They'd probably paid the boy no
notice. And that's how he'd gotten in to kill eighteen people and injure thirty-four.

At the end of the interrogation, the agent said the
guards were free to go. The Afghans seemed hardly to
believe it when Gold translated that bit of news. Perhaps
they'd expected to be taken outside and shot. After they
left, Gold hung around the air ops center until no one remained in the flight planning room. Her cell phone displayed no signal, so she lifted the receiver of a landline
phone. She wondered for a moment if the line was monitored or recorded. Then she decided that was the least of
her problems. Fished the scrap of paper from her pocket,
unfolded it, and punched in the number.

The phone line hissed, clicked, popped. Phone service
remained out over much of Afghanistan, and she'd not

necessarily expected the number to work. But then it began ringing on the other end. After ten rings, Gold started to hang up. That's when someone answered. A male voice said only, "Yes?"

She put the receiver back to her ear, glanced through the doorway to see if anyone was coming in. No one was there.

"This is Sergeant Major Sophia Gold," she said. "I met with the wife of—"

The voice interrupted her. "I know who you are, American. You wish to speak with Mullah Durrani."

Gold collected her thoughts, tried to remember what she'd planned to say.

"That is correct," she said. "My superiors will not likely approve a face-to-face meeting. May we do this by telephone?"

"You may not. The mullah does not use electronic communication. If we allow this meeting, you will see him in person, and only on our terms. Is that clear?"

The answer she'd expected, but it had been worth a try. So she said only, "It is clear."

"Our terms are this: You will come alone. You will come unarmed. Needless to say, we will search you. If we discover anything that looks as if it might be a tracking device, we will kill you. Your body will never be found. We will make no claim of responsibility. You will simply disappear, and your friends and family will never know what happened to you."

The man sounded like an educated Pashtun. Perfect grammar, each word enunciated with precision. Probably middle-aged. As he issued his threat, he did not raise his voice, did not seem excited at the prospect of an easy kill. His tone lacked all bluster, but it lacked caution as well. He spoke with confidence. Gold knew she should not read too much into the sound of a voice on a scratchy phone line. But the man sounded like someone accustomed to taking life, though tired of it.

Careful, she told herself. Don't just hear what you want to hear. If you meet with these people, it could be the most dangerous mission you've ever undertaken. And even if the mission doesn't kill you, it could end your career.

"I understand," Gold said.

"If you agree to these terms, you will see the mullah tomorrow."

"I am not sure if—"

"Then you will not see the mullah." Still no raised voice, no contempt or irritation. Just a statement of fact.

"All right. Tomorrow. How may I find you?"

"You will arrive at the home of Mullah Durrani's wife and daughters at oh-nine-hundred local time. You will be blindfolded and driven to the mullah. Assuming you do nothing foolish, we will return you to your vehicle in time for you to get back to Mazar by nightfall."

Gold wasn't sure how to wrap up the conversation, what attitude to take. She opted for courtesy. It usually didn't hurt.

"It is kind of you to make these arrangements," she said.

A pause on the other end. Perhaps this was strange territory for him, too. The man said, "We do not act out of kindness, American. Know this: We bear you no goodwill at all. However, in this briefest of moments, we may have a common purpose."

"I believe we do," Gold said. She kept assessing what she heard. And she noticed what she *wasn't* hearing—the three words that had come out in nearly every other conversation she'd had with a Talib, usually a man in shackles: *Bitch. Whore. Infidel.* This man clearly did not like her, but he showed no disrespect.

"Please follow our instructions to the letter," the Talib said. "Otherwise, we will eliminate you."

Please? Whatever these people intended, it was certainly different. Without another word, the man hung up.

With Gold loaned to interpret OSI interrogations, Parson made do without her as he helped coordinate medical flights. An Afghan crew in a beat-up C-27A flew in from Herat and picked up a load of patients. Parson tried to talk to the aircraft commander, but the man spoke such poor English that conversation was impossible. He kept talking about grass, and Parson started to wonder if he was some kind of pothead who needed his wings taken away. Then Parson realized the poor guy was just trying to talk shop. The man had seen pictures of the new C-27J. The J model had computer-screen flight instruments—a *glass* cockpit, as fliers called it.

"I hope they get that model for you," Parson said. "Once you've flown glass, you'll never want to go back to round dials."

The man looked at him blankly. Figures, Parson thought. I let Sophia out of my sight and everything goes to hell.

An American C-130 picked up another load of patients—U.S. military personnel and European aid workers. The big turboprop growled off the runway and headed for Germany.

Rashid landed as the sun sank low on the horizon. Parson greeted him inside his aircraft as soon as the rotors stopped. At least Parson could converse with Rashid, however haltingly.

"Good work, buddy," Parson said. "You took some wounded to the hospital in Kabul?"

"We fly sortie," Rashid said. He unbuckled his harness, took off his helmet. His black hair looked matted and sweaty. Rashid's ad hoc crew—copilot, flight engineer, and crew chief/gunner—unstrapped and walked to the perimeter fence to smoke. Rashid watched them as if he wanted to go with them.

"The aeromeds have four burn patients they want to send to Kabul. You up for one more run?"

Rashid unzipped a flight suit pocket and found a shriveled pack of Marlboros. He took the one remaining cigarette, placed it between his teeth, nodded. As he rose from his seat, he patted his pockets until he found his lighter. He moved like he was tired.

He took the unlit cigarette from his mouth, held it in the same hand as his lighter. "We fuel, then we go," he said. Rashid wasn't good about the *sir*s of military courtesy, but Parson did not call him on it.

"I'll fly with you," Parson said.

Rashid brightened a little. "Very good," he said. Then he climbed out of his helicopter, joined his crew at the fence, and fired up his Marlboro.

A few minutes later a fuel truck rolled up to the Mi-17. The truck had TS-1 painted across the tank. TS-1 was a Russian jet fuel similar to American Jet A-1. Didn't really matter, Parson thought. Those Klimov engines would burn anything.

Rashid's crew chief dropped a cigarette butt, stepped on it, and walked back to the helicopter. Parson watched as the man connected the truck's hose to the aircraft and began pumping fuel.

After the truck drove away, an ambulance brought over the wounded. Reyes supervised as medics loaded the patients through the clamshell doors at the back of the aircraft. When Reyes closed the doors, Rashid and his crew strapped in. Parson and Reyes rode in the back with the patients as the helicopter lifted off into twilight.

In the soft light of early evening, the foothills seemed to anchor the mountains below. The pressure gradients that had kicked up such nasty winds earlier had gone away, and now the air lay calm. The Mi-17 flew as smoothly as a simulator set for zero turbulence, and Parson felt safe unbuckling his seat belt and standing at the rear of the cockpit.

Terrain flowed underneath, shadowy in clear night air lit by moonlight and stars. In the reflected glare of instrument lamps, Parson noticed what he thought was a crack in the windscreen. He stared at it until he realized it wasn't a crack but a strand of spiderweb, clinging to the glass at well over a hundred knots. Maybe someday, he mused, we'll figure out how to fabricate material as light and strong as a spiderweb. Then we'll build airplanes with it.

Rashid leveled off at altitude and turned over the controls to his copilot. He slumped in his seat a bit, adjusted his helmet's boom mike. Parson reached over the flight engineer and patted Rashid's shoulder. That guy was turning into a good officer.

"Tough week, huh?" Parson said on interphone. Helicopters didn't spend much time in cruise flight like this. He'd had almost no chance for small talk with Rashid in days. Parson held his interphone cord loosely with his right hand, the talk button between thumb and middle finger.

"Hard days," Rashid said. Rashid's English had improved since Gold's arrival. Parson didn't know if those two things were related.

"At least it's a nice night," Parson said.

Rashid stared out the windscreen, scanned his instruments, gazed outside again.

"It was a night like this that my father . . ." Rashid paused, perhaps searching for words. "Go away."

Parson said nothing for a moment. *Go away* could mean a lot of things, probably none of them good. Finally he said, "What happened?"

Rashid did not talk for a moment, just checked instruments again. Then he said, "My father—fight Taliban with General Dostum." He spoke in halting words. Parson wasn't sure if emotion or lack of vocabulary caused the frequent pauses. But he got the gist of Rashid's story.

During the 1990s, Rashid's dad served as a subcommander in Dostum's forces. Like Dostum himself, the old man was an ethnic Uzbek. One night he picked up his rifle and never came home. Rashid was fourteen.

Years passed before Rashid could piece together what happened. As he matured, he found witnesses and survivors. Their stories varied in some details, but in others they were consistent. Within the consistent parts alone, Rashid learned a story he wished he did not know.

In the summer of 1998, the Taliban pushed north and met Dostum near Maimana. The Talibs routed Dostum's army, but Rashid's dad managed to escape with a small combined force of Uzbeks, Hazaras, and some Tajiks. They hid out in the mountains for a few days, but eventually got caught in a U-shaped ambush.

The Taliban captured dozens of prisoners in the ambush. They loaded some of them, including Rashid's father, into a steel shipping container and drove them south into the desert. There they left the container, chained and padlocked.

When other captives were made to open the container three days later, the stench that rolled out put some of them on their knees, vomiting. All the men were dead, skin blackened by the heat. And they were the lucky ones. The Talibs skinned the Hazara prisoners alive.

Parson could not imagine what it was like to carry such knowledge of your father's fate. How could you think straight, focus on anything other than vengeance, feel anything other than rage? His own dad had died in the Gulf War, one of the relatively few U.S. casualties of Desert Storm. A jet crash, fiery but quick. A painful memory. But Rashid's kind of memories, Parson thought, would have a more caustic effect, corrode you from the inside.

The crew spent the rest of the flight in silence broken only by radio calls and checklists. Parson watched the stars crystallize into pinpoints of ice over ridgelines. As an old navigator, he knew how to use celestial bodies to find his way. Gold had told him how the fifteenth-century astronomer Ulugh Beg had built an observatory in Samarkand. His tables of stars held up pretty well even today. Such heights of learning and depths of brutality, Parson considered, all in the same corner of the world.

When the Mi-17 arrived over Kabul, all the city's lights were back on. The glow illuminated the valley that sheltered the capital. Rashid let the copilot take the landing, and the chopper descended toward Helistrip B1 near the terminal.

Parson had not visited Kabul since the earthquake, and from the look of the airport, supplies were still pouring in. The airport's ramp was sectioned into aprons with designations that made little sense to him. Apron 7A was right beside Apron 1. Pallets stretched across both of them and continued all the way down to Apron 6 at the far end of the field. Tarps covered most of the pallets, but as the helicopter touched down Parson could see some of the cargo included bags of cement, stacks of drywall. He wondered how much would go to rebuild villages and how much would get sucked up by graft. Someone else's problem, he told himself. You have enough of your own.

A bus with a red cross on the side met the aircraft. The aeromed team based at Kabul helped Parson and Reyes carry the wounded from the Mi-17 into the bus. All four patients appeared unconscious.

"Will they make it?" Parson asked Reyes as the bus drove away.

"Three of them might," Reyes said. "I'll be surprised if the other one lives through the night."

Rashid let his crew take a smoke break inside the terminal. Parson and Reyes remained with the aircraft. They spoke little, and Parson stared up into a sky turned jade by the glow of the airport lights.

By the time Rashid and his men returned, Parson was dead tired. He napped on the flight back to Mazar, went straight to his tent after they landed. Parson made a mental note to tell Gold about Rashid's father. But he did not see her in the mess tent at breakfast the next morning. At first that didn't concern him. He'd slept late and got to the chow line just before it quit serving. But after he ate, he saw no sign of her at her own tent or at the refugee tents. Gold was gone.

❧ 19 ❧

Gold started the morning tired. She had hardly slept the night before, thinking of all that could go wrong with what she was about to do. When she'd finally drifted off, the nocturnal sweats and bad dreams returned. But this time she'd not dreamed of captivity and torture. Instead, it was the parachute dream again.

That dream happened the same way every time. She exited the C-130 on a HALO drop, entered a perfect free-fall arch. When she pulled the rip cord she got a streamer: a mass of flapping nylon bound up so that it would not inflate. She reached for the cutaway pillow—and it wasn't there. She had no reserve chute.

As the sun rose now, she drove through the airfield gate in a Humvee checked out from motor pool. Outside the perimeter, alone and without her rifle, she knew she was jumping without a reserve. She had no backup plan, no options if this turned bad.

Diwana, she told herself. This is crazy.

Even if I get some good intel and make it back, she thought, they'll say PTSD skewed my judgment. Well, so what if it has? I do what I do because of things I've seen, things I'd like others not to have to see.

Gold turned off the blacktop and steered the Humvee on the same rutted path the Cougars had taken on the first trip. The vehicle had been upgraded with an Armor Survivability Kit, but it wasn't nearly as blast-worthy as a Cougar. If she hit an IED she'd have less protection—and no way to call for help. Given the Talib's warning about tracking devices, she'd signed out a Humvee that did not have a radio installed, and she did not carry a handheld radio. She had just her body armor, helmet, and MOLLE rig. The rig's pouches contained only writing pads, pens, and bottled water. Not even a knife. *Diwana*.

She drove past a dust-blown village of five homes. At one house, a child of about eight sat in the doorway. The boy wore a soiled brown vest and black pants, and he scraped in the dirt with a stick. Gold waved. The kid waved back but did not smile, then scratched in the dirt again. She wanted to believe he was drawing numbers or letters, perhaps doing arithmetic. But she realized he was probably playing with ants.

Whatever he's doing, Gold thought, he's as good a reason as any for what I'm doing. She considered the Talmudic teaching that had come to mind a few days ago: *To take one life is to kill the whole world.* She liked its inverse better: *To save one life is to save the world.*

What Parson would tell her now, she could well imagine. After he stopped yelling for her to turn around, he'd say, *You're not responsible for saving the world. You do your mission to the best of your abilities, you follow lawful orders, you watch out for those around you. If that's not enough, you can write a check to feed the starving. Maybe even volunteer for the mission to transport the food. But you don't go all renegade trying to beat a terrorist gang by yourself.*

Still, Gold never considered turning around and driving back to Mazar. Rattling along a back road in Afghanistan, she thought of Edmund Burke. She knew a quote attributed to him that he may or may not have said, but it was a great statement nonetheless: *All that is necessary for evil to triumph is for good people to do nothing.* Well, this might be idiotic, she thought, but I'm doing something.

The sun climbed higher as she drove along, brightening the blue dome of sky above her. Parson would call it a good day to fly. Maybe he and Rashid would get a mission today that might keep him busy enough not to worry about where she was. But no, she realized, he'll be angry no matter what.

Eventually she approached the place where the MRAP had run over the roadside bomb. Little remained of the MRAP but charred chunks of steel. The crater opened by the IED had been blown open wider by more powerful ordnance, whatever had been launched from the air. One of those attack aircraft with threatening names like Cobra or Thunderbolt had obliterated the vehicle. The blast had left the soil blackened and burned. The place still smelled of smoke and fire.

Gold steered to avoid the hole. Her right-side wheels sank into a ditch at the edge of the path, and for a moment she worried about getting stuck. But the Humvee had a high enough ground clearance to get over the stones on the lip of the ditch. The Humvee crunched over the rocks, fishtailed just a bit, continued along the roadway.

As Gold neared the village, her heart pounded. Soon enough she'd learn whether she'd entered a baited trap.

She topped a rise and saw the village in the distance. A pickup and three Land Rovers sat parked under the trees. Gold drove closer and saw the pickup was a Toyota Hilux. Two men and a woman stood beside the trucks. The woman wore a blue burka. The men wore *shalwar kameez* and striped turbans—not the usual white or black head-gear of the Taliban. Today, Gold thought, that really means nothing.

Both men held AK-47s. They carried them with the muzzles pointed up. Gold slowed, thinking. At least they weren't aiming at her. She braked, drove the last hundred yards at about five miles per hour. Did not want her ap-proach to look in any way aggressive.

She stopped about forty feet from the vehicles. Felt staring eyes upon her. Drivers waited in two of the Land Rovers; the other sat empty. Gold turned off her engine, removed her helmet, tied her desert scarf into a *hijab*. Whispered a prayer, opened the door, stepped out.

"*Salaam,*" she said. Hoped they did not hear her voice shaking.

"*Assalamu alaikum,*" one of the men said. Same voice she had heard on the phone. He looked at her with an expressionless face. Trimmed black beard flecked with gray. The other man was younger, with no silver in his whiskers or hair. Gold wondered if the younger man was Durrani's son.

"You will find I have followed your instructions," Gold said in Pashto.

"I hope so," the older man said. Then he gestured to the woman in the burka. "Search her."

Gold held out her arms for the pat-down. The woman looked into Gold's eyes from time to time but never spoke. She might have been one of the daughters Gold had met earlier, but it was impossible to tell.

The search was thorough but not rough. The woman took Gold by the arm and turned her away from the men to pat her chest. When Gold turned around again, the woman opened all the pouches in her MOLLE gear. She took Gold's pad and pens, handed them to the older man.

He unscrewed both of the ballpoint pens, examined the springs, dabbed the rolling points on the back of his hand. Apparently satisfied that the pens contained only ink, he reassembled them.

They weren't kidding about tracking devices, Gold thought. The man kept the pens and paper.

"You will not take notes today," he said.

Gold tried to weigh each action, every word. If he'd thrown her pens to the ground, that would have been a bad sign. But maybe they just wanted her to cooperate until they had her somewhere else.

The younger man opened the back door of the empty Land Rover. "Sit," he said. Gold stepped toward the vehicle.

"You are very brave or very foolish," the older man said.

"For now, I will assume the former. We will blindfold you now. Out of respect for your courage, if it is that, we will not bind your hands. But after we begin driving, if you even touch that blindfold, we will shoot you."

"I understand," Gold said. She took her seat. The Land Rover smelled of sunbaked upholstery. The younger man took a white cloth from his pocket, handed it to the woman in the burka. She folded it lengthwise and stood at the open door of the Land Rover.

Gold turned in her seat so the woman could tie the blindfold. When the cloth came over her eyes, Gold felt a flush of panic. Now she'd passed the point of no return; the loss of control was complete. Again she began to question her own judgment. Had she lost her mind? Too late to change anything now. Sweat oozed on her back, her neck, under her arms.

The woman knotted the cloth at the back of Gold's head, over the *hijab*. She tied it firmly, but not so tight that it hurt. Gold took deep breaths, fought her rising fear. She turned in her seat to face forward again, and someone closed the door beside her.

The two other Land Rovers started engines, and Gold realized their purpose. Decoys to head in different directions, in case American drones watched from the air.

Footsteps crunched on the dirt around the vehicle where Gold sat blindly. She heard the driver's door and the rear right passenger door open. Someone sat beside her and someone else up front. The doors slammed. The engine started. The vehicle began to move.

Gold sensed a left turn, and she made a mental note of

it, reminded herself to keep track of the turns. Then she realized that was pointless; they would no doubt take a circuitous route to make it more difficult for her to know where she was. The blindfold itched a little. She sat on her hands to resist any temptation to touch it.

The Land Rover rolled smoothly for a while until a rut bottomed out its suspension. Then more smooth road, then a washboard surface. No one spoke for a half hour.

"Where are your homes, gentlemen?" Gold asked. Couldn't hurt to try to make conversation.

No answer for a moment. Then the older man, sitting beside her, said, "We are not your friends, American. We will not engage in banter."

The rebuke didn't surprise her, so she just sat quietly. But it did surprise her when the older man apparently became bored after another thirty minutes. He said, "You speak Pashto well, American. I detect almost no accent."

"Thank you, sir," Gold said. "For a Westerner, Pashto is difficult to learn. But it is a language filled with poetry."

She let that sink in, take whatever effect it would. No response.

Another hour passed without conversation. The Land Rover slowed, bounced, spun its tires. Then it stopped.

"Remove your blindfold," the older man said.

F ear and anger. Familiar emotions for Parson, but never like this. Had Gold disobeyed his instructions? The thought made him furious. He didn't like giving her orders, anyway. He'd always thought her professionalism put her above direct orders. Now she might have betrayed that trust. Or worse, something else might have happened. She was well-known to the enemy. What if they'd finally caught up with her?

Parson found Rashid in flight planning. The Afghan officer was drawing a course line. He looked up from his charts and said, "We are scheduled—"

"Have you seen Gold?" Parson asked.

"No."

"She's disappeared."

Rashid stared. Confused look on his face.

"I think she might have gone to meet that mullah guy," Parson said.

The pencil fell from Rashid's hand.

"She go alone to Mullah Durrani?" he asked.

"It's the only thing I can think of. We had that bombing yesterday, and maybe she decided— Shit, I don't know."

"Do you report her disappeared?"

Parson thought for a moment. That would ring alarm bells from here to the Pentagon. Not the kind of attention he wanted, but he saw no other choice. He thought he had an idea of what Gold was doing. But all he knew for sure was that someone under his command was missing in a hostile area.

He picked up a phone and called command post, told them what he knew. Then he called the security police and the OSI. Several minutes later, the security forces commander—a captain—called him back.

"Sir," he said, "the gate guards say a woman in a Humvee drove out early this morning."

Parson slammed his fist down onto the flight planning table.

"Why the fuck didn't they stop her?" Parson asked.

"They had no authority to do so, sir. She's an E-9, after all."

Lame-ass excuse, Parson thought. "Do they have authority to use some fucking common sense?" he asked.

"I'm sorry, sir," the captain said. "We'll do all we can."

"You do that." Parson slammed down the phone.

The next call came from flight scheduling. Rashid would get to keep the copilot, engineer, and gunner he'd rounded up yesterday, but the supply sortie they were to have flown today was canceled. Now they would fly a search mission.

"I'm going with them," Parson told the scheduler. A statement, not a question.

He gathered up his flying gear. Parson slipped on his flak vest, donned a survival vest over it. Strapped on his thigh holster, checked that his Beretta was loaded. He got to the helicopter before anyone else.

To help the crew get ahead on the preflight checks, he looked around for hydraulic leaks. Examined the five blades of the main rotor and the three blades of the tail rotor. Though Parson was not a qualified Mi-17 crew member, he'd know a crack if he saw one. The rotors looked good. When Rashid and the rest of the crew showed up, they started the APU and began powering up the aircraft's systems.

Parson plugged his headset into an interphone cord, listened to the crew run through their checklists. He fought the urge to press his talk button and say something like *Hurry the fuck up*. At this point, rushing would serve no purpose except to make them miss something and cause an accident.

Finally, Rashid hit the starter buttons one at a time. Parson looked over the flight engineer's shoulder and watched temperatures and pressures come up, saw the engineer put the generators on line. He knew the crew was working as efficiently as possible, but the start-up procedures had never seemed to take so long.

With the engines on speed and the rotors turning, Rashid spread a VFR chart across his knees. He looked up at Parson and asked on interphone, "Do you think she go back to village?"

"That's the only spot I know to look," Parson said.

"Mullah Durrani may live other place," Rashid said.

"Maybe so," Parson said, "but we gotta start somewhere."

Rashid called for his takeoff clearance, lifted off from the airfield. The walnut-brown expanse of Balkh Province's plain stretched beneath the aircraft, at the foot of the mountains where seasonal streams drained toward Mazar. As the Mi-17 circled over the field, Parson scanned below for a lone Humvee. Nothing there. Rashid leveled on a heading for Samangan.

Cool wind whipped past the door gun and throughout the cabin. Parson closed his eyes and felt the air, tried to settle his mind. Then he adjusted the stems of his sunglasses under the ear seals of his headset. The seals were filled with gel, and if he found the right spot, the headset could clamp his shades into place. That way he could scan outside on a bright day like this without having the wind rip away the glasses. He stood in the rushing air, found a place where he could see over the crew chief sitting at the door gun.

Down below, two dirt roads twisted into the hills. No traffic moved on either of them.

"Rashid," Parson asked, "which of those roads goes into Samangan?"

Rashid checked his chart, conferred in Pashto with the copilot. "The one to left," he said. "It lead to village where Marines go with you and Sergeant Major."

"Let's just follow it. Maybe she's still on it somewhere up ahead." The village was less than an hour's flying time away, but Parson wanted to be there *now*.

Rashid nudged the cyclic to the left, banked slightly. He spoke again in his language and transferred control to the copilot. With his hands free now, he took off his gloves and held his right palm in front of the fan mounted on the top of his panel. Sweating hands, Parson noted, nervous pilot. Maybe he didn't like what this could turn into. If they found Gold, who else would they find?

Parson turned his attention back outside. From this altitude, he had a much better view of the region than during the drive with Gold earlier. Green ribbons of irrigated agricultural land stopped abruptly where terrain rose into knolls and crests, brown and lifeless. Scattered villages and compounds dotted with goats put Parson in mind of the Old Testament. Crumbling ruins also passed underneath, remains from deep antiquity. And still no sign of a Humvee.

Instinctively, Parson checked the navigational radios. Rashid still had his ADF tuned to the Mazar beacon. Now they were far enough from Mazar that the needle had lost the signal. It swung around its compass card, hunting for a beam. No navaid existed close to where Durrani's wife lived; they'd have to rely on Rashid's dead reckoning and Parson's memory of what the village looked like. Old Testament navigation, as far as Parson was concerned. He remembered the place had trees around it. All the villages he'd seen for the last few minutes had been treeless.

The terrain rose higher, became a little greener. Rashid checked his chart and pointed. The copilot banked to the right.

Rashid looked back at Parson, pressed his talk switch. "Is there?" he asked.

Parson bent his knees to see better out the windscreen. A copse of trees sheltered a collection of mud and stone houses. A dirt path led to the village.

It seemed right, but landscape viewed from the air could look entirely different from a ground perspective. The sun was high now, so at least long shadows didn't get in the way. Parson wanted a closer look.

"If you don't see any threats, drop down a few hundred feet," he said.

Rashid gave an order in Pashto, and the Mi-17 descended. And there it was—the back end of a Humvee, visible underneath the trees.

"That's it," Parson said. "I see her vehicle. Let's get on the ground."

The last time they'd come here, things had turned out

all right. Maybe all was well. He'd give Sophia a piece of his mind—not in front of anybody, though. Then he'd decide what to do. He'd try to keep this thing from going any higher up the chain than his own level. No Article Fifteen or anything like that. But he was so angry he was ready to send her home. She'd gone so far off the reservation, there was no coming back. When he gave a lawful order, he damn well expected it to be followed. What bothered him so much wasn't disrespect; he knew Sophia intended nothing like that. It was what might have happened to her.

The Mi-17 landed in a field just off the road. The field had lain fallow for at least a season, and weeds grew knee-high. The crew shut down the aircraft, and Rashid left his men to guard it.

With Rashid, Parson waded through the weeds toward the village. He stepped around a patch of milk vetch, a shrub with spiny seedpods and red flowers. Parson recognized it from photos on his evasion chart, tucked away in his survival vest. The chart, made of weatherproof Tyvek, included a guide to which plants were edible and which were poisonous. Under the photo of milk vetch, it read *DO NOT EAT ANY PART OF THIS PLANT.*

Just like before, the village seemed quiet. But this time, everyone in it had to know the military had just arrived. No covering the noise of a chopper landing.

Parson unsnapped his holster, rested his right hand on the grip of his Beretta. He and Rashid were armed only with their handguns, and they were in for a bad day if it came to a firefight.

No sound came from within the village but the cluck-
ing of chickens. As they neared the Humvee, they saw it
was unoccupied. No blood or signs of struggle. Tire tracks
all around.

"Son of a bitch," Parson said. "She might have left with
somebody."

Rashid raised his eyebrows. Apparently he didn't like
that any more than Parson did.

A Kevlar helmet lay on the Humvee's right seat. Parson
opened the door and picked it up. It was Gold's; he saw the
Emily Dickinson quote. It almost made him shudder. Had
she really written it there as a cautionary note? Maybe
she had a death wish. Sure seemed like it now. Or had her
dedication to this place and its people simply overtaken all
other considerations? Parson knew he was Gold's superior
in rank only, and it was a privilege to command someone
so talented. But their relationship, and their obligations to
each other, had evolved so far beyond the command structure that regulations seemed hardly to apply. He dropped
the helmet back onto the seat.

"Rashid," he said. "Do you want to knock on some
doors and ask if she's here?"

"Where she visit before?"

Parson pointed. "That house right there. Durrani's
wife. I want to know whatever she knows."

Rashid moved to the door, knocked softly. A woman
in a burka cracked the door, did not let him in. Long conversation in Pashto. No raised voices, but the woman
seemed emphatic about something. Finally the door closed.
Rashid walked to the Humvee and lit a cigarette.

"What did she say?" Parson asked.

"She say Gold go with men. She not know where."

"Bullshit," Parson said. "When did they leave?"

"She say she not know."

"More bullshit."

"And she say we must go away."

"Why?"

"She not say. She just say go."

"Fuck that," Parson said. "We're going to wait right here." Then he thought for a moment. "No, we're not," he added. "Let's get in the air and look for any kind of vehicle."

Rashid took a long drag on his cigarette, removed it from his lips, and flicked it away. He exhaled the smoke, waved to his flight engineer, made a twirling motion with his right hand. By now, Parson knew that private signal: *Start the APU; we're going flying.*

⋙ 20 ⋘

Gold pulled off the blindfold, squinted in the glare. When her eyes adjusted, she saw the Land Rover had stopped in front of a compound much like any other in Afghanistan, though perhaps a little larger. The main building was about the size of a twenty-man Army tent. Thick timbers supported walls of stone.

Rock fences adjoined the house, forming paddocks for sheep and goats. Two other houses connected with the fence lines, a network of stone. Terrain fell away in the distance, yielding to patches of green that looked to be irrigated from canals off a river. She tried to call up a map of Afghanistan in her mind, attempted to place the river. The Khulm, perhaps. Gold couldn't be sure, and at this point, the geography really didn't matter.

The younger man got out of the driver's seat and opened Gold's door. She stood as the older man came around the vehicle toward her. Still no threatening moves, no pointed weapons. At the door to the compound, two other Afghans stood guard with AKs. The guards were no more than thirty, and they scowled.

"So this is our hostage," one of them said.

The older man spun on his heel, faced the man who had spoken. "Silence, you fool," he said.

Gold's legs grew weak; she felt sick to her stomach. Had the man just revealed something too early? If so, for her, knowing came too late.

The guard who had not spoken knocked at a weather-beaten wooden door. A voice inside called, "Enter." The guard opened the door, and the older man led the way in.

Inside, a gray-bearded man sat cross-legged, perched on red pillows, at the far end of the room. A rug dyed in intricate patterns covered the floor. A rug not made of jute but of something finer, perhaps cotton or wool. At its center lay a depiction of the Kaaba, the sacred cube-shaped structure in Mecca, purportedly built by Abraham and his son Ishmael.

"I am Mullah Durrani," the man said in Pashto. "I bid you welcome." He motioned for her to sit. Gold and the older man who'd escorted her sat on the carpet.

On the wall behind Durrani hung a *jezail*, an antique muzzle-loading rifle, its stock inlaid with ivory. Gold knew the symbolism of the *jezail*. According to mujahideen legend, Afghans had defeated the Soviets with such primitive weapons, guided by the hand of Allah. But in reality the Afghan rebels had done their best work with Russian AK-47s and American Stinger missiles.

"I thank you for your time, sir," Gold said. "This meeting is out of the ordinary."

"Truly," Durrani said. "You have taken a great risk. In some ways, so have I. Some in my circle advised that we take you captive. And I considered it."

That admission did not surprise Gold, but it still frightened her. She thought for a moment, chose her words carefully. "But you opted for a different approach?"

"I did, for many reasons. For one, I did not wish to make my eldest wife a target for you Americans. For another, I must say I admire your courage, though you serve an infidel government. But most importantly, you wish to protect Afghanistan's young ones. So do I."

Gold wanted to move on to matters of hard intelligence and then get out. But she knew she had to avoid even a hint of impatience or rudeness.

"You honor me with your words, sir," she said.

Durrani adjusted the blanket he wore across his shoulders. Perhaps the woolen *patou* warmed his joints and made old injuries less uncomfortable. The seams across his forehead deepened as he considered his next point.

"As my associate has told you," Durrani said, "we bear you no goodwill. Do not make more of this meeting than it is. But this Black Crescent has gone too far. Jihad is for grown men."

"We agree that young ones should be protected," Gold said.

"Sergeant Major," Durrani said, "do you know my ancestry?"

Gold did not. *Durrani* was not an unusual name. That tribal tree had many branches.

"I know your name has a long history."

"It is that history to which I refer. I am a direct descendant of Ahmad Shah Durrani."

Gold knew that name. Many considered him the founder of Afghanistan as a nation. After the murder of the Persian emperor Nadir Shah in 1747, Durrani united tribal leaders and brought together the lands that became Afghanistan. He ruled for nearly thirty years and was laid to rest in an ornate tomb in Kandahar.

"That is a proud heritage," Gold said.

"Indeed. My ancestor was the father of this country. Now I must think as a father."

"When leaders consider the next generation, that is when they become statesmen," Gold said.

All right, she thought, maybe it's a bit much to call a former Taliban leader a statesman. But better to butter him up than antagonize him.

"And you wish to know what I can tell you of Black Crescent," Durrani said.

Now's the time to be simple and direct, Gold thought.

"Yes, sir," she said.

"I presume you know its leader, Bakht Sahar, from his videos. He goes by a ridiculous nom de guerre."

"Chaaku," Gold said.

"That is correct. He is an upstart who has begun working at cross-purposes to us. Villagers who lose their children will turn to anyone for help, even you Americans. And they may not see the distinction between Black Crescent and Taliban."

"So you feel Chaaku is giving you a bad name?"

"Exactly. You should understand something, American. Sooner or later you will leave our country. When you do, we will return to power. Your departure may happen in five years or fifty. But if the actions of Black Crescent drive the people into your arms, you will stay longer."

Gold could see the logic. This guy was brilliant in a twisted way. He thought far enough ahead to do something no other Talib could get away with. It amounted to his own innovation in military doctrine: counter-counter-insurgency.

And to achieve a short-term goal, however necessary, Gold was cooperating with someone fighting the longer-term goals of the United States. Well, war was messy in so many ways. She had studied the theologian Reinhold Niebuhr, who wrote of "the immoral elements of all historical success." Maybe this was what he meant.

"So we both seek the defeat of Black Crescent," Gold said.

"Yes. It is not so strange. With the mujahideen, I accepted aid from Americans to defeat what I then considered a worse enemy. That aid did not make us brothers and sisters."

Again Gold paused to consider her next phrase. What Durrani just said was probably the best opening she'd ever get. "If we knew where to strike," she said, "we could achieve this short-term mutual goal."

"Black Crescent does not telephone me with their plans. What do you know of them?"

Gold told him about the kidnapping of Aamir's son, Aamir's attempt to commandeer the helicopter and deliver Parson to terrorists.

"I heard of that incident. In all honesty, I wish the plan had succeeded. One less senior officer for the Americans would have been a blow for Allah."

Gold bristled at that remark, but she kept her feelings to herself. This was the enemy. Of course he wished the abduction attempt had succeeded.

"But what of Lieutenant Aamir's son?" she asked.

"Yes, that troubles me, as I have told you."

"Aamir tried to fly to a location along the *Kuh-e Qara Batur* mountain spur. Do you know of any stronghold there Black Crescent may be using?"

Durrani stroked his beard, seemed to consider the question. Gold wondered if he was searching his memory or just deciding whether to tell the truth. Then the expression on the old mujahideen commander seemed to soften.

"There is a fort, actually more of a ruin, near the southeast end of *Kuh-e Qara Batur*," Durrani said. "Beneath the fort is a small set of caves. In the 1980s, the soldiers of God dug out the caves farther, strengthened them with masonry. We worked long and hard in that place. We even brought in a generator and wired for electricity. There, doctors treated our glorious wounded, commanders held councils of war. The ruins obscure the cave mouth, which is why the Russians never found it. It would be difficult to spot if you did not know exactly where to look."

"So Black Crescent tried to make Aamir bring an American officer straight to their headquarters," Gold said.

"Possibly," Durrani answered. "That location would serve handsomely. But it would have been very sloppy tactics to bring an aircraft directly there, under any circumstances."

"Certainly," Gold said. She hoped a brief acknowledgment might prod Durrani to keep talking.

"Such mistakes are born of inexperience and arrogance. This Chaaku is cursed with both."

Gold waited to see if the mullah would say more. He sat silently for nearly a full minute. Eventually he said, "You must look for ruins that lie on a wide outcropping beneath a higher knoll. I know nothing else of tactical value to you."

"I thank you for this, sir."

"I believe I have told you what you need. Do not expect another meeting. Do not contact my wife again."

"As you wish, sir."

"Then leave me."

The older man who had escorted Gold rose to his feet and went to the door. Gold stood, nodded to the mullah, and stepped through the door held open by her escort.

Outside, the two guards glared at her, said nothing. The younger man who had driven the Land Rover sat in the driver's seat. Gold remembered the blindfold in her pocket. She took it out and handed it to the older man. He directed her to sit in the vehicle, and then he tied on the blindfold. The man pulled a little harder, tied a little rougher than the woman had, though Gold supposed he thought he was being careful.

She felt the door slam, the rush of air. A minute later, the Land Rover started and began to roll. They drove the route back to the village in silence. The day was warmer now, midafternoon, and Gold felt the temperature rising in the vehicle. No air conditioner, apparently. Maybe this would be the last warm day before fall deepened and led to the brutal Afghan winter. She lost track of time, but it seemed the better part of an hour passed as the vehicle bounced along.

She startled when a hand grabbed the blindfold. The Land Rover skidded to a stop. Someone yanked her head forward, tore the blindfold from her eyes.

For a second, the scene made no sense. She heard a helicopter, saw an Mi-17 landing on the road in front of the vehicle. Dust billowed from under the rotors; grit ticked against the windshield. Her older escort, who had sat beside her and had seemed so calm, took a handful of her hair and scarf with one hand. With another he held an AK-47 under her chin.

He jerked her by the hair so that her face turned toward the helicopter.

"What is the meaning of this?" he hissed.

B eretta drawn, Parson jumped from the helicopter, landed hard and flat-footed on the soles of both boots. He saw a door open on the Land Rover, and a man pulled Sophia out of the backseat. The turbaned bastard had her by the hair with one hand, and with the other he jammed a rifle barrel against her neck. Shouted in Pashto. Sophia gestured with her hands out, palms toward Parson. *Stop, stay calm,* she seemed to say. The driver sat frozen at the wheel.

Behind Parson, the crew chief trained the door gun on the Land Rover. Those terrorist degenerates had to know that if they shot Sophia, that gun would cut them into halves and quarters. But then it would be too late for her.

Parson aimed at the man holding Sophia, notched front sight into rear sight. He longed to put a round through the Talib's head and drop him. But at this range, maybe twenty yards, the distance was too great for that kind of precision with a pistol. Too much risk of hitting Sophia.

He didn't want the crew chief to be a hero, either—for the same reason. Parson took his left hand off his weapon. Held his hand out toward the helicopter, hoped the crew chief would take his meaning: *Hold your fire.*

It sounded like Sophia was yelling in English; Parson couldn't hear her over the helicopter noise. He glanced toward the cockpit, made a slashing motion under his throat. Rashid was peering forward, hands on the cyclic and collective. His helmet visor was up, boom mike across his lips. He appeared to give an order. The rotors and engines stopped, but the APU howled on.

Better, but still loud. At least Parson could understand Gold now.

"Don't shoot," she yelled. "It's all right."

"Bullshit it's all right," Parson shouted. "Tell that bastard to drop his rifle or I'll kill him."

Gold spoke to the man in Pashto. Whatever she was saying, it was too many syllables for Parson's simple command. Somebody was going to die here. He saw little way out of this without bloodshed, most likely starting with Sophia.

The man yelled at her, a long string of Pashto. Jerked her by the hair again, tipped his chin toward the Mi-17.

We're not a fucking debate society, Parson thought. Just let her go and maybe you'll live.

"He helped me," Gold said. "They're bringing me back from a meeting."

"What?"

"Durrani," Gold yelled. "They took me to Durrani. They're just bringing me back."

"How do I know he didn't just tell you to say that?"

"For God's sake, Michael, nobody needs to get shot here."

The man with the AK shouted again in Pashto. Gold answered with long sentences. Parson racked his brain, tried to think of a way to defuse this. But he hadn't heard enough to give him the confidence to lower his pistol.

"You violated orders," Parson said.

"I know it," Gold shouted. "I'm sorry. But they gave me information, and if you guys start shooting, I won't get to tell you."

What the hell was this all about? Parson inched closer, tried to shorten the range. Shooting still seemed like a good idea to him.

The man yelled in his own language, and Gold shouted, "Stop! He says don't come any closer."

Shit. So that wouldn't work. What else to do? Parson thought of something.

"Does he speak any English?" Parson asked.

"What?"

"Does that son of a bitch speak any English?"

"Only a little, I think."

Good. Maybe something he could use.

"If you're not telling me the truth," Parson said, "if he's just making you say all this, then use the duress word."

Apple. The duress code this week was *apple.*

"I'm not under duress, Michael," Gold said, "other than having an AK-47 in my face."

Parson thought for a moment. She wasn't tied up. Perhaps that meant something.

"Okay," Parson said, "tell him I'll put down my weapon. But if he shoots you, that door gun will rip him apart, and I'll bury the pieces in pig blood."

"I'm not going to tell him that. Just put down your pistol. Please."

Parson considered the situation. A man was holding a gun to Sophia's neck, but she insisted he didn't mean to harm her. About a mile up the road lay the village and Sophia's Humvee. She'd said they were bringing her back. And the Land Rover had been heading in that direction when Parson spotted it from the air.

He saw just two choices: trust Sophia, like he always had, or take a long, crazy shot with a handgun and maybe hit her. Not hard to do that math.

Parson put his Beretta on safe. Eased it down slowly, placed it in his thigh holster.

The man with the AK kept the muzzle at Gold's carotid artery until Parson brought his hands back up, spread his fingers to show them empty. The man lowered his rifle. He held it one-handed at his side, let go of Gold's hair. Then he looked at Parson—a hard look but not necessarily one of hate. The man seemed to take Parson's measure, decide what to think of him.

With several words in Pashto, the Talib addressed Gold. She closed her eyes, let her shoulders relax. Spoke several words Parson could not understand. What else could they possibly have to talk about? Then they nodded at each other like they were drinking buddies, for God's sake.

Gold stepped toward the helicopter. The Talib sat down in the Land Rover and closed the door.

"I'm sorry, Michael," Sophia said as she reached his side. "I should have known you'd come after me."

Parson didn't know what he wanted more, to explode in anger or to question her about what she'd just done. Was it worth her life? Was it worth her career? Instead he asked, "What were you two saying at the end?"

"He said, 'Your Bible says there is a time to kill. This is not that time.'"

"What the hell would he know about that?" Parson asked.

"He also said he wants to watch us leave. My vehicle is right up there." Gold pointed to the village. "I'll drive us back, and you can yell at me all the way to Mazar."

That sounded good to Parson. Maybe the yelling part, but mainly the exit—getting out of here before things got even crazier. And more dangerous.

Parson climbed back into the Mi-17, put on his headset, pressed his talk button, and said, "Sergeant Major Gold and I will drive back in her Humvee. Go ahead and start up, and take off when you see us pull out."

"We wait for you," Rashid said.

"Just orbit over us as we drive. Keep an eye on the road ahead of us and behind us. I'll have my survival radio on. Call me on the guard channel if you see anything. I still don't trust these bastards."

"Never," Rashid said.

"Oh yeah—call back to command post and tell 'em we found her," Parson said. "See you back at Mazar."

Parson unplugged his headset from the interphone cord, picked up his helmet bag. He kept on the headset for hearing protection as Rashid's crew started engines. With Sophia beside him, he walked up the dirt path toward the village, audio cord dangling at his waist.

❦ 21 ❦

At the village, Gold opened the driver's door of the Humvee and sat behind the wheel. Parson took the passenger seat and did not speak. She wished he'd say something, but he only removed his headset, placed it on the floor, and looked through the windshield.

The branches of a St. John's Bread tree stretched over the vehicle, and he seemed to stare at its dangling seed-pods as if they presented some kind of threat. If anyone in the village was home, they stayed indoors. All the houses remained closed up tight, even that of Durrani's wife.

Gold moved the ignition switch from ENG STOP to START. The turbodiesel fired up instantly, and she released the switch to RUN. The military vehicle did not require a key, and Gold realized she was lucky no one had stolen it, even absent the threat of kidnapping.

Down the hill, the Mi-17 waited with rotors turning. When Gold put the vehicle in reverse and backed away from the tree, the helicopter lifted into the air. She lost sight of the helo when it pounded low overhead, but she felt its pulsing right through the steering wheel and into her hands.

The chopper reappeared in front of the Humvee as Gold pulled out into the road. Her tires wallowed through a gully and regained their footing on firmer soil in the path. Finally, Parson spoke.

"I'm sending you home," he said.

That didn't surprise her. He probably meant it, too. She'd never known him to say anything just for effect. Gold waited before responding, to give him a chance to get out whatever else he had to say.

"I can't have you making up your own missions," he said. "Especially suicide missions." Parson glanced at her, then craned forward to look up at the helicopter. He unzipped a pocket on his survival vest and withdrew his radio. Extended the antenna and rolled the thumb switch. The radio began to hiss.

Gold paused for a moment. Then she said, "I didn't get myself killed."

"Not for lack of trying."

Several minutes passed in silence. Gold drove as fast as the rutted road would allow, which was only about forty. The Mi-17 crossed overhead once, twice. Rashid called on the radio.

"I see nothing on road," he said.

"Copy that," Parson said. "Keep me advised." He released the transmit switch, turned toward Gold, and said, "At least Rashid follows orders."

Gold nodded, conceded his point. Waited.

"All right," he said. "What did you find out?"

"Where the Black Crescent leader might be hiding."

Parson let his right hand, holding the radio, drop to his lap. He gaped at her wordlessly. His reaction relieved Gold a bit. At least he seemed to believe her. She knew she'd probably damaged her credibility with him by going on this mission at all. With no recording, no documents, not even handwritten notes, Gold had only her reputation to back up the intel she'd gathered.

"Uh, where?" Parson asked. Blank look on his face, like he was still processing what she'd said.

"In the *Kuh-e Qara Batur*, where Aamir wanted to take you. Durrani says there's an old muj base at the southeast end. The ruins of a fort obscure a cave entrance, and insurgents use the place as a bunker. If you didn't know where to look, you'd never find it from the air."

Parson spread his arms, still apparently dumbstruck. The motion caused the equipment in his survival vest to jangle.

"How on this fucked-up earth did you get him to tell you that?" he asked.

Gold told him everything Durrani had said, how he felt Black Crescent worked against everyone's plans, even his own. Counter-counterinsurgency.

"So he expects us to take out Black Crescent for him?"

"Yes."

"And we probably will," Parson said. "Hell yeah, we will."

Parson looked through his window, out over the hills. Tightened his lips together like he was already planning.

Above, the Mi-17 crossed over the road, banked, flew over the Humvee, and went out of view again. The helicopter trailed a smoky line of exhaust.

"But Durrani wasn't a hundred percent sure?" he asked.

"No. He just thinks that's a likely spot."

"Hmm," Parson said. "We'll have to request some Predator orbits or some other kind of eye in the sky. Watch the place for a while."

"That's what I was thinking," Gold said. She wondered if she'd be stateside by the time the surveillance began.

"I'll have to see what Task Force will approve. We'll tell 'em we got some good human intelligence. We just won't go into a lot of detail about how we got it."

Now Parson appeared more interested than angry. Probably the best thing Gold could have hoped. She could see his wheels already turning, perhaps imagining a reconnaissance flight. She just wished he'd let her see this thing through to the end.

Since she'd managed not to get abducted, an early retirement was probably the worst she could expect. The military did not like to slam recipients of the Silver Star. Gold had set her sights on an academic life after the Army, anyway. But she wanted to finish what she'd started. And Parson still needed her; otherwise, he wouldn't have sent for her in the first place.

"Michael," she said, "I don't know if this intelligence will bring what we want. But I hope I get the chance to help you try."

Parson rode in silence for a minute. Scanned the roadside and looked up at Rashid's helicopter.

"It might not be up to me," he said.

No surprise there. Undoubtedly he'd reported her missing that morning. A lot of people would know about it by now.

"So what do you want me to do?" she asked.

"Just press on like normal. If anybody asks, tell them you were gathering intel from a source. That much is true. Let me deal with the rest."

No surprise there, either. His loyalty again. Sounded like he planned to take some heat for her.

"So you'll try to keep me assigned to you?"

Parson slid back his seat, put his boot up on the dash. "You got fired," he said. "But then I rehired you. Just don't forget you got fired."

He didn't smile when he said that. Gold imagined he was more angry than he let on. She appreciated the respect that implied, and she felt sorry she had tested that respect so sorely. But she'd done what she had to do. Her obligations to the Afghan people ran deeper than military orders.

A miscommunication.

That's how Parson managed to spin it. Gold had been following up on a tip she first got when Black Crescent hit the refugee camp in Samangan. Not absent from her duty post. Not disobeying an order. Chasing down a lead just like she was supposed to do. Parson did not realize she had an off-base meeting that day, and he hit the panic button prematurely.

It made him look like an idiot. What kind of senior officer couldn't keep track of his primary aide? The Joint Relief Task Force commander even made him apologize to the security forces captain he'd yelled at over the phone.

So Parson wasn't in the strongest position when he requested Predator coverage over *Kuh-e Qara Batur.* Three days passed before he received an answer, but on the strength of Gold's specific information, the request got approved. He watched the first video feed from the unmanned drone on a screen in the Air Operations Center.

Gold and an intelligence officer sat with him as the images beamed down. Crosshairs floated over the mountains, with technical data from the aircraft superimposed along the sides of the screen. Parson recognized some of the information: airspeed, altitude, engine manifold pressure. The rest of the data was unfamiliar, but it looked like bearing and range to whatever was under the crosshairs. He'd spent his career in manned aircraft, and though he understood the importance of these remotely piloted drones, he'd never had much experience with them.

Parson did know the Predator launched from a classified location within the theater. Once airborne, a pilot and sensor operator sitting in a stateside ground control station took over. From the United States, the team flew the aircraft via a satellite link. The Predator had a four-cylinder Rotax engine that sounded like a go-cart, but the drone ranked among the most powerful surveillance tools ever invented.

"So what are we looking for?" Parson asked.

"Anything out of place," the intelligence officer said.

"Vehicles that stop for no apparent reason. People walking where there aren't paths to villages."

"Anything there at all is probably out of place," Parson said. "I didn't see any houses or anything when we crashed up there. Just an abandoned canal."

The feed looked like a grainy movie of nothing. Rocks and hills. Trees and scrub. A knoll above some ruins, just like the mullah had said to Gold. But no trucks or cars. Not a single person.

Parson spread a pilotage chart across the table in front of the video screen, and he tried to relate what he saw on video to a position on the chart. But the chart's scale of one to five hundred thousand gave a topographical view too wide to orient with the Predator's lens. He folded the chart and just watched the feed.

In Afghanistan, they didn't need to monitor the video constantly. The sensor operator would make a note if he picked up anything, and intel analysts from Mazar to Al Udeid to CENTCOM headquarters in Florida would examine the recordings.

"How long do we get to look for something?" Gold asked.

"They told me they'd give us twenty hours over the target," Parson said. "If nothing shows up, I don't know if we'll get another chance at this."

Parson would have liked more time, but he understood the limitations. The war continued all over the country, and every commander wanted drone coverage. What battle leader wouldn't want an eye in the sky to warn his guys of an ambush? The Joint Relief Task Force used Predators to survey earthquake damage, too. Parson knew he was lucky to get a drone assigned even for one flight.

All day, the movie of nothing kept rolling. The Predator might as well have probed some arid planet with an environment too harsh for anything but brush and gnarled trees.

The only activity came near dusk when a bird—a hawk or a falcon, most likely—soared over the hills beneath the drone. The infrared camera displayed warm objects on the light end of the grayscale spectrum. The raptor's wings, cooled by the air flowing over them, appeared black against the warmer ground, which had absorbed heat from the sun for many hours. The bird rode the final updrafts of the day, circled as it hunted. Parson never saw it flap once, though it must have when off the screen.

The bird's showing off, Parson mused to himself. He wants us to see he manages kinetic energy so well, he never needs to add thrust.

After gliding for several minutes, the raptor struck. It rolled into a bank of almost ninety degrees, folded its wings, and dropped like a bolt of black lightning. Parson could not see the bird's target, perhaps a mouse or a small snake. The bird did not pull up. It remained on the ground, probably eating its prey. Idly, Parson wondered if he'd been watching a falcon or a hawk. From some corner of his mind he remembered the difference: Falcons killed with their beaks, and other raptors killed mainly with their talons. A distinction by weapons system.

He wished he could see his own target and hit it like that right now. From a distance, he'd once watched an air strike in Iraq with a JDAM launched from a B-52. At the moment of impact, the ground rippled. An orange flash appeared for an instant, followed by the roil of smoke. A beat later came the sound, more thud than blast. And another high-value target answered to Allah.

But this flight was purely recon. These video images came from an unarmed drone. An armed version, the Reaper, carried Hellfire missiles, but a Reaper had not been available. CENTCOM probably assigned killer drones to missions with a greater chance of finding something to shoot.

After full nightfall, Parson and Gold took a break from watching the video and went to dinner in the chow tent. The place smelled like all deployed location dining facilities: the scent of gravy under heat lamps, whiffs of hand sanitizer, with an aftertaste of the morning's bacon grease. At a clipboard just inside the doorway, Parson wrote his name on the sign-in sheet, and he put O-5 in the column for rank. He had no idea why they needed his name and rank to feed him, but he filled out the form just the same.

Third-country nationals from Bangladesh dished out food in the serving line. The TCNs looked out of place with their white uniforms and black bow ties. Gold said little; Parson knew she was probably disappointed not to have seen anything on the video. He sat with her at a long table draped in vinyl, took a few bites from a warmed-over veal patty, and sipped weak iced tea. The food was better than the group rations the chow tent had served earlier in the relief operation, but not by much.

"You said Durrani wasn't even sure himself," Parson said.

"He wasn't," Gold said. She picked at a salad of wilted lettuce. Ranch dressing covered it—her apparent effort to give it some taste.

Parson had seen Sophia a lot of different ways: engaged and in control; frightened and hypothermic; exhausted but still in command of her skills. However, he'd never seen her depressed. He tried to think of the right thing to say. Parson knew his own skills had never included a gift for just the right words.

"So the worst that happens is we waste some gas in the Predator," he said. "Won't be the only time we've acted on bad intel. Remember Saddam's chemical weapons that weren't there?"

Gold pushed away her salad. "I hate to think I got you into trouble with Task Force when I should have been the one on the carpet."

"Not the first time a colonel's chewed my ass," Parson said. "Probably not the last, either."

He tried to think of more words of comfort, but the growl of a C-130 takeoff overwhelmed his thoughts. Parson excused himself, went to the refrigerated dessert carousel. The trays stopped turning when he opened the door. He took out two pieces of chocolate meringue pie.

Back at the table, he stuck a plastic fork into one of the pie sections and shoved it toward Sophia.

"Eat something, Sergeant Major," he said. "That's an order."

She gave that half smile of hers. He had rarely seen her grin broadly or laugh out loud. He knew she wasn't down all the time; open mirth just wasn't part of her nature. But she'd seemed different, a little sadder perhaps, during this entire deployment. Sometimes the best way to keep a crewmate in the game was the little things, small favors to remind them you had their back.

Sophia withdrew the fork, stabbed it into the tip of the pie wedge. She didn't say anything, but she finished the dessert.

"You want to go back and check the video again?" Parson asked.

Gold sighed. "It's like watching paint dry," she said, "but we might as well."

When they returned to the Air Operations Center, they found the intel officer still staring at the screen. But he didn't look bored. He was on his feet. Without any word of greeting, without taking his eyes off the video, he motioned to Parson and said, "Come here and look at this."

The sensor operator had zoomed in so far, it looked like the lens was at treetop level. At the center of the crosshairs was a pickup truck. Two more were parked near it. Men wandered around the trucks, stepped among stone ruins. Some of the men disappeared inside the mountain.

"How long ago did those vehicles show up?" Gold asked.

"Ten minutes," the intel officer said.

"Did they take anything out of the trucks?" Parson asked.

"Not that I've seen."

Gold pulled up a metal folding chair, sat near the screen, crossed her legs. She took a pad from her cargo pocket, scribbled some notes, and put her pen behind her ear. Now Sophia looks more like herself, Parson thought.

He knew the trucks alone weren't reason enough to lob a bunker buster onto those coordinates. It took more than a hunch to turn a point of interest into a target. The officers who made those decisions would need to see weapons, hear radio traffic about enemy operations, or gather some other information to make sure whoever was there needed killing.

But maybe this vindicated Gold's wild-goose chase. At the very least, CENTCOM would probably put up another Predator. Or maybe they'd launch one of those Rivet Joint birds to listen in on any communications coming from that barren spot in the mountains. With just a bit more intelligence, somebody somewhere could push a button and solve this problem.

"Smile," Parson said. "You're on *Candid Camera*, you sons of bitches."

❧ 22 ❧

When the Predator ran low on fuel early the next morning, an MC-12 took its place. Gold didn't care what aircraft watched that mountain; she was just glad something of value had resulted from what Parson called her temporary insanity. But he told her the MC-12 Liberty was a manned airplane—a heavily modified Beechcraft flown by a crew from the Mississippi Air National Guard.

Like the Predator, the small twin-prop aircraft carried video cameras and other sensors. According to Parson, using little planes to gather intel was a fairly new mission for the Air Force, driven by a new kind of war. The military needed a lot of surveillance in a lot of places, and it made sense to take a relatively inexpensive civilian plane off the shelf and stuff it full of electronic gear.

Gold spent the morning with Parson in the Air Operations Center, sipping coffee and watching the downlink. The trucks they'd seen the evening before were gone. But now the flight crews knew exactly where to look. The video mostly turned in a constant circle over the same spot, the lenses not so much searching as lying in wait. Occasionally the sensor operator would slew the camera across the ridge, over the valley. But clearly, after the trucks had shown up, somebody pressed the STORE function on a nav computer, and now those coordinates were locked in.

"Is that boring for the pilots?" Gold asked.

"Probably," Parson said. "But it beats the hell out of taking fire on a low-level run."

Parson watched the screen with obvious interest. Since last evening he had put on a fresh flight suit. On his left sleeve he wore the usual U.S. flag. But on the same sleeve, over the pen pockets where Air Force fliers often put tiny unofficial patches, he had a little black, red, and green Afghanistan flag. Solidarity with the Afghan crews, evidently. He'd come a long way since hating this whole country and everyone in it, and Gold liked to think she had something to do with that.

Right now Parson seemed engaged with the problem at hand, fascinated with the challenges of an assignment outside his normal role as an airlifter. If he still felt any anger toward her for what she'd done, he did not show it.

Gold tried to think of anything else she could do, any other way she could contribute. She was a language specialist, not an investigator or an intel spook. But she knew one thing about investigators: They worked their sources.

Gold excused herself and went to the field telephone in the flight planning room. She lifted the receiver and punched in the number for Sergeant Baitullah with the

Afghan National Police. This time it rang on the first try.
Maybe the phone service had made repairs since the quake.
A police recruit answered, and in Pashto Gold asked for
Baitullah. The recruit did not place her on hold, but simply put down the receiver. Through the line she heard dis-
cussions and then the clomping footsteps of someone
walking on poorly fitted prosthetics: Baitullah coming to
the telephone.

"*Salaam*, my teacher," he said.

"Good morning, my friend. I am sorry I have not called
you again before now, but much has happened."

"Not bad things, I pray."

"Neither good nor bad," Gold said. "We have more
information about Black Crescent. Much of it I cannot
discuss on a nonsecure telephone. But I wanted to ask if
your own investigation on the kidnappings has borne any
fruit."

Baitullah paused as if searching his mind. Gold wondered if he was considering what he should say over an
open line, or perhaps what he should say when other officers knew he was talking to an American. She trusted him
because she knew him. But she did not trust the Afghan
National Police. The U.S. military, along with British
forces and the German Bundespolizei, had worked to pro-
fessionalize the ANP. Success had been slow and spotty.

"The investigation has shown little progress, I fear,"
Baitullah said. "Witnesses will not talk to us. Some of the
parents do not even report the crimes."

"That is unfortunate," Gold said. "They probably received night letters warning them not to go to the police."

"Quite likely."

The thought of letters from terrorists gave Gold another idea. Had there been any more communication from them?

"Sergeant Baitullah," she said, "Black Crescent has released some statements on video. Do you know of any more messages from them in recent days? Video, audio, anything?"

"Not recently," Baitullah said. "They release their statements to news agencies in Pakistan and—"

Baitullah stopped himself in midsentence. But he remained on the line. Gold could still hear the ambient noise of the room: coughs and conversations, smatterings of Dari and Pashto. Why had he grown quiet?

"My teacher," Baitullah whispered, "do you have access to a secure telephone?"

"There is one here in command post," Gold said.

"Let me call you on that phone in one hour," Baitullah said. "What is the number?"

"I'll have to check."

Gold put down the receiver and went to command post. She asked a sergeant for the number, returned to the field telephone, and read the number to Baitullah.

"I thank you, my teacher," Baitullah said. Without another word, he hung up.

A strange turn, but a hopeful one. Maybe he'd thought of something important to tell her. But Gold wondered where he could get to an STU. Secure Telephone Units weren't lying around everywhere, especially not in ANP offices. At any rate, she'd find out in an hour. In the meantime, she could see if the surveillance plane had spotted anything else.

She found Parson still in the intel section, still intent on the video screen. The downlink showed no activity, but the video was zoomed in tight. The circling lens gave a clearer view of the entrance to what was apparently a cave bunker or underground complex, similar to what Durrani had described. Some of the mountain's rock formations ran in straight lines—a clear sign of man-made reinforcement. Defilades, perhaps, defensive fighting positions just outside the entrance. Part of the masonry looked like crumbled fort ruins, but some of it seemed newer, more intact.

"Seen anything?" Gold asked.

"A couple more trucks a little while ago," Parson said. "They pulled up, and four guys got out. Looked like they had AKs."

Interesting, Gold thought, but still not quite enough. Practically half the population of Afghanistan had AK-47s. She told Parson about her conversation with Baitullah.

"I remember that guy," Parson said. "One of the lucky ones who got out after we landed on fire."

A day Gold tried not to think about. She could still see the flames raging through the wreckage of Parson's C-5 Galaxy, black smoke boiling into a clear blue sky. A funeral pyre for too many of her comrades. That scene sometimes woke her up in night sweats.

When the hour had nearly passed, Gold returned to command post and sat by the STU. The phone rang exactly on time, and Gold answered with her name and rank.

"It is I, my teacher," Baitullah said.

"I didn't know your office had a secure phone," Gold said.

"Alas, it does not," Baitullah said. "I am engaging the function now."

"Same here," Gold said. She pressed the SECURE button. The phone's digital screen read GOING SECURE. The receiver hummed and buzzed like a fax machine answering, and Baitullah's voice came back on the line.

"I am in the office of an army friend," he said.

So Baitullah had to go to an army facility to find someone he trusted. The Afghan National Army hardly represented the military ideal, Gold knew, but the army was way ahead of the police in rooting out treason and bribery.

"That was a good idea," she said. "Do you have news?"

"Only a bit. But perhaps it helps complete the puzzle."

To Gold, it was a pleasure to hear Baitullah speak, to see him work. When he'd first joined the force, he could barely write his name. A frightened, uneducated kid. Then he'd lost his feet in the attack on the ANP training center. A life of disability and poverty seemed his fate. But now he sounded like a seasoned detective, not just drawing a government check and watching the clock, but actually trying to do the job.

"Any information will help," Gold said.

"We have analyzed the videos released by Black Crescent and this Chaaku," Baitullah said. He uttered the name with scorn, as if the word carried with it a bad taste. "The media experts believe there was no daylight in the room when the video was recorded—that all the lighting was artificial."

"So they shot the videos at night," Gold said, "or in a dark place."

"Perhaps the latter," Baitullah said. "The analysts also see clues in the masonry on the wall above and beneath the Black Crescent banner. The rough brickwork looks like construction the mujahideen used for bunkers in the 1980s."

Gold felt a moment of satisfaction. She had helped teach this man to read, and his literacy had unlocked his talents. His evidence wasn't conclusive, but it substantiated what Durrani had told her. Just maybe, she and Parson were looking in the right place.

When the MC-12 broke off and landed, a Reaper took its place. Parson still didn't like the way Gold had made up her own mission to gather intel, but he had to admit one thing: The more information she got, the more horsepower he got with CENTCOM and the decision-makers above him. And now he had firepower, too. The Reaper carried four Hellfires and two GBU-12 Paveway laser-guided bombs. Parson could not give the order to shoot; it wasn't exactly *his* firepower. But his assignment as an adviser put him in the midst of what was quickly becoming an offensive operation against a new terrorist threat. Not the usual day's work for someone originally trained to fly cargo from point A to point B.

The Afghanistan war had a way of putting U.S. troops into positions outside their normal roles. Parson knew of young officers who found themselves with nation-building responsibilities—captains with budgets of two million dollars. Now it was his turn to face a new kind of challenge, to learn as he went along.

Gold watched with him as the Reaper circled the *Kuh-e Qara Batur*. The downlink included audio now—the interphone conversations of the pilot and sensor operator at Creech Air Force Base, Nevada, and radio traffic between the pilot and a mission commander at Bagram, north of Kabul. Parson kept a satphone number for the mission commander, but he didn't expect to need it. These guys had their procedures and rules of engagement, and Parson looked forward to seeing them do their stuff.

Killer drones had become controversial in some quarters back home, but not here where bullets were flying. The way Parson saw it, the only difference between a remotely piloted aircraft and a manned bomber was that you didn't put a crew at risk. Those people who had a particular problem with drones maybe preferred to have a crew get shot at. To Parson, that said a lot about whose side they were on.

For hours, the Reaper's sensor showed nothing but trees, rocks, and dirt. Parson and Gold went to dinner in the chow tent, walked back to the Air Operations Center in darkness. The drone had switched to infrared by then, the night imaging clear as day video.

Parson decided to turn in for the night. He zipped on

his flight jacket. Plenty of other eyes would watch this feed, and he could catch up on his issues of *Stars and Stripes*. Maybe even catch up on his sleep.

That's when he heard the voice of the mission commander, reedy on the little speaker:

"Got some signals intelligence that indicates your high-value target may be approaching."

The stateside crew answered:

"Pilot copies."

"Sensor copies."

Parson took off his jacket, draped it over the back of his folding chair. No way he could leave now. On the screen, the lens zoomed out to a wider view.

"What's this?" Gold asked.

"Showtime," Parson said. "Could be, anyway. Maybe our boy got careless with a cell phone and told somebody where he was going."

Gold took her seat beside Parson. She showed no anticipation, no elation at what might be about to happen. No doubt she disliked seeing people die no matter how much they deserved it. Parson knew she wasn't squeamish; he'd seen her trip a trigger more than once. But she would not celebrate a death.

Parson wasn't so circumspect. He didn't like killing, either. But some people needed killing real bad. If not for General Order Number One, he'd crack a beer right now, dig his hand into a bowl of popcorn, and put up his feet to watch. Fuck these bastards.

The image on the screen zoomed in, zoomed out, slewed east and west, north and south. Nothing there. Just night in Afghanistan, with its centuries of ghosts. Beautiful and calm and silent, waiting for the next spasm of violence.

Several minutes ticked by, and Parson began to feel a little disappointed. Maybe they'd been wrong about their sigint. But eventually the mission commander came on the net again:

"Got a confirmation on your HVT. He's in one of two pickup trucks heading roughly southwest to northeast on a dirt path."

"Pilot copies. Sir, do we know which truck?"

"Negative. If I give you clearance to engage, it will apply to both vehicles."

The video zoomed and panned, found the trucks.

"You're starring in your own reality show now, you son of a bitch," Parson said. Gold did not respond.

"Designate target," the mission commander said.

"Pilot copies."

"Sensor confirms."

Parson slid his chair for a better angle. This was going to be good.

The Reaper crew began their prelaunch checklist. Parson didn't know all their terminology, but as an aviator he understood enough to realize they were configuring weapons systems and running BITs—built-in tests—for last-minute function checks.

"Spin up a weapon for me, please," the pilot said.

"Yes, sir," the sensor operator said. They continued their checklist as the crosshairs tracked the first truck.

"AEA power."

"On."

"AEA BIT."

"Passed."

The vehicles labored uphill. Parson thought about the occupants. Smug sons of bitches, probably planning their next raid. Maybe thinking about cutting somebody's head off on camera. With no idea they were on camera themselves.

"Weapon power."

"On."

"Weapon BIT."

"Passed."

This technology was just fucking fabulous. Parson re-called a lecture he'd once attended. A retiring general gave the audience an overview of basic Air Force doctrine. "The Air Force's gift to the nation," he said, "is that sometimes we can defeat an enemy from on high, so we don't have to hurl eighteen-year-olds at him."

And here was a perfect example.

"Code weapon," the Reaper pilot said.

"Coded," the sensor operator said.

"Weapon status."

"Weapon ready."

"Prelaunch checklist complete."

The trucks neared the spot where they'd been parked last time. Parson had stared at that location so long, he remembered the pattern of trees and scrub, masonry walls. Four or five figures stood outside, presumably waiting for their boss. Cool. Maybe that Reaper would blow Chaaku's ass to hell and get a few of his henchmen as a bonus.

"Clear to engage," the mission commander said. "Your discretion."

"Pilot copies."

"Sensor copies."

The video zoomed out, zoomed close. The crosshairs still tracked the first truck. Probably waiting for them to stop, Parson thought. That's what I'd do.

He thought of times when he'd watched a deer or an elk—or a terrorist—through his own crosshairs. You waited for the perfect moment to fire, but you couldn't wait too long. The Reaper crew began their launch checklist.

"MTS auto track."

"Established."

"Laser selected."

"Arm your laser, please."

"Armed."

"Master arm is hot."

The trucks stopped. The video zoomed in. More figures, now maybe a dozen, appeared around the bunker entrance.

"Give me laser guidance."

"Lasing."

Parson couldn't see the laser on video, but he knew the weapon would ride that beam straight down to Chaaku's lap. If anything, it was too good for him. Too quick.

The video zoomed out wider. Now maybe twenty people appeared. Some of them lined up in a row. They were shorter than the others.

"Those are kids," Gold said.

Parson's anticipation turned instantly to dread, as if he'd swallowed some fast-acting poison.

"Oh, shit," he said. "You're right."

He stood and grabbed a yellow adhesive note from the table in front of him, checked the number written across it. On his satphone, he punched in a call for the mission commander. In the eternal seconds before the call connected, Parson thought, Stop, stop, stop, stop. The phone at the other end began ringing, but no one answered.

"Clearance canceled," the commander said over the net. "Hold your fire, hold your fire."

"Pilot copies."

The commander picked up the phone. "We see 'em," he said. Hung up.

"Master arm off."

"Weapon safe."

The truck doors opened. Men got out. Some of the figures gathered around one who seemed to be in charge. He gestured and pointed with his left hand, held something in his right.

It was a sword. Chaaku and his toy. The crosshairs centered on his head, guidance for weapons now disarmed.

Parson kicked over his chair.

"Fuck!" he shouted. "Fuck this whole fucking war."

He put his hands on his hips, walked in a circle. Looked up at the cloth ceiling, down at the floor.

"We had that bastard," Parson said. "We *had* him."

"There could have been children in the trucks. They could always be anywhere around him," Gold said.

"I know it."

He met Gold's eyes, glanced back at the screen. The Reaper circled, still watching the men put the boys through some kind of drill or exercise. One man passed out rifles to the kids standing in a row.

Parson looked into her eyes again. Neither spoke. But he knew they were both thinking the same thing: *We're going to have to do this the hard way.*

✦ 23 ✦

The operation would go down like a hostage rescue. Except Gold feared some of the hostages would be hostile. There was no way to know how many of the abducted kids had been indoctrinated enough to fire on their rescuers. The thought of returning fire at children sickened her. Yet she wanted to take part, to do anything in her power to help bring this thing to a close.

Joint Special Operations Command took control of the op. When Gold first heard about that, she wondered if she and Parson might get left out of the action. Neither of them had ever been a special operator. But JSOC wanted Afghan involvement, and that brought Rashid and his crew—and their adviser and the adviser's interpreter.

Parson sat next to Gold in the mission brief at the Air Operations Center, a faded Air Mobility Command emblem on his flight suit. Blount and his Marines attended the meeting, along with Reyes and a few other Air Force types Gold had not met. A colonel led the briefing on video conference from Al Udeid Air Base in Qatar.

"We're going to come at them in two ways," the colonel said. "The Marines will make an Osprey-borne assault, along with some Afghan troops, and we're also going to airdrop an Air Force Special Tactics Team."

"Sir, what are the blue-suiters for?" Blount asked. Glanced at Parson and Reyes. "No offense," he added.

"Air support will be limited due to the nature of the target," the colonel said. "But we will have air assets on station just in case. You'll have a combat controller to call down fire if it's warranted, and Sergeant Reyes will handle the medical contingencies."

Medical contingencies. The military jargon pointed up the dangers of the mission. Gold wondered how many of the people around her would be dead or wounded tomorrow night.

"If you can get Chaaku," the colonel said, "take him dead or alive. If you take him alive, Pakistan wants to extradite him."

"And then what happens?" Blount asked.

"We don't know," the colonel said.

"Probably release him," Parson whispered.

"We'd like to give Sergeant Major Gold a key role," the colonel continued. "She's done some fine work as Lieutenant Colonel Parson's interpreter, but JSOC wants to borrow her."

Gold didn't know what to make of that. Was she in trouble for her visit with Durrani? Probably not, if she was getting some key role, whatever that was. Parson looked at her. From his puzzled expression she knew he had no idea, either.

"What can I do for you, sir?" Gold asked.

"Sergeant Major, you are still HALO qualified and current, are you not?"

"Yes, sir, I am." Apparently, he'd checked her records.

"We would like for you to jump in with the Special Tactics Team. You will carry an Icom radio like the ones used by Black Crescent and other insurgents. You will relay anything useful you hear."

Gold could hardly believe what she'd heard. It gave her new . . . purpose.

Purpose.

Something in life more important than contentment, than wealth. Even more important than happiness, to Gold. In certain moments of her career, she'd believed she understood exactly why her Maker had sent her here. Those moments had come less often of late. She'd questioned her role, her judgment, even her sanity. But now, as Parson might put it, she felt as if someone had pressed her master reset button.

"I'd—I'd be honored, sir." Parson wouldn't like this, she knew. But it came from a JSOC full bird colonel, so even if Parson fought it he wouldn't win. And it made operational sense. He'd come around to see that eventually, if he didn't see it already.

With a combat jump, Gold would earn a star on her jump wings. Though most paratroopers coveted that star, she gave little thought to decorations. But the opportunity to put all her skills into play gave her a sense of fulfillment she'd not felt in a long time. The mission still seemed dangerous; terribly so. But her awareness of the danger shrank in her consciousness the way pain shrank after a dose of Percodan. It was still there, but the proportions had changed.

"You can draw whatever equipment you need from the Special Tactics Squadron there at Mazar," the colonel said. "Just save your hand receipts for everything."

"Yes, sir."

"Any questions, Sergeant Major?"

"Uh—no, sir. Thank you for the opportunity."

"All right," the colonel said, "let's talk a little about tactics." The colonel's face disappeared from the screen, replaced by a topographical map of *Kuh-e Qara Batur.* "You're going in a little after midnight."

Gold, Reyes, two Force Recon Marines, and an Air Force combat controller would begin the operation by parachuting from twenty thousand feet. On night vision goggles, they would observe the target area. Unless they saw something to speed up or delay the mission, the main force would come in by chopper and by Osprey a short time later. The spot where the trucks had parked now had a new name: Objective Sword.

The colonel gave few specifics on what to expect after the main force landed. No intelligence agency possessed a layout of the bunker complex at *Kuh-e Qara Batur.* No way to tabletop what would happen next. As the colonel put it, the Marines would try to minimize hostage casualties in a kinetic action of unpredictable nature. Tear gas and flash-bangs. More lethal stuff when necessary.

Gold understood what that meant, and it darkened her previously good mood. For the abducted kids—for Fatima's brother, for Aamir's son—the raid would be dangerous, too. Those who fired on the assaulting force would become combatants, lawful targets. Terrible even to think about it. Their captors might kill them. The whole place might be wired to explode.

When the briefing ended, Gold went to check on Fatima. She couldn't tell the child anything, of course, but she wanted to see her one more time before she left.

Shadows were spreading through the rows of refugee tents. Gold felt the temperature dropping as darkness approached, and she thought how tomorrow night would answer prayers or shatter lives. Probably some of both.

She found Fatima lying on her cot, drawing on a notepad. Apparently some well-traveled UN staffer had given her pencil and paper. The pencil bore the logo of the Hotel Splendide Royal in Rome.

"You look very busy, Fatima," Gold said in Pashto.

"Sophia!" the girl cried. She stood up and hugged Gold. They sat together on the cot.

"What brings you to work so hard?" Gold asked.

"I am drawing pictures of the people here I know." She flipped forward to the first page. "This one is you."

The drawing looked like those done by children all over the world. Little distinguished it from the refrigerator art of American kids, except it was all done in pencil for lack of crayons. The picture showed Gold holding a rifle, and the drawing emphasized her hair—depicted in a bun. Apparently Fatima had an eye for detail. She'd put in lines of scribble everywhere Gold wore an insignia: wavy circles for her jump wings and free-fall badge, bigger scrawl where the tapes read GOLD and U.S. ARMY. The face wasn't smiling; Fatima had drawn a straight line for the mouth. Points for accuracy there, too, Gold had to admit. But she smiled now.

"That is very good, Fatima," she said. "I am flattered."

"What means this word, *flattered*?" Fatima asked.

"It means you have honored me."

Fatima beamed, turned the page. "I also drew the giant soldier," she said.

Blount's picture filled the sheet. Fatima had put tiny stick figures behind him, an exaggerated show of relative height. She had turned the pencil lead on its side and shaded the face to represent his dark skin. Clearly the girl remained fond of the gunnery sergeant who had carried her away from Ghandaki that awful night.

"Do you remember his name?" Gold asked.

Fatima shook her head.

"Blount. Gunnery Sergeant Blount."

"Bloo-anht." Two syllables.

"Blount."

"Blutt."

"Close enough."

Fatima turned one more page. "I made a picture of your pilot friend, too," she said.

The girl had drawn a smile on Parson's face. Now, why

did he rate that? Well, he usually looked happy if he was flying and nothing went wrong. And in the picture, perhaps he was about to fly. Beside him, Fatima had drawn a rough helicopter—just an egg shape with a big sideways X for a main rotor and a small upright X for a tail rotor.

After Parson's drawing, the pad was clean. No pictures of her brother, her murdered mother. Too painful to think about, Gold imagined. Instinctively, the girl compartmentalized. A natural coping strategy for post-traumatic stress. That's what Gold's counselors had said, anyway.

Gold thought of the remaining pages in that pad as the rest of Fatima's life, unwritten. The shapes and colors to mark the unused sheets were impossible to predict. But tomorrow night would turn one more page.

I n the twilight outside the Air Operations Center, Parson found Rashid sitting on a stack of sandbags. The Afghan pilot had the kneeboard he kept for making notes in flight. Its leg strap dangled, unbuckled. Rashid was using the kneeboard as a lap desk. He held a pen in his right hand. The heel of his left hand rested on his thigh, a lit cigarette between his fingers.

"Can you see to write?" Parson asked.

Rashid looked at him, maybe thinking through the casual American construction of Parson's English sentence.

"No longer," Rashid said. He looked away. Put the cigarette in his mouth and took a drag. Across the entire apron, not a single aircraft ran engines. The red ember at the tip of Rashid's cigarette brightened. Amid the deep quiet, Parson heard a crackle as the fire burned deeper into the tobacco.

"What are you working on?"

Rashid took the cigarette between his fingers again, exhaled the smoke. Stared beyond the tarmac. He waited so long to answer, Parson wondered if he'd heard the question.

"Words to wife."

Parson knew Rashid was married, but the Afghan pilot had seldom spoken of family. Just that story about his father. And Parson had never known Rashid to write a letter to anybody. It took a moment for Parson to realize what his friend was doing.

"That's not a death letter, is it?"

Rashid took another drag, nodded once.

"Come on, man. Those things are bad luck."

Parson had known crew members to write those letters before. They would leave the letters in their quarters, or perhaps give them to someone on another crew. But he had never written one himself. Whenever he went on a mission, no matter how risky, he had every intention of coming back. Parson was more than willing to sacrifice himself for his friends, and he'd nearly done so more than once. But he started every new operation with the expectation of success and survival. Unlike Rashid, he didn't have a wife. But he doubted he'd ever write such a letter even if he were married.

Self-analysis had never been one of his skills. However, as he considered what he should say to Rashid, he felt the wide gulf of experience and culture that separated him from his Afghan friend. Most Americans, including Parson, were hardwired for optimism. It twisted through the double helix of their DNA.

But in Afghanistan, each family had suffered the losses of conflict. And the deaths went back a lot further than the Soviet invasion. Parson remembered Sophia mentioning that a tribal war had taken place in just about every recorded decade. What would that history do to your view of life? Probably not incline you to assume everything would be all right.

"If writing that letter settles your mind," Parson said, "then do what you have to do." He paused, let Rashid run through his internal translation. "Because tomorrow night," he continued, "you and I are going to kick some ass."

Rashid dropped his cigarette. The glowing tip bounced onto the pavement, scattered sparks that burned out one by one. When only a single cinder remained, he crushed it out with the toe of his boot.

"I like," Rashid said. Left it at that.

You like what? For a second, Parson wished for Sophia to interpret. But maybe this was better. Neither man was entirely sure about the other's words. But Parson knew Rashid shared a goal with him. The rest would come as action, things to do. A language any guy could understand. Maybe what Rashid liked was the thought of kicking ass. Good on him.

Whatever Rashid was thinking, he channeled it into preparation.

"I wish to . . ." Rashid said, apparently struggling for

the English. "I wish to . . ." He put his fists before his eyes and made twisting motions. "My night glasses."

Clear enough for Parson. "You want to get your night vision goggles, get them adjusted?"

"Yes, yes."

Hot damn, Parson thought. This guy's in the groove. You could work with a man like that.

"Let's get you fixed up, then."

Rashid stood up, trotted over to his helicopter. Came back with his flight helmet. Rashid had limited experience on night vision goggles, Parson knew. Parson hoped that in time, flying on NVGs would become second nature for these Afghan aviators, but that would take hours and hours of practice. In the beginning, unfamiliar equipment could hinder more than help. But Rashid would need to use his NVGs tomorrow night, regardless. Maybe he'd had enough experience with them not to kill himself and his crew.

Parson led the way to the Aircrew Flight Equipment section. At Mazar it amounted only to another tent, along with a couple of conex boxes—metal shipping containers large enough to stand up in. He signed for two sets of night vision goggles.

"The Hoffman tester is inside that conex, sir," the AFE tech said, pointing.

"Thanks," Parson said. He worked the handle on the conex, swung open the steel door. Inside, the Hoffman tester—an electronic box the size of a small suitcase—rested on a table. In front of the table was a folding chair.

Rashid sat in the chair, pressed the red power switch on

the tester. The viewing screen on the test box came alive with a faint hum, though with the naked eye Parson could see nothing on the screen. Rashid snapped his NVGs into the mount on his helmet, then donned the helmet. Lowered the NVGs into place and turned them on.

First, he turned a knob on his goggles to adjust interpupillary distance. Rashid's eyes were set wide apart, and he had to open the gap between the two tubes of the NVGs nearly to the limit. Next, he moved another knob to adjust eye relief. Parson worried the language barrier might make it difficult to remind Rashid how to set the NVGs a comfortable distance from his eyes. But the Afghan needed no help. Parson took that as a sign of good mechanical comprehension.

He pulled the conex door shut behind him, which locked in full darkness except for the green backglow reflected around Rashid's eyes. The Afghan peered into the viewing screen on the Hoffman tester. He rolled the diopter rings on his NVGs, fine-tuning them by degrees. People new to the technology always took forever to focus the goggles. Rashid was trying to bring into clarity a set of bars and lines, and he kept turning the diopters, searching for that perfect spot. You never really found precise focus; it was a limit of the equipment. Eventually Rashid satisfied himself and turned off the goggles.

"Now, don't forget," Parson said, "those things rob you of some of your depth perception. You gotta be careful about that." He didn't know if Rashid understood him, but he felt better having said it.

Rashid stood, bumped his way back from the chair.

Parson turned on his own NVGs and used them, unfocused, to find the chair and sit down. Since he wasn't occupying a crew position in the Mi-17, he didn't have to use his NVGs on a helmet. In his flying as an adviser, he preferred to wear them around his neck on a lanyard, the way an elk hunter might wear binoculars. But that meant the lenses were not at a fixed distance from his eyes, so the adjustments were even less precise.

He turned on the goggles, held them in front of his eyes. Two quick turns of the diopters brought the bars into reasonable focus. Not the sweet spot, really. More like the good-enough spot.

Setting up equipment on the eve of battle put Parson in mind of some unknown ancestor sharpening a saber, running a ramrod down the bore of a musket. Procedure and ritual. You had to get your gear ready; if you failed to prepare, you prepared to fail. But the work carried with it a psychic purpose, too. Somehow, focusing the hardware focused the mind as well. Helped dial in the set of thoughts and attitudes you needed when you knew you might have to take a life or give your own. An indefinable mix of determination and acceptance.

Parson switched off the Hoffman tester, rose to his feet. Through the NVGs he found the door handle for the conex, and he pushed open the door. The lights illuminating the airfield ramp had a pink glow now, the result of his eyes' exposure to unnatural night vision. In a few minutes the lights would return to their true white.

"We're as ready as we'll ever be, buddy," Parson said.

Rashid stepped out of the conex, helmet in hand. He

did not smile or respond in any way to Parson's comment. But he wore a placid expression, as if somewhere in his mind, amid all the anger and sadness and bad memories, he'd discovered a corner of tranquility.

Parson knew the place Rashid had found. The Afghan pilot was ready to look into darkness.

❖ 24 ❖

Gold managed to adjust her sleep schedule. It was already dark by the time she woke up, but still hours from launch time. At least she wouldn't have to rush as she put together her rig.

The Air Force Special Tactics folks issued her an MC-4 ram air parachute. Four equipment rings carried her oxygen bottle, an MBITR radio, an attachment for her rifle, and the Icom radio for monitoring the enemy. The Special Tactics people also gave her a wrist altimeter, Nomex gloves, knee pads, and an aircrew-style helmet with brackets to accept the bayonet clips of her oxygen mask. They didn't have a flight suit to fit her, so she'd have to jump in her ACUs. No problem there—she'd just fold the collar inside so it wouldn't slap at her neck during free fall. A Parachutist Drop Bag would carry her body armor, Kevlar helmet, extra ammunition, NVGs, and water.

She stuffed her gear into the PDB, hoisted the parachute over her right shoulder. Outside, she found a cool evening, maybe ten degrees Celsius. No wind at the surface. No clouds above. She figured the current conditions boded well for good weather at the drop zone.

Gold placed her equipment beside the sandbag wall that protected the Air Operations Center. Sat cross-legged and leaned against the sandbags. Closed her eyes and tried to focus, to get herself into that zone where her mind could zero in on the task and let all else fall away. She started with a prayer—for skill and alertness, for competence and strength. *Please let me get this right.* Gold never prayed for safety; that wasn't . . . seemly. Or even practical, given the circumstances. She asked only for help to perform well.

Parson would be asking for the same thing, she knew, in his own rough way. They had eaten breakfast together earlier in the day—right before she went to bed to rest up for the mission. He had changed the unauthorized pen sleeve patch on his flight suit. The new one read DFU. She asked him what it meant. The answer was vintage Parson: *Don't Fuck Up.*

When she opened her eyes, she felt a little more assured that things would go according to plan. Not necessarily *her* plan, or even the JSOC frag order she'd been given, but a concept of operations from higher command. The notion untangled some of her worries and distractions, put her at ease enough that she actually dozed, caught a few more minutes of precious sleep.

The cool, calm evening brought a dream of home in Vermont. Perhaps because Gold was about to fly into darkness herself, she saw night-flying woodcocks migrating south from Canada, silent as death in their passage. They'd rest in bogs during the day, resume their mission after sundown. The russet-colored, long-billed birds flitted overhead in twos and threes. When Gold saw them no more in the black sky above her, she realized she was awake.

A while later, Reyes and the Air Force combat controller showed up. Both nodded to Gold as they entered the AOC. When they emerged, they carried armloads of bags and equipment. Reyes clenched a pencil between his teeth. He put down his gear next to Gold, flipped through a spiral-bound manual.

"We'll have to prebreathe oxygen for thirty minutes," he said.

"Are you going to be the jumpmaster?" Gold asked.

"Yes, ma'am."

That worked for Gold. When translating, when communicating, she was at the height of her powers. But parachuting, as much as she enjoyed it, was an ancillary skill. Especially free fall. Reyes, by contrast, had probably logged hundreds more HALO jumps than Gold. Pararescuemen joked that skydiving was just a way to commute to work, something embedded in their culture. It was even half their job title.

The two Marine Corps Force Recon men—a sniper and spotter—checked in half an hour before scheduled showtime. They looked more than a little surprised to see a woman on the jump stick with them, but they said nothing about it. With all five of the jumpers assembled, Reyes declared it was time to suit up.

He and Gold donned their parachutes using the buddy system. First, Gold leaned forward as Reyes held the MC-4 by its main webs. He placed it on her back, and she threaded and fastened the chest strap. They worked together to tighten the leg and shoulder straps. She stood up straight, stretched, pulled at her sleeves to try to get more comfortable. The weight of the canopy felt good on her shoulders.

She picked up Reyes's rig, held it for him. He put it on in half the time she'd taken. The cinching of straps seemed to draw up cords within him, as if the rig had become some natural part of him. The pararescueman's ease with his equipment gave Gold even more confidence about following his lead through the jump.

The two Force Recon guys geared up together, and Reyes helped the combat controller. They attached their kit bags, double-checked security of rifles, oxygen bottles, and radios. Though the jumpers represented three different services—Marines, Army, and Air Force—their procedures for HALO drops were nearly identical. Reyes glanced at his watch, led the way to the flight line.

An MC-130 Combat Talon had flown up from Kandahar for them. Gold had jumped out of C-130s many times, but this special ops variant, named for the talons of a bird of prey, had a strange look. It sported a funny-looking nose, or radome, as she knew Parson would call it. Probably contained some kind of super terrain-following radar used during the insertion of special ops forces. In the world of special ops, Gold had worked only around the edges, advising and interpreting. Now she found herself in the middle of it.

She walked up the Talon's open ramp with her fellow jumpers. The aircraft's loadmaster had already installed a six-man prebreather, a green metal box marked AVIATORS' BREATHING OXYGEN. The prebreather was secured to the floor with five-thousand-pound-test cargo straps. Six hoses extended from the device. Two Air Force physiological technicians checked the hoses and fittings. The phys techs would not jump, but would ride along to make sure no one showed signs of hypoxia or other problems.

"It won't take much more than half an hour to get to the DZ," Reyes said. "We'll have to start prebreathing on the ground. Go ahead and arm your CYPRES and get all your gear set before you start on oxygen."

Gold checked the control unit for her Cybernetic Parachute Release System, mounted on her right-side lift web. It was a silver box not much bigger than a lipstick container, with a single button and a numerical screen. If a jump went very, very badly, with an unconscious parachutist plummeting toward earth, the CYPRES would automatically deploy the canopy when the parachutist passed through a certain altitude beyond a certain speed. The latest generation of what old-school jumpers called AODs, or Automatic Opening Devices.

Gold remembered an instructor at Fort Bragg who liked to say, "Don't depend on an AOD. Because what's AOD spelled backward?" Still, Gold felt safer knowing her chute would probably deploy even if she couldn't open it herself.

She pressed the button on the control unit. After one second a red light glowed. She pressed the button again, repeated the sequence two more times. That put the CYPRES into a self-test mode. The device checked good.

The drop zone at *Kuh-e Qara Batur* was at about a five-thousand-foot field elevation. Gold intended to open four thousand feet above that. She programmed the CYPRES to fire at twenty-five hundred feet above ground level if she was still falling faster than sixty-five miles per hour. So many details to remember, procedures to get right. If you missed something and got yourself killed, you were just doing the enemy's job for him.

Next, Gold strapped the altimeter to her left wrist and checked its internal light. The face of the instrument glowed yellow with the electricity from a fresh battery. She switched off the light to save power.

When she looked up, she saw the Talon's aircrew gathering in the cargo compartment.

"Who's the jumpmaster?" the aircraft commander asked.

Reyes stepped forward. The aircraft commander and navigator briefed the takeoff time, time over target, and emergency procedures. Reyes nodded, wrote a couple of numbers on the heel of his hand. To Gold's relief, the mission required no last-minute changes.

She sat on a troop seat and strapped in. Gold seated the hose from her oxygen mask into a connector on the prebreather. Her four fellow jumpers also plugged in as she placed her mask over her face and fastened its bayonet clips. One of the phys techs connected his own mask to the six-man prebreather, and the other phys tech hooked up to an oxygen regulator mounted on the wall of the aircraft.

The pure oxygen felt like a tonic as it filled her lungs. It went down a little cold, and Gold could almost sense it reddening her blood cells and flowing through to her brain. But though the oxygen woke her up fully and made her feel alert, that wasn't the reason for prebreathing.

By saturating her bloodstream with oxygen, Gold could prevent decompression sickness. When a parachutist or aviator flew to high altitude in an unpressurized aircraft, the effect resembled a diver surfacing from deep water. As air pressure decreased, nitrogen in the blood could come out of solution and form bubbles. Very painful and potentially lethal. But not an issue if pure oxygen replaced the nitrogen.

She checked her watch. Now that she'd started prebreathing, she could not take off the mask. If she inhaled ambient air, which consisted mostly of nitrogen, she'd have to start the thirty minutes all over again.

Boot steps thudded up the ramp, which remained open to the airfield's stadium lighting. In the glare, she saw Parson greeting the Talon aircrew, backslapping like old friends. Probably former squadron mates from his days as a C-130 navigator. After handshakes and happy words Gold could not quite make out, he pulled himself away from the fliers and sat beside her. The crew headed for the cockpit, presumably to begin their own prebreathing from hoses on the flight deck.

"Keep your mask on," Parson said. "Don't start over on my account."

Gold nodded, tried to shout hello. Her verbal communication couldn't go much beyond that, so she debated what gestures were appropriate. Settled on a thumbs-up.

"Everything's good on our end," Parson said. "Rashid's ready to launch with some Afghan troops, and I'm flying with him. Blount and his Marines are coming in the Osprey."

He paused, as if he wanted to say more but could not find the words. Finally, he spoke again.

"Be careful, Sophia," he said. "You've done a lot of good work on this deployment. Maybe too good. If anything happens to you now, I'm going to be really, really pissed off."

Gold smiled inside her mask, realized he couldn't see that. Then Parson did a surprising thing: He lifted her hand off her right knee, held it in both of his—all three hands gloved in Nomex and leather.

"Give 'em hell, Sergeant Major," he said.

He squeezed her hand slightly and released it. Stood up and walked down the ramp, silhouetted in the severe light of halogen lamps. Tonight, his limp was hardly noticeable, more like a rolling gait.

A loadmaster flipped a switch, and a hydraulic pump began whining. The man wore a flight helmet and oxygen mask as he worked, trailing a long extension hose. He moved a lever, and the ramp groaned closed. Thunks echoed from underneath as the ramp locks engaged.

The lights in the cargo compartment dimmed. Gold listened to the sounds of an aircraft preparing for engine start: the whooshes of bleed air and the hum of electronics. Outside, a propeller began to turn. It occurred to Gold that if she survived the next several hours, the Form 1307, her parachutist's record, would carry all kinds of notations for this jump: *N* for *night*, *H* for *HALO*, *O* for *oxygen use*, *F* for *free fall*. And *C* for *combat*.

Parson watched the Talon lift off into the night. The aircraft flew with all its lights off, so darkness swallowed it immediately. The rumble of turboprops continued long after the plane had vanished. The disembodied engine noise gave Parson a vague unease that did not square with his knowledge of tactics. The aircrew and jump team were safer, of course, if bad guys couldn't see them; Parson had done a hundred such blacked-out departures himself. But he'd seldom seen one from the ground, and the effect unsettled him.

His anxiety, he knew, had more to do with who was on board than anything else. He didn't know if he could handle losing any more friends, especially Sophia. The rational part of his mind recognized emotion worming its way into his judgment, or at least his assessment of risk.

The Air Force's psychologists and grief counselors might call it a form of delayed stress. But so what if it was? Parson still had a job to do. He didn't have time to sit around talking about his feelings; he had time only to suck it up and press on.

Inside the Air Operations Center, he found Blount and a Marine captain watching the video downlink. Parson guessed the captain was a commander from Blount's unit, trying to glean any last-minute intel. Blount had grabbed some food from the midnight chow line. He sipped from a half-pint carton of milk and chewed on a fried potato cake. His rifle hung from a sling around his shoulder. Unfamiliar shapes bulged from his web gear: canisters and cylinders. Nonlethal weapons, Parson assumed. Tear gas and flash-bangs the team hoped to use to incapacitate rather than destroy.

On the screen, an image of the target zone streamed from the sensors of the Predator orbiting on station. Two figures, ghostlike on infrared, moved about the ruins and masonry structures outside the bunker complex. With nothing for size comparison, Parson couldn't determine their height with any accuracy, but he took them for grown men. They moved like adults, held their rifles in a manner that suggested long practice. Sentries, maybe. If those sentries stayed put, Parson imagined, they probably had about an hour to live.

Blount studied them without comment. His eyes betrayed no emotion as he watched the feed, but Parson could guess what he was thinking. The big Marine had made clear how he felt about Black Crescent and its abductions.

I'd hate to have this guy coming after me, Parson thought.

The sound of jet engines rose from the flight line, drowned out the routine chatter on the Predator feed. From the throaty rumble of the turbines, Parson figured it was the pair of A-10 Warthogs supporting this mission. The relatively slow ground attack planes had a sound distinct from the higher scream of supersonic fighters. Parson wondered what they'd sound like from the ground if they strafed you. He was glad they were on his side. A lucky break that repairs by civil engineers had opened enough runway for Warthogs to land and take off at Mazar.

"There goes our air support package," Parson said.

"Yes, sir," Blount said. "But I doubt they'll do us any good."

"Maybe not," Parson said. In truth, almost certainly not. This mission's entire concept turned on minimizing casualties. Otherwise, the Reaper could have done the job the other night. But it made Parson feel a little better to hear the A-10s take off on time. All the parts were clicking into place.

When the twin roar of the attack jets died away, the Predator crew and their mission commander were talking again:

"Give me a wider angle, please."

"Yes, sir."

The lens zoomed out to show a broader view of the target area. Slewed left and right. Parson thought he saw something. Apparently, so did the sensor operator. The camera slewed again. It revealed a pickup truck heading for the bunker complex.

"What have we here?" Parson said to no one in particular.

"At least we'll know they're home," Blount said.

Another vehicle followed the pickup. A bigger, commercial truck, maybe. Parson wondered if it was one of the jingle trucks he'd seen all over Afghanistan's roads.

Another truck appeared, the same size. Then another, and another. Now Parson was worried. Jingle trucks didn't usually run in convoys. But military-style vehicles did. Especially if they were carrying arms or reinforcements.

"What the hell are they doing?" Parson asked. "Did somebody warn them we were coming?"

"Unlikely, sir," the Marine captain said.

"If they knew we were coming, they'd just move," Blount said. "I've seen insurgents do that three times at least. Tipped off by the Pakistani ISI or some traitor on the take in the Afghan government."

"Just bad timing, then?" Parson said.

"Just timing," Blount said. He didn't seem fazed at the prospect of hitting a stronger target than expected. But Parson didn't like it at all. What were Sophia and the others jumping into?

"The weather's great tonight," the Marine captain said. "If the conditions are good for us to run an operation, conditions are good for them to move around."

To move around four extra truckloads of . . . what? Kids? Rocket-propelled grenades? Battle-hardened jihadists? Sophia and the Special Tactics Team would be over the drop zone pretty soon. But it wasn't too late to abort.

"Let's see what JSOC wants us to do," Parson said. Please let them call it off, he thought. He'd never shied from a tough mission, but Sophia wasn't supposed to be in the middle of a damned firefight to begin with. Let alone one where the odds had suddenly gone south. She was a linguist, for God's sake.

"I'm on it," the captain said. Dialed a secure phone.

He began to explain the situation, but then stopped, as if the officer on the other end had cut him off. Apparently the mission commander was watching the same feed and already knew what was happening.

"Yes, sir," the captain said. He glanced at the screen, at Parson and Blount. Parson followed the end of the conversation he could hear: "I think so, Colonel . . . Affirmative . . . So we're still go? . . . Thank you, sir." The captain hung up the phone and said, "Boss says we know where they are tonight. We might not get this chance again."

Dear God, Parson thought, why did I ever let Sophia get involved in this? Why did I ask her to come back here at all? She's already done more than her share. Selfish of me. I sent for her because it would make my job easier.

He wanted to call the Talon crew and tell her not to jump. Let the shooters go without her. But now she was chopped—Change of Operational Control—to JSOC. For the purpose of this mission, she was no longer his to command. Parson had helped set these events into motion, and now he'd have to see them through and live with the results.

"Let's saddle up," Blount said.

It was nearly launch time for the main assault force—Blount's Marines and the Afghans. By the time they got there, Gold and the Special Tactics Team would be observing from the knoll just to the north of the target area. Blount's team would arrive in their Osprey and hit the bunker complex, while the Afghan troops from Rashid's chopper would set up a blocking force. The idea, Parson knew, was to keep bad guys from getting in or out of the area during the attack. More of them were in the area now, though. Nothing for it at this point but to strike them hard and fast.

Parson gathered up his gear. He buckled on his body armor, slid his survival vest over that. Hung his NVGs around his neck. He already had his Beretta in a thigh holster, and he'd signed out an M4 carbine. He lifted the carbine and headed for the flight line.

A dozen Afghan soldiers were already seated in the Mi-17. Rashid and his crew briefed in Pashto. When they finished, Parson told Rashid what he'd seen on the Predator feed.

"This thing just got a little harder," Parson said. "Might as well tell them what they're up against." No changes to the orders. Just changes to the hazards.

Rashid spoke in his own language again. Some of the troops looked scared; others looked resigned. Three began to pray.

Down the tarmac, the Osprey already had its rotors turning. Rashid and his crew strapped into the Mi-17, and Parson took a seat at the front of the helicopter's cargo compartment. Plugged in his headset and listened to the crew's chatter.

Though he couldn't understand the words, he recognized the call and response cadence of starting up an aircraft. So their checklist discipline was getting better. And they probably knew tonight, of all nights, was not the time to make a mistake.

The rhythmic whomping of the Osprey's rotors deepened, vibrated inside Parson's rib cage. He looked outside and saw the Marine Corps bird lift off. Raised his NVGs and watched through them.

Sparkles swirled at the tips of the rotors, the corona effect of blades striking dust particles. The phenomenon appeared first as double circles. But as the Osprey climbed and entered translational lift, the glow spread down the length of the blades. On night vision, it gave the image of stars caught in a whirlwind, as if the aircraft had stirred a galaxy.

With his own rotors on speed now, Rashid eased up on the collective and twisted its grip throttle. The more time Parson spent around rotorheads, the more he appreciated their hand-eye coordination. Simultaneously, Rashid had to adjust power, change blade angle, and feed in a little torque pedal to keep the nose straight. It took both hands and both feet to keep this contraption pointed in the right direction.

Rashid nearly always flew well, and Parson hoped he could count on his Afghan friend again. Above all, Parson wanted to get to the target as quickly as possible. Gold was somewhere out in that night, maybe over the drop zone by now. And ultimately, he had put her there.

❖ 25 ❖

When her ears quit popping, Gold knew the MC-130 had leveled at drop altitude. She swallowed one more time just to make sure everything was clear. You couldn't do this kind of work if you were congested at all. Good way to rupture an eardrum from the inside.

Gold didn't have that problem now, so she wondered why she felt anxious. The open ducts of the unpressurized plane at high altitude let in cold air, but despite the cold, she was sweating. Then it dawned on her she was sweating *because* of the cold.

Cold was one of her triggers. The worst pain, the deepest fear she'd ever felt had happened during that blizzard when she was shot down with Parson.

Not now, she told herself. Deal with it later. She had to push through anxiety the way a marathon runner pushed through the hurt to reach the finish.

Reyes stood up. From this point on, she'd get her cues

from his hand signals. With the rushing wind, roaring engines, and oxygen masks, talking was impossible, shouting pointless. He placed both hands at waist level, then extended his arms to his sides: *Unfasten seat belts.* Time to go.

Time to focus.

She switched on the light in her altimeter, mentally congratulated herself for not forgetting that step. Though Gold planned to use her night vision goggles later in the mission, she could not wear them in free fall. The manual specifically warned against it because NVGs could restrict a parachutist's ability to find the rip cord and cutaway handle.

Gold released her seat belt and kept her eyes on Reyes. The two Marines and the combat controller did the same.

Reyes placed his right thumb on his right cheek, rotated his palm and fingers over his oxygen mask, across where his nose and mouth would be. Normally, the signal for *Don your mask.* But since everyone was already prebreathing through the pressure-demand masks, this time it meant *Disconnect from the prebreather and go to bailout bottles.*

Gold took a deep breath, held it. Unseated her hose receptacle, snapped it into the bottle connection. Exhaled, drew another breath. No resistance, no leaks. She gave a thumbs-up to Reyes and the phys techs.

Please don't let me screw this up, she thought. The government had spent a tremendous amount of money, and she had spent a great deal of time and effort, all to prepare

her for a moment like this. The lives of her teammates—
and of Fatima's brother and Aamir's son—could depend
on how she acquitted herself.

At the back of the cargo compartment, a red light
blinked on. The aircrew was running their pre-slowdown
checklist. Reyes tapped his left wrist with his right index
finger. Held up ten fingers.

Ten minutes.

Somewhere on the ground beneath her existed the result of some of man's worst impulses. Gold was about to
head straight for it at terminal velocity. She just hoped
training and instinct would take over, that her own impulses would lead the right way when she didn't have time
to think.

The luminous hands on her watch seemed to accelerate.
Ten minutes melted away in seconds. Reyes extended his
arm straight out to his side, then bent his arm to touch
his helmet: *Move to the rear.*

Gold stood, shuffled with the other jumpers toward the
back of the aircraft, awkward with her drop bag and other
gear. The Talon's engines seemed to sigh as the flight crew
reduced power, slowed to airdrop speed. So now the crew
was in their slowdown checklist. The whine of a hydraulic
pump started again, shrill enough to pierce all the other
noise. The ramp dropped open to wind and blackness.

Reyes moved his fist in an arc over his head: *Stand by.*
Fifteen seconds.

The jumpers stood in a line on the ramp, Reyes in the
lead, Gold next. No light shone on the ground, no stars

overhead. Gold couldn't tell if high cloud cover had moved in or if her eyes simply weren't adjusted. Either way, she saw only darkness. As if nothing remained in the universe except the back of this aircraft. And the cold.

Gold tried to clear her mind. No outside thoughts. Just concentration, pure as innocence.

Green light.

Reyes disappeared. Gold made a diving exit behind him. Caught her boot on the lip of the ramp. Dropped into the void, tumbling.

She rolled, spun, with no sense of up or down. Her inner ears' natural gyroscopes, useless. Wind whipped at her as she plunged through an abyss. In this out-of-control plummet, she could not open her parachute.

Gold spread her arms, arched her back. Rolled. Arched harder.

Her body steadied, seemed to fly. Though she could see little, she knew she'd entered a stable free fall. Her spatial references returned. The wind yet lashed at her, but from directions that made sense. Now Gold felt she dropped not through a limitless abyss, but through the atmosphere of the earth.

She relaxed the arch a bit, thankful the emergency procedure came to her when she'd needed it. No conscious thought intruded, just muscle memory. In the arch position, she'd managed to control her center of gravity and thus stop the tumbling.

Clumsy of her to make such a lousy exit. No doubt caused by bumping her foot. Better now.

Her altimeter needle swept through fifteen thousand feet. She could not see the other jumpers. The terrain below loomed as dark nothingness.

With her stable body position sustained for a few seconds, Gold seemed to float, cushioned by air. She checked the altimeter again, dropped past ten thousand feet. Shapes appeared in the corner of her eye, just a thickening of the night. Her teammates, falling with her.

Just a few seconds to go. Watching for four thousand AGL . . .

Look. Reach. Pull. Clear.

Time—which had rushed ahead of itself inside the Talon—now seemed nearly to stop. Gold sensed every step in the sequence as her canopy deployed. She noted just a small tug when the pilot chute inflated. As she fell through the night, the pilot chute lifted the main canopy's bag and lines. Ruffling noise as the canopy emerged from the bag. More pull now, as the slider controlled the canopy's rate of opening. And finally, a rapid deceleration as the canopy cells inflated.

The wind blast hushed into silence. Gold felt nothing but the pressure of her own weight against the harness. Heard nothing but the faint luff of other canopies. A moment of peace above a war zone.

She looked up, inspected her chute. A dark rectangle. It held an even shape—no twists or line-overs. Good canopy. Thank God.

Dim outlines of her teammates and their chutes took form in the darkness. All the men were above her. She must have opened just a bit lower than the others.

Indistinct patterns on the ground hinted of a bald knoll with scattered trees east and west. The Talon's navigator had done his job; he'd put her out right over the DIP, the Desired Impact Point. Parson would appreciate the precision. The target area to the south showed no activity Gold could see with the naked eye—just a deep, black pool.

She pulled a steering toggle to set up a downwind leg toward the drop zone. Her free-fall rig was more than a piece of nylon with lines attached. The ram air parachute generated lift like an aircraft wing; the chute was actually a high-performance glider, and learning to use it had taught her some of Parson's language.

With the canopy's full-forward speed of about thirty miles per hour, Gold flew alongside the knoll. Glanced at her altimeter, though now she was going more on feel than anything else. Pulled a toggle to turn onto a base leg. Pulled once more to set up a final approach.

She popped a quick-release snap hook to lower her kit bag. Felt the line run out beneath her. With the bag hanging several feet below her now, she wouldn't slam into it if she landed hard.

Gold did not land hard. As the ground rushed at her, she drew both toggles down toward her waist, went to full brakes. Stepped onto the earth like stepping off a curb. The canopy collapsed around her. Dull thuds to her right and left as the rest of the team touched down.

She'd always spent most of her time and thought on the big picture, the long-term and the eternal. But she took a little pride in a good HALO landing—about the only instant gratification she allowed herself. That she'd pulled it

off in a combat zone, after a rough exit, made the glow
that much warmer.

She let herself feel it just long enough to shrug out of
her harness and remove her mask and flight helmet. Then
she locked her oxygen switch in the OFF position, daisy-
chained her suspension lines, rolled up her canopy. Opened
her drop bag, dug out body armor, Kevlar helmet, night
vision goggles. Unstowed her M4.

"Everybody all right?" Reyes whispered.

"I'm good," Gold said.

The other jumpers made affirmative noises. Gold donned
her ground equipment and switched on her NVGs. But
what she could hear was more important than what she
could see. She plugged an earpiece into the Icom handheld, turned on the radio, and listened to the enemy frequency. Nothing. She also turned on her MBITR so
she could talk to the friendlies, positioned the hands-free
mike over her mouth.

The rest of her team began to unpack their gear. One of
the Marines assembled his rifle. As the weapon came together, Gold saw it was a Barrett M82—a .50 caliber
monster with an effective range of nearly two thousand
yards. The combat controller switched on some kind of
radio she'd never seen, worked with other electronic gear
unfamiliar to her.

Gold moved to the edge of the knoll and found a
place where she could look down the hill on the bunker area. The Marine sniper and his partner set up next to
her.

She trained her NVGs on the target. Gold saw four

trucks parked among the ruins of what might have been a fort or stronghold since antiquity. Ancient warriors would have liked the spot for its remoteness and adjoining caves, just as the mujahideen did in the 1980s and Black Crescent did now. A narrow valley dropped away behind the ruins, appearing on night vision as a deep green cleft in the landscape.

In all the hours of watching this spot on the surveillance feeds, she'd never seen this many vehicles. They looked like cargo trucks, with tarps over steel frames. Figures began to jump down from the tailgates. All looked like full-grown men. All carried weapons. Gold began to count them: four, six, ten, fifteen, twenty.

"Are you seeing this?" Gold whispered.

"Got 'em in the reticle," the Marine nearest her said, sighting through his nightscope. "I'd love to start firing, but we'll let 'em be surprised when Gunny Blount shows up."

Gold keyed her MBITR. "Golay flight," she called, "Seraphim is in position at Objective Sword."

The Marine commander in the Osprey answered immediately. So they were airborne and inbound. "Golay has you five by five, Seraphim. What do you see?"

"Approximately thirty armed personnel. They just arrived in four trucks."

"Copy that, Seraphim. Keep us advised."

The commander did not sound startled by the news. That Predator was probably still up there, its infrared eye unblinking.

In Gold's left ear, where she monitored the Icom, the

squelch broke. A voice spoke in Pashto: "Chaaku has re-turned with more holy warriors."

Through his NVGs, Parson saw the lobe of ridgeline that marked *Kuh-e Qara Batur*. Taller mountains loomed beyond it, vast folds of rock that knew no national border, undulating until they flattened into the steppes of Russia. Rashid flew a path dictated by terrain, dipping into valleys when he could, crossing peaks when necessary.

Ahead, the Osprey cruised like an airplane, with its rotors in the forward position. In Parson's goggles, the blades appeared to turn almost languidly, not caring if they generated propulsion or not. Just an illusion, he knew, but it looked strange as hell. A flying machine invented by crazy men.

Near the target, the Osprey rotated its nacelles to place the rotors overhead. Banked and descended.

Rashid said something in Pashto, and the Afghan troop commander repeated it. The troops gripped their rifles more tightly, placed hands over their seat belt buckles. Then Rashid said in English, "Two minutes."

As the Osprey overflew the fort ruins, ground fire erupted. Tracers spat upward, burning needles directed at the aircraft. The Osprey's gunner returned fire with a cas-cade of light. Still on night vision, Parson watched scin-tillating particles slam against the hillside, a storm of air-to-ground tracers. He could not tell what damage it did to the enemy, and the Osprey itself did not seem to be hit.

The Mi-17 descended toward a dirt path that led to the ruins and bunker complex. Rashid touched down smoothly. The troop commander shouted, *"Zah, zah, zah!"* and half his men leaped from the helicopter. Parson pressed himself against the cockpit bulkhead, gathered up his interphone cord to let the men get by him. With a twist of the throttle and a tug on the collective, Rashid lifted off again to place the rest of the soldiers on the other side of the target area.

Aloft once more, Parson strained to see the Osprey. It was on the ground now, gun blazing from its open ramp. So much for catching the enemy asleep. Ground-to-ground tracers flashed singly and in threes—Blount and his Marines opening up on semiauto or with short bursts. Seen through NVGs, the bullets cut brilliant vectors, a bizarre geometrical show of illuminated angles.

The Mi-17 banked. Figures ran among the trees and rocks below. Some looked to be armed; with others it was hard to tell. Were they insurgents attacking the troops who'd just disembarked? Captors chasing kids trying to escape? Parson struggled to think, to make sense of what was happening. It was an officer's job to understand in the midst of confusion, to bring order to chaos. But the scene below him defied understanding: random gunfire, innocents among enemies.

He heard Pashto chatter on the interphone. The crew chief began firing the PKM door gun. Expended brass dropped away, tumbling green cylinders in the pixels of Parson's NVGs.

Dear God, Parson thought, I hope he knows what he's

shooting at. And he hoped Gold stayed safe, unseen up on
that knoll, with nothing to do but observe.

The landscape blurred as Rashid accelerated. He flew
an arc around the southeastern end of *Kuh-e Qara Batur*,
descended for another landing. Metallic cracks echoed inside the aircraft. Bullet strikes.

A liquid burning sensation seared Parson's neck. He
dropped his NVGs, let them swing from their lanyard.
Placed his palm to his throat. His first thought was blood,
but it was too hot for that.

Hydraulic fluid. A round must have punctured a line.
Warm, slick ooze covered his hand, dripped down his
flight suit.

More babble on interphone, nothing Parson could understand. But he could imagine: *What's wrong with the
aircraft? You've lost hydraulics, sir.* An oily odor filled the
cabin.

The crew chief let loose another burst of fire. Swiveled
his gun left and right. Kept firing. Then he slumped over
the weapon as if he'd suddenly grown tired of fighting
and had fallen asleep. Parson pulled him by the shoulders.
The man's head lolled back. He'd taken a round through
the face and died instantly.

Rashid was having trouble controlling the chopper. The
helo yawed, pitched. The standby hydraulic system should
have kicked in, but with battle damage, maybe backup hydraulics weren't working. Pashto chatter grew more heated
on interphone. Rashid was fighting an aircraft that was
bleeding out, approaching the moment when its controls
would lock up and fail.

Two of the Afghan troops unbuckled their seat belts. They helped Parson pull the crew chief out of his harness and away from the gun. The Mi-17 banked left, pitched down.

"Put it on the ground!" Parson shouted. "Land it while you still can."

Rashid dumped the collective, touched down hard. Gave an order in Pashto. The copilot rose from his seat. Took the crew chief's place in the door and began firing the PKM.

More orders in gibberish. The APU started, and the engines whined to a stop. The flight engineer got up from his jump seat.

"What the hell are you doing?" Parson asked.

"Engineer fix," Rashid said on interphone.

The copilot kept shooting, laying down suppressing fire. The flight engineer pulled a flashlight from his helmet bag. He swung himself out the door. When the rotors stopped, he climbed atop the helicopter. Parson heard bangs from overhead; the engineer was using the flashlight as a hammer. Beating a valve into obedience, Parson supposed.

The crew's actions started to make sense. Standby hydraulics should have engaged but had not. The engineer needed to force the standby system to work and replace the lost fluid. To do that, he had to get up top to the hydraulic reservoir. Which he couldn't do with blades spinning.

They know their aircraft better than I do, Parson thought.

But now that he understood, he knew how to help. He

fumbled in the dark, found the extra quarts of hydraulic fluid. Gunfire chattered as he clawed two aluminum cans out of the bin of spare fluid. Slipped in the spill on the floor, scrabbled back to his feet. Doffed his headset.

He ducked past the copilot firing the PKM and heaved himself, grasping for handholds, up the side of the Mi-17. This job normally belonged to the crew chief, but the crew chief was dead.

Bullets cracked overhead as the engineer flipped open the hydraulic reservoir. Parson drew his boot knife, stabbed two holes into one of the quart cans. Poured the fluid, spilled half of it on himself.

He tossed away the empty can. The heat of the engines burned him through his flight suit and gloves as he spiked holes in the remaining quart. Parson dumped in the fluid and climbed back down for more. Stabbed two cans, handed them up to the engineer.

Tracers speared the night as the engineer poured the rest of the fluid into the reservoir. More tracers cracked around him as he slid down the side of the helicopter. The PKM door gun answered the enemy's weapons with a rate of fire so rapid, it sounded more like a tornado than a series of shots. Parson figured that door gun was the only reason he and the engineer had come off the top of the Mi-17 alive. The insurgents couldn't shoot accurately because they'd had to keep their heads down.

Back inside, Parson put on his headset as the engineer scrambled into the cockpit. Parson pressed his talk button and said, "You got more fluid, Rashid, but I don't know how long it'll last."

"Marines call," Rashid said. "They want Afghan soldiers at bunker."

Must be getting hot up there, Parson thought. The plan called for the Afghans to provide only a blocking force. But no plan survived contact with the enemy.

Rashid punched the starter buttons. The turbines took forever to spool up again. When they finally reached idle, the engineer leaned over to shut off the APU. Then the engineer took over the gun, and the copilot strapped back into his seat. Rashid opened the throttle, lifted off.

The climb revealed a battle gone to hell. Through his NVGs, Parson saw bullets burning paths all over the hillside. Not from organized lines, but from everywhere. Worse than any shoot-house scenario a trainer could concoct. The Osprey, flying again, orbited the target area. Probably looking for a chance to use its gun from the air.

"Where you gonna put 'em down, Rashid?" Parson asked.

Rashid spoke only in his own language. The PKM quit firing. Too hard to tell Marines from insurgents, Parson thought.

The helicopter began descending. Now Parson could tell where Rashid intended to land. Not much choice under the circumstances.

Right in the middle of the firefight.

❦ 26 ❦

From her knoll above the target area, Gold watched the Mi-17 touch down. An insurgent crouched behind the remains of a rock wall, sprayed the aircraft with gunfire. The sight turned her stomach. Was Parson hit? Rashid?

"You see that shooter?" she called to the Marine sniper and spotter.

"We're on him," the spotter said.

The Barrett rifle barked once, a deep booming slam underneath the cackle of lighter weapons down the hill. Flame spat from the muzzle brake. The expended cartridge flipped through the air, landed with a thud as heavy as if someone had dropped a wrench.

The .50 caliber round did not so much drop the insurgent as flatten him. The bullet stomped the man into the ground. Not a classic sniper head shot, but a round through the back that took him apart. With a bullet that size, where it hit didn't matter.

The sight revolted her. Through his own choices, the insurgent had asked for it. Gold understood the justice. But even justice looked like murder when delivered through a jacketed round a half inch across, striking with nearly ten thousand foot-pounds of energy.

Troops poured from the helicopter. Two fell as they emerged, did not get up. Through her NVGs, Gold could not tell if Parson was one of them.

The sweating returned, that unfocused anxiety.

She drew in a deep breath, forced herself to think rationally. Gold didn't know a lot about small-unit tactics; that wasn't her field. But she did know the best way for Blount's Marines to straighten out that mess down there was to establish fire superiority.

Gold could help with that. And it was the best way to help Parson, if he remained alive. She could fall apart over this when she got home. But right now, she would tolerate no weakness in herself. She was still a New Englander. God helped those who helped themselves. Tonight on this mountain, certain things needed doing.

She listened closely to the Icom radio hissing in her right ear. Nothing on that freq at the moment. The Barrett rifle slammed again. This time she didn't see its target, but she heard the spotter say, "Good hit."

In the green imaging of her night vision goggles, she saw two insurgents firing toward the Afghan troops scrambling for cover. Gold flipped up her NVGs, took aim. Her rifle's optic put her at some disadvantage; it was a standard ACOG, not a nightscope. But she could see where to aim because the bad guys kept shooting.

All right, she told herself. Mind control, breath control. She inhaled, held the air within her lungs, fired. The trigger break felt crisp, like cracking a matchstick. She fired again, twice more. Scanned through the NVGs. One terrorist down and not moving, the other crawling away.

More fire came from near the base of the knoll, immediately downhill from Gold's position. Additional ruins there, remains of another wall. Only this wall stood higher than the stone foundations near the cave entrance. Behind such ideal cover, several Black Crescent shooters blasted at will with little exposure to themselves. From a position like that, they could do a lot of damage. Gold saw three figures fall to their bullets.

Blount must have seen the same insurgents at the same wall. In her left ear, through the connection to the MBITR radio, she heard him suggest an air strike. Behind her, the combat controller made it happen.

"Raven," he called, "Seraphim with a fire mission."

Gold wasn't on that channel, so she didn't hear the answer. But over the gunfire, she heard the controller's next call.

"Target is riflemen at the base of a knoll to the north of the cave bunker. Target is stationary. Will mark my own position with a buzz saw. Request strafing attack, heading zero-niner-zero, pull out right. How copy?"

Another pause, then, "Friendlies to the immediate north and south, danger close. Don't fire if you can't identify that stone wall."

The whine of jet engines rose almost immediately. The

A-10s must have held on station close by. Gold could not see them yet.

The combat controller bent a chem light. Gold heard a pop when its inner vial broke. Blue neon filled the controller's hands. He tied a length of parachute cord to the light stick and spun the light over his head.

Those pilots can't miss that, Gold thought, but neither can the insurgents. A calculated risk.

With his free hand, the controller keyed his radio and said, "You're cleared in hot. Confirmation code Hotel Alpha. Call with target in sight."

Deepening growls of turbines filled the night. Gold scanned overhead, spotted one of the Warthogs. It rolled into a steep bank and pointed its nose at the earth. The attack jet fell from the sky in such drastic fashion that for a moment Gold feared it had been shot down.

Then it began to fire.

A ripping sound overpowered all other noise, as if the mountains themselves were rending. Flame shot from the nose cannon in an unbroken stream; the weapon appeared to spew burning oil instead of metal. The base of the knoll exploded into a churning mass of dust and smoke. The top of the knoll, where Gold lay, shook so violently that it triggered in her some dormant animal instinct. She dug her fingers into the dirt to hold on, shut her eyes.

When she opened them, dust obscured everything in front of her. She could not assess the results of the strafing, but it seemed impossible that anything under that gun could have survived. The engines screamed a shriller note as the Warthog pulled up, powered away from its target.

"Good hit, Raven," the controller called. After a pause, he added, "Negative. Just give me a couple dry passes in a show of force."

The chatter of automatic weapons continued down the hill. The air strike had not ended the battle, just changed its calculus. Gold knew children likely remained among the enemy, perhaps some of them firing. She wished she knew if any could be saved. And she wanted very much to know if Parson was all right.

Clicks in her earpiece, the one from the Icom. Then a voice in Pashto: "What is happening, what is happening?"

"The infidels have struck from the air."

"Send out the young martyrs."

"Three of them have their bomb vests on now."

"Tell them to walk to the infidels with their arms raised as if to be rescued."

Suicide bombers, Gold thought. Warn the Marines.

She reached for the MBITR's talk switch. Turned to her left, raised up to better find it.

A hammer blow struck her shoulder. Spun her, hurled her to the ground. Heat scalded her chest as if she'd inhaled boiling water.

Gold wanted to get up, make the radio call. Tried to push herself up with her arms. Her body would not respond. She lay on her back, tried to cry out.

Not even her voice worked. Her throat, her trachea, would not propel her words. She remained fully conscious, but could not make sense of things.

I've been shot, she told herself. But why can't I talk?

She put her lips together to form the word *medic*, but she still could not get enough air to speak.

Why can't I breathe?

Gold could not understand. She knew she'd been hit in the shoulder by a bullet. But she felt she was drowning. What was happening to her? Interpreting this strange set of agonies was like reading a text poorly translated.

She coughed, felt blood spray into her throat and nostrils.

The A-10s roared over her. Tracers followed them, perhaps from the same rifle that had shot her.

Her chest tightened, wrenched. She opened her mouth, tried to gulp air. Breath would not enter her lungs.

The drowning sensation made no sense. But as her oxygen debt deepened and her vision blurred, she realized the obvious.

This is what it feels like to die.

Through air gauzy with smoke, Parson peered through his NVGs. Held the goggles with one hand, his rifle with the other. On night vision, the smoke gave the appearance of a green toxic gas, the atmosphere of a cursed planet devoid of life.

He tried to think clearly, understand what these bastards were doing and where they were. The A-10 had rocked their world, that was for damn sure. But some of them were still firing.

The ruins of some old structure, a wall only inches

high, gave him a bit of defilade. Ahead of him, Blount found similar cover. From there, the Marine used that badass weapon of his with deadly effect. His Squad Advanced Marksman Rifle had put down at least three of these sons of bitches.

But his team had taken casualties. When Parson first jumped out of the helicopter, he saw two Marines on the ground. And some of the Afghan troops had been mowed down before they ever fired a shot. Parson remained outside the aircraft, trying to help make up for the loss in firepower.

Rashid should have lifted off by now to get his aircraft out of harm's way, but the Mi-17 still sat on the LZ. The helo's rotors turned at idle, stirring that otherworldly smoke. The door gun stood silent.

Someone threw a grenade. When it detonated, the photoflash effect illuminated a still image of the firefight. Parson saw Blount, prone, aiming. Beyond him, an insurgent pulling a boy by the arm. And at the cave mouth entrance to the bunker, a man with an RPG launcher.

Parson fired a burst. The man, now a dim figure in the dark, crumpled. His RPG flew wild, cut a harmless path over the top of the helicopter.

The glare of the rocket's passage reflected in the windscreen of the Mi-17. Bullets had pocked the glass, round holes with edges crazed white. No wonder the chopper was still there. A dead or wounded crew.

In a crouch, gear rattling in his survival vest, Parson sprinted the few yards back to the helicopter. The engineer lay beside the door gun, one gloved hand over the breech of the PKM. Hard to tell where he'd been hit; black blood soaked most of his flight suit. Parson put down his M4, felt the engineer's neck. No pulse.

In the cockpit, someone was moving.

"Rashid," Parson called. "Are you hit?"

"Copilot dead," Rashid said. His voice was weak, like a man just emerged from sleep.

Parson stumbled over the engineer, kicked the folding jump seat out of the way. The backlighting of instrument panels revealed blood on gauges, bits of glass on the console. The copilot hung in his harness, head twisted at an unnatural angle. Rashid had managed to release his own harness. He turned in his seat.

A bullet had nearly severed his right hand. The hand hung by tendons, bled from exposed arteries and torn muscle. Another round, apparently, had mangled much of his forearm. The night was growing cooler. In the chill, the blood gave off vapor.

Rashid would probably lose the hand. And if the bleeding didn't stop, he'd lose his life. Parson looked around for a first-aid kit. He didn't have to improvise a tourniquet; the new kits had specially made combat tourniquets. He found a kit on the cabin wall, pulled it from its mounts. Broke the seal and unzipped it.

The tourniquet amounted to a Velcro band with a windlass rod for tightening. Parson looped the band over Rashid's arm just below the elbow.

"Damn it, I'm sorry, friend," Parson said. "I know that hurts."

Rashid said nothing. Parson fastened the band around

itself. Turned the windlass, watched for the bleeding to stop. When no more drops fell from Rashid's wrist and bloody sleeve, Parson locked down the windlass with a clip.

Outside, gunfire still sputtered. And the cockpit was a bullet magnet.

"Let's at least get you out of that seat," Parson said. "Can you stand?"

Rashid didn't seem to comprehend, so Parson pulled on his good arm. "You need to get down on the floor," he said.

The Afghan leaned on Parson, pushed himself up, and let Parson back him out of the cockpit, holding him by the armpits.

Parson lowered him to the floor. Hated to put him down on the bloody plating between his dead crew chief and engineer, but that seemed the safest place.

The engines of the Mi-17 still whined, and all of Parson's instincts told him to let them idle. You didn't shut down under fire. But Parson couldn't fly the helicopter, and its running engines with flowing fuel could do little now except start a fire if a slug hit the right place. He leaned into the cockpit, reached overhead, and pulled the stopcocks.

Out the left cockpit window he saw stabs of flame from muzzle flashes. Rounds slapped into the side of the helicopter like thrown gravel.

Now Parson was angry. He might not know how to fly this contraption, but he could damn sure work its gun.

He turned, stepped aft to the door. Pushed the engineer's hand off the weapon. Released the PKM from its mount, lifted the old-school wooden stock to his shoulder. The belt of ammunition dangled to his feet. Shoot my friends, will you? Maybe shoot at Sophia? He waited for those muzzle flashes again . . . There they were.

Parson pressed the trigger and held it down.

❧ 27 ❧

Gold wanted more than anything to make that radio call before life left her. Warn Blount and the others. But she could not talk, could barely breathe. What little air she inhaled, she coughed right back out in a bloody spray.

She sensed someone kneeling beside her. Reyes. She was probably beyond his talents now. She hated to leave this way, with a job undone—one so critical. But like every mission, her entire life had been just a frag—a fragmentary order—that was part of a larger op plan she was not cleared to know.

Her mind stopped racing, settled into something like acceptance. This wasn't so bad. It hurt, but the pain wouldn't last much longer.

Scattered images, sensations came to her. Vermont's Green Mountains, aflame with sunset and October. A rocky coast in Maine, lobster with corn on the cob. A banana milk shake with almonds and dates, a gift from students in Kabul. Quite a blessing, she thought, to have such memories to ease her passing.

Reyes pulled a knife. He slashed away her MOLLE gear, pushed aside her radios, cut the fasteners of her body armor.

"Your lungs have collapsed, Sergeant Major," he said. His words only half registered, as if they applied to someone else.

One of the Marines held a penlight for Reyes as he worked. The Marine shielded the light with his hand to hide the glow from the enemy. Reyes unbuttoned her ACU top, cut open her bra.

"Sorry, ma'am," he said. "Also, this might hurt a little."

He reached into his medical ruck, withdrew a catheter needle so large, it resembled a nail. Gold noticed the silver glint of stainless steel, thought it strangely pretty.

Reyes pressed his fingers into the flesh just above her left breast. Found a spot between ribs. Aimed the needle. Pushed it in all the way.

A faint pop sounded as the needle pierced her chest cavity. Then came a long rush of air.

The fist that had crushed her lungs let go. She drew half a breath. Coughed blood. Drew a full breath.

Dear God, it hurt. But now her chest rose and fell. Reyes slid the needle from the catheter, left the catheter inside her.

"I think that bullet glanced off your clavicle or something," Reyes said. "It got at least one of your lungs, and it exited your back."

"I've seen bullets do weirder things," the Marine said.

"You just got a needle decompression," Reyes said. "Don't pull out that catheter."

Gold drew another breath, spat blood and saliva. "Give me my radio," she said. "The MBITR." The sound of her own words scared her. Like she'd choked them out through gravel in her throat.

"Just rest and—"

"Now, Sergeant!"

She tried to rise up on her elbow. Cords of reddened mucus dangled from her nose and mouth. Reyes looked worried, but he stopped arguing. He put the MBITR in her hand, moved her boom mike back into place over her lips. She pressed the transmit button.

"They're sending—they're sending out three kids in suicide vests," Gold said. Inhaled again. It felt like breathing fire, but she was breathing, nonetheless. "They told them to come out"—another burning breath—"with their hands up."

Gold released the button. She heard Blount respond with one word, devoid of emotion: "Copy."

The PKM's bolt latched open. That told Parson he'd fired the last 7.62-millimeter round in the ammunition belt. The weapon smoked in his hands. He'd emptied the machine gun on the insurgents who were firing up at Gold's position on the knoll. Now, no more muzzle flashes came from those bastards. Parson put down the PKM and drew his handgun. The team had to clear the cave eventually, and his Beretta made a good close-quarters weapon.

Blount rose from the stone ruins just yards from Parson. Moved closer to the cave entrance. He spoke into his microphone, but Parson could not hear the words.

Three figures stepped out of the cave together. In the dark, Parson couldn't see them well, but they were not tall enough to be adults. All the children had their arms raised. Good. Maybe this thing was ending.

"Zaai peh zaai wudregah," Blount shouted. Parson remembered that phrase; it was one of the few things he knew in Pashto. *Stay where you are.* Gold had taught Parson a few useful words in recent days. Someone had taught Blount, as well.

The kids continued toward him. *"Zaai peh zaai wudregah,"* he repeated. "Stop! Now!"

Blount backed up several steps. Why was he being so cautious? Of course these kids would come toward their rescuers.

"Wudregah," he called. "Please!"

Blount shouldered his weapon. With quick semiauto shots, he cut down all three children.

"What the fuck are you doing?" Parson shouted. He pointed his Beretta at Blount, who had apparently lost his mind.

Before Blount could speak, one of the small figures on the ground turned into a geyser of orange flame.

Heat, noise, and debris hit Parson. Flying grit stung his face, lashed his arms. The blast so overwhelmed his ears that their membranes transmitted not sound but pain. Parson's mind seemed to lock up and cage like a navigational instrument getting bad data: *Marines don't shoot children. And children don't become pillars of fire.*

He flattened himself, waited for another explosion. Nothing. As the smoke and dust cleared, in the moonlight he saw two of the kids on the ground. The other had simply disappeared as if vaporized. The two that remained wore bulky vests. Suicide bombers.

Somehow Blount had known. And maybe he'd saved Parson and the Marines behind him. Blount had been even closer to the explosion. Now he lay on the ground, supported himself with one hand. His cheek bled from a deep gash. Tears and sweat mingled with the blood. He pushed himself into a kneeling position, shouldered his weapon, and fired more rounds into the two boys who had not detonated themselves. They were probably already dead, Parson realized, but Blount had to make sure.

Three of his men emerged from the darkness. "I think we got the hill secure, Gunny," one of them said. "Are you hurt?"

"I don't think so," Blount said. "We still gotta take the inside."

"What's in there?"

"No telling," Blount said. "Just stragglers, I hope. We caught a lot of them outside."

"Only one way to find out," another Marine said.

Blount leaned on his rifle for a moment, steadied himself. Then he stood up and took a flash-bang grenade from his tactical vest.

"God only knows what we'll find," Blount said. "If it's kids, let's try not to kill any more of 'em."

The gunnery sergeant made his way to the cave entrance, stepped over the broken bodies of the two boys. Pulled the pin on a flash-bang. Threw it inside.

The flash-bang made a weak pop compared to the suicide detonation moments ago. The Marines activated the rail-mounted lights on their weapons, charged into the cave bunker. Parson was not as well equipped. He found his SureFire in a leg pocket, turned it on, and used both hands to hold it next to his Beretta. He still felt stunned from the suicide blast, and his head hurt like hell. Parson just hoped he could see, think, and move fast enough for whatever waited inside that cave.

As soon as he stepped inside, two quick shots rang from up ahead. He rounded a dogleg entrance and saw the Marines crouching. Dim light bathed them from an electric lamp mounted on the cave wall, perhaps powered by a generator tucked away in some stone recess. A flashlight beam illuminated a fallen insurgent, facedown, AK-47 in the dirt beside him.

"Look alive," Blount called. "There might be more." He rose from his crouch and led on, taking half steps through the dark. At another bend he froze, raised his fist. The other Marines stopped. Parson held his breath, waited. Blount swept with his rifle, searched with the light beam. Fired two shots.

The team held their positions, listened. Parson heard nothing but a single moan. When they moved forward, he stepped past a dead insurgent slumped against the cave wall as if in repose. White beard and tunic. Camo field jacket. Radio in one pocket.

Parson realized neither of the dead insurgents looked like Chaaku. That meant little, though. The Black Crescent leader could have died in the firefight outside, or fled. The thought of that lowlife getting away infuriated Parson. It was time for a reckoning, one way or another.

Beyond the glow of the wall-mounted lamp, pure blackness loomed. The Marines' flashlights probed the cave bunker like the beams of divers exploring a deep shipwreck. Brickwork reinforced the walls in places. A conduit carried wires along the ceiling. Powdery dirt made up the floor, soil so dry it retained only vague hints of the Marines' boot prints.

"Preston," Blount called, "keep a watch behind us. Shirer, you watch up ahead."

"Aye, aye, Gunny."

"Will do, boss."

A few steps deeper into the cave, they came to a metal door. Parson guessed that it opened into a side room dug out of the rock. The cave's natural passage continued past the door into darkness. Blount tried the rusty lever. Locked.

"Shotgun man," he ordered. "Get up here and breach it."

One of the Marines carried an M1014, a twelve-gauge semiauto. He placed the weapon's muzzle to the latch.

"Watch your eyes," shotgun man said. Turned his head to the side and pulled the trigger.

In the confines of the cave, the blast hurt Parson's ears nearly as much as the bomb detonation earlier. From the other side of the door came the screams of children. Parson shuddered. What kind of misanthrope would lock kids in such a dungeon? Blount tried the lever once more. The door still wouldn't open.

"Hit it one more time," Blount said. "Be real careful. Y'all be careful when it opens, too. They could have more suicide vests for all we know."

Shotgun man positioned his weapon at an angle so that any buckshot penetrating the door would slam into the ground. Parson turned away to shield his face and eyes from metal shards. Held his pistol in one hand, pressed the other hand over his ear.

Since he was ready for it this time, the shotgun's report sounded more like a loud thump. Sparks danced off the metal, burned out in an instant. Blount kicked the door. It clanged open.

Flashlight beams and the bores of weapons came to bear on a group of six boys. The children cowered in a corner. They cried and shouted in Pashto.

Parson tightened his finger around the Beretta's trigger. Scanned with his SureFire. The boys held no firearms, but Parson worried more about detonators. He watched their hands, looked for a tiny thumb over a switch. Saw only grubby fingers, dirty faces streaked with tears and mucus. The children squinted against the flashlight glare. They wore tennis shoes and baggy pants. No bulky vests or wires. Thank God.

"*Zoy,*" Blount said. "*Zoy, zoy, zoy.*" Parson tried to remember what the hell that meant. Oh, yeah. Another of the simple words Sophia liked to teach the Americans. *Son*.

That's better than nothing, Parson thought, but we need to get Sophia in here once we have this place under control. Get these poor kids calmed down.

Blount kept repeating the one word he knew to say, which seemed to help a little. The children quieted, but remained huddled together. Blount kneeled in the doorway. Stretched out his hand toward the boys.

Automatic weapons fire ripped from deeper within the bunker. The Marine with the shotgun fell against the wall. Blount twisted out of the doorway, brought up his rifle, and fired. Something knocked him backward as if kicked in the chest. He dropped to the cave floor. The two other Marines whirled, opened up. The boys screamed, huddled into the corner to escape the shooting.

Flashlight beams wavered, spun, bounced off cave walls. Voices shouted in English, Pashto, and Arabic. Two, no, three insurgents charged out of the darkness. Parson fired his pistol three times. Sprayed more than aimed.

The firefight in such tight confines tapped a madness within him. Parson struggled to think, to hold on to reason. Trapped in a hole filled with gunfire and screams, his universe closed down to nothing but the urge to kill. He squeezed off four more shots.

One of the insurgents went down. Then two others fell to rifle fire. Parson pointed his flashlight, saw one of the men raise himself onto his knees. The wounded insurgent aimed a handgun. Parson shot again, twice more. One of his rounds struck the base of the insurgent's throat. The terrorist collapsed.

Blount lay stunned. Rounds to his body armor had

knocked the breath out of him. He got up on one knee. Shotgun man sat up, bleeding from an arm wound. The two other Marines stood with rifles poised, but the shooting seemed to have stopped. The boys cried and shouted words Parson could not understand.

"Get those kids out of here," Parson said to the Marines left standing. "Blount and I will cover you."

The two Marines looked at Blount.

"I'm all right," Blount said. He coughed. Then he added, "Do what the man said."

One of the Marine riflemen extended his hand toward the children. "Come on," he said. "Nobody's going to hurt you."

The other rifleman slung his weapon and kneeled, stretched out his arms. "Let's get out of here, guys. This ain't no good place for you." Perhaps the kids found the tone reassuring. One of them stood and moved toward the Marines. The rifleman on his knees picked up the smallest boy, and the two men led the kids out of the cave. The moment brought a brief scene of normalcy: two adults taking children on a stroll.

"Can you walk?" Parson asked shotgun man.

"Yes, sir." The wounded Marine got up, held his M1014 with one hand.

"Go on," Blount said. "Let the corpsman check out that arm. The lieutenant colonel and I will be right behind you."

"Aye, aye, Gunny." Shotgun man stumbled toward the cave mouth.

Parson's mind reeled. His thoughts raced to catch up

with time, to account for all the bloodshed and choices made in the last ten minutes. Lives saved, taken, or scarred in split-second decisions. He couldn't believe he'd aimed a weapon at children, nearly pulled the trigger. Couldn't imagine what Blount was thinking. Whatever Blount thought, the big man just kept it in. Parson watched him eject from his rifle what must have been a nearly empty magazine. With hands covered by black tactical gloves, Blount started to reach into his vest for more ammunition.

Then a voice shouted, *"Allah-hu akbar!"* A man charged forward from the darkness of the corridor.

Glint of silver. A sword slashed down toward Blount's head.

The gunnery sergeant rolled. The blade caught the throat protector of his body armor.

Chaaku, Parson realized. Field jacket over a white tunic. Black beard and blazing eyes. The man drew back the sword with what looked like the practiced motion of a fencer. Poised to strike again. Parson fired at center mass.

Chaaku fell back. Clutched the sword with both hands, lunged again. So the son of a bitch had body armor, too.

Still on the ground, Blount swung his left leg, caught Chaaku in the knees. Chaaku dropped to the cave floor, still holding the sword. Parson tried to aim for a head shot, but Blount was in the way. He considered whether to just jump on the terrorist, but Blount seemed to be holding his own. Parson steadied himself, waited for a clear shot.

On his back, Chaaku swung the blade once more.

With both hands, Blount thrust his rifle into the path of the sword. Steel glanced off steel. Rasp of scraping metal. Blount brought his weapon's muzzle toward Chaaku's neck. Chaaku writhed to his side in a manic frenzy. Took one hand off the sword's grip, scooped up a handful of the powdery dirt. Flung it into Blount's eyes. Looked at Parson. Swung his sword just as Parson fired again.

At a better angle, with a little more force, the blade might have clipped off Parson's hands. But lying on the ground, Chaaku lacked leverage. The sword slashed Parson's right forearm and spoiled his aim. The bullet flew wild, and Parson dropped the pistol.

Chaaku and Blount both sprang to their feet as Parson stumbled backward, bleeding. The terrorist lifted the sword high to deliver a death gash.

Blount fired from the hip. Chaaku had attacked as Blount tried to change magazines, and the round in the rifle's chamber was the only one left. The bullet struck Chaaku's body armor, knocked him off balance. Blount turned his weapon around, rammed the stock into the terrorist's chest. Then he dropped the rifle.

In a move like Parson had never seen, Blount swept upward with his palms, locked Chaaku's elbow and wrist. Twisted Chaaku's arm. Kneed him in the groin. Released the terrorist's forearm. Wrested the blade away with both hands.

Blood dripped from Blount's gloves. He shoved Chaaku against the cave wall, jammed the sword's point into Chaaku's thigh. The terrorist screamed. Blount stabbed the blade in deeper, then yanked it out and flung the sword away.

Parson placed his left hand over the sword wound on his right arm. Blood ran between his fingers, saturated his sleeve. The cut burned all the way to the bone. He looked for his weapon, did not see it on the darkened cave floor.

Blount rammed the heel of his left hand into Chaaku's chin. The insurgent's jaw made a crack as it broke. Chaaku let loose a keening sound, as if he couldn't open his mouth enough for a full scream. Blood from Blount's soaked glove smeared the face of the terrorist.

Chaaku's hand dropped to his side, came back up with a dagger. Blount tried to block it, but the blade entered under his right arm. The gunnery sergeant growled something unintelligible, slammed his fist into Chaaku's neck. Chaaku slashed with the dagger again. This time Blount blocked it squarely.

Blount held on to Chaaku's arm. With a maneuver that seemed too fast and finessed for a man his size, the Marine pivoted and kneeled. He brought his enemy's arm over his shoulder, elbow down. Yanked hard.

Bones crunched as the arm bent the wrong way. The jagged point of a fracture tore through Chaaku's sleeve. The terrorist made a series of high-pitched yelps. The dagger fell from his hand.

Parson had heard cries of pain in many forms, but not like this. The yelps expressed not just pain but panic, and Parson saw why. Blount could have killed Chaaku by now. He was toying with him, taking his time. The gunnery sergeant was not just large and powerful, but apparently skilled in a martial art. A big cat with a mouse, and the mouse knew what was happening.

Not many things scared Parson anymore. But he had never witnessed vengeance in quite this form. And it actually frightened him.

With his boot, Blount hooked Chaaku's knees from behind. The terrorist fell flat. Blount stomped Chaaku's fingers. More snaps of bones.

Parson considered whether to try to stop this. It had crossed the line from combat into something else. He knew what Gold would want him to do now: Follow the rules to the letter. But Gold had broken the rules herself when she'd seen the need. And their orders were to take Chaaku dead or alive. One or the other.

Blount lifted the insurgent up over his head and threw the man's body against the cave wall. Chaaku's back slammed into the stone.

Parson heard another crack. This time, the spine.

"You like edged weapons?" Blount shouted. "Lemme show you mine."

Blount reached to his side, unsnapped his KA-BAR. Crouched beside Chaaku. When Chaaku saw the fighting knife, he began to mumble, *"Ash-hadu anla ilaha . . ."*

"You praying to God?" Blount asked. Feebly, Chaaku raised his hand. Blount slapped it down. "Maybe you're asking for mercy? You put suicide vests on children."

Chaaku looked at Parson. Not exactly a look of hate, but something worse than that. Madness. Serial killer eyes. Take him dead or alive? Parson made his choice, held his silence.

"Maybe you're saying you like my knife," Blount said. "My grandpa carried it on Okinawa. Since you like knives so good, I'm gon' let you look at it close."

Blount raised the KA-BAR over Chaaku's face, the leather-bound handle in a bleeding fist. The Marine's blood trickled over the hilt and down the matte black finish of the blade, dripped off the tip.

The gunnery sergeant swept downward with his fist, plunged the point between Chaaku's eyes. Drove in seven inches of carbon steel.

Chaaku's limbs trembled, then stilled. His eyes remained open and fixed on the last thing he saw—Blount's knife.

Blount stood, placed his boot on the Black Crescent leader's face. Leaned over and pulled out his KA-BAR. Wiped one side of the blade on his trousers, then wiped the other side. Blood and brain matter left stains on his uniform.

He looked at Parson with eyes cold as flint. Eyes that reflected rage like Chaaku's, but from a different place. Not from love of killing. From fury at being forced to kill.

"He made me shoot kids, man," Blount said. The Marine bled from his hands, his right arm, his cheek.

Parson did not know how to respond. Blount looked around for his rifle, found it in the dirt. He took the weapon by the barrel. Swung it like a maul, smashed the buttstock into Chaaku's head. The skull split open with a spatter of pink.

"It's over, Gunny," Parson said. "He's dead."

"I won't ever get over what he made me do."

Tendons and veins stood out on Blount's neck, visible

even in the poor light. Muscles in his face twitched as if he struggled to contain his wrath or hold on to his sanity.

Parson tried to think of something to say to bring him back, to pull him out of whatever dark night his mind had entered. Before any words came to Parson, four Marines came into the cave.

"Gunny," one of them called, "are you all right?"

"Yeah," Blount said. "Clear the rest of this hellhole."

"Aye, Gunny."

The Marines disappeared into the darkness farther down in the cave bunker. Parson heard no shots, nothing to suggest any insurgents remained alive inside. He saw his Beretta in the dust, and he holstered the weapon. Left bloody smears on the pistol's grip.

"Let's get out of here, Gunny," Parson said.

The two men stumbled to the cave mouth, their wounds dripping. Just outside the cave, Blount stopped. He looked down at the remains of the boys he'd shot. Two of them lay where they'd fallen, blood congealing around them. Something had blown most of the face from one of them, either Blount's bullets or shrapnel from the suicide bomb.

Of the child who had detonated himself, Parson saw only a torn leg. EOD will probably come in and blow up the other two, Parson thought. Simpler than defusing two suicide vests. Blount swayed on his feet, went down on one knee.

Voices in Pashto came from farther outside. The boys rescued from the cave babbled among themselves.

"Gunny," Parson said, "listen to me. You're going to see

this the rest of your life. I get that. But when you see the kids you killed"—Parson pointed to the dead children— "I want you to see the kids you saved." He pointed to the six boys. "They're here because you did what needed doing. I'm giving you a direct order to remember that."

Blount looked over at the children, now starting to gather around Rashid. The gunnery sergeant's lips moved, and Parson understood Blount was counting the children.

"That's right, Gunny," Parson said. "There's six of them. Six boys who'll get a chance at becoming good men. My order to remember that stays in force even when you retire to a bass lake down South."

"Aye, aye, sir," Blount said. He stood up, made his way over to the kids.

Parson found a corpsman, pulled up his bloody sleeve to expose the slash wound on his forearm. The corpsman placed a clean dressing over the cut, and he wrapped an Israeli bandage over the dressing.

"That'll need a lot of stitches once we get you back to Mazar, sir," the corpsman said.

"I know it," Parson said.

The radio in the corpsman's tactical vest must have been tuned to some common frequency the medics used. Parson recognized Reyes's voice.

"I have a critical patient with a gunshot wound," Reyes said. "Tension pneumothorax. I put a ten-gauge catheter in her thoracic cavity, and she's breathing all right."

She? Gunshot wound? Critical?

That could mean only Sophia, Parson knew. He had brought her here. What had he done to her?

◆ 28 ◆

The air entered Gold's lungs heavily, as if it had an altered density. But at least the drowning sensation had gone. She lay on her back, and she guessed she was passing in and out of consciousness. Reyes had put dressings on the entrance wound where her arm met her shoulder, and on the exit wound in her back. But she didn't remember him doing any of that.

Nearby, the combat controller and the Marine sniper and spotter still watched the target area through scope and NVGs. However, the gunfire downhill had stopped. A welcome stillness settled on the mountains. Reyes kneeled beside Gold.

"What happened?" she asked him.

"They just called clear," Reyes said. "They got Chaaku."

Gold inhaled slowly, sought the strength to speak again. "What about . . ." Paused for more air.

"Blount heard your warning, and he stopped the suicide bombers. You're one tough blonde, I'll give you that."

The news eased her pain like morphine. She silently thanked a higher command. Forgot to ask after her own health, but there'd be time for that.

Reyes answered a call on his radio, spoke words Gold couldn't quite make out. Then he said, "Pave Hawk is inbound, guys."

The night grew fuzzy around her. Gold sensed she was about to lose consciousness again. But she had to know. She forced her awareness to hold on another moment, took in enough air for one word: "Parson?"

Reyes said nothing. Did that mean something had happened to Michael, or did Reyes just not know?

"Are you talking about the lieutenant colonel with a limp?" the Marine spotter asked, gazing through his NVGs.

"Yes."

"He's okay," the spotter said. "I see him right now."

Gold smiled, felt stickiness on her lips. Her own blood.

She relaxed her mind, let perceptions and memories wander. A stray thought came to her—Mullah Durrani's storied ancestor, Ahmad Shah Durrani, was also a poet. He wrote of his devotion to Afghanistan:

By blood, we are immersed in love of you.

Gold did not necessarily love Afghanistan. But she loved many of its people as much as she loved her comrades in arms.

"I wish I could give you something for pain," Reyes said, "but narcotics might suppress your respiratory function."

Nature did what drugs could not. Gold's vision turned hazy; her hearing dulled. She let herself pass out again.

Where was that damned Pave Hawk? An eternity had passed since Parson learned Sophia was hit. He paced outside the cave entrance, cursed, condemned himself for bringing her here at all. He wanted to climb to that knoll, go to her right now. But it was too steep to scale without gear, even for someone without a slash wound to the arm and a bad leg. The quickest way to see her was to wait for the HH-60. The waiting hurt worse than the cut.

A few Marines watched over the other injured—Rashid, Blount, shotgun man, and a half dozen wounded Afghan troops. The rest of the jarheads manned a perimeter, waited for the Osprey to pick them up. The six rescued boys sat on the ground, chattered in Pashto with Rashid. Gutsy of him, Parson thought, to find the strength to comfort those kids with his hand nearly blown off. The corpsman had given Rashid a fentanyl lollipop. Maybe that helped. Now the corpsman was taping dressings onto Blount's bleeding palms and fingers. The gunnery sergeant made no sound.

Rashid turned to Parson, pointed with his good hand to one of the boys.

"That one Mohammed," he said.

So what? Parson thought. He felt relieved some of the kids had survived. Blount's sanity might depend on that. But he was too worried about Sophia to care about their names. Half the boys in this part of the world were named Mohammed. But then he remembered.

"You mean that little girl's brother?" Parson asked.

Rashid spoke in his own language again. The boy nodded. He wore a round hat, along with a woolen vest over a ragged and oversize shirt.

"Fatima his sister," Rashid said.

Well, that was something. Sophia would be happy about that. At least Parson would have some good news for her. Dear God, please let her live to hear it.

"What about Lieutenant Aamir's son?" Parson asked. "What was his name?"

"Hakim," Rashid said.

Mohammed uttered a few syllables, began to cry.

"They give him bomb," Rashid said.

And sent him out to Blount's rifle, Parson thought.

The faint thump of helicopter rotors sounded from a distant valley, grew louder. Finally. Blount rose and stood beside Parson, opened his mouth to speak. He hesitated, had trouble with the words. Eventually he said, "Sir, if you gotta report what you saw me do in there . . ." Paused again. "I mean, there ain't gon' be no hard feelings. You just do what you think's right."

"We did it together, Gunny," Parson said. "I was the highest rank there. And our orders said dead or alive. Let's just not do it that way again."

Blount pressed his lips together, thought for a moment. "Yes, sir," he said. "Unless it needs doing."

Good point, Parson thought. Unless it needs doing.

Parson listened to the Pave Hawk's approach. Looked down at Mohammed and the other boys. Up at the dark knoll where Gold lay wounded. She was in critical condition because of Chaaku and Black Crescent. Yeah, Parson considered, Blount did what needed doing. Damn straight. Parson wished he'd done it himself.

The helicopter circled *Kuh-e Qara Batur*. Parson watched through his night vision goggles as it descended toward the knoll. Within several meters of the ground, the main rotor kicked up dust. Arcs of green formed at the blade tips. From his vantage point about a half mile away, Parson watched the corona effect shimmer into a full halo as the Pave Hawk touched down to pick up Gold.

Reyes and the combat controller lifted her. Sophia's arm swung from the litter as they carried her into the aircraft. The sight looked far too much like images of the dying Parson had seen all over Afghanistan, and it worried him sick.

The helicopter lifted off, gathered speed. It banked, then descended toward the cave bunker where Parson stood with the Marines and Afghans. The broken Mi-17 remained on the LZ, and the Pave Hawk had little room to land. But Parson had seen choppers put down in less room.

Grit flew into Parson's eyes as the Pave Hawk settled next to the Mi-17. Without waiting for a signal, Parson ran to the HH-60's open door. Sophia lay on a litter, IV in her arm, some kind of needle in her chest. Dirt and dried blood across her pale skin.

"How is she?" Parson shouted to Reyes over the engines and rotors.

"She got shot real bad," Reyes said. "But with this kind of wound, if they make it this far, they usually hang on." Matter-of-fact. Like she was just another patient. Reyes arranged a blanket across her torso, kept the fabric clear of the needle. He rolled up another blanket and propped her feet on it. Treating her for shock, Parson realized.

Parson kneeled beside her, took her hand. She did not open her eyes or respond in any way. But her fingers felt warm, and he took that as a good sign. Maybe she wasn't in deep shock.

Reyes and the corpsman helped load some of the other wounded onto the aircraft. They placed Rashid on a stretcher, put him down across from Gold. One of the other Afghans had a bloody bandage covering most of his head.

When the corpsman motioned for Blount to board, the gunnery sergeant waved with a hand wrapped in white. "I can wait for the Osprey," he said. "Take some of these boys. They been here longer than I have."

"Bring that one," Parson said. He pointed to Mohammed. Reyes and the corpsman collected Mohammed and two other kids. Buckled them into web seats at the back of the Pave Hawk.

The Pave Hawk's flight engineer slid the door shut, took his seat behind his gun. Two turbine engines above Parson's head howled in unison, and the helicopter lifted off. *Kuh-e Qara Batur* dropped away, receded in the darkness.

A few minutes after the helicopter leveled at altitude, Gold opened her eyes.

"You did good," Parson said.

She blinked, inhaled and exhaled as if getting ready to expend great effort. Parson leaned close to hear whatever she might say amid the noise of the aircraft. Finally she asked, "The kids?"

Parson nodded toward Mohammed.

"That's Fatima's brother," he said. "They got five other boys out, too. You did it. You and Blount and the Marines."

Gold closed her eyes, clasped his hand. The strength of her grip encouraged him. She took another deep breath. Then she said, "We did it."

Parson shook his head. "I never should have brought you back here, Sophia. It wasn't fair."

She gathered herself to speak again, inhaled deeply. That made Parson feel even more regretful. He realized he shouldn't encourage her to talk right now.

"Michael," she said, "this is what I do. This is what *we* do."

Reyes adjusted the blanket covering her. The effort revealed pallid flesh, heaving torso, and in the pale light, bandages soaked in the color of rust. Loose blond hair spread across her bare collarbone, some of the strands clotted with blood.

"You do what you can do," Reyes said, "and that's all you can do." He spoke in a soothing tone, like he wanted Sophia to stop thinking and just relax.

Gold drew a rasping breath. Seemed to summon all of her strength. "One save at a time," she said.

"That's right," Reyes said. "Now rest, so we can work on saving you."

The helicopter banked to the left. Without letting go of Sophia's hand, Parson looked toward the instrument panel and watched the attitude indicator register the turn. Rashid said something to Mohammed, and whatever it was made Sophia give that half smile. Despite the ravages of a high-velocity round, Gold looked more content than Parson had ever seen her. Because she'd done all she could do, he realized.

The Pave Hawk rolled out of the bank, onto a heading to Mazar-i-Sharif. Parson gazed through the window and into the night outside.

A crush of stars overlaid charcoal ridgelines. Among those mountains, villages still needed to rebuild, to recover from the earthquake that had given Black Crescent an opening. Parson hoped the faults beneath the ridges would lie quiet, that those kids would grow to old age without seeing another quake.

Without seeing another war.

Not likely, Parson thought, but at least we've given them a chance.

He felt Gold press his fingers together. That brought him back to immediate problems, so he did what he could do. Squeezed her hand back. Thought about what to do once the helicopter landed: Make sure they get her on the first medical flight to Germany. Get his arm stitched up. Then pack up all of Sophia's stuff and send it to her at

Landstuhl. Save her notes about finding a home for Fatima and Mohammed.

Parson would get started as soon as the Pave Hawk touched down. He looked ahead through the windscreen, watched for the lights of Mazar.

THE STORY BEHIND
The Renegades

Michael Parson has had some rough missions. In my first novel, *The Mullah's Storm*, he evaded capture in the midst of a blizzard while holding on to a Taliban prisoner. In *Silent Enemy*, he flew a doomed aircraft more than halfway around the world. And in *The Renegades*, he and his partner, Sergeant Major Sophia Gold, battle a violent Islamist splinter group.

On these missions, Parson has held different jobs. He began his fictitious career as an Air Force navigator, then cross-trained to pilot, and now appears as an adviser to the Afghan military. Some may think I've used artistic license to put him in these varied roles. However, Parson has taken a fairly realistic career path for an aviator and officer.

Air Force fliers don't just fly. As their careers progress, they take on different duties such as training managers, safety officers, and diplomatic liaisons. Just like Parson in *The Renegades*, one of my West Virginia Air National

Guard squadron mates deployed as an adviser to Afghan fliers, trying to help them create a modern, professional air force. Another of my colleagues worked as an aviation liaison to the Iraqi Ministry of Transportation, helping put Iraq's civil aviation system back together. He was a pilot, not a bureaucrat. But he used what he knew—sometimes under fire—and he helped bring Iraq a little closer to normalcy.

When service members take on such special duties, they tackle jobs for which there is sometimes no specific school, no War College course. They call on their experience and judgment in situations where they must think on their feet. In *The Renegades*, Parson faces a number of challenges: The Afghans fly aircraft unfamiliar to him, he doesn't speak the language, and he's never worked so closely with foreign forces. But he knows how to lead, and he tries to impart that knowledge to Rashid, a promising Afghan officer. And he knows someone who does speak the language, his old friend Sophia Gold.

In this situation, it's not outlandish that he'd call on Gold for assistance. In *The Mullah's Storm*, they were thrown together by ill fortune. In *Silent Enemy*, they met again by chance. But this time, Parson sends for her by name. That could happen in real life. By now, the public is familiar with major deployments that call up entire units. However, military personnel can also take combat tours as individual augmentees, the way Gold does to help Parson in *The Renegades*.

Once Gold arrives in Afghanistan, she and Parson find themselves working closely with different branches of the armed forces. Gold, of course, is an Army translator serving with Parson, an Air Force officer. They encounter Gunnery Sergeant Blount, who leads a team of Marines. The Marines get air support from an Air Force combat controller and medical support from a Navy corpsman.

That sort of interservice cooperation happens in the modern military. People from different branches train together to leverage their combined strengths. Hollywood stereotypes notwithstanding, soldiers and airmen don't get into fistfights every time they meet in a bar. They're more likely to swap stories about the last time they worked together. My own helmet bag carries a collection of patches from past missions that included Navy SEALs, Marine riflemen, and Army paratroopers.

Even though I've served in the armed forces for almost twenty years, I'm still learning about different specialties in each of the branches. One job I got to explore in *The Renegades* is pararescue. Air Force pararescuemen are referred to informally as PJs, for pararescue jumpers. Represented in *The Renegades* by Sergeant Reyes, PJs are medics trained to do whatever it takes to reach a wounded soldier or downed airman. They attend schools that include scuba diving and free-fall parachuting, in a program so tough, its washout rate can exceed ninety percent.

You would hate to need the services of a PJ, because that would mean you were having a really bad day. But in a training environment or a social situation, it's a pleasure to meet people so capable and upbeat.

Another skill crucial to the modern military is winning what counterinsurgency experts call the human terrain.

Making friends, essentially. Gold has dedicated her life to it. And younger troops follow in her footsteps, like my characters Ann and Lyndsey with the Lioness team. That's a real program, and that's its real name. (Don't worry; it's not classified.) The role of women in combat zones has expanded greatly in recent years, and not without controversy. But real-world counterparts of Ann and Lyndsey, in meetings with Afghan women, have made contact with a segment of Afghanistan's population essentially sealed off from American men.

One specialty I'd like to learn more about is working with military dogs. I've often flown dogs on airlift missions. When the animals get loaded on board, they usually bark constantly in their kennels until takeoff. Then they go right to sleep. On landing, the barking starts again. Those canine passengers inspired the Belgian Malinois that survived the Mi-17 crash landing in *The Renegades*. That breed makes good military dogs. I met one several years ago at a base in the Middle East while waiting for cargo and troops to show up at my aircraft. A dog handler and his bomb-sniffing Malinois arrived early. The rest of the troops got delayed for several hours. We passed the time by playing with the dog and feeding it pizza.

Sergeant Major Gold's high altitude/low opening parachute drops also come right out of the real world. Back in my C-130 days, I got more of a kick out of HALO drops than any other flight operations. I have especially fond memories of a training mission well before 9/11 at the former Indian Springs Auxiliary Field, Nevada (now

Creech Air Force Base). My crew flew Army Special Forces jumpers on HALO drops for about a week.

Each day we'd do two drops, break for dinner, and come back for a night drop. All at high altitude, unpressurized, on oxygen. With no higher rank present than a captain, we had no adult supervision at all. Just a bunch of young guys who thought we were bulletproof, and an airplane and parachutes to play with. It was glorious.

As it happens, I got my first look at a Predator drone during that training mission. The Predators were still fairly new then, developed in a program at Indian Springs. I saw them next in Bosnia, and later in Southwest Asia.

Like my previous novels, *The Mullah's Storm* and *Silent Enemy*, I wrote *The Renegades* for two reasons: First, I wanted to create a compelling story that readers would find entertaining; I've always loved fiction. But through these novels, I also wanted to convey something about the motivations and mind-sets of American servicemen and -women. I hope my books do justice to their dedication, and to the expertise their work requires.

> *Tom Young*
> *Alexandria, Virginia*
> *January 2012*

ACKNOWLEDGMENTS

If you enjoyed reading *The Renegades*, thank my wife, Kristen, who took pen in hand, put her feet up on the ottoman, and ripped the manuscript up one side and down the other. She's done the same for all my books. Thanks also go to my parents, Bob and Harriett Young, for a little help copyediting and a lot of help getting the word out.

I also received helpful input from Barbara Esstman, Jodie Forrest, Liz Lee, and Robert Siegfried. A special tribute goes to Dick Elam, who has given me good writing advice for thirty years. Even now I look at his comments on my manuscripts and think, Damn, I should have thought of that.

My squadron mates in the 167th Airlift Wing, West Virginia Air National Guard, have provided inspiration, moral support, and comradeship. Joe Myers enjoys a well-earned retirement now, and he edits copy with the precision you'd expect from a military instructor pilot. Pete

Gross offered generous descriptions of his time as an adviser to the Afghan Air Force, and his observations were tremendously helpful. James Freid-Studlo also gave valuable descriptions from his experiences in Afghanistan—and darn near wore me out on a bike ride through rural Germany as we waited for our airplane to get fixed.

Like Parson, all of my helicopter time has been as a passenger, so I called on some experts to keep me straight on rotary-wing flying. They included Adam Albrich, Keith Olson, Sean Roehrs, Michael Adair, and Rob Tatum.

Brandon Forshaw and his colleagues at the 920th Rescue Wing, Patrick Air Force Base, Florida, schooled me on the pararescue career field. I received other valuable medical tips from my cousin, Billy Perry, and from the world's greatest flight nurse, Sandie Duiker.

If the novel contains any errors about medicine or helicopters, those errors are mine alone. With other technical aspects, I have taken artistic liberties. For example, some of the operations described in *The Renegades* would probably involve more personnel, and especially more officers, than depicted. However, I chose to limit the number of characters for the sake of the narrative.

Were it not for my agent, Michael Carlisle, my novels would be nothing more than files on my computer. Thanks also to Lyndsey Blessing, who has helped bring my stories to readers in Europe and Asia. Author and professor John Casey helped me get this adventure started, and I owe to him continued thanks.

As always, it's a pleasure to work with Putnam publisher

and editor-in-chief Neil Nyren and company president Ivan Held, as well as Thomas Colgan at Berkley. Thanks also to Michael Barson, Victoria Comella, Sara Minnich, Kate Stark, Chris Nelson, Lydia Hirt, Caitlin Mulrooney-Lyski, Alexandra Israel, and everyone at Penguin Group.

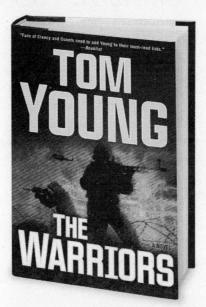

THE
MULLAH'S STORM

by THOMAS W. YOUNG

A transport plane carrying a high-ranking Taliban detainee is shot down in a blizzard over Afghanistan's
mountainous Hindu Kush. The storm makes rescue impossible, and for two people—Major Michael Parson,
the navigator, and Sergeant Gold, a female Army interpreter—the battle for survival begins across some of
the most forbidding terrain on Earth with a prisoner who
would very much like the three of them to be caught...

www.thomaswyoung.com
www.penguin.com

M1039T0112

M14G0610

Penguin Group (USA) Online

What will you be reading tomorrow?

Patricia Cornwell, Nora Roberts, Catherine Coulter,
Ken Follett, John Sandford, Clive Cussler,
Tom Clancy, Laurell K. Hamilton, Charlaine Harris,
J. R. Ward, W.E.B. Griffin, William Gibson,
Robin Cook, Brian Jacques, Stephen King,
Dean Koontz, Eric Jerome Dickey, Terry McMillan,
Sue Monk Kidd, Amy Tan, Jayne Ann Krentz,
Daniel Silva, Kate Jacobs...

You'll find them all at
penguin.com

Read excerpts and newsletters,
find tour schedules and reading group guides,
and enter contests.

Subscribe to Penguin Group (USA) newsletters
and get an exclusive inside look
at exciting new titles and the authors you love
long before everyone else does.

PENGUIN GROUP (USA)
penguin.com